THE
LEGEND
OF
ZELKOVA

UMBRAS

By S.L. Vaden

ISBN-13: 978-1-7336254-2-5

Library of Congress Control Number: 2020901048

Place and Character Name Translations:
Ager - Latin = Field
Arbor - Latin = Tree
Aria - Italian = Air
Aurum – Latin = Gold
Carya - *Carya laciniosa* = Hickory
Cedrus - *Cedrus atlanica* = Cedar
Elementum – Latin = Element
Fraxinus - *Fraxinus americana* = Ash White
Ilex - *Ilex verticillata* = Holly, Winterberry
Inane – Latin = Void
Ingens - Latin = Vast
Jardin – French = Garden
Kasai - Japanese = Fire
Lignum - Latin = Wood
Litore - Latin = By the Sea
Malus - *Malus sargentii* = Crab Apple
Montis - Latin = Mountain
Nati - Haitian = Nature
Omnia – Latin = All
Opima - Latin = Plentiful
Petra - Latin = Rock
Pyrus - *Pyrus communis* = Pear, Bartlett
Ruri - Latin = On the Farm
Silva - Latin = Forest
Solaris - Latin = Sun
Spero – Latin = Hope
Sten - Danish = Stone
Tempus - Latin = Time
Tuuli – Finnish = Wind
Umbars – Latin = Shades
Unda – Latin = Wave
Vatten - Swedish = Water
Vako – Finnish = Furrow

Place and Character Name Translations (cont.):
Ventus - Latin = Wind
Vindby - Swedish = Gust
Yang – Chinese = Positive / Bright
Yin – Chinese = Negative / Dark
Zel – Aztec = The One
Zelkova - *Zelkova serrata*

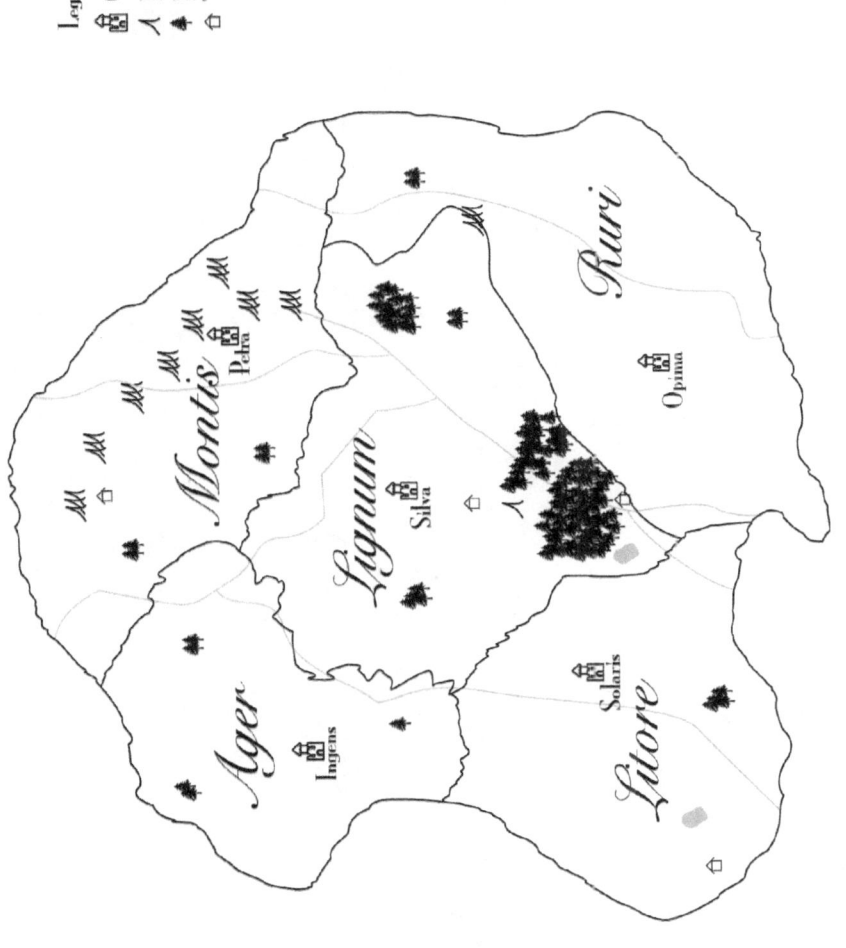

Montis

Petra

Ager

Ingens

Lignum

Silva

Ruri

Opima

Litore

Solaris

There is a world just out of view, hidden from human eyes. This is where the elements wait for a day even humans don't see coming, when everything is in harmony once more. But before the light, the dark must come...

The kingdom of Litore had prospered greatly in the two hundred years after Zelkova's death. The prosperity was all due to the Aurum family, who had a deep connection to the stories of Zelkova. Even though most who held the Aurum name were too humble to own their contributions throughout several generations, Litore and the capital of Solaris would have long been laid to waste without them.

The borders of the city had expanded significantly, along with the trade market, which the Aurums had a hand in as well. The lush vegetables and fruit Litore became known for was highly sought after in all the different kingdoms. In the capital and the countryside alike, rumors abounded about how the Aurum family managed to maintain such abundant farmland. One such rumor is that their founding great-great-grandfather made a deal with a witch...

A young red-haired man with chiseled facial features entered a large indoor garden where a fiery-haired lady sat brushing a wilting flower with the back of her hand. "Mother! There you are. I've been looking everywhere for you."

The lady turned a bright smile to the young man. She lifted her hand from the wilting leaf, which gradually turned green. "Have you now? I am certain you will always find what you are looking for in the last place you look." She winked at him and beckoned him near.

He returned her smile and walked closer. Once he reached her side, he took his mother's hand and kissed the back of it. "Mother, I have come to speak with you on behalf of…"

She waved to silence him. "Now, now, Spero, my dear. Out of all my children, you are the one who should know above all else that once I set my mind to something, there is no changing it. The more someone tries to change it, the more I sink my roots in. Come, take a turn around the garden with me, as I explain once more why I decided to do as I did."

He nodded as she wrapped her arm around his. "Spero, my son, the reason I have canceled your engagement is because I feel that you are not fond of this young lady." She must have noticed the expression on his face because she tapped her nose with a laugh. "See, a mother knows."

His smile faded. "It doesn't matter if she is what I desire in a wife. To unite our two families would benefit us greatly."

"That may be so, but have I ever pushed any of my children into a marriage they did not desire? Despite what benefits we might gain?" She grinned at him. "If I felt that you really liked this girl, then I would have no objection, but I will not have any of my children wed to someone they do not love. Yes, yes, feelings can grow. But it is hard to build a house without a foundation, is it not?"

Spero nodded grudgingly. "I suppose so."

"Do you really want to marry this young lady for the land she comes with?" He sighed deeply, looking down at his feet. Before Spero could answer, his mother asked, "Is that what your father would have wanted?"

They both paused. She could tell her son was struggling with this, so she wrapped her arms around him in a strong embrace. "Spero, listen to me. Your happiness is what matters, not any piece of land. I will give you time to think on it. Now, shall we speak of other things?" She paused and released him from their hug. "I have heard a rumor of a floating island…"

Spero turned his head as if he were looking for it, then stared at her in shock. "What? When? Where?"

She laughed. "Calm yourself. It's only rumors."

"How can you say that, Mother? The rumors you hear are usually true. Do you think it's the island from the tales?"

She nodded. "I do. There is no other one it could be."

"That also means the stories of Zelkova were real as well?"

"I've always believed so. My great-grandfather was adamant on teaching us all that they were true. I was a small child when he passed. Before he did, I remember he gathered us all around to tell the story of Zelkova once more. And how the floating island had only ever appeared in the sky during his time. There is no record of it in the history books, nor of the Elementals that live atop it."

After listening in awe, Spero asked, "What would you have me do?"

"The Council meeting has been moved up to next week because of it. I spoke with the king and there is no one he trusts more than you to investigate the situation. Make certain no one tries to start a war over this."

"Yes, Mother."

"Listen, Spero..." She paused, gathering her thoughts. "I need you to be on your guard. I feel a great shift." His mother took his hand in hers, squeezing reassuringly. "No matter what may lay in the future, I want you to always remember the kindness our family is based on. Never turn a blind eye to those in need. When we can step in to help another, we must do what we can to ease the pain of those who are suffering." She moved forward and kissed him on his forehead. "Come, we must speak with the others about this."

Spero stood in his study. Gazing out the window, he scanned Solaris, which was busy with people going about their day. He admired the people's resilience. So many of them had been brought so low, only to fight their way up again and out of their troubles.

He turned his head toward another part of the city. This area seemed to seethe with darkness. Knowing there were good people in the world, Spero also knew how easily people could, and would, turn. Fear and hate were such strong emotions. They ruined not just people but entire countries.

After hearing his mother's admission to feeling things shift within their world, Spero began to connect more to the elements. He also felt a slight shift. It was faint, but he could feel something looming unseen in the distance. It was hard to explain the feeling, but something was amiss within the balance of things.

Whatever it was seemed to be waiting for a moment to strike. It also had a darkness about it. The sinking feeling in the bottom of his stomach seemed to grow with every breath. He didn't know how long he stood staring out at the city, but he knew standing around would solve nothing. Spero needed to set up a plan. But how could one plan for something that was just a feeling, a rumor?

Shaking his head, he turned toward his study, glancing over to the bookshelf. His eyes scanned the literature. After a few moments, his gaze landed on a book he had not seen before. He reached out his hand, and the tips of his fingers lightly touched its binding. As they did, a surge of energy ran through him. He stepped back, surprised, nerves standing on end. But that feeling turned into a warm sensation, making him feel like he was being wrapped in a warm embrace, putting him at ease as it flooded his body.

Resolving to look at the book, he pulled it from the shelf and sat at his desk. Light from the midday sun shone in through the window, the warm light illuminating the book before him. As Spero was about to open its pages, it started to rapidly turn on its own. He gasped as the pages turned before his eyes. Seconds later, it stopped.

As he leaned forward for a better view of the page the book had opened to, a vision filled his mind's eye. Like the pages that had just unfolded before him, images flooded his mind. A young girl with blonde hair and a dark complexion reached for him, her eyes begging for his help, seeking him out. A dark outline surrounded her.

A voice echoed in his mind. "You of great heart will bring hope to those who are lost. You have felt the darkness that looms on the horizon. You must play a part in this war of shadows. Spero... Help this girl. She will need the light that naturally surrounds you. You two... are the tipping point. Seek her out, seek out the legend... And never lose your light of hope, Spero."

He sat there blinking.

The vision faded, but the image of the girl's image remained, slowly fading. The images and the voice did not frighten him. This vision was for him and him alone. To speak of it would change things, and not for the better. As he turned his gaze down to his desk, he realized the book had vanished. He stood and looked for it in the bookshelves, but there was no sign of it anywhere. It was as if it had never existed...

Spero once again sat at his desk and wrote several delegates about how eager he was to speak with them at the upcoming Council in Silva. So many thoughts ran through his mind. When he rose from his desk, the light from the sun was starting to fade.

He could not shake the image of the girl from his mind. Who had spoken to him? He dared not speak to anyone of the book or the vision. Knowing things doesn't always make them better.

As the days passed, preparations were made for his departure. Spero went over what to say on behalf of the king of Litore. On the day he was to depart, Spero stood in the courtyard next to his carriage.

His mother took him by the shoulders, worry and love filling her expression. "My dear son, be careful. And know you can do all that you set out to. We will all be awaiting your return." She hugged her son and backed away.

He nodded to her with a slight smile. "Thank you, Mother. I will be back soon."

Their tight smiles masked the worry and unease they both felt within. As Spero sat down in his coach, he looked out the window to the city he was leaving. Around the stone and wood building, people stirred.

For a reason he couldn't explain, he felt the world was on the verge of change…

2

In the cover of darkness, a shadowy figure moved within a cave. They knelt next to a pond. Light streamed in from holes in the ceiling. A rock sat beside the water with symbols of all the elements engraved on the surface. The figure brushed its hand over the engravings and it slowly changed, the symbols morphing into those for time, dark and light.

The shadow transformed into dark fog, which faded into the rock and disappeared.

A bird flew overhead, looking down on a large castle. It soon came to perch on the edge of the roof. The castle could no longer be recognized as it once was. Its original stone walls now composed the inner chambers. The castle had doubled in size since it was first built, the original structure hidden by large limestone slabs that glistened in the sunlight. Land that had once been a forest was now engulfed by the expanding town. Cottages and shops now occupied the space where trees once stood.

The bird took off into the sky once more. It circled, then dove down to the ground to catch a mouse that ran from a shed toward a young lady hanging clothes nearby.

The commotion startled her. She had a slim frame, caramel-toned skin, and golden hair. Her eyes were deep blue, like the deepest ocean.

Because of her petite stature, she looked younger than she actually was. Someone who didn't know her would think she was a child of thirteen or fourteen instead of a young woman of seventeen.

Because of her unique look, she caught the attention of many eyes, even some of the royals she worked for. The men tried to take advantage of her while the ladies made her life as hard as they could. Despite her poor upbringing and circumstance, she kept her sweetness, not letting anyone take away her happiness and joy in the small things. She knew her parents would want it that way, even though she had never known them.

The castle was in a state of chaos. Everyone was preparing for the yearly Council meeting among the kingdoms, which would be held within two days' time. As usual, she had been sent to do the tasks others thought were beneath them.

That afternoon, she was sent into town to buy herbs. The castle's garden had already been stripped of them, and there weren't enough for the banquet. The town seemed just as busy as the castle, if not more so. Carts, horses and people flooded the streets. There was one main street where everyone gathered and the majority of shops were. Side streets extended out toward homes and smaller shops.

She tried her best to keep out of the way, but she was soon pushed out into the middle of the street by the crowd. She tripped over the uneven cobblestones. Just as she regained her footing, a cart barreled toward her. Stumbling, heart racing, she moved out of the way just as it was about to hit her. One thing she disliked about her stature: she was easily lost in the crowd.

Breathing hard, she finally reached the herbalist and took a rest inside the doorway. Reaching into her dress pocket, her stomach sank as she realized she'd lost her list of herbs.

She went back to where she had fallen, but there was no sign of the note in the street. Giving up, she went back and bought the herbs she could remember from the list. Finding the main street even busier than before, she decided to take side streets back to the castle.

She soon found out she would have fared better in the main streets of Silva.

After reaching a bend in the road, she ran into three men who were laughing over a bottle of alcohol. They stumbled toward her, and she broke into a run toward the town center. She saw the busy people in the distance, but before she could reach them, someone pulled her back by her arm. She screamed and dropped her herbs.

"Where are you going? The fun is here, not out there," the man slurred as he pulled her closer to him.

"Please, sir. I need to get back to work. They'll be missing me." She looked for some way out, but there were no windows looking into the dark narrow street.

"We won't keep you that long, will we, lads?" Laughing, the man looked at his comrades, who stood behind him.

"I don't know. We'll all want a turn. Might take a while, can't promise I'll be gentle." The shorter of the two got closer and rubbed her arm, smiling through decaying teeth. The three of them started pawing at her. One held her arms, while the one who had just spoken stroked her cheek.

Her heart raced, and panic filled her mind. "Someone help, please help!" she yelled at the top of her lungs. The three men laughed.

They tugged at her clothes as she continued to scream. "Yell all you want, no one will hear you."

Tears started to fall down her face as she struggled to get away. The men pushed her to the ground. She closed her eyes and turned her head, prepared for the worst. Fear ran through her, so many thoughts running through her mind that she hoped to go insane before they touched her more. But then she heard a scream and the man who was holding her down released his grip. Opening her eyes, she saw the other two men being thrown by what looked like roots. As the roots pulled back, she looked to see where they had come from.

She saw a young man walking toward her. He stood almost a head taller than her and had broad shoulders.

Before she could speak, he yelled at the three men who landed, slumped, against a wall. "No wonder this country is turning into a cesspool with the likes of you. None of you deserve to live, but luckily for you, I'm not one to kill. But I will hurt you so that you never do this again."

The man rushed past her to the three men. He blocked her view, so she was unable to see why the men suddenly screamed in anguish. As they fled, limping, the young man turned to her and helped her up. With a kind smile, he asked, "Are you all right? They didn't hurt you, did they? Did I make it in time?"

His smile warmed her heart and eased her fears. She had never been so happy to see someone in her life; she tried to return his smile, but tears once again filled her eyes from the thought of what could have occurred. The man grabbed her and wrapped his arms around her, trying to comfort her, but his actions seemed to take them both by surprise.

"I'm glad you're unharmed." He gently stroked her head, which still rested against his chest.

His heart beat quickly underneath her ear. She looked up and asked, "Your heart is racing. Are you all right?"

He looked away in embarrassment. "Yes, I was just so angry from what I saw. Come, we should go back to the street. May I ask your name?" He released her from his embrace, and they began walking.

"My name is Omnia, and yours?" she answered, looking up at his face, noticing he had a rugged yet regal look about him. He had a slight shadowing of a beard and stood with confidence.

"Spero. Nice to meet you, my lady." He half-jokingly bowed and as he rose back up, she finally got a look at how he was dressed. He wore a long brown jacket embroidered with gold leaf. His vest was a deep red, and his tan pants were tucked into his black boots.

As she looked him over, another young man came running toward them. He was not as well dressed. "My lord, we've been looking for you everywhere! Where have you been?" He then eyed Omnia and said, "Please, my lord, come back to the carriage and leave the filth in the street where it belongs."

She knew she must look like a mess. Before Spero could react, she quickly said, "Oh, my herbs. Thank you again."

Omnia bowed and rushed back to the alley to pick up the basket she had dropped. Then she began to walk back toward the main street. Omnia saw someone in the shadows and froze with fear, thinking one of her assailants had returned.

The figure emerged from the shadows, his hair seeming to catch fire as sunlight shone down on his tall form. "Good, I'm glad you were able to get them. I could have taken you to buy more."

She sighed at the sight of Spero but quickly remembered his rank. "My lord, you should have gone on."

He stepped forward, taking the basket from her hands. "Come now, I thought we were past all of that. Call me Spero. I don't see ranks when I look at people. I just see people."

Smiling at her, he started to walk, beckoning her to follow. She did and as they reached the main street, she reached out to take her basket. But he turned just as she did, making their hands meet. He met her eyes with a smile and asked, "Where is it you're taking these herbs?"

"Oh, to the castle. I'm already so late, they will be upset." Omnia looked down, thinking of what they would do to her. The shouts, slaps and no food echoed through her memory.

"Then I must insist you accompany me in my carriage. I am headed there anyway. It won't be any trouble."

"But, my lord..."

He smiled. "Spero."

Blushing, she looked down. "Yes, Spero, but I will get in trouble if I come with you."

"I will make certain that doesn't occur." He reached out his hand for hers. "I insist."

She nodded in agreement, and he guided her into the coach. The two of them sat in silence, but it was broken by Spero after a few moments. "So, tell me. How long have you been at the castle?"

"Ever since I can remember."

"Your parents live there as well?"

"No, I never met my parents. I am a servant. You do know this, don't you?" She looked down at her hands, which were anxiously intertwined.

He saw her fidgeting and put his hand on top of hers, making her look up. His eyes were a deep green, and his hair was auburn-colored, like maple leaves in the middle of autumn.

"Like I said before, I don't see ranks as others do. That's how I was raised. Tell me, how do they treat you at the castle?"

"Oh, well enough, I am certain." She knew she couldn't tell him what they did or what they were certain to do if she arrived with him. "Would you please drop me off before we reach the gates?"

"If you wish, but I would like to see you again. Would that be possible?"

Omnia nodded. "Yes, I'm certain we will meet again. Where is it that you are from?"

"I'm from Litore, I sit on the Council for the king there. Don't look so nervous. I already told you, ranks don't matter. They're just made up by people to keep themselves in power. I look at my rank as a job, not who I am. Really, I'm glad I met you today."

She looked down, but he reached out for her hands once more, making her eyes lock with his. "I must say, Omnia, you have such pretty eyes. They look like a story yet to be told. I would like to know more of you and your story."

"Story? I already told you. I work at the castle. There's not much else to it."

"I'm certain there's more to you than that. You might not have found it yet. Looks like we're almost there. Please promise me we'll meet again before you go."

Omnia nodded and said, "Yes, I promise."

He let go of her hand as she exited the carriage, which continued toward the castle gates. She took a shortcut through a small patch of woods situated next to the kitchen yard meant to block the view of servants at work from the king's road. Thinking back, she forgot to ask about the roots that hit the men who attacked her. But once she was in the kitchen, her mind turned to other things. She set the herbs on the table. Thankfully, everyone was too busy to notice her; she went to the top of the stairs that led to the courtyard and looked out.

The queen was facing the gate, and Spero was walking toward her. "Welcome, Lord Spero of Litore," she greeted him. "Welcome to Silva. I hope you find it to your liking and that you will return to your country with great stories to tell your king."

Just as Spero was about to respond, someone grabbed Omnia's shoulder. Turning around, she saw the head housekeeper glaring at her. The look in her eyes was enough to scare the largest of men.

"What took you so long with the herbs?" she rasped. Not waiting for a response, she continued, "You shouldn't have been lollygagging around now of all days. I'll think of how to punish you later. Too busy today. Go help with the dishes. Once you are done, go clean yourself up. You will be helping serve tonight. Go!"

Before Omnia could respond, the lady disappeared. She did as she was told. After dishes, she went and changed into a dark gray dress. It was shapeless and did not flatter her in the least. That was the way she wanted it. She fixed her hair in a bun, then headed back to the kitchen for instructions.

As the evening progressed, the nobles gathered in the large Great Room to mingle. Omnia and a few other young girls were assigned to serve drinks and appetizers. She knew the reason why only young girls were sent. Some would be chosen to keep the nobles' company after the night's festivities were over. She tried her best to keep out of sight and to not make eye contact or smile at anyone, hoping it would deter any unwanted fondling.

She saw Spero that night. He smiled in her direction, but she averted her eyes each time, trying not to draw any attention to herself.

All her efforts to disappear were in vain. Right before everyone began to turn in for the night, an older gentleman pulled her into the hallway. The events of earlier that day came rushing back, making her break out in a cold sweat.

The man tugged her by the arm, then pushed her up against the wall beside a stained-glass window. His words were slurred as he spoke close to her face, his breath rank with alcohol. As he touched her, he said, "I saw you trying to hide from me. I do love a good game of cat and mouse. Playing hard to get only made me want you more." As he pressed his body against hers, her pleas of protest landed on deaf ears. She had to be stern and stand her ground. To find the inner strength she knew was inside her.

"Please, sir. Please stop." She pushed him away with all her strength, knocking him back to reality. He stumbled a few feet from her, then glared at her.

"How dare you! Who do you think you are to refuse me?" he yelled so loudly people came out of the Great Room to see what was happening. "You should feel honored to be chosen! How dare you say no to me!"

Omnia saw the queen and Spero out of the corner of her eye. Just as she glanced at them, a large hand slapped her across the face, the force knocking her to the floor. Her vision blurred. Her heart raced so much that it was the only thing she could hear. Tears started to roll down her face as she tried to catch the breath that was knocked out of her.

Someone grabbed her, gently lifting her up. She knew not who it was; her vision and mind still reeled from the force of the hit. If it were the man, she'd have no choice but to do his bidding.

Her life as she knew it would be over. Her mind poured over the possibilities. If she were to have a child by this man, the child would only end up like herself. Or worse, it would be taken away at birth, never knowing a mother's love. She would rather die than let that happen, but she had no strength left to fight. Even if she could, she wouldn't win. She would only receive more of a beating. Closing her eyes, she released her thoughts to the darkness that overcame her.

3

Omnia awoke with a start, sitting up in bed. She looked around and noticed she was in a large guest room with vaulted ceilings and windows that came to a point at the top. She looked down to see she was still dressed in her clothes from the night before.

When she stood, her head started pounding, forcing her to sit back down. Just as she put her hand to her head, the door opened. Fear struck her heart. Too nervous to see who entered, she closed her eyes and waited.

"Ah, good. You're up! I brought some food and drink for you. How is your head feeling? It was quite a jolt you got." Surprised, she turned to see Spero with a bright smile on his face. The light from the morning sun streamed in, illuminating his hair. The sight of him eased her heart. "That must have been a shock last night, but let's not speak of such things. Here, drink this."

He came toward her, offering a glass of warm milk with honey, which she accepted. "Spero," she asked, "how did I get here? I was sure..."

"You were sure you had been taken away by the madman? No, once he hit you, several of us stepped in. We found him a willing girl, which pleased him. Some of the men pushed more drinks on him, though, so he probably fell asleep before he could do any more harm. I spoke with the queen who agreed to let me take care of you." He had taken a seat beside her and was scratching his head, chest puffed out.

Omnia blinked in shock. "She did?"

"Is that surprising to you?"

Nodding, she smiled. "Yes, quite."

"Nevertheless, I've come up with a plan." He winked.

"A plan? A plan for what?"

"To get you out of this place. With what I saw yesterday, not just once but twice, I can't leave you here. How would you feel about joining me in my country? It's a lot safer there." He beamed with pride as he stared at her.

"But, why? I'm just a maid. What would you get out of it?" Omnia looked down at her folded hands, afraid to look up and see his reaction.

Spero gently patted her hands. "A friend and knowing you are safe. Please let me help you."

She nodded and smiled up at him. "First, tell me of this plan."

"I won't be able to come with you, not yet at least. So, I will have a trusted friend meet you and take you to Solaris."

"Not one of the men you have with you?"

"No, they aren't men I would trust alone with you."

The word *alone* stuck in her mind. Looking around, she realized they were alone together. Before she could stand in protest, Spero rested his hand on top of hers once again.

"It's all right. People are going to think what they want no matter what we do, and besides, you won't be here to hear their whispers. So, as I was saying, there will be someone to meet you at a cave near here. But when you meet him, keep an open mind; don't judge him by his looks. He looks different than most people, but he has the gentlest of hearts. I have made a map for you to follow to the cave from here. I gave him a passcode that I will now tell you."

She nodded to indicate she was listening. He continued holding her hand as he spoke. His smile was captivating. His mannerisms were gentle and made her feel safe. She was happy he kept talking; that way, she could keep staring at him and admiring his handsome face without feeling guilty.

"The passcode is a question and an answer. You will ask him, 'What was the name of one of the four companions who traveled with Zelkova, the one known for his smile?' He will answer, 'Cedrus, the one with the gift of nature.' Make sure he says it just like that."

"All right, I will." All of this felt surreal to her, but she had to admit she didn't want to stay here. And she did trust him for some reason. "Are you a fan of the legend of Zelkova stories? I've only heard the tales a few times in passing." The stories of Zelkova had long been told for over two hundred years. Some say the events that happened were true, others say it was merely a child's tale.

"Yes, you could say that. It's getting late. We should get ready. Go pack some things you think you might need but pack light. I will meet you at the back of the castle past the kitchen yard."

She stood to leave but then turned to look at him and asked, "Why are you doing all of this for me? We only met yesterday. You hardly know me."

"Because there is something in your eyes, a fire just waiting to be lit. I don't want that light to be lost due to the cruelness of this world."

He smiled at her then headed out the door. Omnia questioned the feelings growing in her heart. Was this fluttering of her heart only because she had never been subjected to such kindness before, or was there more to it? She hoped not; Omnia wanted this warmth within her to remain.

It was just past noon when she headed out of the kitchen and into the gated yard. Just as she reached the gate, she heard screams from the courtyard. Before she could make her way there, something in the sky caught her eye. Looking up, she saw something she had only heard of from stories of old. A large floating island loomed above the castle. The bottom was made up of jagged stone. The top was covered in trees from what she could see. The island was longer than the castle and twice as wide. Omnia's heart sank at the sight of it.

Figures came down from the island, as well as more screaming. She was about to take off running toward the screams to see what she could do to help when someone grabbed her arm. Looking to her right, she saw Spero, who had a frightened look on his face.

What he said next made her more frightened than he looked. "It's too late. There's too many of them. Where did they all come from? Was all of what my great-great-grandfather did for naught?" he said, like he was addressing someone unseen rather than her. He turned her toward him. "You must go. I will try to help out here and hopefully meet up with both of you. Go to the cave I told you about. He will be waiting. I will meet you in two days' time."

"But you just said it was too late. Why take such risks?"

"I have to find out who is behind all of this. Now, go. Before they see you. Go, run!" He shook her shoulders, trying to get her to listen.

"Yes, yes, I will see you in two days. Please be safe." She tried to smile as they parted ways, but it was barely a smile. As she ran into the woods, he took up his sword and ran into the castle. So many questions raced through her mind. Would she truly see him again? What was happening to the people of Silva? Were the stories of the island and Zelkova true?

Omnia followed the map to the nearby cave, but no one was awaiting her there. As she sat outside the entrance, she noticed how clear and calm the day was. There was no indication of what was happening at the castle, and there had been no forewarning. Everything around her was silent when suddenly, she heard a cry from within the cave. Turning, she called, "Hello. Is someone in there?"

She listened and heard more crying, like that of a scared child. She stood and entered the cave. Instead of turning to the right, where holes in the ceiling illuminated the pathway, she went to the left, down a narrow shaft toward the cries. The light was faint. She fell several times and cut her hands. Minding her footing was hard, but she continued forward. After what seemed like ages, she reached a large cavern that was brighter than the passageway. Light once again streamed in from the ceiling. In the corner of the cavern, there was a pool of water.

Stepping forward, she knelt beside the pond to clean the cut on her hand. When she did, she heard the cry once more. Looking to her left, she saw a large stone with a flat surface. The stone had symbols carved into it. Some she had seen in books when she had snuck into the library as a little girl. One symbol was for time, another one for light. She couldn't make out the others.

Was the crying coming from the rock? How? Why?

Omnia reached out her hand and just before she touched the stone, it flashed and changed from four symbols to eight. One side of the rock glowed with a bright white light, while the other was shrouded in deep darkness. The symbols continued to transform before her eyes. She tried to pull her stretched hand away, but it felt as if the stone was pulling her to touch it. The force became stronger, and her palm pressed against the surface. She couldn't see which symbol her hand was on because the light and darkness surrounding the stone had now enveloped her body.

She screamed in fear and pain. The sensation took over her body and mind. It felt as if she were being pulled in two. The light and the dark seemed to be fighting for control, consuming her from the inside out. As she screamed, half of the room turned bright like a midsummer's day. The other half fell into pure darkness, like the side of the moon where light never reached. Her body started to float as the battle of light and dark continued.

Soon, both light and dark faded to gray and she glided to the floor, unconscious.

Upon waking, Omnia saw the cave just as it was before she touched the stone. She looked at the rock, but the engravings were gone. There was nothing to indicate if what she had just experienced was real or not. Did she imagine all of it due to stress? How long had she been out? As she climbed to her feet, her body ached. Her mind became foggy. She looked down at her hands. The cuts that had been there moments before were now gone, just like the symbols on the stone.

Needing air and sunlight, she moved slowly back the way she had come. For some reason, the path wasn't as dark as before. Once she made it out of the cave, she sat down near the entrance. Sunlight streamed through the trees. She heard a rustle of leaves and jumped to her feet.

Looking in the direction the noise had come from, she saw a shadowy figure among the trees. In a clear voice, she asked, "What was the name of one of the four companions that traveled with Zelkova, the one known for his smile?"

The man replied, "Cedrus, the one with the gift of nature." He stepped forward, and she realized he was not a man at all, at least not a human man. Even though his facial features were like a human's, his body was made of bark and wood. "Miss Omnia, I assume? Pleasure to meet you. I am Arbor." He half-bowed.

"Have you heard from Spero? A floating island came out of nowhere and people started screaming. Is he safe? He ran to help." The look of him made her wonder, but she thought it rude to ask about his appearance.

"He is safe. He will meet us soon. Come, we are still too close to the castle. They could find us here." Arbor held out his hand, motioning for her to follow. "I'm certain you have many questions. I was told you have never met an Elemental, which is now common in the world we live in. Elementals have kept hidden for the most part of two hundred years. I only show myself to Spero and his family."

"Why just them, if I may ask?" She stared at the tree-shaped man as they walked.

"I've known his family for many generations. I promised Spero's great-great-grandfather I would look after them all." He smiled sweetly at her.

Her eyes widened. "Wow, great-great-grandfather? And who was that?"

Arbor smirked at the question. "You really don't know much of our world at all, do you? Most people know who his great-great-grandfather was. His name was Cedrus and most of the stories are true, but some are over-exaggerated. Come. We should move faster. Things are amiss... I will help you. We aren't going to make it to the capital. We have to head somewhere safer."

"Safer than Solaris?" His words surprised her. Even though everything was moving fast and she knew she should be frightened, Omnia felt strangely at ease.

"Yes, trust me. I will keep you safe. Don't be afraid." Arbor moved the loose leaves under her feet. They lifted her slightly off the ground. She remained still as the leaves propelled her forward. "I will explain more once we get there."

They moved fast through the trees, going eastward until they turned and started heading north, which prompted Omnia to ask, "Are we headed to the Forbidden Forest?"

"So, you know of that then?"

"Yes, I have heard many people speak of it, how some go in and never come out. And that the trees are larger than normal trees. Is that where Elementals live?"

He nodded at her question, then asked one of his own. "Are you scared of me?"

"No, I put my trust in Spero when he asked me to trust you. Therefore, I am trusting you. I admit I wasn't expecting an Elemental from stories of old, but it seems like my life is taking many unexpected turns. Like Spero coming to my rescue, not just once but twice, then the island, meeting you and the strange thing at the cave. A lot has happened…" Omnia was surprised at how well she was handling it all. In some odd way, it was all like fate.

Arbor stopped her mid-sentence as the leaves beneath her feet slowed to a halt. "You went into the cave?" She nodded. "Please tell me what happened in there."

He looked stern but almost scared as he listened to her story.

Tentatively, she said, "I heard a child crying so I went toward the sound and found myself in a place with a pond. There was a rock that had symbols on it and I must have passed out and had a dream because what happened doesn't make sense."

"Tell me, what is it that you think you dreamed?"

"When I touched the stone, the symbols changed from four to eight symbols. Then a deep darkness and a bright light took over my body, as if they were fighting to see which would possess me. I felt like I was being pulled in two."

"We must really hurry then." His eyes were fixed on her, shoulders tense.

"Wait. Why? It was just a dream, right?"

Omnia felt as if he were trying to look into her soul. "I wish it were. Stand still. I will move you with leaves again."

They started moving again toward the Forbidden Forest. Omnia wanted to ask Arbor more questions but knew that it would only worry her more. The thought of what happened in the cave gave her chills. Surely, it was just a dream.

When Arbor and Omnia reached the edge of the forbidden forest, the sun was beginning to set, readying for the moon to take its place. Just before they stepped from one forest into the other, Omnia screamed. Arbor turned to see her kneeling on the ground. Half of her hair had become white, the other half black. He reached out to help her, but an invisible force pushed him back.

Arbor got up and approached her again, but a cloaked figure moved closer with unnatural speed. As it reached them, it knelt next to Omnia. This figure was immune to the force that had pushed Arbor away. It reached out, touching Omnia's cheek, causing her to scream in pain again. The cloaked figure seemed to be whispering something to her, but Arbor was unable to hear its words.

The figure lifted Omnia into the air. As the two of them hovered above the ground, something caught its eye. Something behind Arbor seemed to scare the creature so much that it dropped Omnia's unmoving body to the ground. And in the blink of an eye, it was gone.

Arbor turned to see nothing behind him. He rushed to Omnia's side, lifted her into his arms and headed into the thick forest.

4

After Spero left Omnia in the garden, his heart sank with unease, not just for her but for himself as well. He'd heard tales of the floating island, but he wondered how it managed to return and why. Was another Elemental uprising brewing, like the one over two hundred years ago? Was there going to be another war between humans and Elementals?

He ran up the back stairs into the courtyard where several small Elementals had emerged from the island. Many of them looked like shadows; he wasn't familiar with the type and he didn't know how to defeat them. Instead, he ran toward the Elementals he knew, fighting them off frightened people. Guards tried to fight them off best they could with swords, but that only worked on the nature ones.

"For fire, use water! For nature, use fire! I will take care of the water Elementals." Thankfully, there were no air or rock Elementals. Soon, the few fire, water, and nature Elementals were defeated, leaving the group to face off against the shadow ones.

Just as Spero and the others were ready to take on the dark forms, a bright light came from the sky, blinding them all. When their eyes finally adjusted, the shadows and the island were gone. The only evidence that anything ever happened was the damage done to the castle and its people. There were small fires about the yard, holes in the stone walls, roots protruding from the ground. People cried over lifeless bodies. Some were burnt beyond recognition. Others searched for loved ones they could not find.

Spero contacted Arbor through his gift of nature, which he and his family kept a close secret, telling him to head to the Forbidden Forest for the time being; he would meet them there after the cleanup and the meeting of the Council. But he soon learned that the Council was canceled in light of what had happened.

As Spero walked the halls of the castle, he overheard other Council members from different countries speaking of a war between regions. Everyone was throwing blame at the others' parties in hopes of flushing out the true source of the chaos.

"It must be Lignum." One of them glanced in his direction.

"No, no. I think it's Ager, haven't heard from them in years. What about Montis? They could have found a new king..."

The whispers continued as Spero left his party, who traveled back to Solaris without him. He would travel alone to the forest above Silva to meet up with Arbor and Omnia.

With the help of his gift, he moved faster than he would if he had a horse. Spero glided by moving the leaves under his feet. At times, he beckoned tree limbs to lift him up. As the afternoon turned to evening and the last glimmers of sunset faded, he decided to rest for a while. Leaning against a tree, he spoke to Arbor telepathically. He was thankful for his gift. It made connecting with Arbor and his family easier. Like well-connected roots, their thoughts could be shared effortlessly.

She what?

She went into the cave. Afterward, right as the sun was setting, her hair turned half white and half black. A dark figure appeared out of nowhere and whispered to her, but it was scared away by something unseen. It disappeared like a puff of smoke. She seems fine now, but she has yet to awaken. Arbor sighed.

I will reach the forest before sunrise. Let me know if anything changes or if she awakens. The questions that plagued him now were agonizing. Where did the island come from? What happened to Omnia, and who was the figure that appeared? As he puzzled over the day's events, a strong gust of wind blew past him. Spero stood, arming himself. Fog appeared in front of him, spiraling upward until it reached his height.

The cloud took the form of a man. Dark gray clouds formed his body, with even darker clouds on top of its head. The figure appeared almost human. He bowed to Spero and said, "I have heard of you on the wind. It's nice to put a face to a name. I was sent here to speed up your travel to the forest. My name is Ilex."

Spero put his sword away and bowed, knowing from the tales of old who this was. "I am honored. I have heard many stories of you and my great-great-grandfather. Is Aria with you?" Ilex and Aria were both air Elementals known for their connection to Zelkova. The thought excited him. It meant his hero was not just from a fairy tale but from history.

Ilex smiled at the name. "No, right now she's taking on an impossible task. I will tell you of it later. Right now, we should head to the forest. We should reach it in time for sunrise to see how Omnia will fare."

"You know of..."

"Yes, I hear many things from many sources. Come, stand by me. I will lift you up. Hope you're not afraid of heights!" Without waiting for a response, Ilex lifted both of them up into the night sky.

As they glided through the air, Spero was in awe of what he saw. The tops of trees were below them, looking like a green blur because of their speed and height. "I have so many questions I want to ask. First, did Zelkova really die? Where did the island come from? What are those shadow creatures?" Spero didn't stop to breathe between questions. When he finished, he sucked in air.

"You are an excitable one I see, but before I answer some of your questions, I have one for you."

"Please, go ahead."

Ilex looked at him. Narrowing his eyes and tilting his head, he asked, "Why did you rush to help Omnia? I understand the first two times. But why move her to your city, a whole country away? Why go to such lengths?"

Spero smiled, then looked up at the stars and with a thoughtful sigh said, "If I could help every hurting person in the world, I would. I'm in a good position to help people, so when I can, I do. As for Omnia, something about her... She's polite, shy, yet there's a wildness to her. It is as if there's something lying in wait within her, hoping for the day to show itself. Maybe it's her inner strength. I'm not certain. But I would like to see the day she becomes more of her true self, rather than hiding it due to the circumstance around her." He thought back on the book that appeared in his study but thought best not to speak of it. "Wait, how did you know?"

Ilex seemed a bit surprised by Spero's reply but sweetly smiled as he looked forward. "Air is constantly around you, is it not?" He paused. "Everything has become suspiciously still. There is a change in the wind."

"So, about my questions," Spero prompted when Ilex lapsed into silence.

"Oh, yes. First, the island and shadow creatures. The island has been off the coast for the last two hundred years and, by all accounts, should still be there. We're not certain how or if it even moved or if it is a completely different island entirely. The shadows are a different concern that we are still uncertain of ourselves. As for Zelkova..."

Right as her name left Ilex's lips, a gust of wind came from behind them. They both turned to see a large island. Black shadows formed from it, moving toward them.

"I didn't even feel them nearby. How?" Moving just as fast as Ilex, the shadows quickly caught up to them, surrounding them and the cloud they sat on. Soon everything around them was in darkness.

"Ilex! What do we do?"

"I'm uncertain. I've never encountered them before. I didn't feel them coming. I'm trying to push them away but they're not budging at all."

Spero and Ilex used their gifts to try to make the shadows back away or make a hole through the pitch-blackness to escape through. Nothing worked. Soon Spero felt pressure around him. Spero cried, "Are they trying to crush me?"

"It's not just you. I feel it as well. Seems like they are trying to enclose us. Maybe crushing is the result they are looking for. I can't tell."

Spero had swung his sword so much that he was gasping for air. "Who are you?" he shouted. "What is it you're after?" Nothing answered from the deep darkness, and the pressure only became stronger.

Spero saw townspeople suffering, the village and its people on fire. Others cried over their dead loved ones. The pain that pulled at his heart was excruciating. Image after image made him fall to his knees and grab his head, screaming in pain. "So, you want everyone to suffer? Is that your plan? If that is your endgame, I will fight you till the last!"

Despite their efforts, neither of them could push the nightmarish visions from their minds.

Suddenly, Spero heard a whisper that sent pleasant chills through his body. The voice spoke to his mind rather than his ears. *Think not of the pains of the past, nor the fears of the future. Remember the time you were most happy, the hope you felt for the future that lay ahead of you. Pull out those thoughts, push out the darkness that swirls in your mind with the light of hope and love.* As he heard the words, a light started to shine around them, pushing out the shadows.

Gradually, he pulled himself back to the reality of their surroundings. The two of them were no longer on a cloud in the sky, nor were they surrounded by darkness;

they were now on top of a mountain on a large flat ledge beside a cave where they could easily see the peak. Soon it would be sunrise, but the moon gave little in the way of light to show them their surroundings.

"Ilex, where are we?" Spero stood and neared the edge, looking down to see only faint clouds among the darkness. He turned back to see Ilex walking toward the cave. As Spero neared the entrance along with Ilex, they saw a small fire. It hovered in place above the ground, burning without any wood to fuel it.

Nearing the fire, he saw a bowl of food. Ilex sat down as if waiting for something. "Sit down, Spero. Eat. It was prepared especially for you."

Spero sat down near Ilex and picked up the bowl. "For me, by whom?" As he said this, a shadow crossed near the opening of the cave. Spero reached to draw his sword, only to realize it was no longer there.

Ilex smiled. "Looks like Aria was successful in some of her endeavors."

Spero looked to Ilex and then back to the shadow that came into the light.

5

The light from the flames cast shadows toward the entrance of the dim cave where the figure now stood. Spero stood beside Ilex, who wore a calm expression with a hint of a smile. As the figure stepped into the light, Ilex bowed. Spero's eyes widened in shock.

A tall rock creature in the form of a woman came toward the them. Her eyes were white with black pupils, hair of ivy tied behind her in a long braid, flames playfully laid on the tips of the leaves, not setting them ablaze. Small water droplets hovered among the flames, together, but not touching. He was surprised the ivy didn't catch fire and that the water didn't put out the flames. All the elements seemed to intertwine, making a sort of armor that wrapped around the stone body.

As Ilex rose from his bow, he smiled. "I'm glad to finally see you after so many years."

"As I you, Ilex. It feels like a lifetime ago but also feels as if it were yesterday."

Ilex turned to Spero. "Here is an answer to one of your questions. Let me introduce you to Zelkova. Zelkova, this is Spero, which I'm certain you already know. She is the one from the stories, the human turned Elemental. Only one of us to possess all of the gifts."

"Nice to meet you, Spero. There are many questions running through your mind. Which will you start with?" Zelkova moved toward the fire and sat down, and the others followed suit.

Spero looked at Zelkova in amazement. "All the stories I've heard, everything my father and grandfather passed on from Cedrus true? I had always hoped, but I never thought I would meet the one behind the legends. I do have many questions, but we need to get to Omnia before sunrise."

"True, and we will make it in time. Don't worry. Ask your first question."

Spero looked at Ilex who nodded, agreeing with Zelkova and urging him to ask his questions. "I guess the first one would be, how did we get here? What happened to the shadows and island? Sorry, I'm overzealous. That was two questions." He smiled and scratched the back of his head.

"To your questions, the answers are intertwined. I've been trying to hunt the island down since it started moving, but my view is blocked most of the time. When it connects with certain people, I can find it, which was the case at Lignum and when it attacked both of you. You both got here by my doing, but the island is once again blocked from me. I have spent all these years searching..."

She paused at the thought. Sadness was written across her stony features. "For over two hundred years, I've searched for the cloaked figure and for Carya. I only received a glimpse of the shadowed ones but none of Carya. And then the island moved. So many things are changing. I could try and stop it, but there's one issue. I can't get on the island. The one who started all of this is there, and they are blocked from me as well."

Ilex glanced at Zelkova. "Is it the same island you moved off the coast that disappeared?"

Zelkova looked up at him. "Yes and no. I need to talk to the one who made the island, but I have to wait till the next total solar eclipse."

Spero questioned, "Why then? Can't you just make one happen?"

"Because that's the only way to change what has been done. At least that is what I was shown. It's not that easy to make one happen. I have to think of the repercussions of my actions. If I made one occur, it would affect the natural balance of our world. I limit myself on how much and when I use my gifts. I could go around doing as I please, but where would that leave humankind?" She smiled at Spero.

"Tell me then, what happened to Omnia? How can we help her?" Spero asked in concern.

"I placed a seal on a stone in a cave. If it was touched by someone worthy, they would see a peaceful vision and I would know at once. But when I felt her touch the stone, I felt a darkness enter her. So, she wouldn't be taken over, I filled her with light. It was the only way to save her. She is battling the light and dark within her now. I fear there are more stones like that one placed throughout the countries but not by my doing. Once I visit Omnia, I will go and hunt down these stones."

Ilex nodded slowly, digesting that. "When is the solar eclipse supposed to be?" he asked.

"In several weeks' time. I may need Omnia's help if you think she will be up for it. She might be our way onto the island. Ilex knows I don't like to involve people unless there is no other way."

"That is true. Zelkova would rather do everything alone so that no one gets hurt, but she needs to learn that she's not alone."

"Very true, Ilex. That is something I need to work on. So, Spero, what other questions do you have for me?" She turned from Ilex to Spero.

"Tell me of the Elementals."

"That might take some time…" Eyeing him, she went on. "As you know, there are the elements of fire, earth, air, water, nature, light and dark. Of those elements there are Elementals. The First is, of course, the first of their kind, the first one made. There are other levels, Second, Thirds and Fourths. With each one comes different control of their element and the power they have over it. Ilex here is a Second where I am on the level of a First. I can see through all the elements, and he can see and hear through most of the air but is still limited at times."

"And of the others who were with you during your first travels? Such as Malus. I'd like to hear what happened to the others and my great-great-grandfather. Why didn't he turn into an Elemental like Ilex?"

"Instead of telling you, let me show you. But be forewarned, some images you see may be unpleasant."

He nodded in agreement. She placed her cool stone hand on top of his hand. As she did, visions shared from her mind went into his.

The first was of a middle-aged Malus who was sitting in his room looking over a stack of papers when suddenly, he couldn't catch his breath. He looked fearfully around the room as he fell to the floor. A dark, clouded figure appeared in the corner. It seemed to be in a shape of a man, the height of a young adult. But this was no man.

The figure knelt next to Malus who gasped, "Ventus."

"Ah, so you remember me. You're probably asking why I am doing this." Ventus grinned and whispered, "Because I hate humans. Well, I hate everything to be honest, and you just happened to be first on my long list of many."

And with that, the vision faded, bringing on another one. The next image he saw was of his great-great-grandfather. An elderly Cedrus rested in bed as a breeze blew through the open window next to him. He turned to see Zelkova in her new form standing beside him, smiling.

He gave her a bright yet weary smile. "It's nearing my time, isn't it?" he asked her in a whisper.

"Yes. I have come to say my farewell and to ask if you want to become a nature Elemental, to live with them for hundreds if not thousands of years. Or do you want to go to the afterlife and be with your parents, wife and, in time, some of your children?"

He smiled at the thought of his children. He knew some might turn into Elementals after their bodies passed.

"Even though becoming an Elemental is tempting, I'd rather be with most of my family."

"If I take your element now, your body will only last for a few hours. Are you ready for that, or should I come back later on?"

"I am ready. I've made my peace."

Zelkova leaned over him and kissed him on his now white-haired head. And as she did, he could feel his strength leave him. "Thank you for everything, dear friend. You will be greatly missed but always remembered. The legend of your bright smile will live on for eons." They smiled at each other one last time.

As someone else entered the room, Zelkova was no longer there and the vision faded from their connected minds. Spero blinked. "It felt like I was in the room with them! So, this Ventus killed Malus? Is Ventus still around?"

Zelkova shook her head no. "He seems to be out of my reach, just like the island and Carya."

"Who is Carya?" he asked.

The question brought a somber look to Zelkova. "She is someone dear to me. I would have long been lost without Carya. She has been lost to me for centuries. I have been looking for her for over two hundred years."

Silence fell upon them until Spero said, "It must be dawn. We should get to Omnia. How long have we been sitting here?"

Ilex smiled. "For about two hours. Don't worry. Zelkova put us in a time bubble where time passes at a different speed than outside."

Zelkova and the two men stood to exit the cave and the time bubble; it would soon be dawn.

Zelkova, Ilex and Spero traveled through the forest. But the way they traveled was different from anything Spero had ever experienced before. They moved at unnatural speeds. One second, they started off the mountain. Spero blinked and they were down in the woods. Blinked again and they were twenty yards from their last position. Within just a few moments, they were at the edge of the Forbidden Forest. Soon, they were beside Omnia, who laid on a bed made of intertwined tree branches.

A small group of Elementals was gathered around her. Arbor was among them, but Spero didn't recognize the other three, who Zelkova bowed her head to in greeting. Spero was too worried about Omnia to be concerned with introductions, knelt beside his unconscious friend. And noticed her hair was half white and half black. He moved to touch her hand but Zelkova stopped him.

"Not yet, might not be safe." She reached her own hand out toward Omnia. As she did, a force started pulling and pushing Zelkova at the same time. She looked distorted, as if she were in front of them yet somewhere else at the same time, struggling to be in one place.

Zelkova was experiencing much more than what they could see. In her mind's eye, Omnia was being torn in two. There was a shadowy figure kneeling on the opposite side of the unconscious girl, whispering to her. The others could not see this.

This figure spoke in a voice that was hauntingly familiar. It sounded like two separate voices, yet one in the same. "Everything must end in darkness; no light shall remain."

Zelkova's vision changed. She saw a lovely green field with all her family and friends there awaiting her. Looking down, she saw her hands were once again made of flesh. But as she looked up, everyone turned into shadows. Then everything went black.

This was someone else's memory, not her own. Zelkova tried to push through the new darkness that filled her mind. She tried to find more memories. And then found herself on top of a cliff beside a waterfall that flowed to a large river below. Had she been there before? Looking further, she saw Yin and Yang, the Elemental of dark and light, floating around her flesh body. The black and white orbs hovered in front of her.

They spoke in unison. "We have come to give you our gifts. But these gifts aren't to be taken lightly. You must not give in to one more than the other. If they are not in balance, you will be consumed by one or the other. You must keep a peace of mind. Do not let one emotion overtake you. Keep all in check. No more of one than the other. Together yet separate." This vision faded into yet another.

Zelkova was seeing memories from the past, but were they her memories? She was certain she'd never experienced the scene unfolding in her mind. This time, she was on a battlefield, sword in hand. She looked to her right and saw Carya being cut down only a few feet away from her. She glanced at the sword in her hand to see it enveloped in darkness. Was this her hand or someone else's?

The darkness gave way to a scene inside a cave, the same cave where Vatten used to live. Omnia was lying on the ground in a fetal position.

Zelkova spoke to her. "You are stronger than you think. You can give into the pain, but to what end? Is that the ending of your story, or will you fight to write a new one? The choice is yours. Give in and fade away or fight and overcome it. Find a balance. Remember the peace that a sunrise gives and the sadness of sunset. Take the good with the bad, welcome all these feelings yet let them go. Come to a place where all is in order. The light and the dark, together yet apart."

Zelkova continued to speak to Omnia as the others watched on the outside, not knowing what was going on in either of their minds.

Zelkova's body returned to a stable form. She no longer seemed to be flickering between one world and another. But she continued to stand, silent and still, at Omnia's side, who did not stir.

After a few moments, Ilex broke the silence. "Oh, yes. Spero, let me introduce you to everyone."

He went from left to right. "This is Aria, First of Air." Aria had the figure of a woman formed by dense gray clouds. Fluffier white clouds made up her hair. "You already know Arbor. This is Zelkova's mother, Nati, First of Nature. And beside her is Fraxinus, Third of Nature and Zelkova's father."

Spero's eyes lit up. "What are the differences between Firsts and Thirds?"

"Firsts are the first of their kind. They have the most control over their elements and have powers that Second, Thirds and Fourths do not, such as being able to see everything their element touches."

Fraxinus then explained that he'd met Nati again after the war two hundred years ago, and she'd given him the gift of nature. But he had only connected with the nature element for a few years before his human body passed, which made him into a Third. And that the Forbidden forest had been made forbidden after the war by Zelkova, making it a sanctuary for the Elementals.

The morning turned to midday as the group talked, watching Omnia and Zelkova all the while. Right before the sun fully set, Zelkova finally opened her eyes. Omnia still lay asleep, her hair still half black and half white. Zelkova turned and walked to the group. She sat down next to Spero in front of the fire.

Before he could ask his first question, she said, "All we can do now is wait and see what she does. She can either give in, which would be easier for her." Spero's eyes went wide. "Or she can fight and learn to control it. I gave her the tools she needs, but it's up to her now."

Omnia felt as if she were being torn in two. Voices cut through the pain that surged through her. One told her to give in to the darkness and allow it to consume her. To give in to the hate that was trying to flood her mind, so the pain would stop. That voice didn't last long, but it sounded similar to the next voice that followed.

It came to her in soft waves. "Find balance, light and dark co-existing. No more of one than the other. Together yet apart. United yet separate. Find harmony among the chaos. Believe in yourself. You are stronger than you know."

After the voices faded, she tried to will herself to be at peace. She tried to will the pulling and pushing to halt.

When everything started to ease, she heard yet another voice. This voice was her own, but it was different somehow. It was as if she now had two voices, the one she'd always known and this new side of her.

"Why are you still sleeping? You shouldn't be so lazy."

Omnia looked around for the source of the sound, even though she knew it came from inside her. "I'm not being lazy. I can't control all of this..."

"Why can't you? It's your own mind, isn't it?"

The realization shocked her. "Yes, that is true. Before I wake, though, shouldn't I try to get a better hold on this?"

"I guess you're the realistic one then." The other voice laughed.

"And I'm guessing you are one to act now and ask questions later."

"Yes, yes. Now let's do this, imagine yourself in an empty room sitting cross-legged on the floor. I will do the same." As Omnia did as the other voice suggested, she cleared her mind and pictured herself sitting in an empty room. Opening her mind's eye, she saw herself sitting across from a figure that was her mirror image — only this other self had a dark shadow around her, along with pale skin and dark hair. Different from her own darker tone and lighter hair.

"Since it seems you are different than me, shall we call you by a different name?" Omnia smiled.

"A different name? I guess you are right, Omnia sounds too cheerful for me..." She nodded in agreement. After thinking for a while, she looked to Omnia and said, "Call me Inane."

"And that name doesn't sound cheerful?"

"Better than yours." They both laughed at each other, or at themselves. They decided to practice throwing a light and dark ball of their making back and forth to control it, so that neither of them would be overtaken by its energy.

After several moments, Inane threw the black matter ball to Omnia. When she caught it, the darkness started to consume her. "You made it stronger!" she shouted to Inane.

"It was getting boring! You can take it. I believe in you!" Just as Omnia was about to be overtaken, she was able to push it back into a shape of a ball. Afterward, she fell to her knees, letting the matter roll toward Inane, who put her hand over the darkness and absorbed it.

She went over to Omnia and placed the light orb over Omnia's head, which she then absorbed. "I think it's time..."

Omnia looked up at Inane's words and replied, "But we have no idea what will happen when we wake up."

"There's only one way to find out!" Inane replied. She paused, sensing Omnia's apprehension. "Don't worry, you made me. Come."

Inane reached out her hand, and Omnia took it.

7

Night fell. The flames of the campfire cast long shadows. Zelkova stood, startling those around her, who were deep in thought.

Spero was about to speak when Ilex stopped him with a whispered, "She senses something."

The shadows around them started to shoot unnaturally toward the light of the fire. Zelkova turned around. Spero followed her gaze to see Omnia standing next to the bed. Black fog surrounded the side of her body where her hair was white. Her other side, with black hair, was glowing. Her eyes flickered and finally settled with black pupils.

Spero was about to approach her when Omnia spoke. Her voice sounded the same, but somehow different, as if it were an echo rather than her actual voice. "Spero, you made it here safely. Omnia is so glad to see you safe but who are all these..." She couldn't think of the word Elementals.

"Wait, what do you mean Omnia is? You are Omnia." Spero frowned.

"That statement is true, yes. I am Omnia and she is me, yet I am not her. We are different yet the same."

Spero was even more worried and confused when Zelkova stepped in. "To combat the light and dark, Omnia made you to help control both. To keep light and dark together yet separate."

She nodded. "Yes, she did. We are still uncertain of what is happening inside of us. Oh, yes. Omnia just reminded me that I have forgotten to introduce myself." With a slight curtsy, she went on. "Please call me Inane when I am in this state."

Spero smiled and stepped closer. "Let me introduce Zelkova. She's the one who gave you light so the darkness wouldn't overtake you. Next to her are Nati and Fraxinus, her parents. You know Arbor. Aria and Ilex are the ones next to him."

"It's a pleasure to meet you all. Tell me, Zelkova. What happened to us?" Spero was taken aback by the tone and mood of Inane. She was clear to the point, not shy and graceful like Omnia.

"Come, sit." Zelkova motioned for everyone to sit near the fire then continued. "I put a stone in the cave over two hundred years ago. I put it there so anyone who found it would be shown visions of what the world would look like without war. If someone found it, I would sense them. But when you touched it, I felt you and another. The other was trying to fill you with darkness, which I believe would have turned you into a shadow like the ones we've seen."

"People are the shadows?" Spero voiced in concern.

"I believe so." She paused, thinking. "There are other stones like it, but I didn't create them. I didn't know where they were until I felt someone touch them, and by that time, it was too late. I think someone has created these stones and enchanted the one I made to turn humans and even

Elementals into these shadow creatures. They wish to have their own army. I know you are wondering why I don't or can't stop them. When I reach the shadows, just like the island, they disappear out of my sight. I am unable to track them down until they appear again to someone else. Like I told Spero, I've been on the search for over a hundred years, but I think there may be a way to reach them now."

"What do we do about it?" Spero asked.

"First, there are a few Elementals I need. I must go and wake them up. After they join us, we will split up to find the stones that are turning people into shadows. Until then, I think it's best if Omnia and Inane practice more with their newfound gifts. Come, Inane. I will try and overtake you with light. You push it back."

"How did you know I was dark and not light?" Inane asked.

Zelkova's smile held secrets. "I can tell these things."

Zelkova stood to go train with Inane but Nati's words stopped the two. "It's been so long since we've seen you. I wanted to talk to you about something." She paused and then went on, knowing Zelkova was listening. "I've noticed a shift in what I can control. It feels like my power is weakening yet again. Have you felt this shift? Didn't our powers change two centuries ago? Does that mean they're shifting again?"

Zelkova sat back down, looking at the fire flickering in front of her. The fire was no longer burning the wood beneath it. It seemed to draw its fuel from thin air. "I have felt the shift. It started when I was on the island for that one year long ago. It started out slow, but in the last few weeks, the change has become more rapid."

Fraxinus looked at his daughter. "What is shifting?" Everyone's eyes lock onto Zelkova, waiting for her answer.

"The powers seem to be changing for Firsts again. From what I can tell, the elements are shifting to be controlled by one Elemental, not all."

"So, Elementals will no longer have control over their own element?" Ilex spoke the question on everyone's mind.

Zelkova let out a thoughtful sigh. "The power over the elements seems to be shifting to myself and to another. The other is the cloaked one you saw, Arbor. I do not know who they are, and I can't find them because their powers allow them to block their location, just like all the Firsts. It's just like you explained centuries ago, Mother."

"So, you and this cloaked one are becoming the Firsts. And the other First and Seconds, where does that leave them?" Spero voiced in concern.

She stared into the fire, as if searching for something. "I have been trying to find the cloaked one for almost two hundred years. But I have an idea. This person probably still wants Omnia and Inane as their disciples. It's probably interested in the fact that Omnia wasn't instantly taken over by darkness. If Omnia and Inane are taken to the island, I will be able to follow them. Then they won't be so easily blocked from my view. Before that happens, Inane and Omnia need to learn to control their gifts more or else the darkness will overtake them." Zelkova studied Inane. "What do you both think of this idea?"

Inane nodded in agreement, her eyes shining with determination but then changed to concern in an instant. "Omnia wants me to ask, will we... will she ever go back to being normal?"

Zelkova glanced at everyone in turn and then her eyes landed on Inane. "Once we find the one who controls the shadows, my hope is to return everything back to normal. But to do this, I need your help. I cannot and will not look at my own future again. I don't know the outcome that faces us all. But with everyone working together, my hope is to overcome this darkness." Zelkova studied the group. One by one, every head nodded in agreement.

So, they laid out a plan. First Zelkova would help train Inane and Omnia, while Arbor and Nati trained Spero to use his gifts of nature further. They would train as much as possible in the two weeks before the eclipse. Then they would head to the shore of Ruri. Zelkova, Omnia, Spero and Arbor would go on foot. Zelkova would only use her speed of travel in dire situations, not wanting to shift the elements more than they already were.

After the two weeks, they left Nati and Fraxinus who were setting off on missions of their own. Ilex and Aria had left several days before to seek out any changes in the elements. As Zelkova and her group moved from the forest toward Silva, Zelkova heard a message on the wind from Aria and Ilex, that they overheard of a stone being near Brandton. So, they would detour to the town below Silva.

The four of them reached the town just before nightfall to find it deserted. Not a soul was to be found within the borders of the city. Because Zelkova could not sense the stones through the ground, they split up to look around the edges of the town. Zelkova and Arbor, Spero and Omnia. Inane had traded control of her body back to Omnia at dawn but would be returning once the sun set.

Zelkova and Arbor went up above the town and into the woods, carving a path down to the right. Returning to this place brought back memories Zelkova longed to forget. Seeing Carya through the vision of time passed made her heart ache with pain, knowing she had lost the love of her life and may never see her again.

Arbor noticed this and reached his hand out to her. He smiled as she took it. "Come, let us not think of the past. You most of all know it won't bring back loved ones," he said.

She nodded at his words and they moved on through the forest. The sun soon set, and their surroundings became dark. It seemed like they had been walking for hours when they stumbled across a large rock where the forest met Brandton's main street. It stood taller than both of them and cast an even larger shadow from the moonlight. Arbor started toward it but Zelkova grabbed his arm.

"No," she warned. "Let me."

"But what if something happens to you?" he protested. "We can't lose you."

She smiled and shook her head in disagreement. "We are all important. We all have our place in this world. I have encountered a stone like this before. If it tries to overtake me with darkness, I am better equipped to combat it with the gift of light."

He nodded as she moved closer to the stone. "Be careful, Zelkova. You said yourself you don't know who is behind this. You don't know all they are capable of."

"Yes, I will. Thank you. You be careful as well. If the shadows come, do not stand guard. I would rather you retreat than be taken." They embraced and parted.

Just as she placed her palm on the stone, her surroundings changed, just like it did when she had touched the first rock over two hundred years ago.

Zelkova found herself in an empty field. Elements were mixed together in a whirlwind nearby. She tried to discern what time she had traveled to, but because this was only the second occurrence, she wasn't unable to pinpoint anything concrete. Nearing the tornado of elements, she saw a man on his knees in the middle of the vortex. He covered his head with his hands to protect himself from the raging winds.

Zelkova stood outside the force of the whirlwind, willing her voice to be heard by the ailing young man within. "Calm your senses. Focus on my voice. Nothing else. Clear your mind. Hear my words." Zelkova continued speaking to him. As he started to calm down, she was able to break through the vortex toward the middle where the man knelt.

Kneeling, she touched his shoulder. Visions of his life flashed before her eyes; the events that brought him to his current pained condition shook her to the core. The Elementals had done to him what they had done to her long ago, changing his life forever. But he was unable to control his gifts. Now knowing what timeline she was in, she could now assess how to make the least effect possible.

The man had calmed down and looked up at her. He started at the sight of her. She knew she didn't look as the other Elementals did. Zelkova had all the elements making up her body, taking him off guard. "How—who are you? How do you have all those elements? Please, don't give me any more ele…" He sobbed, unable to get the words out. "I can't…"

Zelkova smiled at him and took his hand in hers. "You have been through a lot, more than anyone ever should. You have fought bravely. I can help you if you wish."

"Help me? How? Who are you? Are you with the others?" The man stared at her, his eyes wide and scared.

"My name is not necessary for me to help you. I only wish to ease your burden. Is that what you wish?" Zelkova smiled sweetly at the man.

"Yes. I never wanted this. It is all too much."

"Tell me, out of all of the elements you have, which one do you feel the most connection with?"

He looked down in thought and soon lifted his head. "If I had to choose one that eases my mind the most, then I would choose nature." His voice was clearer and more controlled.

"I see." She stood and walked in front of him. He stood in turn, which made the remaining wind dissipate. "Throughout your years, you must not speak of this event to anyone, nor should you search me out. In time we will meet again, but to do either of those things before then could change both of our timelines, and not for the better. Do I have your word that you will never speak of this to anyone, nor search for me until our timelines cross and we both know of this moment? Give me your word..."

He nodded in agreement. "I give you my word. I will never speak of this, nor will I search for you."

"Good. Now, I will leave you with one gift. The Firsts will want to know how your gifts were taken. Do not speak of this. Say you woke up and they were gone. You have a place in this world, a much bigger part than you know. You must keep strong and keep moving forward. I look forward to seeing you again soon." She smiled and embraced him, relieving him of all his gifts but that of nature.

Zelkova released him from their hug. Her surroundings started to change. "Keep your word. Tell no one. Keep strong..." As she said those last words, she faded away and her vision went black.

Spero and Omnia moved to the left of the village as the light of the day started to fade. "Spero, I'm sorry for all of this. I feel that it's somehow my fault. I shouldn't have gone into the cave. I shouldn't..."

He turned to her, putting his finger to her lips. He smiled down at Omnia, seeing her bright eyes look up to him in surprise. "I never want you to be sorry for any of this," he said. "None of what is happening is your fault. You are only a victim of circumstance in all of this. I want to help you. Come, we don't have much light left." Spero took her hand and tugged her forward.

"Spero, thank you so much for your kindness. It's something I have very little experience with. Also, when Inane comes, please keep in mind her actions and words are not always my own. Sometimes I disagree with what she says and does. Please know this."

He turned to her once more and took her other hand in his. "Omnia, I understand. We will get through all of this together. I promise." They shared a tentative smile.

The light shifted around them, changing day into night and Omnia into Inane. He released her hands. Before either of them could say a word, the area around them became ever darker, even though the moon still shone brightly above them.

Spero looked around and saw a man walking their way. The outline of him was very dark, as if darkness seethed out of him. Taking out his sword, he shielded Inane behind him. "Whatever happens, stay behind me."

"I understand, but you have to let me help. I might be able to change him back."

He glanced back at her. Her eyes shone with determination. Reluctantly, he nodded. "All right, but don't push yourself too far. If it's too much, I want you to stop immediately."

Inane nodded. "I understand."

She stepped from behind him and held out her hands. As she did, the shadow that outlined the man's body responded to her. The darkness seeped out of him and crawled toward her. In seconds, the pitch-black darkness blocked out all light.

"Inane! Omnia!" Spero cried, feeling around him for her. Not a sound was heard, not even the wind through the trees. "Inane! Are you there? Call out to me, Omnia, please!" Sword in one hand, he reached out his other hand but found only darkness.

As he continued searching, he saw something in the distance that was even darker than his surroundings. Nearing it, he heard a man groan. "Hello? Who's there?"

As he neared the prone figure, he heard a faint voice. "Help me... I'm in so much pain... Kill me..."

"I can't kill you. But I don't know how I can help either."

"Please... Kill me," the man begged.

"No, I won't..." The man's words shook Spero to the core. Even though he carried a sword, he had never killed anyone in his life, nor did he plan on it. But the cry for help, the agony the man was in, pulled at his heart.

Even though Spero protested, the man continued to beg. "Please, help... Please, kill me... It's the only way..." The man groaned.

"No, there has to be another way. Inane? Zelkova? Can you hear me? Please help him!" Just as he called out, the man's outline neared him and before Spero could even react, the dark shadowed figure was in front of him. Spero tensed, mentally preparing to defend himself. Before he could so much as blink, the man lunged forward and impaled himself onto the sword. Spero gasped and jerked his sword away.

The shadows faded from the man. Spero grabbed him as he fell to the ground.

"Thank you, and I am sorry..." the man rasped.

Spero didn't have to ask why he was sorry. The darkness swarmed Spero, engulfing him.

"You killed him," a malicious voice whispered in the back of his mind. Pain consumed his body, feeling like a thousand knives slicing his skin open. "It's your fault. You weren't brave enough. You killed an innocent person. How can you face the world now? How many more people are you going to kill? You are a waste. How can you live when he is dead?" Spero screamed as another wave of pain blasted through him. "Killer! Murder!" the voice hissed," You should die, just like he did at your hands."

Spero could hardly stand the pain ripping his heart into pieces. He didn't want to kill, he never wanted to do such a thing. "Inane... Omnia... I'm so sorry," he cried.

Just as he was giving in to the darkness, warmth washed over him. A bright orb appeared.

"You are no murderer, nor a killer. You are kind and a warm-hearted man. Don't let these lies deceive you." Memories came into his mind: one of him helping a stranger who had a broken leg, another where a horse was caught in a raging river. With each memory, the darkness around him faded piece by piece.

When it faded completely, he saw he still sat in the woods near the town of Brandton with a dead man at his feet.

8

When Zelkova returned from the past, night had fallen over the woods, and there was no sign of Arbor. She touched a nearby tree to sense him but felt no sign of him nearby. Turning back to the rock, she stretched out her hand. As she did, a beam of light hit the stone. An outline of light and dark formed around it. She hoped the light would help combat the darkness and block the shadows

Feeling a shift in light and dark near the town, Zelkova moved toward the disturbance. When she reached the edge of the forest, she went north where a dense black fog covered the area. She swiped at the shadows with her hand, but the darkness remained. Zelkova sat down at the edge of the fog. Crossing her legs and resting her palms on her knees, she concentrated.

Zelkova closed her eyes and searched for Spero and Inane. "Spero, Inane, Omnia... Hear my voice." There was no answer. She tried again, but this time, it came out as a whisper floating through the air, piercing the fog.

"Spero, Omnia, Inane, hear my voice. Fight the darkness feeding your mind. Push back the bad memories. Reach toward the bright days of the past and the ones that are to come. Omnia, Inane, you can move the shadows. Think of bright thoughts. Think of Spero. He is combating the fog all alone. Help him. You can do it. You have the power, now make the will. Believe in yourself."

Inane screamed in pain. Surrounded by nothing but darkness, she could neither hear nor see. She could feel nothing but sadness until a faint voice came to her ear. "Inane, Zelkova is calling to us… Can you hear her?" Omnia whispered within Inane's aching mind.

She shook her head and closed her eyes. Pain still consumed her body and mind.

"Listen, Inane. Open your mind and heart. You are not alone. I am here with you, but I need your help. We must save Spero. Please, help me…"

Inane opened her eyes and looked around. She saw a faint light beside her. Taking it in her hands, she let it engulf her with the warmth of an afternoon sun. Inane could now see Omnia in front of her, shining brightly in her mind's eye.

"Come, take my hand, Inane, and think only happy thoughts."

A faint light slowly dispersed the black fog. Once it had lifted, the moon shone down on a scene no one expected. Men and women of the village laid around them as if a battle had been fought and these people had lost. Most were unmoving, some were slowly showing signs of life. But thankfully, they were all breathing. All but one. A man laid lifeless at Spero's feet, staring into nothingness. These people had been the fog itself, not just within it.

Zelkova found Inane and shook her out of her daze. "Listen, Inane, Spero needs to hear from Omnia. Can you do that? Go comfort him. Feed him with warm light. I will help the others."

Inane nodded and headed to Spero's side as Zelkova filled the area with heartfelt, soothing light to fight off any remaining darkness that lingered in the villagers' minds.

Inane sat next to Spero and pulled him toward her, making him look away from the dead man. "I'm to speak on behalf of Omnia. So, the next words I speak are hers."

Spero said nothing but nodded to acknowledge that he heard her. All the while, Zelkova listened from afar on the element of air and watched through the earth. This was something she rarely did. But this wasn't a normal situation.

"You mustn't focus on what happened tonight. The darkness that seeped into their minds, the voices you heard. All of that was the cloaked one's doing. That man was trying to ease his suffering the only way he knew how. He took his own life. The only one to blame here is the source of the darkness and shadows. We must help Zelkova and the others find and dispose of this shadowed one. We can't do it without you. We are all a part of this now, and we must work together."

Inane turned Spero's face to look at her and then took his hands. "Spero, I need you. I don't think I can get through this change without you. Please, Spero. Don't let the darkness take you as well."

Spero blinked blankly at Inane and then turned his head away, returning to looking at the ground. "Omnia, Inane, how can I get through this? How do I have the right to live when this man does not?"

Zelkova quietly knelt beside them. Her stone body glistened in the moonlight, and a smell of fresh spring rain passed through the air around them. It brought a peace of mind and ease of heart to those who sensed it.

Zelkova smiled at them. "You both have a place in this mission and in this world. You have to live, not just for yourselves but for those who have lost their lives. If you give up, their loss will affect the world more than it already has. Live the best life you can for you and for the ones who we've lost."

Inane turned to Spero. Tears were forming in his eyes.

Zelkova smiled and stood, leaving the two of them to talk. She went to the townspeople to speak with them to see if they remembered anything of what happened. They had awakened and headed back to their village. She carefully approached an older woman, not wanting to frighten the lady with her appearance. "I am here to help, but I was hoping you could help me as well by telling me what happened. What do you remember?"

"I don't know how it all started," she said weakly, rubbing her frail hands together. Most of the people had what looked like soot covering them. But she knew it was shadow residue. "It was late at night and I was about to go to sleep when someone knocked on my door. I thought it was odd and that they surely must need help, coming by so late. When I opened the door, all I saw was deep darkness, like every light in the world had gone out. After that, all I remember is pain. Pain and anger." Her voice cracked on the last two words.

Zelkova took the lady's hands in hers. "I'm certain all of this was hard for you, but do you remember if there was a voice trying to reach out to you? To order you to do things?"

A warm light surrounded Zelkova and those around her as she willed peace into the air. The sweet smell of jasmine was meant to calm frayed nerves and ease the people's fears.

"There was a voice," the old lady said, her voice shaky. "It told me to give in to the fear and hate, to find others and hurt them, to fill them with the same emotions that I felt."

A nearby middle-aged man overheard their conversation and stepped in. "I heard the same things. The hate in me kept growing. I felt if I could just spread the darkness, it would ease some of my own pain."

Soon, more and more of the townspeople gathered around Zelkova. She used the elements to sooth those around her, knowing sweet smell of lavender would calm their emotions. The sun was now peeking through the trees as a new day began to dawn. As Zelkova listened to the stories, she noticed Omnia and Spero sitting outside of the circle. They listened yet whispered amongst themselves.

A younger timid-looking couple came forward with a story of their son. "I remember it was mid-morning. I was taking care of our laundry and getting lunch ready when our son went out to play."

The husband cleared his throat. "Yes, and I was out in the garden weeding when I saw him enter the woods."

The women continued. "I came out to tell you lunch was ready, and that's when we saw it: a black form about the height of our child, exiting the forest and coming toward us."

Every eye was glued to the couple. "We didn't know what it was or that it was even him. We were scared, so we ran to our house. We heard screams and then silence. After a while, we thought maybe it was safe, that the thing was gone. So, we exited our home. It was midday and we didn't see anyone around. That's when we started calling for our son, hoping that the figure really wasn't him, that he was safe."

She fell silent. The husband looked to the edge of the group where several children played and laughed, and Zelkova followed his gaze. She was blocking out the stories the adults were telling and putting happy thoughts into the children's minds with the gift from yin and yang. They didn't need to experience any more trauma.

The man looked back to the group. "We walked around the town and saw the black fog. We ran from it, but we were soon overtaken. That's when we felt the hate, the sadness, the loneliness. I heard a voice, too, telling me to give into the hate and fear. That I shouldn't suffer alone, that I should spread what I felt. It kept speaking until I heard your voice, Zelkova, along with that young lady over there. I am assuming that was her voice."

He nodded to Omnia who still sat with Spero. She smiled sweetly in the direction of the group then turned her attention back to Spero, who still seemed to be shaken. Zelkova continued speaking to the group and even fixed them an afternoon meal, one with herbs that would help them rest and ease their minds and bodies.

Omnia came back once the sun started to rise. She still held Spero's hands as Zelkova gathered the townspeople.

"Spero, are you all right? Is there more besides the man?" She wouldn't let him look at the body near them. She stood up, making him stand with her. They went to sit near the group of people while some of the men went and took dead man's body away.

"Even though I'm trained in swordsmanship, I've never taken a life before. I never wanted to," Spero said finally, his voice low and haunted, avoiding Omnia's gaze.

"Spero, you've helped me so much, even though we just met. You are a strong, kind-hearted person, and you would never kill someone needlessly. Not willingly. What happened was not your fault."

His lips upturned in a hint of a smile, making her heart skip a beat. "Thank you, Omnia. It seems we have both saved each other."

"Yes, it seems that we have." They went on talking until the sun set.

"Will you walk with me?" he asked suddenly, offering his hand. She took his hand without hesitation. They walked to the outskirts of the small town, circling its perimeter.

"Thank you again, Omnia. You are stronger than you appear. I know you are scared by everything that is happening. I am as well. But like you said, if we're together, we can get through it all, right?"

During the two weeks they took to train, a friendship had blossomed between them. Spero made her feel things she'd never felt before, and she knew he felt the same. She'd caught the glances he'd stolen when he thought she wasn't looking. In so short of a time, he'd become important to her.

Smiling, she nodded. Spero lightly brushed his knuckles across her cheek. She tried to look away, but he took her chin between his fingers and made her face him. He drew closer, so close she could feel his breath, and in a split second, he had pressed his lips against hers.

9

They spent the whole next day and night in Brandton, helping the townspeople recover. And the three of them needed to recover as well. Zelkova again fixed them all meals: a vegetable stew to warm their bodies and hearts, along with some sweet bread. Omnia and Spero took small strolls during the day, talking and holding hands. Zelkova smiled at the sight. The flourishing love warmed her heart yet made it freeze at the same time. She shook her head, not wanting to think of things she could not change, of the love she lost long ago on the island.

After lunch, children rushed up to Zelkova and surrounded her, peppering her with question after question. "All right, all right. One at a time, please. We'll start with… You, little one. Go ahead. What's your question?" Zelkova smiled at a small little boy who seemed to be younger than the rest.

He smiled back at her, showing a missing front tooth. Ignoring what the older children yelled at him to ask, he asked, "Is it true?"

Zelkova crouched to his level. "Is what true?"

"Is it true that you were a human once?" His big, round eyes studied her curiously.

She grinned at how adorable he was. "Yes, that is true, but don't worry. Not everyone changes as I did."

Another child screamed, "How long ago were you human?"

"Over 200 years ago."

An older looking boy with bright eyes raised his hand. Zelkova nodded for him to go ahead with his question. "Do you miss it?"

Zelkova sat down on a log nearby, motioning them to gather around her. "At times I do, but there is a reason for everything and I mustn't dwell on the past."

"How do you make the food? Without using our gardens?" a curly haired girl questioned.

"I grow what I need myself. By using the gift of nature." Zelkova put her palm out flat. The children watched in amazement as a small flower grew in the center of her hand.

They eagerly gathered at her feet and sat down, continuing to ask questions, wanting to see more of her gifts. She answered them the best she could but then turned to telling them stories of old missions as a knight of the king's guard.

As Zelkova told them stories, the men and women gathered with their children to hear the stories as well. As she went on, her eyes caught sight of Omnia and Spero walking past. They didn't see the townspeople gathering. They only had eyes for each other.

Just as dusk was falling upon the town, Omnia and Spero returned. The villagers had finished the dinner Zelkova had made for them and were headed back to their houses when a gust of wind came out of nowhere, almost blowing the people off their feet.

Aria and Ilex were soon in front of Zelkova. Even though they didn't have the facial expressions of humans, Zelkova could still tell that they were both worried and frantic about something. "What is happening that I haven't felt?"

"Someone you've been on the lookout for is also hiding in the cloaked one's shadows. That's why you haven't been able to find him," Aria whispered hurriedly.

"Ventus?" she asked in surprise. "How did you find out?"

"Vindby, Second of air, has been in contact with him this whole time because he didn't see him as a threat. Now he has gotten his power back from when I weakened him. It has grown to mirror my own."

"The one making the shadows helped him regain his power, and in return, Ventus has been helping the cloaked one," Ilex said, frowning.

Zelkova looked down, searching for signs of Ventus but she could find none. "So, he has been helping them the last two hundred years, and because of that, he has been blocked from my view. I think they might have taken Arbor as well," Zelkova said sadly, feeling the pain of loss deep in her chest.

"Why? How?" Aria asked in surprise.

"When I touched the nearby rock, I was transported in time, and while I was away, something must have happened." Zelkova sighed. "When I got back, he was no longer here, nor could I sense him anywhere. Both of you be on your guard. If you see a stone like the ones turning people and Elementals into shadows, don't touch it. I'm still not certain how to get rid of them or how they work. They seem to have a different reaction with me. Since you are both here, why not stay the night and we can all head out in the morning?"

Ilex and Aria shared a glance. "We would love to stay," Aria said, smiling.

Ilex and Aria nodded in agreement to the idea. The three of them stayed up talking as everyone else went to sleep.

"How long have you known of this shadowed one?" Aria asked in a whisper.

"I've felt them for quite some time. But I do not know where or what they are. It worries me."

"Are you certain bringing Omnia and Spero along a good idea? I know I've told you for a long time to let others help, but..." Ilex voiced in concern.

"They can help where we cannot. We were once humans but are no longer so. To interact with people and to help others understand how this effects the human world as well as the Elementals, they are crucial."

"And you said before that Omnia may be able to help you locate the island. But she will have to be taken by the shadowed one, correct?"

Zelkova looked to Aria, nodding gravely. "I'm afraid so. But no harm will come to her while she holds light within."

The next morning, Ilex and Aria helped Omnia and Spero travel in the clouds along with Zelkova. They floated above the trees, high in the sky. As they traveled, Zelkova searched for Ventus and the floating island. This method of travel allowed them to arrive at Ruri's beach a lot faster than they would have otherwise. Zelkova could have moved all of them on her own, but that went against the rules she had set in place for herself long ago.

On the way, they intended to stop by Opima to see the king and queen. While Spero and Omnia saw to that, Zelkova and Ilex would watch from afar, not wanting to alarm anyone. Aria would go in with them. She could make herself invisible to the human eye and guard Spero and Omnia. Aria would also be able to send messages back to the others.

It was midday when they landed near the gates of the city. The city had grown almost three times the size in the last two hundred years, making it one of the largest capitals. The city was built in a circular pattern, expanding out in all directions.

As the three of them entered the city, Zelkova and Ilex stood nearby, leaning against the castle wall. Zelkova could blend in well with the stone, and Ilex could make himself nearly unseen, disappearing into a faint mist.

Ilex looked to Zelkova with a questioning gaze. "Why did you isolate yourself for so long? You hadn't seen a human in person before Spero, and you only came down from your mountain twice a year. We wanted to see more of you. All of us missed you."

Zelkova's gaze remained fixed on some unseen object in the distance. Ilex knew she wasn't looking with her eyes right now. She was looking with all her elements, searching; she was always searching.

Zelkova finally glanced at Ilex. "I had changed. These gifts can be hard to control. When I changed into what I am now, I didn't know how much power I had. I didn't want to hurt anyone or the world around me. I thought it best to hide away while I learned to control these gifts I was given."

Ilex wanted to say more, to tell her that she wasn't alone, that they could have tried and helped, but he knew she had her reasons, and he respected that.

"So, Spero is Cedrus' great-great-grandson? I can see the resemblance. I hope all of this doesn't change his cheery disposition."

"I hope so as well. If he resembles Cedrus in more than just in looks, he will be fine. Has Aria said anything to you?"

Zelkova heard and saw most of everything, but she still chose to act as if she couldn't. She held onto the hope that what she saw, any visions of the future, could still change. "They are entering the castle now and waiting for an audience with the king and queen."

"Like all of us so many years ago..."

Spero and Omnia entered the Council room and awaited King Dane and Queen Alys of Ruri. Omnia lightly touched Spero's hand. "Have you met them before? Are they nice? Do you think they'll be willing to help?"

"I have met them. They like to meet delegates in here rather than the throne room. More personal. I think they will take what we have to say into consideration, but I don't think they can help much. Maybe just warning their people will be enough help."

The guards came in, followed by the monarchs. The queen was tall with long black, flowing hair. The king, much like the queen, had an olive tone and high cheek bones. Both looked as if they were bronze statues.

As the two rulers sat down, Spero and Omnia came forward and bowed. Spero straightened and stepped forward. "Your Majesties, I have come here from Lignum and I wanted to warn you and your country of what we encountered — both in Silva and at the border of your land."

King Dane whispered something to the queen who then waved them on. "Please, go on. Tell us what you are wanting to warn us of."

Queen Alys eyed Omnia's hair. From the corner of his eye, Spero saw Omnia shift uncomfortably under the scrutiny.

Spero politely bowed. "My travelling companions and I, including this young lady beside me, have had a firsthand encounter of a strange harmful darkness invading the lands. It seems to be coming from large stones placed in unknown areas. We encountered one in the town of Brandton. Whoever touches it is taken over by shadows. When these individuals encourage others, they spread the darkness and the shadows then take them over as well. The whole town was in darkness."

The queen sucked in a breath. "What happened?"

"Luckily, we have several in our party who combat the darkness. We aren't able to stop the stones without someone else's help; we are now traveling to find them. Because of this, we want you to warn your people. If they see a large stone with strange markings anywhere, even within the borders of your city, they should not touch it for any reason. The darkness grows at an alarming rate and without someone here with the gift of light, your whole city could be taken over within a few days. Just like Brandton." Spero hoped his words would not scare them but help them understand the severity of the situation.

The king stood, his tall stature prevalent. "Who is it that has the power to control the darkness?"

Spero hesitated. "I wouldn't say control. They are able to help those who have been taken by it..."

A voice inside his head interrupted him. It was so faint he hardly heard it. "Tell him, if someone is taken by the shadows for too long, they might not be able to come back." Spero was still amazed by Zelkova's powers and how far they could reach.

"They can help, yes, but if someone is taken by the shadows for too long, there might not be a way to recover them. We are on the lookout for the source of the stones and the shadows. They seem to be on a floating island that is hidden from us. Once we can locate and defeat them, you and your people will have nothing to fear."

Queen Alys stood and put her hand on the king's shoulder. She leaned in to whisper something to her husband that Spero couldn't hear.

"She wants one of the people who can control the light to stay," Aria whispered to Spero and Omnia. Spero jumped slightly, having forgotten about the Elemental's presence.

"Tell them I can put a border around their city, but if someone leaves the boundaries, I won't be able to help them," Zelkova's voice murmured in his mind. "I have power but not so much that I can protect each living thing."

Spero turned the attention to him before the king could react. "The leader of my group should be able to put a barrier around the city," he said, "but if someone steps out of it, they won't be able to help. None of us can stay and stand guard. We have to find the source and meet up with more of our companions."

King Dane's eyes flashed in anger at being denied his will, but the queen put a soft hand on his shoulder before he could act. "Do what you can for us. I hope you are able to find what is turning people into these shadows, as you call them. We will tell our people to be on their guard." She smiled, her radiance glowing. "Would you both be able to stay and have dinner with us?"

"We would be honored." Spero dipped into a bow.

10

Ilex stood by Zelkova as she peered into the future, the past, or the elements. Maybe all three. Ilex was never completely certain. Just before dusk, she turned to him. "We should go inside. They are to eat with the king and queen. I hope what I see won't happen, but we should be there if it does."

Ilex faded away even more and entered the city. Zelkova entered through the stone wall by melding into it and reforming on the other side. She blocked people's view of her as she walked down the streets.

They soon reached the dining hall to see everyone sitting down to eat. Zelkova, Ilex and Aria stayed hidden from others' eyes, even Spero and Inane as they enjoyed the company of King Dane and Queen Alys. Even though Omnia was now Inane, Spero continued to call her Omnia, not wanting to confuse the monarchs. The four of them spoke of the shadows and how it affected the townspeople they saw.

During dinner, Zelkova continuously moved her fingers.

"What are you doing?" Aria murmured, softly so the others wouldn't be able to hear.

"In time, you will understand," Zelkova responded simply.

They didn't push the subject and merely watched. Zelkova soon stopped her motions and stood by with them, watching the dinner commence.

After dessert was served, King Dane started to get anxious. Beads of sweat rolling down his stricken face, he spoke with a guard who then left the room. After coming back, he whispered to the king, who then stood up and started to pace the floor.

Queen Alys stood and asked him what was wrong. He whispered to her. Aria and Ilex heard what he said, and they then understood what Zelkova was doing. The king had planned on drugging Omnia and Spero and holding them in their city in the hopes it would keep them all safe from the shadows. They were to have been dosed with a sedative in the first course. The king had started to panic now that the four-course meal was over. Ilex whispered to Spero and Inane, telling them what had occurred.

Zelkova stepped from the shadows, showing herself to the monarchs. The guards drew their swords and placed themselves in front of the king and queen.

"I am disappointed in your actions," Zelkova told them bluntly. "To try and take my friends hostage to save your city wasn't the correct action to take. I understand your reason, but I still hoped you wouldn't choose this path."

"What? I did no such…" King Dane turned stone pale at the accusation. Zelkova held up her hand to silence him, but the king didn't take too kindly to that. "How dare you!" he yelled. "Who do you think you are?"

When the guards advanced toward Zelkova, she moved her fingers in a circle. Following her will, the men's swords bent inward on themselves. The guards dropped their weapons to the ground. A chorus of swears and exclaims of shocks filled the room.

She bowed to the king and queen. "I mean you no harm, but I will not allow you to impair any of my friends. We are here to help, despite what you were trying to do to Spero and Omnia. I will still put up a barrier around your city. I wish I could do more, but even I have limits."

"Who are you?" the king demanded, his tone dripping with authority and command. This was a man who was used to getting his way. "*What* are you?"

"I guess I should introduce myself. My name is Zelkova. I am what is called an Elemental. Most of us are now hidden from human eyes but you might have heard of us through stories passed down through generations. If you would like, we could sit down and talk more, or my companions and I could just leave. What would make you more comfortable?" Zelkova schooled her features, making herself look less intimidating.

King Dane seemed embarrassed at his actions. "I did not realize they were with you. If I had known…" He paused, almost blushing. "Your name. I have heard stories passed down from our families." He motioned to the queen. "Please, stay and let us speak further." His actions and words changed after learning who she was, making Zelkova wonder what stories he had heard. Zelkova, Spero and Inane sat with the king and queen in front of their hearth, Ilex and Aria still out of sight.

"Have you always been this Elemental thing?" the queen asked Zelkova, breaking the silence first.

Zelkova considered her words, making certain to phrase her answers just right. "No, not all Elementals were born that way. Some were humans at first."

"I heard of stories about a Zelkova from my grandfather," the king piped up, eyes roaming over Zelkova. "He said he heard it from his father, who lived in the time from when the stories came. He said that there was a human girl who received gifts from Elementals. She tried to make peace between Elementals and humans, but in the end, she died."

Zelkova remained silent, neither confirming nor denying the statement.

"But she really didn't die in the end, did she?" King Dane asked smartly. "It seems she is still wanting to save everyone. Am I correct in my assumption?"

"It seems your great-great-grandfather saw the better parts. Some stories don't hail me a hero but a villain."

"I always loved to hear of your adventures," the king confessed, and Zelkova couldn't stop the smile that spread across her face. "I'm so glad you became an Elemental. I want to thank you for helping my great-great-grandfather and this kingdom. Who knows where this land and its people would be without you."

Zelkova bowed her head in thanks. She didn't like to be thanked for something she felt was her duty.

They talked late into the night. Eventually, Inane, Spero, and the king and queen went to bed. Zelkova asked

Ilex and Aria to keep guard. She would go outside the wall and set a barrier while the town slept.

She walked the empty streets, deep in thought. Some buildings stood from two hundred years ago, but where wooden buildings used to stand, there were now stone and brick buildings in their places. Zelkova remembered they day she had spent here before everything had changed. Before she had changed. Breathing deeply, as if she still had lungs, she went through the stone wall again and stood outside the city.

The wall stood twice her height. It seemed to be made of thick limestone. The city had grown and expanded over the years. Zelkova had never tried to put a barrier over a city. She wasn't even certain if she could, but she had to try. Never backing out on her word, she knelt beside the wall and moved her hands in a circle. After a moment, a bright orb appeared.

Zelkova held it in front of her for several long moments. The longer it hovered, the brighter and larger it became. She closed her eyes and as she did, the orb floated above the wall toward the center of the city. Once there, it rose ever higher in the sky. Eyes remaining closed, Zelkova moved her arms out then in, one after the other. The light orb expanded outward. With each fluid movement, it stretched to cover the city as if a dome of light was raining down from the heavens.

It was nearly sunrise, and the light almost covered the city. Right before the walls of her light shield hit the ground, Zelkova felt something stir. The island was nearing, and black shadows were quickly rising toward her and the city. She concentrated even more, closing off Opima with light just as shadows overtook her. She heard Ilex and Aria but told them to stay within the light wall. Everything around the city was covered in black fog. It was like the starless night sky had fallen around her.

The fog only expanded a few hundred meters in each direction if Zelkova was correct. Within the darkness, she heard a voice intertwined with muffled cries.

"I've been looking for you yet I've been hiding from you. Why are you protecting that city and its people? What have they done to deserve this protection?" the voice hissed.

"Why have you been looking for me yet hiding at the same time?"

"Because I want to know you, but it's not time for us to meet yet."

"Who are you?" As soon as the words left her mouth, pain and dark thoughts flooded her consciousness, much like those who were turned into shadows. "Are you trying to turn me into one of your shadows?" she gritted out through clenched teeth.

"I would love for you to join me, and I'm certain you will. If not now, then in time."

"Who are you? What happened to Tempus?"

"You know very well what has happened to Tempus. You've felt the change. You just don't want to admit it. As for who I am, time will tell."

"How can you control time itself? Tempus should have stopped you..."

When the voice dissipated, Zelkova heard hundreds of voices around her crying out in pain and anger. She even recognized some of the voices. "Yin, Yang! How? I don't understand..."

Zelkova heard Yin and Yang's voices more clearly than the other screaming ones. "We don't understand either, and we can't fight them. They seem stronger than both of us. Help, help...."

She concentrated to cast out the darkness with happy and peaceful thoughts. The pain eased.

"Omnia, I mean Inane, is trying to leave Opima," Ilex informed her in alarm. "It's like she's possessed."

Zelkova stood from her kneeling position and moved her arms from her side in front of her, palms open. Beams of light shot out from both hands. One moved to the left and the other to the right, fighting back the darkness.

"How?" the voice from before demanded. "I knew you would be strong, but this? It seems we might be equally matched. No matter, I will see you again soon."

As quickly as it appeared, the darkness retreated along with the island, as if it were never there.

Zelkova stopped her beams, letting her arms fall to her sides.

"Spero, he's being taken over by Inane's darkness," Aria cried.

Zelkova swiped her hand in front of her face, as if taking off a mask. She blew into the palm of her hand as she extended it toward the city. She looked out into the fields where the darkness had been and saw several bodies laid out. They were not just the bodies of humans but of Elementals as well. Just as she stepped forward to help them, everything went blank…

Spero awoke from deep sleep to see Ilex floating above him. It looked as if a ghost had taken form and was haunting him.

"Wake up!" Ilex shouted. "Omnia —I mean, Inane is trying to leave! Hurry! The island and the darkness have shown up. They may be controlling her."

Spero sprang to his feet. He ran out of his room and tripped in the process of putting his shoes on. Following Ilex, he ran down the halls and stairwells. Down the streets, the two caught up with Inane. Aria was trying to hold her back with air. She had to put up one wall of cloud after another, having to release each layer because the darkness would overtake them just as fast as she put them up.

Spero reached out to Inane, touching her shoulder and turning her to face him. When he gripped both shoulders, darkness crept up his arms. "Inane, Omnia, listen to me! You can't listen to the darkness trying to take you over! Listen to me instead! I am here for you. Don't give into it. Please hear me!"

The shadows reached his shoulders and upper legs, leaving only his torso and head. Soon, a bright orb appeared, floating in front of him. It entered his chest, casting out the shadows and enveloping him and Inane with light as a new day dawned.

Spero found himself in a bright area, like a whitewashed room. He stepped forward, calling out, "Omnia! Inane! Are you here? Can you hear me?"

After walking a while, it seemed like he wasn't moving, the scenery around him remained unchanged. White nothingness stretched for miles. But then in the distance, a black aura appeared. When he reached it, he saw Omnia and Inane sitting on the floor, leaning against each other, back to back. Omnia looked like her old self, no longer with the black and white hair. Inane had hair as black as night and pale skin, a stark contrast to Omnia's blonde locks and bronze tone.

Spero sat down beside them, but neither looked at him. Their gazes were fixed on something only they could see. "Omnia, I am here for you. Do you remember me speaking of the light within you? You still have that. Use it to fight the darkness trying to take over. Think of a cool morning breeze on a hot summer day. Think of our first kiss."

As he reached out to Inane and Omnia, a bright light extended from him onto the two of them, casting out the shadows. It got brighter and brighter. He blinked, and they were back on the streets of Opima. Ilex and Aria were helping Omnia, lifting her off the ground.

Spero rushed to her. He wrapped his arms around her, hugging tightly. "I'm so glad you are all right. I was so worried. How are you feeling?"

Omnia nodded then looked up at him. Her gaze locked onto his head. "Spero... your hair. What happened? Did I...?"

"Huh? My hair? What about it?" Spero ran his hand through his hair and felt nothing out of the ordinary.

"It seems you were given the gift of light," Ilex said, glancing over at him. "You have streaks of white in your hair."

"I was gifted light? By whom?" Spero looked at the three of them, wondering, but already knew the answer.

Aria floated around the other three. "It came from outside the wall, so it must have been Zelkova. Zelkova, are you there?" No reply came.

Spero looked down at Omnia, squeezing her tightly once more before releasing her. "Omnia, none of this was your fault. It was the cloaked one and their shadows. We should go find Zelkova now."

They headed out the front gate, leaving the protection of the light barrier. After searching the surrounding area outside the castle walls, Ilex found Zelkova leaning against the wall. Lying around her were dazed people and Elementals who had been released from the shadows Zelkova had cast out.

"We need to wake up Zelkova. Try and reach her through light. Touch her and think of light entering her body," Aria said urgently

Omnia and Spero nodded and knelt next to a nearly lifeless Zelkova. They both placed their hands on her arms. Closing his eyes, Spero focused as Aria had instructed. When he opened them, they stood in a dark room. The walls were seething in dark shadows. Omnia and Spero held hands as they stepped forward, looking around for any sign of Zelkova.

"I recognize this place. It's the library in Silva. I snuck in there once as a child," Omnia whispered.

After scanning the room, he looked to the right. Where a window should have been was only darkness except two books atop a table.

When Spero reached out to touch one, a voice came from behind them. "Don't... Don't touch them."

Turning, he saw Zelkova in human form. Black fog covered her, making it hard to tell it was truly her.

"Why—why can't we touch them?" Omnia asked, failing to hide her nervousness when she stuttered.

"Never touch the books. I have tried for two hundred years to burn them, to get rid of them, but they always reappear, always two... No one should have the knowledge they possess. I wish I didn't."

Omnia tried to reach out to her, but Zelkova drew back, hissing. Omnia smiled hesitantly. "Please, we're here to help you. You remember us, don't you?"

Zelkova looked down and hugged herself. "I know no one," she said, voice far away, "yet I know all. Pulled in too many directions. Expected to do all but can do nothing..."

Spero turned again to pick up one of the books again when another voice from the corner of the room stopped him. "As she said, you shouldn't touch them. Who knows what would happen to you."

Zelkova emerged from the darkness, her stone form more familiar. She went and stood next to the shadowy version of herself. "This looks familiar, doesn't it, Omnia?"

Omnia nodded. "Very familiar."

Spero studied both Zelkovas. "What is going on? Why are there two of you?"

Zelkova smiled then looked at herself. "There are always two sides to every coin. One that leans more toward the light and one that leans more toward the dark. It's the actions we take and the decisions we make that turn us into who and what we are. The other one of me you see here is what could have been."

Spero tilted his head in question. "If you were aware, why haven't you woken yourself up yet? Why are we here?"

Zelkova left the side of herself and went over to the table where the two books laid. The other Zelkova hissed, "Don't."

As Zelkova reached the books, she scrutinized them closely as if seeing them for the first time. "She's right. I've tried to get rid of them, but it seems they are in this world for a purpose. Oh, yes. Your question… Why did you come and why haven't I woken up yet?"

The two of them stood in between both Zelkovas. One stood strong and sure while the other seemed to be trying to shrink into herself as the darkness increased.

Zelkova reached out as if to touch the book, before snatching her hand away. "You know, I haven't slept in over two hundred years. Now that I have, I can understand why I don't sleep. Tell me, before you touched me, did any of the elements seem out of balance?"

The question confused Spero, and he was uncertain how to answer. "No."

Omnia shook her head in agreement.

"You two should leave," Zelkova said, surveying the library.

Omnia went to touch Zelkova but quickly drew her hand away when their eyes met. Omnia swallowed and asked, "Why should we leave? We came here to wake you up. There are a lot of humans and Elementals who have escaped the darkness. They need your help."

A hush fell over them. Only the human Zelkova's harsh breathing could be heard.

Spero finally broke the mind-numbing silence. "We need you back with us to help save everyone. This darkness is growing stronger. We all feel it."

Zelkova whispered, so soft they could hardly hear her over the other one's breathing. "I know..." She sighed as if trying to let go of countless years of stress that lay on her shoulders. "I know. I'm coming."

She wanted more time. A thousand things flickered across her face, but she kept it all in. Spero wondered if she continued this way, would she turn into the hard-breathing dark form to their right?

Zelkova turned to where the window should be and said, "Go."

A bright light rushed in from outside the window, engulfing everything around them.

Spero awoke with a start. He looked around, blinking away the haze. Aria hovered nearby. Ilex, Zelkova and a few guards were helping the dazed people and Elementals.

Spero rushed over to Aria, Omnia close on his heels, concern written on her face. "Is Zelkova all right?" he asked anxiously.

"When she woke up, did she seem any different?" Omnia asked.

Aria looked at Zelkova then back at the two of them. "No, same as usual. Come, you two. Use your light to comfort whoever you can."

Guards and people from the city came out to help those who were found in the field. Zelkova left the humans for Omnia and Spero to help. She went to the Elementals instead. After some time, the people were ushered into the city. The ones who didn't survive were carried in on carts to hopefully find their families, but Zelkova informed the guards that some of the dead had been in darkness for longer than they should have lived in human form. As for the Elementals, they were sent into the Forbidden Forest to seek aid from Zelkova's mother Nati, the First of nature.

Spero helped an older man walk into Opima, taking his hand in his own. "Tell me, is the war over?"

"War?" Spero questioned. There hadn't been an all-out war since the last one Zelkova was in. Battles here and there, but not war.

"There were Elementals about and humans chasing them. Then there were others helping them. Everyone was confused about what side to be on. Is it still going?" His voice was weak with age.

"No, sir. The Elemental war ended over two hundred years ago..."

They both fell silent. The weight of what this meant for many of the new arrivals weighed on them all.

They took the rest of the day and the night to help any way they could. And when night fell, Zelkova took Spero and Inane aside to speak with them. "What you saw, please don't let it trouble either of you. Now that Inane is awake, the two of you should practice. Spero, this will be your first time, so you two will throw a light and dark sphere back and forth. Don't worry if one of you is overpowered. I am here to help. But the name of the game is to avoid being dominated by one or the other. Now, form a light orb in front of you, Spero, and you, Inane, a dark orb."

Spero frowned. "Why is it that I don't have two of myself, like Omnia has Inane, now that I have the gift of light as well?"

Zelkova paused, choosing her words. "Spero, you have less light than Omnia. When I gave her that gift, it was to combat the darkness, so I had to give her the same amount of darkness that was given to her. For you, you didn't need as much light to fight off her shadows. I hope that clears up any confusion. Please feel free to ask me anything. I don't mind."

Spero smiled in gratitude. "Thank you."

With that answered, the practice began under the watchful eye of Zelkova. The tossing of the spheres continued for some time. Eventually, with one swift movement, Zelkova snapped her fingers, and the two orbs disappeared in an instant. "It's getting late. You should both get some rest. Go on now."

Before Inane or Spero could speak, Zelkova walked off in the direction of the castle.

Zelkova's feet carried her down to the dungeons, which was thankfully empty. Meeting with the shadows full-force had been trying for her. Sinking to the floor, her insecurity overcame her, filling the whole of the chambers with a thick choking fog. Thoughts of the past came flooding back like a tidal wave of bitter emotion.

The insecure voice in her mind whispered, *You can't save anyone. Look at who you lost. No one can save you from what lies ahead. You must face all your hardships alone or risk losing even more of your loved ones.* This was the dark side of her, the side she had to suppress.

So many thoughts consumed her, eating away every wall of resistance she'd put up over the long lonely years she had spent in isolation. Zelkova started to question herself. *How can I get through all of this? How can I save those around me when I can't even save myself? I never wanted this... I never asked for this...* The darkness surrounding her deepened, like the darkest abyss.

She must have closed her eyes because now there was a small orb of light floating in front of her. Zelkova reached out to touch it, but when she did, her hand was on a flat stone, just like the one at Brandton. In a blink of an eye, she found herself in another place. The castle dungeons were gone. Zelkova stood, taking in her new surroundings.

The landscape was a vast desert, something she'd never seen before despite her connection with the land... What trees and bushes had once grown there were long dead, filling the air with the stink of decay. There was no sign of life, at least not as far as the eye could see. She started walking, the dry hard dirt mixed with loose sand underfoot.

As Zelkova walked up a slight hill, she realized where she was. Lignum, near what used to be the Forbidden Forest. One lone tree stood among twigs that were once budding trees. Past it was the mountain she called home. Everything was a barren wasteland.

A storm brewed in the distance above the mountain. A bright light flashed, and lightning hit the tree in front of her. Seconds later, a loud clap of thunder shook the surrounding area. She had never experienced thunder or lightning before. Storms were rare in Elementum because the Elementals controlled everything, keeping everything in balance.

Which meant this Elementum was in chaos.

She couldn't even tell where she was in time or what universe she stood in. When she reached out to the elements, pain riddled her body as if they were showing her how they felt. This place was dead. Just as the thought crossed her mind, an image flashed by her mind's eye. A verdant green garden with people working the fields, picking the ample crops. Just as she tried to look closer, some force pushed her back.

Darkness flooded her mind as two voices fought to be heard.

"You must move forward. You must save this land…" the softer of the two said, almost in a whisper.

"This world is doomed, no matter what choices you make, no matter what path you follow," a harsh, pain-filled voice countered, out of breath.

In unison, the two voices told her, "You can't control all. Others have choices that dictate the future outcome."

"Be strong. Push through…" The soft voice surrounded her like a summer breeze.

The harsh one felt like winds from a raging storm. "You will sacrifice more than you know."

The voices faded and Zelkova was back in the damp dungeons of Opima. The stone she thought she had touched was nowhere to be seen. The darkness that had engulfed her was now gone. She sat in the abandon cells, deep in thought, until sunrise.

12

Hours later, the capital finally settled down. As the sun rose over the horizon, the five of them headed out of the city and to the sea.

Aria and Ilex lifted Omnia and Spero into the clouds, and Zelkova followed. They floated in silence, all of them seemingly lost in thought. Were the others thinking of the future as Spero was?

The sun rose high in the sky, and the shadows hid from the sun. The party landed near a stream so Spero and Omnia could eat and rest.

Spero took a seat next to Omnia on a hill close to the nearby stream. He silently handed Omnia a piece of bread Zelkova had made for them. She accepted it with a quiet thank-you. Neither of them spoke, uncertain how to act.

Omnia finally broke the silence. "So, you have the gift of light now? How do you feel about receiving it?"

Spero looked out toward the woods and the stream before them, pondering the answer. "It's interesting how I see the world around me now," he finally said. "It's probably also easier to deal with than what you have. I don't have as much light and dark as you have."

"How you see the world?"

"I see the aura of living beings. I see both dark and light. I can tell if an animal or plant is close to death from its aura alone. I try not to see people though. I would rather not know how close someone might be to death. I can also see better at night."

Omnia nodded, taking in his words. "I guess I haven't tried to see the aura of living things. I'm not certain if I want to. Inane says she sees better at night as well. Do you mind that Zelkova gave it to you?"

Spero looked at Omnia. When their eyes met, she shyly turned away, a blush staining her cheeks. "I don't hold any resentment toward her for it. I know she had good reasons. Zelkova knows and sees more than she lets on. She'd rather not burden others, so she shoulders all of it on her own."

Omnia glanced over to where Zelkova, Ilex, and Aria sat down the hill toward the stream. After a moment, she bashfully gazed back at him. "You see all that by looking at her? She seems strong and certain, not burdened at all."

"You are looking with your eyes. Look with your gifts. There's always more than what we can see on the surface." Spero took Omnia's hand with a smile. "Just like what I saw in you the first time we met. I look forward to getting to know more about you."

Omnia smiled sweetly. "And I you, Spero. I must admit, though, I am a little frightened. Why is all of this happening?"

Spero sighed. "I don't know the reasons behind all of this. I just know we're a part of it now, and we have to help stop this darkness."

Omnia looked away. "Can't we just walk away? I didn't want a part of this."

"We can't just walk away from all of this. Zelkova and the others need us," Spero told her and then added quietly, "I need you. We have to help. We don't want this world to end up in darkness." Spero studied Omnia, hoping his words reached her. After a moment, he glanced over at the other three, who hadn't moved.

"I want to just walk away. I just want to turn a blind eye to all of this. Pretend that none of this is happening," Omnia said softly.

"That's understandable. I'm scared as well. But if we turn our backs on something that is hurting others around us, it may hurt us as well. If we have the power to stop it, we have to try, not just for ourselves but for the world around us and everything in it."

Omnia nodded. "To stand up to the injustice of this world. If we have the power to help, then we have to try, right?"

Spero smiled brightly at her, nodding in agreement. "Yes. Are you with me? Will you help me?"

"Yes, Spero, I will help you."

"And once everything goes back to normal, we can make a new life for ourselves. Together." His smiled widened at the thought of making a wonderful life together. As Omnia blushed and turned shyly away, he hoped she felt the same as he did.

Once they were done resting, they packed up and headed to the beach. Once again, they took to the air to move faster toward the large rocks at the edge of the ocean. Zelkova studied the skies as she moved ahead of the others. They would have to spend the night on the beach to wait for the solar eclipse that would happen the next day. Zelkova thought on this, thought of what she must do to get back the ones she loved.

A few hours before sunset, the five of them made it to their destination. The sight of the two stones almost brought tears to Zelkova's eyes. She had seen them several times in person and hundreds of times in visions. Yet, the sight of the two of them frozen in time, and the past that led up to finding them, teemed in her mind.

As the other four set up camp at the edge of the beach and the field, Zelkova went to stand in between the stones. Placing her hands on each stone, she whispered, "Pyrus, Sten, you will come back to this world. I will make certain you get your lives back, and I will protect you to the best of my ability."

Omnia, Spero, Ilex, and Aria stood at the edge of the field, looking onto the beach where Zelkova was walking.

"Aria and I are going to check the surrounding area while the two of you set up camp," Ilex said.

Spero nodded, though he thought Ilex had a hidden motive in wandering off with Aria. They were leaving words unsaid, so as not to worry them. The sun would soon set, and Omnia would turn into Inane. So, Spero wanted to make every moment he had with Omnia count.

"You said you lived in Silva all your life? What about your parents?" Spero asked as they started setting up the tent.

"I'm not certain where they came from. I hardly know anything about them. I was told my mother had a kind heart and that my father was very humble and quiet. That's all I ever really heard of them, and that they worked at Silva as well. Doing what, I don't know."

The subject was a bit gloomy, so he tried to brighten up the mood by telling a story. "Maybe I should tell you more about the legend of Zelkova and her companions."

Omnia smiled. "I would love to hear it."

Spero grabbed one of the poles and jammed it in the earth. "It was almost two hundred years ago. A farmer's wife told a story of encountering the legend. It was said that Zelkova gave the lady seeds. She was told to plant only three at a time in a dark corner of her house, giving them one drop of water each day, and no more. The farmer's wife did as instructed, and the vegetable it produced was like nothing anyone had seen before."

They finished the tent and went about starting a fire. He went and collected wood while Omnia put stones in a circle. Spero hoped he could finish the tale before sunset. "The vegetable was the size of a well-formed eggplant, but the color was unusual. It was a dark red and when opened, the inside was dark purple. Its texture was kind of like that of eggplant as well, but the taste was much sweeter. At least, that's how it tasted for those who wanted something sweet.

For others, it was savory or spicy or even bitter. It seemed like whatever the person wanted to eat, the vegetable would end up tasting very similar to what they craved."

"What happened to the plant?" Omnia asked, eyes bright with curiosity.

Looking up at her, he said, "It was said that the want of them became too great. The lady was told to plant only three at a time or the plant would not grow. So, she hid the seeds. Others who had harvested the seeds from the vegetables could no longer grow them. No one has seen the plant in over a hundred years."

Omnia smiled. "It turned into a legend as well, then?"

"Indeed." Spero looked at Zelkova, who stood in between the two large stones in the shallow water of the ocean.

"What of the island we saw? Where Elementals came raining down from." Omnia's eyes were wide with wonder.

"It had to become a legend. Not very much is said about it, just that the time Elementals used to live there and rumors of Zelkova using it to form her Elemental army, which was not true." He stretched his neck, thinking. "Yes, there's not much to say about it because it was rarely seen, even when Zelkova was human. It only appeared a few times."

Omnia's eyes shifted as the sun set. She gradually turned into Inane right before his eyes. "What are the stones? Is there a story behind them as well?"

By then, Aria and Ilex had returned and took form next to Spero.

"I didn't know the first time I saw the stones," Ilex answered, coming up behind them. "It wasn't until much later that I found out one is her brother Pyrus, once the prince of Lignum. The other is Sten, the First Elemental of stone. She has known how to turn them back for two hundred years, but she wanted to wait until the natural cycle of a solar eclipse would occur. She has the power to make an eclipse on her own, but abuse of her power can bring great consequences. Even though she has great control, there is always a limit to powers, even hers. She is not one to risk the lives of every living thing for just two. So, she waits, knowing her patience will pay off in time. Zelkova still doesn't know how they were turned into stones. She hopes to find out once they have returned to their natural forms."

Spero sighed. "To have lost a loved one like that..."

"She sacrificed a lot. She didn't get to age as a human as I did. She saw her human death and could do nothing to stop it. And Carya..."

Spero wanted to ask more of Carya. He knew very little of what happened, but he thought it best to wait until Zelkova brought up the subject.

They stood in silence, watching Zelkova and the two stones.

Zelkova stood motionless between the large rocks as the sun sank in the distance. She continuously scanned the elements for any sign of the cloaked one or the shadows. Something seemed off, but she saw no sign of the shadows or their maker. As the others rested for the night, she sat on the sandy beach, looking into the past and very little into the future. She wanted to limit her knowledge of the things to come because knowing future events didn't always make or break the outcome. Zelkova wouldn't let herself be excited about finally seeing her brother and Sten, not until she saw them in front of her eyes.

Just as the sun was starting to rise, she went back to camp to see Omnia and Spero waking. "Good morning to you both. I will fix you breakfast if you like."

Spero yawned and started packing up his tent. "That would be wonderful. Thank you."

Omnia smiled in gratitude. "Yes, please."

Zelkova knelt. She cupped her hands, and within a few seconds, a wooden bowl formed. Smokeless flames crackled under the bowl. She motioned her hand above the mixture as if stirring it. Zelkova conjured two wooden bowls and spoons, then poured half the mixture into each. She handed one to Spero and one to Omnia and sat down near them.

"How did you both sleep?" she asked. "Well, I hope. Oh, let me know what you think of the food. I haven't eaten food in a long time, so I'm not even certain what tastes good anymore." She smiled slightly, watching them each take a spoonful.

A bright smile came to Spero's face. "I'm speechless at how good this tastes. I have never tasted anything like this."

By the time Omnia and Spero finished their breakfasts, Aria and Ilex had returned.

"As we traveled the borders, it was quite strange," Ilex said, floating in front of the group. "There was no motion, no wind, no birds. No wildlife, Elemental, or human to be seen for miles. There were no signs of the cloaked one or the shadows."

"It was like everything was asleep or hiding," Aria interjected.

Zelkova stood and looked out at the ocean. "I did feel something unnatural last night, but I couldn't quite place my finger on what it was. I still can't..." She looked back at them. "The solar eclipse will be upon us soon."

Zelkova turned back toward the beach and the two large stones in knee-deep water. The sun was rising between them.

They waited for the eclipse for a bit longer. Omnia, Spero, Ilex and Aria stood on the hill, watching. Zelkova kept searching for what was causing the unusual feeling, and she didn't have to wait long. A dark fog appeared out of nowhere off the coast and rushed toward them. First, it overtook the two rocks and then the beach within seconds.

"Watch out!" Zelkova warned, conjuring a light bubble to protect the five of them and not a second too soon.

The fog surrounded them completely, rising higher and higher, blocking out the sun. Nothing could be seen outside the bubble of the light. Zelkova glanced around to make certain everyone was safe. Omnia was holding her head, screaming in pain. The dark force was stronger than the last time she had encountered it.

As if by instinct, Spero surrounded himself and Omnia in another layer of light. Omnia fell to her knees, clutching her head. He knelt beside her, whispering.

Zelkova's only thought was to get the others out safely and not let the darkness consume them. She heard countless voices coming from the shadows, all of them full of pain. The screams echoed in the fog. She scanned the dense blackness, searching for the one controlling it.

"Are you scared? Don't be. You will join me soon," a voice rang out above the others.

No matter how much Zelkova searched, she could not find the person or the floating island. They were both hidden from her. Her enemy was getting strong... Why did their power seem to grower ever stronger, and why would they not confront her? Was the cloaked one waiting until they had gained as much power as they could?

She didn't know the answers, but Zelkova did know something. She was not the scared one; they feared her, and they both knew it.

She stood, searching the elements, as Aria and Ilex watched Spero and Omnia, who still knelt in pain. Zelkova went over to Omnia and placed her hands on either side of Omnia's head, close but not touching. A soft light floated around Omnia, encircling her and the light Spero had surrounded her with. Seconds later, sharp pain lanced Zelkova's chest. Ilex and Aria both gasped.

Not moving her hands from the sides of Omnia's head, Zelkova looked down at herself. A black spike impaled her midsection. How had the darkness invaded so many levels of the protective light without her notice?

In a daze, Zelkova tried to find the source of the spike. All of this was happening too fast; her control was lost. Who could cause her to lose so much power? Falling to her knees, Zelkova glanced up. Inane's face showed sheer delight at the sight of the darkness seeping into the light. Not Inane, but the cloaked one who seemed to be controlling her. In a blink of an eye, her vision went blank.

She could feel their agony and fear. Every living thing seemed to be in pain. So much pain...

14

Everything happened so fast, so much so he could hardly react to the events as they unfolded. First came the fog, then Zelkova made the light bubble. He'd looked to his right and saw Omnia screaming in pain. It was like all Spero's senses were blocked. He couldn't hear anything, saw things in slow motion, and could not react fast enough. His body acted on instinct and put another light shield around himself and Omnia before his mind grasped what was happening around him.

He tried to help Omnia, and so did Zelkova, but in an instant, everything went black. Spero heard and saw nothing in the darkness around him. He moved his hands in a small circular motion, hoping to form an orb of light. Thankfully, it worked, and he saw his hands holding the orb. There was nothing else around him, only dark shadows.

"Omnia! Inane! Anyone?" Spero yelled, hoping for a response but none was heard. Trying again, he yelled, "Answer me! Can anyone hear me?" He saw some movement near him. A patch of darkness to the right was even darker than the rest, though that seemed impossible. Spero moved toward the deeper blackness, not knowing what he would find once he reached it.

As Spero edged closer to the dark outline, the blackness shifted, as if it were alive and breathing. As he reached the darker space, he felt a pulse of emotions coming from the figure in the abyss. He reached out to them, and they turned. To his surprise, he could make out the person's features, despite the darkness.

His shock forced him back a step. "How?" Staring back at Spero was himself. At least, it looked like him, but he had dark circles under his bloodshot eyes. His skin had a pale purple hue to it. "Who are you?"

The dark form smirked at his question. "What kind of question is that? It should be obvious who I am. I am you."

"No, you are not me."

The figure glared at Spero. "No, you are the one mistaken. I am you."

For a moment, words failed Spero. "Fine. If you are me, where are we? What is this place?"

The figure kneeling before him motioned for Spero to look around at the nothingness around them, but Spero only glared, causing this dark version of himself to grin. "You don't even recognize your own mind? Are you certain you're the real Spero and I'm the fake?"

The darkness seemed to ooze negativity. "You're saying this is in my mind? If that's true, then I can control my surroundings." He closed his eyes and thought of light chasing away the darkness.

The other Spero stood and neared him. He remained focused on bringing in light. "You don't deserve the light," the other Spero hissed, fighting Spero's light with darkness of his own. "You killed that innocent man. You belong in this darkness. How can you continue to live when he is dead? Dead because of you." The dark figure circled him. "Do you actually believe you can save this land? That you truly can help others? You're insignificant. One pebble in a sea of stones. What can you do? You are nothing."

Spero's eyes remained closed, but his brow creased at the words. The battle raging in his heart seemed to have caused the surroundings he was in now. If this was all his doing, then he had control.

He could control his feelings and his mind. "Remove the darkness. Replace it with light." He repeated this over and over, squeezing his eyes shut, blocking out the words his other self was spouting.

He slowly opened his eyes and looked around. There were still spots of black, but light now shone in. His heart eased at the sight. Looking down, he saw himself start to fade. Spero knelt beside his darker self. Putting his hand on the other's shoulder, Spero smiled and asked, "Are you all right?" The dark shadow around him was gone. "You seem shaken. How can I help?"

His other self hissed. "You want to help me? Don't you see that neither of us deserves help?"

"Everyone deserves help. No one is too far gone to not be reached by the light of hope." Spero stood up and extended his hand to himself. They locked eyes and both of them smiled. As they took each other's hand, a bright light filled the vastness around Spero.

Blinking, he saw the other version of him had vanished along with the fog.

Omnia's body filled with pain as the darkness seeped into her eyes and mind, taking over her entire being. She felt Spero and Zelkova trying to push light into the darkness, but she had already fallen too deep.

"Inane! Are you here?" she cried. It felt as if she were drowning in a whirlpool of endless darkness. "What's going on? Someone help! Is anyone there?"

Panic sunk in when no one responded to her calls. How could Inane not be there?

"Inane! Where are you? Please answer me!" She couldn't see anything. Everything was the same shade of black. Was she in her mind or somewhere else? Omnia reached out her hands, hoping to feel a wall or something solid. But all she felt was air. "Spero? Zelkova? Is anyone there?"

She breathed, trying not to let dread take over. She thought of how she made orbs of light before. Cupping her hands, she concentrated, trying to make one appear. Omnia tried over and over without success. She even pinched herself to see if she were awake. *If you pinch yourself in a dream, does it wake you?*

"Someone help me! Inane, Spero, Zelkova. Anyone!" She didn't know how long she had been in the darkness. There was no sense of time. Thoughts ran through her mind like wildfire. She tried again to form an orb of light and this time, a small flicker appeared, like the flame of a candle. With the end of her finger, she moved it around. After a while, she tried to form a larger orb of light, but again, nothing happened.

In an instant, the darkness disappeared, giving way to light like dirt falling away from limestone. The fog was lifted not by her but by someone else. Looking around, Omnia saw lush trees and large, flat rocks. Behind her were clouds. These clouds were at the level of the land, which seemed to vanish a few feet from where she stood. Was she on a mountain top? But then fear struck her at the realization that she was on the island in the sky.

She heard movement toward the trees she'd just seen. Turning, her eyes fell upon a cloaked figure with a glowing outline. The realization of who this person was set her nerves ablaze.

Could this cloaked person be the one the others spoke of? She must truly be on the island Zelkova was searching for. Omnia searched for a way out, all the while hoping she'd spot her companions nearby. The cloaked one came closer and, in a blink of an eye, was standing directly in front of her. The figure stood almost a head taller than Omnia. She tentatively took a step back, eyeing them.

"I'm glad you made it here in one piece." The voice sounded familiar to Omnia, but she couldn't quite place it. "Most people go insane by the process. You were even able to make a faint light. Quite extraordinary, I must say. Even though I wasn't expecting you to receive light along with dark, it's working out much better than I planned." The person snickered.

Omnia started shaking, not just from fear but also from the cold. Wherever she was now was much colder than where she had been, making her think she was higher in the sky than she had first thought.

"Oh, my apologies." The figure moved closer to Omnia. In one motion, it looked as if they removed their cloak and put it around her. Omnia felt warmer, but the cloak remained on the figure's shoulders as if they had made a duplicate.

Looking at her own shoulders, she saw a thinner, cleaner version of the dark cloak. "How did you—?"

The shadowed one interrupted Omnia. "Sometimes it's best not to know the answers to your questions. Come, we have a lot to talk about and very little time to do it." The person extended their hand for Omnia to take. As she reached out her hand, she caught a glimpse of the cloaked one's hand, causing her to hesitate. The hand was almost as dark as the void she'd just came from, with cracks of light running through it. The cloak did its job of hiding the person underneath. Omnia couldn't see any features as they walked further into the cover of the trees.

They walked through a thicket of trees and came upon a clearing. A log cabin stood in the middle. From the outside, the cabin looked as if it should be a single room, but it was a lot larger on the inside than it appeared. Inside, there was a large seating area to the left. To the far right, there was a kitchen and a spacious dining area. There were stairs leading up and down and doors to other rooms. Nothing was of this era or the eras before. She had never seen the likes of it.

A fire blazed in the hearth inside the sitting room. To her surprise, there was no smoke or wood. The figure motioned for her to sit and went into the kitchen. As Omnia waited, she continued to look around. She still could not hear Inane's voice.

The cloaked one came over and set a plate of food in front of Omnia along with two books. Omnia noticed the cloaked one's hands and wrists again. Where skin should have been were flecks of deep blackness with cracks of white showing through. It looked like dry ground cracking under the heat of the summer sun. Or cracks in a painting that had too much light exposure.

Omnia studied the two books on either side of the plate of fruit and vegetables. One book cover had a tree in the middle and an island with a rock beside it. The sky was split between night and day. The other one looked almost the same, but the tree stood on a large rock surrounded by water; the tree leaves were engulfed by fire. The tree itself was untouched by the fire.

The cloaked one cleared their throat, making Omnia look up but she could still not see their face.

"Pick a book. Either one will do. Because once you have looked at one, you will then look at the other," the figure said, pointing to the books.

"But why? What are these? What do they have to do with me?"

"Just pick up a book. The faster you comply, the better off you will be." Those words sent chills down her spine, and she stiffened.

Omnia picked up the first book. It felt like dead weight in her hands, as if it were made of metal. It even felt cold to the touch. Once she touched it, the pages turned rapidly, and a vision filled her mind. She saw herself at the age of ten. She was dancing around an unknown hallway with people who looked like they could be her parents. Her father's dark skin and light hair were much like her own. The person she perceived to be her mother took her hand and led her down the halls. Her mother had light brown hair. Her dark eyes were deep and full of knowledge.

Blinking, she found herself back in the room with the shadowed one. The sight of what her life could have been made her wipe away stray tears. Omnia didn't realize wanting something could hurt so much.

"What did you see?" The person leaned forward, their cloak still concealing their face.

Omnia wondered if who she saw were her parents. She had been just a baby when they both had passed. Omnia shook her head.

"Tell me..." The shadowed one's voice got louder. "Tell me, or you will lose your other half." Omnia looked to where the cloaked one pointed. Stepping out of the shadow of the kitchen was Inane. She was visibly shaken, but her gaze was full of strength and determination. Omnia looked back at the figure and nodded her head.

Seeing Inane caused the fear she'd been trying to suppress to surge to the surface. "I saw what looked to be myself..." She paused, trying to clear her throat of the fear that threatened to choke her. "I was around ten years old, dancing through halls I've never seen before. People who seemed to be my parents led me down the hall. That's it. That's all I saw."

The cloaked figure motioned for Inane to come closer and sit down next to Omnia. "Now, Inane, you do the same. Pick up the book."

Fear gripped Omnia more and more with every breath she took.

A moment later, Inane sat the book down and shook her head. "The pages turned, but I saw nothing."

"Look at the other book, Omnia. Inane, look at it with her. Maybe you will both see the same thing."

The girls nodded and took the book in hand. If felt different than the other one. It felt like it was alive, like energy extruded from it.

Once she took it in her hands, the pages turned, just like the one before. This time, she saw herself as a child, crying in a lonely room, wanting to see her parents who would never come. Then the vision rapidly turned to the day she met Spero, which brought about a flood of emotion. But again, the view in her mind faded away to another. This one was of her and Spero, and they were both older. They were walking around the forest Arbor had brought her to. The Forbidden Forest. The vision expanded, showing the forest and the mountain on the edge of it. But outside the forest was a deserted wasteland.

The book closed with a thud, shocking Omnia back to reality. She glanced at Inane, who nodded. Omnia told the cloaked one of what she saw, but she omitted the last part. The shadowed one sat back in the chair. They seemed to melt into the background as if they were truly a shadow.

Inane looked down at her hands, and with wonderment, she asked, "How do I have a body separate from Omnia?"

"You may think and feel as if you have your own body, but you are just an image. We see you through our minds, therefore you are. You and Omnia are still one and the same. I have just put a barrier between the two of you, so you cannot talk to one another without me knowing."

Inane stood and paced. Omnia stared at her while the cloaked one sat motionless. Inane turned to the cloaked one. "Why are we here? Where are the others?"

The shadowed one leaned forward. "They are all safe for the time being. The reason you are here is because you are not consumed by the darkness. By some form of luck, you were given light, which helped you control the darkness. I want you to join me."

Before they could say more, Omnia rose to stand next to Inane. "Why would we do that? You are the one turning everyone to shadows."

The cloaked one laughed. "Is that what she has told you?"

Before she could respond, the shadowed one screamed in pain. As they fell to their knees, Omnia saw their hands and wrists once again. Before she could see any more, a black fog excreted from the shadowed figure. The darkness soon surrounded Inane and Omnia, returning them to the nothingness from which they came.

15

Zelkova found herself in darkness. Nothing could be heard or seen. She scanned her mind and surroundings, but no one was near her. They were somewhere else, blocked from her. The cloaked one was doing this, but why? Why now of all times, and how could they block her from searching the elements?

She sat down and formed a watery orb in front of her. Because of the increase in her powers, she no longer needed the element near her to form it. Waving her hand in front of the orb, she muttered, "Vatten..." After a few moments, the orb shaped into a man's face. He had a somber look about him as he looked at Zelkova.

Zelkova smiled slightly at the look on the man's face. "I know you are still upset about what happened, but I need your help."

"I'm not the one still holding a grudge. You are the one keeping me here, locked away in a small pond. Never able to leave, only observe."

"True, I haven't had a chance to come free you from your prison, and now is not the time to talk it over. Right now, I need to know what you see. Is the world taken over by darkness or is it just me and my companions?" Zelkova waited on his answer, her eyes fixed on his form.

"It seems to be just you and the others. But I can't see where some of them are. I just know that the land is the same as it was. I see no great mass of darkness."

"And what about the rocks in front of me?"

"They still are just that, rocks."

Zelkova nodded and started to pace. "What about the eclipse, is that still happening?"

"Not that I can see… Wait, something… Someone…"

The orb of water splashed down at her feet, but it wasn't Vatten who broke their contact, nor was it Zelkova. Looking around, she saw a darker fog nearing her. In mere seconds, it engulfed her. She could no longer see. The gift of Ying and Yang did little to help her.

"Why are you fighting?" a voice whispered next to her ear. "We could work together. We could become one."

Pain filled her body. The pain was much worse than what she had felt when her human form was dying.

"Give in to the pain, then you will join the others," the voice said, sharpening. "You will never feel alone again. Just give in."

"You think I'm scared of feeling alone? I've been alone for over two hundred years," Zelkova gasped. It felt like someone had punched her hard in the stomach.

"Why must you fight this? This is what you wanted. Give in."

Her body felt as if it were being torn apart. "What…" She gasped in pain. "What do you want…" Her legs felt like they were being crushed under heavy rocks, her arms being pulled from their sockets. "Tell… me…"

"I already told you. Give in. Join me." A laugh erupted around her as her screams of pain went on. "Give in."

Zelkova heard another voice. This one was much softer and not as clear, but she still heard it through her screams. "Giving in won't bring about what they think. Instead of thinking of it as giving in, think of it as absorbing..."

Zelkova could hardly breathe through the pain. Even though she did not need air, it felt like she was suffocating. As she struggled for breath, she listened to the other voice. Instead of giving in, she would absorb...

Going limp, she thought of taking in what was hurting her, to accept and absorb it... As she did, her pain ceased, and she heard screams. Opening her eyes, she saw holes of light coming through the darkness.

Zelkova stood on shaky legs, and with a motion of her hands, the fog surrounding her was no more. She found herself on the beach near the two large stones in the water. The eclipse had started. The day had turned into night as the moon blocked the sun, creating a bright circular outline. But Zelkova didn't have time to bask in its beauty.

It must have been put on hold somehow — she'd been in the fog a lot longer than a few minutes. She should have missed it. But it was not the time to think of that. She had one thing to do before the solar eclipse passed. Just like the book had shown, she raised her arm in front of her. A tree grew in between the large boulders, then with a snap of her fingers, a fire blazed on top of the water's surface.

Motioning both arms from left to right in opposite directions, she summoned a wind that blew from the north and south. Zelkova waited to see if her vision would come true. She turned and saw the black fog nearing her once more.

She wouldn't let the fog interrupt her again. This was her one chance to get her brother and Sten back. Zelkova wouldn't let anything stop it.

She put one arm out toward the stones, the other arm toward the fog. The fog stopped, hitting the barrier Zelkova had put up around her and the stones. The fog moved to try and block out the eclipse.

Turning, Zelkova put her arms up then pulled them away from each other. This pushed the fog back from the sky. She dropped to her knees as she fought against the fog that threatened to destroy what she'd worked toward for the last two centuries.

She gasped in pain and strained under the battle she was fighting. Somehow, the cloaked one matched her in strength.

Just as the eclipse passed, a bright light shone down on the rocks, nearly blinding her. It pushed back the fog, releasing the pressure from Zelkova. She stood and walked toward the rocks. She could no longer see them in the bright light. She hoped it worked.

As the light faded, she saw stone figures in the shape of men standing just off the shore.

A smile came across Zelkova's face. She couldn't remember the last time she had smiled. She fought the urge to go up and hug the two figures now standing in the stones' place. Knowing they'd gone through a lot, she waited for them to get their bearings, all the while keeping watch over their surroundings.

The sun was now shining normally. Zelkova stared at the two stone figures standing in the water. She held her breath, waiting for them to come up to the shore. Longing to see their faces and hear their voices burned in her heart. In the back of her mind, she worried they would only be taken from her once again.

The mist created by the fire and wind gradually cleared away. As it did, she stepped closer to see the two stone Elementals. One was taller than the other. The shorter of the two had wavy hair made of dirt, the color reminding her of his human form. When he turned, the curls moved slightly like his hair would have. She smiled at the recollection of her brother, but that smile soon faded.

"You!" a voice boomed. "I trusted you. You said not to tell her, not to warn her. So, we didn't, and look what happened!" The shorter of the two waved his arms in Zelkova's direction. "You said you could handle them. That no one could take you on." He stepped closer to the taller one and looked up at him. He shoved his finger into the other one's rocky chest and yelled, "Guess you were wrong about that! Someone could take you on and did! All of this..."

Zelkova's eyes widened. "Pyrus..."

The shorter of the two, the one with the wavy dirt hair, turned and glared. He put his hand up to her, making her stop mid-sentence. Zelkova had never seen Pyrus like this. Sten was the one with the short fuse, not Pyrus. He wasn't easily angered, which made this even worse; this meant he had something to be angry over, and it worried her. She looked to Sten to see how he was handling this rare side of Pyrus.

Sten stood tall and stared down at his beloved, who continued shouting at him. "I should have warned her. How long have we been set in stone?" He turned to Zelkova for the answer.

"Over two hundred years..." Zelkova sighed as her brother clenched his hand into a fist.

In one swift movement, Pyrus punched Sten. It caused a small shock wave when Sten hit the ground. Pyrus stood above him, glaring down. "The anger I feel has left me speechless, and all of it is aimed at you." Pyrus walked to Zelkova and took her into his arms. Pyrus had grown taller in his Elemental form, her head now resting against his shoulder. "I'm so sorry, Zelkova," he whispered, fighting back tears. "You weren't meant to face all this alone. We were supposed to be here with you... I don't know what happened. I just know it's not what either of us wanted." He sighed and stepped back, looking down at her with a weary smile.

She didn't know what to say to him, so she simply nodded and smiled sadly back at him. The only person she showed her weak side to was finally standing in front of her. Tears streamed down her face.

Pyrus grabbed her again and brought her in for a long, strong hug. Like always, his arms shielded her face from anyone who might see. He had always been her shield. Not from swords or arrows; he was not one to fight. He shielded her from the ugliness of the world, from the glares and words people threw at her. He would always guard her against that. It was safe to let her sadness show in front of him and him alone.

After a few more moments of his strong, reassuring embrace, Pyrus let go of Zelkova. The two of them turned to see Sten walking toward them. Pyrus shook his head, indicating he was not ready to speak with him. Pyrus lifted his hand and pushed his palm forward, sending Sten flying back into the waves.

He studied Zelkova for a long moment. "What has happened?" he asked heavily.

Zelkova sighed. "Too much." Instead of telling him, she showed him—not everything, of course, because that would overfill his mind. She selected the most prominent events, then put her finger to his temple and let the images flow from her to him, keeping them easy and clear.

As she shared her memories with him, she also used the elements to search for the others, but she was still unable to find them. Their locations were still blocked from her view. If this was the work of the cloaked one, how did they have such power? And where could the others be?

She stared at her brother sitting before her. Zelkova hadn't seen or spoken to him for over two hundred years and she wasn't certain where to start.

Once Pyrus allowed Sten to come ashore, he sat down next to the two of them. Zelkova felt like a child again, being in the presence of her brother and Sten. Just before the sun was to set, a dark fog rolled in from the nearby trees. It crept across the field between them and the beach. Zelkova shot to her feet, holding out her arm to halt Sten from moving forward. "Don't. This one is too strong for you."

Before Sten could protest, Pyrus walked next to Sten and put his hand on his shoulder. "If this is the one you faced before, I would listen to Zelkova," he said.

"How is she to face them now?" Sten questioned.

Sten looked down at Pyrus then at Zelkova. Pyrus nearly laughed. "She is stronger than you know. I must say, she is even stronger than you."

"Me? But I'm a First."

Again, Pyrus patted Sten, laughing. "Despite all your efforts, you no longer have the power of a First. Now, that title belongs to Zelkova. But this moment is not the time to tell you about the last two hundred years. I will explain later." Pyrus shook his head at Sten's confusion and then asked, "Don't you think it's time we tell her what she's facing?"

Before he could go on, Zelkova jumped in. "Maybe after I handle this. Hopefully, we'll have more time to talk about this matter then." The three of them looked to the nearby field they stood at the edge of. In front of the dark shadows was a cloaked figure.

The shadowed one spoke in a soft voice, as if weakened. "I see you two are finally free."

"Yes, it seems so. I am still not who you think I am. I am different from the one you knew. Just like you are different from what you are now," Pyrus said, shocking Zelkova.

She looked to her brother, then to the cloaked one.

"I wouldn't be so certain of that, dear brother," the shadowed one said

Zelkova again looked between the two of them. She slowly realized what was going on and who the person might be.

The shadowed one looked at Zelkova and laughed. "So, you think you know who I am? Depending on what you imagine, that might hinder you from fighting me, don't you think?"

Zelkova shook her head. She had no words. So many questions ran through her mind and nothing she searched for would give her answers. Who was this person? Were they related? If so, how?

"It doesn't matter. You will join me," the harsh voice said. "As for the two of you, you will die. I was far too nice last time." With that, the dark shadow moved past the cloaked one and toward the three of them.

Zelkova stood ready, and in an instant, she cast a white orb around Pyrus and Sten.

Sten tried once again to move forward to help but he was held back by Pyrus. "We must trust her," Pyrus said. Sten nodded and stepped back once more. Zelkova narrowed her eyes at the shadowed form. There were no people among this fog.

She had to protect Pyrus and Sten. She wouldn't lose them again. She straightened her right leg out behind her and bent her left knee in front. She extended her arms out and raised them toward the sky, looking up. Her rock body shone brightly in the moonlight.

She lowered her arms slowly. The left one extended out in front of her, palm facing up. She cupped her right hand and moved it in a circular motion. The fog slowly lifted, revealing the shadowed one once again.

Unexpectedly, the cloaked one shot rocks at the three of them. Underfoot, roots reached out to grab their legs. Zelkova quickly lifted Pyrus and Sten with air, which served as a barrier along with the light.

Zelkova moved the rocks with a flick of her hand so they wouldn't strike her. She stomped her feet on the roots, freezing them in place. Putting both arms out, palms flat, wrists touching, she twisted her arms to the left and then to the right. Water came out of nowhere, hitting the cloaked one from both sides. In turn, they wrapped themselves in stone.

Zelkova pulled her arms apart. The rock shield around the cloaked one immediately split. They put their arms out straight, palms down, and from their hands black matter shot at Zelkova. She crossed her arms in front of her face. Bright light blocked the darkness.

The cloaked one put more force and energy into the darkness. As it whirled around Zelkova, she dropped to her knees but managed to keep her barrier up.

"Stop this, Vako!" Pyrus yelled.

Zelkova turned her head to look at her brother "Vako... Vako," Zelkova whispered.

In a blink of an eye, she stood and pushed back the darkness. She stretched out her arm and cupped her hand, as if choking someone. The cloaked one screamed. Their body lifted off the ground as Zelkova willed it.

She walked toward them. "So, you're Vako." An outline had formed around Zelkova, mixing the glow of sunlight with the darkness of the blackest night. "I thought it might be the case, but I was never certain. You were always blocked from me. Tell me..." Zelkova was only a foot away from Vako, slowly closing the distance between them. "Tell me, where is Carya? What have you done with her?"

Vako coughed a laugh. "This... This is what I've wanted all along. Yes, give in to the darkness that grows in your heart. We can become one."

Zelkova's anger grew. "Tell me where she is!"

With another laugh, the form in front of her faded away, taking the shadows with them, leaving only a cloak lying limply on the ground. Zelkova lowered Pyrus and Sten to the ground but couldn't look at them. She was searching her mind for any sign of Carya or Vako.

Pyrus stepped forward. "Zelkova," he whispered carefully, as if he didn't want to upset her more than she already was. She turned toward them but walked past, back to the shore of the beach. Sitting down, she cupped her hands over the sand and made a small fire that floated just above the ground. Even though she didn't need to see her surroundings, it brought her a strange sense of comfort to see the flames in front of her casting out the darkness of the night.

Pyrus and Sten sat down near her. They looked like three stone statues sitting on the shore. After a while, Zelkova looked up at her silent companions. "So, tell me. You knew of this Vako, and they called you brother." She sighed. "How do you know them? And why did you think you could take them on?" Zelkova looked from Pyrus to Sten, not certain who would answer first.

Sten cleared his throat and looked her in the eye. "After I found your brother, I did some searching. I found a rock in the forest I didn't make."

"Yes, I saw that stone. It took me to another world."

"Wait, you found it? You touched it? Another world?" Sten looked like he was about to jump to his feet, filled with restless energy. Instead, he sat still as a stone.

Zelkova looked up from the fire to see confusion written across Sten's face. "Yes, I am starting to connect everything and what the stones mean. And yes, there are now more than one. But please, go on."

"Um, yes. I found the stone. It was freshly made. Pyrus and I followed the path of the person who made it. They made their way into Ruri just before you went there. That is when we met them. They told us to meet them here and so we did, right after we talked to you."

Pyrus stopped Sten by touching his shoulder lightly. He smiled at him then at Zelkova. The feeling Zelkova always got from Pyrus was that of a kind leader, someone who would always listen, no matter how small the problem. He wouldn't jump in to fix it, but he would comfort and help if needed. If he were in a room filled with a thousand people, he would stand out among them all. That's just how he was, how he always had been. Kindness radiated from him. Sitting there, staring at him in this new form, she wished she could have seen him as king, to see him rule with compassion. Zelkova admired that about him.

"The look of the person shocked us both. It was like they had charcoal for skin, and underneath were flakes of white. But it wasn't their skin. Their skin was gone..." Pyrus looked toward the water, cleared his throat, and went on. "Their whole body is made of dark matter intermixed with light. They have no body. That is why they wear the cloak, to give the impression of having one."

She nodded and pushed the conversation further. "Yes, I understand. But how did you know each other? They called you brother. You knew their name..."

Zelkova wouldn't tell them about the letter she found in Carya's rooms two hundred years ago. She pushed the memory out of her mind, not wanting to think of the event that caused her such pain. That wasn't something they needed to know.

"When Vako showed up at the beach, they introduced themselves to me. Sten confronted them about the stone. And that is when we found out everything, we are about to tell you..."

16

Ilex and Aria found themselves much like the others, in deep darkness. As the two of them floated in the abyss, their cloud bodies were missing. They were reduced to air with a consciousness, hovering in the nothingness surrounding them.

"Ilex, are we dead?"

He chuckled at Aria's question. "No, I've been in this before. It's the shadowed one's doing. We just need to find a way out. It will be hard without the gift of light, but we have to try."

They worked together to make a whirlwind, trying to push against the darkness, but their surroundings only grew darker.

"This isn't working. Even at our highest speed, there are no cracks in this pitch-black place." Before Aria could say more, the darkness around them lifted, letting beams of light through.

The shadows around them faded, revealing a large field bordered by trees. Ilex and Aria formed their bodies once more and floated just above the ground. Without having to look, Aria sensed someone close by, unseen. Aria grabbed Ilex's arm as dark fog rolled in. It wasn't like the dark shadows that entrapped them before. It was something different. Something unexpected.

"So, we meet again," a familiar voice said. "You were fools not to kill me all those years ago. I would not have made the same mistake." The dark fog took shape of a large man, making his clouds denser to mimic muscles of a human body and taller to intimidate humans and Elementals alike.

Aria sighed despondently. "It has been quite a while, Ventus, but I do not regret my decision. So, you are in league with the cloaked one? How did you regain your strength?"

Ventus snorted. "In league? I guess you could say that, but I'm using Vako for my own means…" He paused, seeming to think about his plan before continuing. "They were able to help me grow stronger somehow, even though Vako can't control the wind. A favor for a favor, as it were."

Aria stared at him. "Why are you telling us this?"

"Because Zelkova gave your man a hint, one he hasn't explored yet. At least that's what I was told. And if what Vako told me is true, I would rather go with the two of you. Even though Vako has helped me, they are insane… I used them to regain my strength and now I want to get as far away from them as I can." Ventus smiled.

Another cloud silhouette formed alongside Ventus. It took a shape similar to his, just as dark, if not darker.

"It's been a long time since we've last seen each other, my lady," the second cloud form said, bowing.

Aria nodded her head in reply. "Yes, it has, Vindby. I have often looked for you, but you were hidden from me, along with your brother." Aria motioned to Ventus with a jerk of her head.

"We've been concealed until the time we revealed ourselves," Vindby said. "It is as my brother has said. He has been helping the shadowed one, Vako, but they have continually grown madder. They don't want to stop at the destruction of humankind; they want to destroy our kind as well. To turn everyone and everything into shadows. Even Ventus thinks they're going too far, and that's saying something."

"Enough of this," Ventus said impatiently. "I overheard Vako speaking of going past the mountains of Montis. Whatever lies there, Vako cannot touch. We must go at once."

Ilex, who had quietly stood by listening, sighed. "If it is as you say, why should we trust you? Why change now? Is Vako so strong that they scare even you?"

Ventus's tone held grim promises. "If you had seen what I have, you would know that what is ahead of us is worse than anything we've ever seen. I don't think even Zelkova can defeat them."

Omnia could no longer see or hear Inane. She lost all sense of time in the darkness around her. Her heart ached at the thought of Spero and Inane going through the same thing she was. But the darkness didn't last forever; it gradually faded.

Omnia blinked her eyes as they adjusted to the light. She was back in the cabin with the shadowed one standing before her. Inane stood behind them. The cloaked one seemed weak when they walked over to the chair. Once more, they motioned to Omnia and Inane to sit across from them.

"I've been rude. I haven't introduced myself. Call me Vako." Vako's voice sounded frail; their shoulders slumped forward. "Omnia, I wanted to tell you what Zelkova has been keeping from you."

She looked up at Vako, then to Inane in confusion. Inane shook her head, obviously not knowing what Vako meant.

"What do you mean?" she asked, focusing her attention on the seated shadow.

"You see, Zelkova knew your great-great-grandparents, at least one of them, very well, and she has yet to tell you of your family's past, which is your right to know."

Omnia frowned. Did Zelkova know her great-great-grandparents? "Why would she hide such a thing?"

"That I'm not certain of. Maybe to use it against you at some point?"

"That doesn't sound like something Zelkova would do." *She isn't someone who manipulates others.*

Vako laughed. "As if you really know her."

"I know and trust her more than I do you," Omnia snapped. She wouldn't let this Vako corrupt her thoughts. She knew better and was smarter than that.

Again, Vako laughed at her words, the sound condescending. They moved to sit at the table in front of Omnia and Inane. Omnia tried to see their face, but it was cloaked in darkness.

"I will show you what Zelkova and the others are hiding from you," Vako whispered in a calm voice that hid a hard undertone.

Vako blew dark mist from their palm into Omnia and Inane's faces.

As the mist settled over Omnia, visions filled her mind. The vision showed Omnia as a toddler, holding her mother and father's fingers as she walked in between them, laughing. They were walking in the courtyard of Silva toward the servant entrance when someone yelled at them from behind. Turning, they saw Queen Malin—who was a princess at the time—nearing them.

Hurrying toward them, the princess whispered, "You must leave. Grandfather is in a horrible mood, screaming about your father and how you disgraced us. If he sees you, it might be your end. Hurry. Hide."

"What have I done to displease him? To make him so angry?"

Malin shook her head, fear darkening her eyes. "Dearest cousin, we do not have time to speak of such things. Hurry before he finds you."

Her father nodded and picked Omnia up, then rushed alongside his wife toward a cabin on the edge of the woods by the kitchen's garden.

After entering the house, her father locked and barricaded the door behind them. Omnia's mother hugged her and her father, whispering, "I've never seen your cousin so scared before. I know your grandfather can be cruel, but to attack you? Us?"

"He has his father's temper, and he's spoiled, which seems to have made it worse. Hopefully, he'll pass out from his drunkenness before he comes here." Her parents played with her until just before nightfall when they heard voices from outside. One stood out from the rest, his voice strong but slurred with drunkenness.

"Open the door!" King Markus slammed his body against the door while the others around him urged him to stop and go back to the palace.

"Please, Your Majesty. You might get hurt," someone voiced hesitantly.

"Let us go back. We can find some fine women and more wine," another offered.

He ignored the counsel of his men. Turning to a man with a torch, he grabbed it and neared the cabin. "Come out, or I'll burn you alive!"

Grimly, her father stood, resolve hardening his features. Her mother anxiously grabbed his arm, stopping him halfway to the door. "Please, darling, don't go. Who knows what the king may do. Stay with us," she pleaded, tears swimming in her eyes.

"Dadda!" Omnia cried, fat tears rolling down her cheeks.

He turned, looking back at his wife and child. A sad smile ghosted across his face. "I love you both."

The moment he opened the door, his grandfather grabbed him and flung him to the ground. "I can't believe Father let my brother live, much less have a child," he shouted. "You are an insult to our family and our name!"

Her father didn't attempt to defend himself. "What did I do?"

"Ha!" the king scoffed. "Don't play a fool. You know full well what you did. Handing out food to the poor in our name."

Omnia's father interrupted his uncle's outburst with a calm voice. "I didn't put a name to the food. It was my own money that I used."

King Markus reached down and slapped him. "People know who you are! You made a fool out of me to my own people! How dare you!" He kicked him in the stomach and turned to the house.

His anger burned brighter than the torch he held in his hand. The king threw the fiery torch into the open cabin without an ounce of hesitation. Instantly, the floor caught fire with a *whoosh*. Omnia's mother screamed and held her tight as the flames quickly spread to the wall, climbing up to the ceiling. Omnia could almost feel the heat from the scorching flames.

"NO!" her father yelled, the sound torn from him. He made to rush toward the cabin. Halfway there, one of the king's guards forced him back and he fell, hitting his head hard on the ground, knocking him unconscious.

Several onlookers tried to rush to the cabin to help Omnia and her mother, but King Markus would let no one get close enough, no matter how vehemently she screamed. Her cries echoed into the night, then came the deafening silence.

A day later, after the fire burned out, they found Omnia under her mother's body, alive and unharmed.

Omnia had no memory; the trauma of the event had made her block out all recollection of her parents from that day forward. King Markus and his family would use that against her. A few days later, her father was hanged for the murder of his wife, even though he was nearly dead from his fall days before.

Omnia sat blinking as tears fell down her cheeks. Inane sat next to her, arm around her shoulders, whispering calming words.

Vako laughed without pity. "If only he hadn't been so kind, if he hadn't fed those poor people... Omnia, I want you to listen. Kindness is a weakness. No one ever told you of your birthright, not even your hero Zelkova."

Omnia looked up at Vako. "I don't believe you," she sobbed, her heart breaking into a million tiny pieces. "You are the weak one, thinking only of yourself."

Vako stood. The room filled with darkness that seethed from Vako, plunging them into blackness.

Zelkova had trained her on how to get out of the shadows, so Omnia did as she was taught. She closed her eyes, cleared her mind and thought of light driving the shadows away. She opened her eyes to a bright sunny day in an unfamiliar forest. Inside her, she felt Inane's presence, easing her aching heart.

After listening to Sten and Pyrus, Zelkova searched for Omnia and Spero by connecting and listening to the elements. A thorough search showed no sign of either of them. After waiting most of the day, Zelkova heard from Ilex and Aria, who reported that they'd encountered both Ventus and Vindby. The three of them agreed that Aria and Ilex would go with the other two air Elementals past Montis. Zelkova felt uneasy letting them go, knowing Ventus was not to be trusted. Listening and speaking on the wind, Zelkova and Ilex told each other of their plans.

"Aria, Ventus and Vindby and I will go seek out this place you and Vako spoke of. I will check in occasionally on my findings." Ilex paused and laughed. "As if you need notification of my whereabouts."

"But I would like to hear it from you, nonetheless." Zelkova sighed heavily. "I have yet to hear from Omnia and Spero. They are still blocked from me. While I await their reconnection to the elements, Sten, Pyrus and I are going to head to the capital of Silva to find the stone I came across two hundred years ago and destroy it."

"Be careful, Zelkova. Ventus is even scared of the cloaked one. And he doesn't scare easy."

"And watch your back, Ilex. Call for me if the wind shifts in the slightest. We don't know how far Vako's reach is. And Ventus could be leading you and Aria into a trap. Both of you be on your guard. I know I am the one who told you to travel there, but they could use it against us."

"We will be on guard. Talk soon."

As they traveled toward the border of Lignum, Zelkova continued searching for Spero and Omnia. She watched out for Ilex and Aria as they journeyed past the mountains of Montis. She thought of what Sten and Pyrus had told her while at the beach. Zelkova re-watched the scene all over again, replying it in her mind.

The three of them sat on the beach. Zelkova had made a fire for light and because it was a habit. Pyrus took over the conversation, refusing to look at Zelkova. "As I said before, we met them here and they called me brother because, in their world, I was."

"In their world?" Zelkova searched through the past again to see if this new information played out. And for a split second, she saw two Vakos in the memory of when Vako visited Carya. The two Vakos were an echo of each other. In the next instant, the vision was blocked, and she could no longer see the image.

"Vako asked us to join them," Pyrus continued. "As their brother, I didn't have to join the shadows. I could go on as I was, but I had to work under them. Sten would be able to join as well. Vako spoke so sincerely. They actually believed we would join them. And when we refused, Vako attacked Sten. That was when we were transformed into stones."

Zelkova was brought back into the moment as they neared their destination. The memory of the conversation on the beach was pushed down.

They had reached the large stone in the forest of Lignum. Looking to her brother then to Sten, she wondered if all of it was real. Were they really in front of her after so long? Zelkova shook her head, blocking out the thoughts that tried to fill her mind. Not having the two people who kept her most grounded had been harder than she first realized. Now that they were in front of her, she was reminded of how much they meant to her.

Sten walked over to the stone. He put his hand in front of it, hovering a few inches above the stone. Slowly, he walked around it as if looking for something. He spent several moments inspecting the stone. "You said you went to another place when you touched the stone?" he asked Zelkova, looking back at her.

She nodded. "Yes."

"Yet you didn't make it?"

She shook her head. "I did not."

Sten looked at the stone then at Zelkova once more. "The reason you couldn't figure out who made it was because you are too closely connected to them."

She tilted her head in question. "What do you mean?"

Sten paused. "The stone seems to be made by you or someone very similar to you. Try to sense the stone again. See if you feel it."

Before nearing it, Zelkova touched her index finger to Pyrus and Sten's forehead, giving them a spark of light to combat the shadows in case they came while she was away. With a somber look, she turned to the stone.

Right before she touched it, Zelkova turned back to Sten. "Would you be able to destroy it?"

He shook his head. "I'm afraid not. Only the one who made it can."

"I see. Oh, and Sten? Don't try to take on the shadowed one—Vako. If they come, run from them because you have someone counting on you." Her eyes shifted to Pyrus then back to Sten. "Running from a fight you can't win doesn't mean you're weak. It means you're smart. Use your brain and not your brawn this time around."

She winked and turned back to the stone. Reaching out, she brushed her fingertips against the rock's surface. Immediately, the scene around her changed.

The world whirled around her, making everything a blur. As things gradually slowed, Zelkova found herself just where she was. Everything looked the same but felt different. She tried to see through the elements, but it didn't work. She looked down at her hands to see flesh instead of stone. Which was odd. She had yet to change her form during these travels. Deciding to see why it took her to where it did, she headed toward Silva to see if it had changed.

As Zelkova neared the town, voices and the sound of horses' hooves upon the road met her ears. Within the cover of the line of trees, she watched, trying to see their riders. Three horses trotted past. One urged the other two into a race. His red hair gleamed in the sun. It was Cedrus along with Ilex and Malus. It seemed they were headed to see her father for the first time. Why was she in this place and in this time?

Zelkova walked back to the rock. When she was about to touch it, a memory came to her. One of Carya with Vako near the pond at the castle. If she remembered correctly, they would be meeting today.

Zelkova headed back to the castle and waited in the woods that outlined the pond and the lone tree beside it. The way her heart pounded in her chest made her feel alive. She hadn't felt that way in over two hundred years. Excitement welled within her. She couldn't wait to look upon her lost love once more, but the anticipation she had felt soon gave way to pain. She feared this might be the last time she'd see Carya with her own eyes. She had viewed her through memories and visions countless times, but none of that could hold a candle to the actual sight of her. The love and pain that battled for control of her soul made her weak at the knees.

Soon, the moment came. Carya strolled into view.

The sight of her chocolate-toned skin and long wavy hair took Zelkova's breath away. Time seemed to slow as she took in every inch of her. A stray tear fell down Zelkova's flesh cheek. She'd already experience the events in person and a million times in her mind, and now, the events from that day were playing out in front of her once more.

"Zelkova could come at any moment. It's not safe," Carya said, and Zelkova froze at the sound of her voice.

"It's fine. I know her movements, remember?" Vako said dismissively. The sound of their voice made her blood boil.

"Yes, I forget sometimes. You act so differently."

Zelkova stood by listening, waiting, but for what? She was uncertain. After Vako left, Zelkova remained among the trees watching Carya, not wanting to blink, not wanting this moment to end, willing it to last a lifetime.

"Zelkova," Carya called suddenly, causing Zelkova's heart to skip a beat, "why are you hiding in the trees? I thought you were headed to the kitchens and the armory."

Her voice pulled at Zelkova's heart, making her instinctively turn in her direction to see her near the edge of the woods. Zelkova sucked in a surprised breath.

"Where are you going? Come out of the shadows. Did something happen? Did you see—?"

Zelkova stepped out of the cover of the trees, making Carya stop mid-sentence. She eyed Carya while fighting the urge to hug her. "How did you know I was here? You couldn't have seen me."

"You're right. You were hidden in the trees. I didn't see you. I felt you through water…"

At that time, Zelkova hadn't recovered the gift of water yet. When Carya stepped back, Zelkova automatically stepped closer like a magnet and bridged the distance between them. Their eyes locked.

"Your eyes?" She paused, expecting an explanation, but Zelkova only stared at her. "They have seen many years, years beyond what I've seen. You are from a different time. The future? But how?"

Before Carya could ask another question, Zelkova lost all restraint. The hundreds of years of loneliness and loss came flooding through. She wrapped her arms around Carya. All she wanted was to fill the void, to never let Carya go again.

Pulling her closer, Zelkova leaned in and kissed Carya. The kiss was soft yet passionate. Carya wrapped her arms around Zelkova's neck, lifting her higher and bringing their bodies flush against one another. The moment seemed to be frozen in time. Zelkova didn't even try to figure out if that was her doing. All she wanted was to focus on Carya and their kiss. The softness of her filled her body with heat. Feelings she had forgotten existed rushed through her, making old memories creep into her mind. Zelkova tried hard to push them firmly down.

Eventually, she pulled away, though she never wanted it to end. She would fade from this timeline soon. She'd never spent so long in a different time before. Looking down at Carya, Zelkova took in every inch of her, her heart aching in her chest. How she missed her, yet she felt betrayed. But the love she felt had not diminished in the slightest, despite Vako.

Carya opened her eyes. "I've been waiting for that kind of kiss for years," she whispered.

Zelkova half-laughed, the sound raspy. The kiss had temporarily knocked her off balance. "Not as long as I have waited. You mustn't tell me about this, nor this Vako. I've done too much by revealing myself to you. Who knows what ripple effect it will cause when I get back."

Voices sounded in the distance, getting closer with every second. That was her cue to leave. Zelkova blinked back tears as she kissed Carya's forehead. "Always remember I love you…"

Carya turned to greet a group of maids, and Zelkova took the opportunity to glide back into the woods.

Why did she have her flesh body, and why hadn't she returned to her own timeline yet? Why hadn't she gone after Vako instead of kissing Carya? She knew her reasons. With two of her here, who knew what could happen and how it would affect everything in this time and the next. With some disappointment, she decided to head back to the rock.

Walking back to the stone, Zelkova thought back on the kiss. How she wished she had done that so much sooner. That was the biggest regret of her past. Not loving Carya fully. Maybe if she had, Carya wouldn't have turned to Vako. Another stray tear fell down her cheek, and she quickly brushed it away. Zelkova knew she had to stay focused, to think of what was at stake.

When she got back to the rock, it seemed to pull her toward it, making her hand touch the cool surface.

Her surroundings changed and once everything settled, Zelkova found herself at the pond where she had sealed Vatten away. To her right was another stone. *The stones must be connected*, she thought. Looking down at her hands, she saw they were stone again. All her senses were working. She was back in the right time.

"I guess now is a good a time as any," a voice said from behind her.

Turning, her eyes met Vatten's. He was almost a watery blob. With a wave of her hand, the form of Vatten became more solid, which freed him to walk onto the shore for the first time in two hundred years. Zelkova's feelings were still raw with the emotions of seeing Carya. Her heart ached to touch her again, to see her face, to hear her voice, to kiss her.

"It's been quite a while." He surprised her by moving closer, so close he wrapped his arms around her and pulled her in for a hug, one she reluctantly returned.

"Let the past be what it is, the past. Let us not give it the power to define our new future," he whispered into her ear, sending uncomfortable chills down her spine. Zelkova nodded slightly and started to pull back, but he held her tight. "It's been so long since I've seen you in person. I've imagined this moment ever since I realized how I felt."

Her heart continued to ache as the thoughts of Carya consumed her mind. Zelkova wished she could go back, to be with her again. To touch her skin, to feel her against her body, not Vatten. She had the power to do so but knew better than to use it. That hurt more than anything. Having the ability to change things but knowing you couldn't—and shouldn't. The outcome could become like Vako.

"I was always fascinated by you, but the more I thought about you and saw you, the more I realized my fascination had become so much more. Now that we are face to face, I want to tell you…" He finally pulled away, looking down at her with a smile. "I love you. I want to be with you. I don't expect an answer right now. I will give you time to think it over."

Looking down at her feet, Zelkova nodded. So many thoughts whirled in her head, all fighting for priority.

She was lonely and had admittedly isolated herself.

Then there was Carya. Was she actually gone? Or was she with Vako? Should she let her go? It had been over two hundred years.

There was something off with Vatten that didn't sit right in the back of her mind. She looked at him. He still wore a smile.

Then there was Vako and the shadows. They had been there all those years ago. And here again. They seemed to know more than her, and yet they didn't have all the gifts. She had to save this world from them before it was taken over by shadows. And that was what she needed to focus on. Nothing else.

Shaking her head, she told herself Vako was where her attention had to be.

"Yes, time is what I need. I sense Sten and Pyrus are on their way here. We will wait for their arrival. Then I will touch this stone to see where it leads. I assume you know what has been occurring."

Nodding, he released her and backed away. His expression had changed when she mentioned Sten, becoming hard and closed off.

That night, she meditated, searching for any sign of Omnia, Inane, Spero, and Arbor. The sun was soon to set when Sten and Pyrus arrived. A fire hovered above the ground, illuminating the area. The two silently joined Zelkova and Vatten around the blaze.

"I don't think we've all sat together like this before. In our true forms, that is. It's kind of nice," Pyrus commented, obviously trying to lighten the mood. His smile fell when no one responded.

Zelkova finally got in contact with Spero and Omnia and gave them instructions to continue their mission to warn the other countries. After speaking with them, she stood and headed toward the large stone. As the others stood to follow, Zelkova held up a hand to stop them.

"I need to look into these stones more and learn how to stop the shadows that come from them. You three should meet up with Spero and Omnia. They are going to warn the other capitals about Vako and the shadows. I will meet up with you all when I can."

"Wait," Vatten instantly objected. "One of us should go with you to help."

Zelkova shook her head. "You can be of more help here. I thank you for your concern."

As she reached out and touched the stone, Vatten grabbed her hand, taking both of them on a whirlwind ride through time. Zelkova turned and hugged Vatten against her so he would not get lost in an unknown time loop. As they tumbled through time and space, Vatten pulled closer and wrapped his arms around her. In an instant, his lips were touching hers.

Zelkova wanted to pull away but couldn't. As her mind turned to Carya, their travel slowed. Zelkova instantly pushed Vatten away and looked around as the scenery around them came into focus. It wasn't just the timeline that had changed but their location as well. They stood next to the ocean on a high cliff. A line of trees stood several feet behind her at the edge. It was late night and a violent storm raged in the ocean. Before she reached the edge of the cliff, Vatten grabbed her arm, turning her around. His facial expression had dramatically changed from just a moment ago. His eyes showed deep concern, but for whom?

Zelkova concentrated on the storm out in the sea. She noticed something strange. There were clouds over a ship but no wind around it. The waves and rain seemed to be controlled by something. The realization occurred to her as she stared at Vatten. Before he could speak, she reached out her fist and then closed it, freezing Vatten in place.

Turning back to the cliff, Zelkova looked over the edge to see the other Vatten on the beach below. She glared back over her shoulder to the frozen Vatten and then focused again on the boat out in the ocean, seeing through the elements.

She saw the wood that made the ship, the water that pushed against its frame, and the air that hovered all around it. What she saw shook her to the core. People screaming and crying in fear. It wasn't just seamen. It was women and children as well. The men feverishly worked on the boat, desperately trying to keep it afloat, to keep it from tearing apart. The women held their children tight.

Judging from the grim, resolved look on each face, they all knew there was no saving it or themselves.

Her physical form shook with anger. Zelkova wouldn't let the other Vatten know she was watching. The ship gradually sunk into the dark depths, and her heart sank with it. She wanted so badly to recuse everyone, but it would only change the future. Maybe not for the better.

But there was one person she had to save, meaning she had been here all those years ago. Traveling through time was a scary thing, which made her more determined to stop the shadows and break the cycle.

It was almost dawn when Vatten disappeared off the shore Zelkova stood above. The future Vatten still stood frozen behind her, wide-eyed. She had been blocking his gifts, so he couldn't warn his past self. She knew this frightened him, to not have control.

Just as the sun rose, Zelkova saw a group of fishermen head to the shore from a nearby trail. She had to hurry so everything would be timed right, just as it had come to pass so long ago.

Zelkova moved her hands rapidly. Soon, a bubble floated toward the shore carrying a small child with chocolate-toned skin and black hair. Just as the villagers reached the beach, the bubble burst, laying the child out to be found. Zelkova sighed and turned back to Vatten. She grabbed his wrist and touched the stone. For a split second, she noticed she was stone as well, not flesh like before. She shook her head and focused on the lake near the border to see if it would respond and take her there.

When she gripped Vatten's wrist tighter, she found them back where she had planned. Zelkova threw a frozen Vatten to the ground, shattering him. Pyrus watched in silence.

"You just left. What happened?" Sten asked, confused.

Pyrus grabbed Sten's arm, urging him to step back. "Not now," he murmured.

Vatten reformed into his watery self. Zelkova glared at him. "If I had known, I would have killed you two hundred years ago!"

"Zelkova, listen, it's not what it looks like." Vatten tried to sound calm, but the cracks in his voice showed he was anything but.

"Really? So, it didn't look like you killed people on the boat to try and kill Carya?"

Sten stepped forward with clenched fists. But Pyrus held him back, shaking his head.

"You don't understand. The books—" Vatten started desperately.

Before he could finish, Zelkova cut him off. "Books?" Her glare became more thunderous as she stepped closer to him. "You told me what the first book showed wasn't set in stone. Yet you go and kill people because of an image one of the books showed you? How dare you! Why? What did it show you? Leave nothing out." There was nothing else in the world she wanted to do more than to rip him into pieces at that moment, to fill his mind with pain like she had felt with Tempus. The one he had sent her to face. The one that had taken Carya from her. Her anger toward him built even more.

Zelkova scowled at Vatten as he hesitated, but Zelkova wouldn't give him enough time to think of a way out of this. Not this time. "Vatten, stop wasting time. *Why* would you kill people because of the books and how did you have both? Don't test my patience. You may lose your life faster that way."

"The books showed me that if Carya was around you, you would not become what you were meant to be. You even told me so."

Her glared intensified. "What?"

"Yes, your future self came to me one day, right before you left to find Pyrus. That's when I tried to talk Carya out of going with you."

Zelkova stepped closer to Vatten and in a low voice asked, "Did this person look like I do now?"

Vatten shook his head. "No."

"Did the person wear a cloak?" She grabbed his arm, pulling him closer. Vatten's eyes met hers, and she saw the truth. "You idiot, that was Vako! How could you? Out of everyone… I trusted you. I gave you so many chances to tell me the truth. Was everything you ever said a lie? And how could you have been so easily fooled?"

The anger building inside her made her see spots. She threw him away from her in disgust. A keen sense of betrayal stabbed at her. She *had* trusted him. Zelkova paced, excess energy demanding to be released.

Vatten stood as still as a statue, not making eye contact with Zelkova. "I didn't lie about loving you!"

She stopped and scowled at him. "What I've gathered is that you tried to kill Carya as a child because of the books, and you told her to stay away from me because Vako somehow tricked you into thinking they were me from the future. And then you hid or killed Carya after her human body died?"

Vatten's eyes grew large.

"Is what Zelkova is saying true, Vatten?" Sten asked quietly, his voice shaking with emotion. "You actually did all that? Where is Carya? Did you kill her?" Sten grabbed Vatten by the shoulders and shook him as if he could shake the answers out of him.

"Tell us!" Pyrus went over to Zelkova and put his arm around her shoulders, hugging her.

"I… I killed her…" Vatten whispered, then frantically told Zelkova, "You have to listen to me! It's not like it sounds. I did it to save you. To make you become who you are now. I love you. That is why I did all of this. I love you…"

Without looking at Vatten, Zelkova laughed. It was not her typical laugh. It was filled with deep pain. "You killed her because you love me? Is that love to you?" She looked up and locked eyes with Vatten. She laughed again. "You call that love? Hurting the person you love? Making them suffer because they never knew what happened to the person they loved? You are insane! If you truly love someone, you let them go. You let them find happiness even if that means without you..."

Sten let go of Vatten and backed away. Vatten also stepped back, perhaps sensing the turbulent emotions swirling inside her. Flames shot from her clenched fists.

"Love... You killed her because you love me..." Darkness coated her words and enveloped her body. "You killed her..."

Anger brought out the darkness she had held in place for so long. Zelkova had lost so much and had never really let herself grieve. The loneliness of it all was now crashing down on her like a mountain she had been holding up tirelessly. She had finally given in to feelings she'd bottled inside for years.

In an instant, flames engulfed Vatten. He screamed in pain. "Zelkova! What are you doing? You don't kill. You didn't even kill Tempus!"

A smirk came across her face. "Isn't this the way you wanted me? Isn't this the reason for your actions? So I would become who you wanted me to be? Well, take a good look. You got what you wanted."

The flames around Vatten intensified as he tried to escape the vacuum that whirled around him, his screams mixing with the howling of the wind. "Zelkova, don't do this! This isn't you! This isn't what I wanted. Sten, Pyrus. Help! Zelkova! Please."

She observed him without pity. He'd brought this on himself. He had wanted this outcome for Tempus. Vatten had lied over and over again. Manipulated her for his own gain. Little had he known what she would become, that she would be his downfall.

"This isn't what you wanted? If Tempus was in your place, you would be happy with my transformation."

"Someone, help! Don't just stand there!" Vatten's form slowly started to evaporate.

Zelkova looked at Pyrus and Sten to see if they would intervene. Neither of them moved a muscle.

Once his legs disappeared, leaving him at knee-height, Zelkova stepped closer to the flames surrounding him. She raised her arms and then swiped back, making the fire disappear. Zelkova dropped to one knee, crossing her arm in front of her body. Leaning in close, she looked Vatten in the eyes. He was weak and scared. She could see that now, but it was too late to go back; all traces of kindness had disappeared.

She reached out her other arm. She opened her mouth to speak, but then she looked away. She made a fist, and Vatten's body fell into a puddle. Zelkova stood and walked toward the stone. Touching it, she stayed in place, not moving in time. Taking her hand away, she snapped her fingers, and the stone collapsed into rubble.

Zelkova briefly looked at Sten and Pyrus before the weight of her grief made her drop to her knees. She screamed, tears pouring from every inch of her, putting out the flames on her hands. She lifted her head to the sky, screaming even louder, and let out two hundred years of grief as the darkness consumed her.

17

As Omnia looked around the unknown forest, there was no sign of Vako, the island or the shadows. It was like she had never been on the island. She walked toward the sound of rustling leaves. Reaching a small stream in the forest, she saw someone coming toward her. Shadows concealed the figure. She froze, fearing it was Vako. As the person stepped into a beam of sunlight, red hair and a bright smile drew Omnia's eyes.

"Spero!" She rushed over to him, holding herself back from hugging him.

Spero didn't hold back. He wrapped his arms around her, swinging her in the air before letting her back down. Looking down at her, he kissed her forehead, causing them both to blush.

"I'm so glad you are all right. I tried to find you for hours. Where were you?"

She looked up into his green eyes, which were bright with the relief of seeing her. "I was with Vako, the cloaked one. On the island, Inane had her own body, or at least it looked like it. Now, she is back in my mind. So many things happened..." Omnia fell silent as pain of recollection assaulted her.

Spero wrapped his arms around her, hugging her tight. He kissed the top of her head. "If you want to talk about it, I'm here for you."

She nodded and explained what had happened with Vako.

"I'm sorry, Omnia. That must have been hard to see." He hugged her even tighter, making her feel safe and warm. Spero made her look at him to see his smile. "But you have a new family now. I'm your family. And I will never leave you."

She nodded, hoping his words were true, hoping she had finally found a family to call her own. "What do we do now? Are we going to your hometown? Is it all over? Where are we?"

Spero frowned but then grinned again. "Yes and no. We have to head to my home capital to warn them about the shadows and Vako if they haven't been invaded already. It's starting to get dark now. We will head out in the morning. It seems we are in the forest near the field and beach of Ruri's coast. Here, sit. I'll build a fire." He winked at her and headed out to get some firewood.

Omnia looked in the direction Spero had gone, hoping she could find the strength within her to fight this fight that wasn't even hers. When he came back, he put the branches on the ground and hovered his hands above them. After a few minutes, the fire blazed to life.

Omnia looked at him in wonder. "What were you doing just now?"

"I was thanking the limbs for helping keep us warm," Spero answered without looking at her as he fed more wood into the flames.

Omnia was in awe of him. She watched his arms break apart the limbs and place them in the stack. His sleeves were torn, showing his muscles. She found herself staring at the exposed skin. Spero saw her studying him and smiled when their eyes locked. After the fire was going strong, he sat down beside her, so close their arms touched.

"I'm sorry I don't have our tent or blankets. I lost our gear when Vako took us. But I can make you something."

He stretched out his arms and waved his hands as if he were sowing seeds. Omnia looked out past the fire and saw leaves coming together from different trees, forming a large blanket that came and wrapped around both of them.

She smiled at his kindness. "I don't understand how you can be so nice, always thinking of others when others think only of themselves."

Spero gazed down at her with soft eyes, making her heart skip a beat. He reached out and tenderly brushed her hair out of her face. The air around them was hot and damp. Just as their lips were about to touch, the fire roared out of control, ruining the moment.

Spero jumped to his feet, pulling Omnia with him. He lifted them into the trees and watched as a nearby stream surrounded the raging flames.

As day shifted into night, so too did Omnia shift into Inane. Dumbfounded by what just happened, Spero felt the shift of dark and light. Looking at each other, Spero knew she felt something wasn't right just as he did. The elements were shifting, but why and how?

"What's happening?" Inane murmured, clutching onto his arm.

"I don't know." He frowned. "I have a feeling it has to do with Zelkova."

Both Spero and Inane called out to her on the wind, but no response came.

After calling a few more times, Spero heard the voice of Ilex in his mind, and from the look on Inane's face, she heard him as well. "It seems Zelkova is in trouble. We're not quite certain what is going on. We only know what her brother Pyrus and Sten have told us. They seem to be near her."

"Do you feel the pull of the darkness?" Aria asked.

"Yes," Spero and Inane said simultaneously.

"Then go to that place; that is where you will find Zelkova. Help her if you can. Hurry..." Ilex said, and just like that, both of their voices vanished with the breeze.

Spero wrapped his arms around Inane. He held her against him as they jumped from limb to limb, following the pull of the darkness.

All Pyrus and Sten could do was watch the darkness overtake Zelkova's body. But that was the least of their worries...

Fire shot out of the ground, whipped up by the wind into a tornadic vortex. The lake swelled out of its banks and rushed toward their feet. Zelkova floated in dark matter above the rising water.

Sten grabbed Pyrus's waist and lifted them both up on a stone pillar. Thankfully, the fiery vortex stayed swirling in place, unmoving. All they could do was watch.

"I knew Vatten was going mad, but I never expected any of what just happened. And now this." Sten sighed and hugged Pyrus close.

Pyrus looked up at Sten. Despite the chaos surrounding them, he smiled at the fact they were able to touch and talk after so long. "Thank you, Sten. For protecting me."

Sten choked back a laugh. "Much good that did. We were stones, actual stones, for centuries and there was nothing I could do about it. I'm so sorry. That's time you will never get back. Time you could have spent with your family. I never meant for any of that to happen."

"Nothing that happened was your fault. No one knew of Vako or what they intended. Even now, it's still unclear. You protected me the best way you knew how, and I am forever grateful. I love you, Sten."

He turned his gaze from the dark orb to Pyrus and, with a smile, said, "And I love you. I never knew what love was until I met you. I will always be by your side."

Pyrus' breath caught in his throat. He didn't think he would ever get used to how captivating Sten was. He leaned in, eyeing Sten's lips. Noticing, Sten grinned and took Pyrus's lips with his own.

As everything around them swirled with chaos, for a moment, they were in their own little world.

Darkness consumed Zelkova as everything around her changed. Anger and sadness filled her heart while visions swirled in her mind. They looked like memories from the past, but she couldn't remember the events. Had Carya or Vatten removed these from her mind? Carya had done it once before.

She slowly floated through the visions, clearly seeing the events playing out before her. Zelkova was in her human body, or so she thought. Both she and her brother stood in front of their father. She was looking up at the king who towered above her. She was only a child in this memory.

"Father, you have to understand. Vako—" Pyrus said in a determined voice to their stern-looking father.

"Don't use that name." Fraxinus looked from the older child to the younger. "We will not use that name in this castle. Vako doesn't exist as far as I'm concerned."

"Father, please listen," Pyrus said, stepping forward.

"No, I will listen no more. Vako is gone and that is final." Fraxinus stared at Zelkova, and if looks could kill, they would have been dead on the floor.

That scene gave way to another that seemed to take place years later. She found herself at the edge of the pond under the tree. Carya was making ripples in the water. She wore a lovely green dress with her hair flowing in the wind.

Zelkova was so taken in by her beauty she was unaware of her father's approach. Soon, he stood over her, glaring down. In an instant, he had her by the arm, pulling her to her feet. "How many times have I told you not to wear trousers? You are not a man!"

He flung her to the side and pulled out an ax from behind his back. He started chopping at the tree Zelkova had been sitting under.

"Father!" she cried, distress written all over her face. "What are you doing?"

"I have to get through to you somehow," he said grimly, glancing back at her.

"Not Mother's tree!"

"Your mother abandoned you. Us. It's time to let her go and let go of what or who you think you are." He continued chopping at the tree, merciless in his pursuit.

Zelkova rushed to stop him. He threw her to the ground, and Carya came running from the pond. When she reached Zelkova's side, Fraxinus pushed Carya away from her.

Fraxinus started toward Carya. "I will get through to you, even if I have to take all that is precious to you away."

"Don't touch her!" Her father didn't listen. "I said stop!" Zelkova jumped to her feet. "Enough!"

As the word left her lips, a black shadow emerged from the tree and shot toward her father. It took the shape of a human and lifted Fraxinus off Carya. It dangled him in the air, holding him by the neck as Zelkova walked toward him.

"You no longer have power over me or Carya. We are no longer under your control. Vako is now in charge."

Her father glared at the figure then at her. "Vako doesn't exist."

The vision faded and moved to yet another. Even though it felt like she was in her own body, it seemed like she was seeing the visions through someone else's eyes. Her eyes once again adjusted to the world around her. It was her world yet different.

She found herself in her bedroom at the castle, looking herself over in the mirror. She wore brown pants with a baggy tan shirt. A belt slung over her shoulder sheathed several small knives. As she looked at her face, it seemed different from before. Her hair was cut short. Her face was sterner and sharper.

There was a knock on the door and Carya came in. She wore a tight tan dress. She shut the door behind her and shyly looked at the floor as Zelkova moved toward her. Zelkova realized, though she was watching through this body, she had no control whatsoever.

Carya looked up and whispered, "I've missed you. Why must we sneak around like this?"

Zelkova lifted Carya's chin. "You know I can't control my father or his men. This is the only way I know how to protect you. I'm lucky he hasn't had me killed yet."

Carya nodded. "What are we going to do? I've heard whispers that someone has put a hit out on you." A tear ran down Carya's cheek. Zelkova kissed it away, and then their lips met. The kiss was long and passionate.

The images around her faded to one she had seen before. She stood in a field, surrounded by an army. Across the field, someone cut Carya down. Blood drenched her dress. As Zelkova looked down, the sword they held turned black, and shadows consumed everything. She screamed.

Pain in her mind and body replaced the visions. The agony of losing Carya, not just in the visions she saw, but in her world as well, nearly destroyed her. Vatten's words rang in her ears as she floated in the darkness. That pain, accompanied by the thoughts of how Vatten had betrayed and lied to her, made her feel like her heart was ripping in two. How could Vatten kill Carya's family and then kill Carya yet say he loved her? The confusion that gripped her mind made the ache in her heart grow.

All the pain she had held in for over two hundred years finally came out in a gnawing scream that could shake the world. Zelkova had held out hope beyond hope that somehow Carya was still out there somewhere, waiting to be found. Now that hope was gone, leaving an abysmal hole in its place.

"You can pull through this," a little voice in the back of her mind whispered. "Think of those who need you. Vako will destroy this world."

She opened her eyes to see a human form cast in bright light standing before her.

"Let them," she responded to this version of herself. Her tone could ice over a summer day. "Let Vako destroy this world. There's nothing left for me there."

"You don't mean that. You just got your brother back…"

Zelkova screamed in pain, and the figure of light disappeared.

"He killed her because of you. And you killed him because of her. He lied and betrayed you, and you took his life for it. How does it feel? Do you feel guilty? Do you feel happy about it?" The voice sounded so familiar, but pain consumed her thoughts.

Tears fell from her eyes as the last image of Vatten filled her mind. So many thoughts ran through her mind, eating away at her like water against a stone. How could she have killed him? He had helped her, but he lied. Had she gone too far?

Slowly but surely, the strength that had kept her going would break, leaving behind nothing but a pebble to show her existence in the world she'd leave behind.

Sten and Pyrus stood watching their surroundings change. The water in the pond beside them stopped rising, but the surface of the water bubbled and waved. Suddenly, the water receded back into the pond and returned to normal. But all the rest of the elements still raged out of control.

Seconds later, a watery figure emerged from the pond, standing a little shorter than Zelkova. Her watery hair was long and wavy, flowing behind her when she walked onto the shore of the pond.

Sten lowered them back to the ground. He and Pyrus almost ran to her as she sweetly smiled at them. She looked around at her surroundings and then to the black sphere that held Zelkova. Sadness swept across her face. She made her way over to the shadowed circle that seemed to breathe in and out like a living being.

Pyrus grabbed her arm, stopping her. "Carya? How?" he asked in a whisper. "Vatten said…"

She looked at Pyrus and Sten. "Yes, Vatten thought he killed me," she said, her tone soft and gentle. "He tried to absorb me, but I stayed hidden within the depths of his subconscious. I was able to reach out to Cedrus a few times right after it happened but couldn't speak to him."

"So, you were pretty much a prisoner all this time, unable to contact anyone for fear of detection from Vatten, yet you saw everything he saw?" Sten asked.

Carya nodded, looking at the sphere again. "I wanted so badly to reach out. It was torture to see Zelkova suffer. I'm thankful seeing her was rare."

"Why didn't you reach out when Zelkova locked him in the pond?" Pyrus interrupted with a confused expression.

Carya looked up at Pyrus, who was more than a head taller than her. "I was too weak then. If I had tried to reach out, he would have been able to kill me without Zelkova even knowing. I had to wait to gain strength. When Zelkova concentrated on weakening Vatten, I was able to separate from him. I was still trying to regain my body when Zelkova…"

They all looked at the sphere as Carya stepped toward it. Sten tried to grab her arm to stop her again, but his hand slipped right through.

"Don't worry. I trust her," Carya said simply.

When she reached the sphere, she raised herself with a pillar of water to make her level with the darkness. Carya reached out her hand and the shadows separated, letting her step into the sphere. The darkness swallowed her whole.

Carya's heart lifted and sank all at once when she saw Zelkova. She floated among the darkness, her eyes reflecting the same color that surrounded them. But her stone body gave off a faint glow. Once she was near enough, Carya reached out and touched Zelkova's cheek, making her own heart flutter. Their surroundings reacted. She felt movement as if the orb was lowering itself. When the dark fog around them cleared, she saw they were ground level next to the lake. The elements had returned to their normal states.

Zelkova's eyes cleared and closed as her body went limp. Carya caught her and lowered them both to the ground, cradling Zelkova in her arms. She lovingly stroked her cheek with her fingertips, making certain this moment was real. That, after all this time, they were finally together.

Pyrus and Sten ran over to them. Pyrus knelt and gingerly touched Zelkova's cheek with the back of his hand. Concern filled his face as he looked up at Carya.

Carya leaned into Zelkova and whispered in her ear, "I'm back, my love. I'm sorry it took so long to get to you. I never meant for you to suffer so."

Carya leaned in and kissed her. A tear fell and hit Zelkova's cheek. Her heart raced and ached. The woman she loved was in her arms but had suffered so much, and alone at that. Carya knew how Zelkova would shoulder the whole world if she could—and would blame herself for Carya's disappearance. Because that's how she was, always trying to make things better, even when the odds were against her.

The sun was high in the sky when Spero and Omnia reached the group to see Zelkova lying on the ground surrounded by Elementals they didn't know. Two large stone Elementals and a water one. He had never met a water Elemental before and would have been excited any other time.

One of the stone Elementals rose and met the two. He bowed slightly to show he meant them no harm. "My name is Pyrus, Zelkova's brother. I'm glad you both came. Ilex sent us a message saying he sent you to our aid. Aria said you helped awaken Zelkova once before. It seems we need your help again."

Omnia and Spero followed his gaze to the comatose Zelkova.

The three of them walked over to the group, and Pyrus made quick introductions. Spero and Omnia knelt on opposite sides of Zelkova while the other three stood watching. Omnia and Spero locked eyes as they put their hands on Zelkova's stone arms.

Closing their eyes, they said in unison, "Zelkova... We're here. Let us help. Let us in."

When Spero opened his eyes, they were in a thick forest. It was so dense Spero grabbed Omnia's hands so as not to get separated as they pushed through the thick foliage.

"Spero, where are we?"

Spero pushed through thick bushes intertwined with trees, Omnia following behind. "We're somewhere in

Zelkova's mind. It's worse than last time; a lot more chaotic. Stay close to me. We don't need to lose each other. We might not find our way back."

They walked through the dense, dark forest, getting cut by thorns and branches scratching at them. They soon stumbled upon a waterfall. The waterfall fell into a small pool below, which was surrounded by thick brush. Spero was taken aback by the dark water that flowed from it. Omnia held onto Spero's arm as their eyes took in their surroundings. Everything oozed black matter. Dark fog filled the air.

"Is she here?"

Spero nodded. "Can't you feel the sadness? The grief?"

Before Omnia could answer, a low raspy voice came from the other side of the little pond at the bottom of the waterfall. "I feel distrust..."

Spero looked to where the voice came and saw a black figure stand up as if emerging from the fog itself.

Omnia leaned against Spero even more. "Is it Vako?" she whispered.

The figure laughed, causing Omnia to shiver. The figure stood taller, looking as if it were made of coals from a fire. "I am not Vako. I am much worse." The word *worse* was drawn out, shaking the tree leaves near them.

Spero stepped forward and Omnia followed his lead, still holding onto his arm. "We're here to help you, Zelkova. Carya sent us." He was about to say more when the embers on the dark figure turned a blue color.

The figure of Zelkova moved closer, hovering over the pond. Black steam rose from the surface of the water, making their surroundings ever darker.

"Don't speak that name." The voice had changed, becoming deeper and darker.

Spero wasn't going to back down though. "Zelkova, you have to listen. She wasn't killed. She was in hiding. But you set her free. She's alive and waiting."

"Silence! I will hear none of those lies!"

"Please, listen," Omnia said hesitantly, her voice shaking. "Spero isn't one to lie. You know that. She made Vatten believe —"

A strong wind blew through the trees at Vatten's name. The air around them whirled, and Omnia squeezed closer to Spero.

Spero had to scream so his words would be heard over the strong windstorm. "Listen! Carya is alive and waiting! You can finally be together!" He paused to see if she would respond. When she didn't, he went on. "You are no longer alone! You have people waiting, wanting to be with you! You no longer have to be alone."

Omnia leaned over to Spero, whispering, "Can you help me walk on water?"

He looked down at her with a surprised look that turned into a bright grin when he realized what she was thinking. He nodded, and she stepped forward until her feet reached the pond. Leaves floated atop the water, making a path for her.

Zelkova looked down at the path of leaves then up to Omnia who slowly bridged the distance between them.

"Please, Zelkova," he said, trying to distract her from Omnia. "Carya is waiting."

When Zelkova looked past her to Spero, Omnia quickly jumped forward and wrapped her arms around Zelkova. "You are not alone," she said. "We are all here for you. Pyrus, Sten, and Carya are waiting. We all need you."

Spero had been concerned about the heat from the embers burning Omnia, but her skin was unharmed by the contact.

Zelkova looked down at Omnia, who had a weary smile on her face. Zelkova's charcoal face flaked away, revealing her stone physique. The scenery gradually changed as her body transformed into the stone figure they knew. Light shone through the tops of the trees and glistened off the top of the water, chasing away the dark fog. The water turned clean and clear. A cool breeze filled the air.

Zelkova slightly smiled down at Omnia, then looked at Spero. "Thank you both. It seems I let my emotions get the better of me..." She looked down at the water with a sigh. A tear fell from her cheek into the water, making a ripple appear. "It's time for both of you to head back. I will join you soon enough."

With those words, a bright light shone, making them shield their eyes.

Just before sunset, Zelkova finally twitched. It was not long before she opened her eyes, much to everyone's relief.

Pyrus scooted over and hugged her. "Welcome back. You had us worried for a while."

Zelkova nodded. "I'm sorry I worried you all. I let my emotions get the better of me. I won't make the same mistake again." She scanned the group in front of her, and Zelkova's eyes landed on Carya.

She froze, staring at Carya's new form. Her features remained the same, but where skin once was, there was water in its place. She took in every inch of her. Carya stared back with a smile. Zelkova couldn't believe her own eyes; was what she beheld even real? Was Carya really there, alive and sitting in front of her? Or was this all a dream? Despite no longer having a heart, she still felt flutters, as if it were still there and she were still flesh and bone. She wanted so much to go over to her, to touch her and see if she was truly real, but Zelkova held herself back.

Carya broke the silence, her voice soft and certain just like Zelkova remembered. "I am real, and I am here Zelkova. Vatten tried to kill me by absorbing me when my flesh body died, but I was able to hide in his subconscious. When you weakened him, I escaped into the pond. It took longer than I wanted to regain my form. You were always on my mind, seeing you through Vatten's eyes, to see the..."

Zelkova knew she was wanting to say kiss but was too embarrassed to say so. Without a second thought, Zelkova stopped time for the others then leaned over to Carya and kissed her on the lips. She leaned in even more, gently pushing Carya onto her back. Zelkova hovered over her, happily gazing into her eyes. *I never thought her kisses could feel this good.*

"Don't be embarrassed," Zelkova told her, smiling. "We've waited long enough to declare our love. I will never let you go."

Carya wrapped her arms around Zelkova's neck and tugged her down, slanting her lips against hers once more. She slid her stone hand down Carya's watery form. When Zelkova leaned up from her kisses, she studied Carya, noticing she was truly a water Elemental.

"I have a request," Carya said shyly.

Zelkova nodded. "Anything."

"I feel quite odd with nothing over me, like clothes…" Zelkova's face lit up with a bright smile, and Carya turned her head away. "Don't laugh. I feel strange without it. I know I'm an Elemental now, but…"

Zelkova put her finger to Carya's lips. "No need to explain. I understand."

She wanted to ask her about Vako and how she could even believe that it had been her, but it had been two hundred years. There would be no use in asking. It would only make them remain in the past when they both needed to focus on the future.

Zelkova hovered her hand over Carya's chest, waist and then hips. After a few moments, a dress appeared over Carya. It was green leaves intertwined. The straps were wide at the top of the shoulder and tapered to where it was attached to the dress. It hugged tight around her stomach and flared slightly at the hips. The hem ended above her knees and had a few leaves that rained down to the ground.

Zelkova saw her looking it over. "Does it not suit your taste? You know I've never been one for dresses, so my styling may be a little off."

Carya shook her head, smiling up at her. "No, it's quite lovely. I like it. The leaves remind me of you." She wrapped her arms around her once more, whispering, "Thank you. I will never let go. I will be yours forever."

She leaned in for another kiss. Afterward, she stood up and helped Carya to her feet as well. Time resumed to normal. Only Zelkova and Carya knew she had put the two of them in a time bubble. The others saw only a split second of a blur, not realizing time had moved at a different pace for herself and Carya. Zelkova leaned in for another kiss, one everyone saw.

"It's about time. I'm so happy to see you both accepting your love and declaring it. Never be scared to hide who you are or who you love." Pyrus stood up as well and looked at Zelkova and Carya with a smile.

"Not everyone is as brave as you are, dear brother."

He winked at her. "I'm not certain if that is the word I would use. I just knew I loved Sten, and I wouldn't let others control my life, even our father." Smiling, he grabbed Sten by the arm. Sten grinned slightly at everyone but went back to his somber look within seconds. Pyrus and Zelkova laughed.

"Always the somber one, aren't we, Sten?" He looked down at Pyrus in confusion as Pyrus nudged him with his elbow, still amused. "Wait. When did Carya get a leaf dress?"

"I made it for her. It only took a second." She winked and took Carya's hand in her own. Zelkova couldn't remember the last time she had held hands with her. She never wanted this moment to end.

They settled down for the night. While Inane and Spero slept, the others walked to the pond, discussing their plans. Omnia and Spero would still go to Solaris to warn the kingdom and report back to Zelkova of any shadows they saw along the way. They would not confront them without contacting her first.

Sten and Pyrus were to seek out an island off the coast. It was hidden from humans. Zelkova had only seen it through the elements. If what Vako said about the land where Aria and Ilex were going was true, this was something to look into as well. Zelkova and Carya would travel in search of the dark stones and destroy each one. She was sad to leave her brother and Sten after not seeing them for so long.

"Don't worry, we will see each other again soon," Pyrus said reassuringly.

It was hard to return his smile. Zelkova had this sinking feeling that this happiness would not last. Despite blocking her view of the future, the foreboding sensation only grew. Just like the shadows she chased...

18

The next morning, they all set off in their own directions. Sten and Pyrus went southeast off the coast of Ruri. They moved fast across the countryside with the ground beneath their feet helping them move at unnatural speeds. They went past Opima to see the shield of light still holding and no darkness around the capital.

After traveling all day, they stopped to rest just past the city. They found a wooded area to use for cover. Sten looked at Pyrus almost shyly. "It wasn't just Zelkova and Carya who were separated for two hundred years."

Pyrus smiled at Sten. "That is true, but it was like we were asleep. Zelkova was living without Carya, and Carya saw the world from someone else's eyes. Not quite the same for us."

Sten nodded, looking down at his hands. Pyrus grinned and scooted over to him. He put his head on Sten's shoulder and took Sten's hand in his.

"I missed you, too," Pyrus said, feeling a flutter in his chest. "I know it can be hard for you to express yourself. I think it's really cute when you get frustrated, though."

Sten shook him off, and Pyrus laughed. Sten opened his mouth to say something but shook his head and wrapped his arms around Pyrus instead. Pyrus wasn't certain who moved first, but in the next instant, they were kissing. One hand laid on the small of Pyrus's back, the other rested on the back of his head, pressing him close. Their bodies tangled together, the need for one another growing.

When the sun rose, Pyrus woke up in Sten's arms. Sten never slept, but he had stayed still all night for Pyrus' sake. Pyrus hadn't been an Elemental for long before turning into a rock, so he was still used to sleep. In time, he wouldn't need it. Pyrus contacted Zelkova before they headed out again to make certain everything was all right.

Once he talked to her, the two of them moved toward the same coast where they laid as stones. When they reached the spot, Pyrus couldn't tell if Sten was as nervous as he was to see the place where they were imprisoned. As they were about to travel to the nearby island, a dark fog crept over the beach. Pyrus glanced at Sten, who showed a hint of agitation rather than fear.

He smirked at how calm Sten could be when facing danger. He stood face to face with threats of all kinds but never showed a hint of fright. They stood there, waiting. For what, they weren't even certain.

Could they combat the darkness that loomed ahead, or would they become a part of the shadows themselves?

Ilex and Aria flew alongside Vindby and Ventus, both keeping their guard up. They didn't fully trust either of them or the reasons behind their desire to team up. None of them spoke.

Below them was an endless ocean. Blue waves mixed the darkest parts of the ocean, so deep it turned the aqua color almost black. The unknown depths of the ocean sent a chill through Ilex. Give him the blue sky any day. Wherever this land was, it wasn't near where any of them had ever been.

The group knew nothing of what they were looking for. Zelkova just said to go past the mountains of Montis. Vako said there was a land beyond Elementum. They didn't give much detail to what it was they were really seeking. If there were lands beyond the one they lived on, no human had ever found it. Ilex pondered this as they flew along.

The four of them traveled for many days with nothing in sight.

Ventus was the first to voice his concern. "I think Zelkova might be as mad as Vako. They both made up this land to make us go on a wild chase."

The others seemed to have the same thoughts but hadn't voiced them.

"Why would they do that? Zelkova isn't one to play with others' minds," Vindby said.

Ventus stared at Vindby, annoyance filling his features. "The only reason I tolerate you is because you are my brother."

Vindby shrugged unconcernedly. "I am only speaking the truth."

"You act like you know Zelkova. You know nothing about her beyond what she chooses to show you."

Smiling, Vindby nodded. "Yes, that is true, but her actions speak volumes, brother dear."

Ventus glared at Vindby as if he was trying to make Vindby fade into nothingness before his eyes.

Aria noticed the tension between the two and tried to ease it. "We've already come this far. Let us try for a while longer," she said. "Since everything is so vast, maybe we should split into two groups to make our search more effective."

Ventus turned his glare on Aria. "I'm not letting either of you out of my sight. We will all find it together or not at all. I don't trust either of you. If you find it, you could make Zelkova hide it from us before we even lay our eyes on it."

"All right, but can we at least spread out a little? We can stay within view of each other, but we can cover more of an area that way." Ilex tried for a compromise to fit everyone.

"Fine," Ventus grumbled reluctantly.

Everyone agreed and they all spread out several hundred feet. They all concentrated on the air around and before them, searching for any interference that would come from the land they are looking for.

Even though Ilex tried to concentrate on the job at hand, he was still worried about Zelkova. He knew she had come back from the darkness, but what would happen if she wasn't able to combat the shadows that might linger in her heart and mind?

"Do you feel that?" Aria asked, shaking him back to the moment.

Ilex glanced at Aria. He focused on the air in front of them and felt a change in it, one he had never felt before. "Have you felt anything like this in all your years?"

Aria shook her head. "No, this is quite unusual. Let's continue forward to see if it has a form."

As the four of them moved forward, they came upon something Aria had never seen before. Giant white and gray clouds towered over them. At first, it looked like normal clouds, but as they pushed further through the first layer, they emerged into a world beyond the one they had just left.

The clouds looked to be cumulus mammatus, large storm clouds. The lower level made them look like huge towers in the sky reaching unknown heights. The clouds felt unstable, but everything became more solid further up. The structure surrounding them took shape. Aria gasped in amazement. Ilex's eyes widened at the sight. Ventus cussed and Vindby laughed.

Aria wasn't even certain if what she was seeing was even real; were her eyes deceiving her? The clouds surrounding them had taken on the form of large, connecting castles made of large towers of dense clouds with columns connecting the long halls. It was beyond description.

The three of them looked at Aria in astonishment.

"Did you do this?" Ilex asked.

She shook her head. "This wasn't me."

"Do you know who did then?" Ventus asked.

Aria shook her head again. She was just as confused and amazed as they were. "I don't feel any air Elementals. Do any of you?"

"No, but something seems off. It feels completely different yet familiar at the same time," Ilex noted.

They lapsed into silence for a few moments, taking it all in.

"I don't sense that," Ventus blurted out. "It all feels very strange to me. I think everyone should be on their guard. This could be a trap."

"By who?" Vinby asked.

Ventus answered, "Zelkova or Vako. Maybe both, but I'm not taking any chances either way."

"Then why did you take us all here?" Ilex asked, frowning. "You were the one who wanted us to find this place so badly."

He snorted. "Let's keep looking, shall we?"

The four of them floated around the castles, looking in the rooms. There were dining rooms and bedrooms with cloud furniture. Hallways and stairs shaped with sharp edges by soft clouds. It was almost as if things were made of soft marble. Dark and light clouds mixed with gray, soft and sharp edges throughout. High vaulted ceilings in some areas. In others, it was open to the blue sky. What appeared to be the throne room had large open windows with pointed arches. It was all formed with clouds. Everything was made in the design of human structures, but this clearly was made by no man.

Aria came upon a great high tower that sat in the middle. "Here, I think the feeling is coming from here."

They climbed the cloud staircase. At the top, a small misty figure stood in the middle of the hallway. The figure turned around, eyeing the four of them as they cautiously approached.

The figure smiled and floated around them. "You are early yet late. You came together yet alone."

"What are you talking about? Who are you?" Ventus mumbled.

It giggled. "I am here yet I am not. You may call me Tuuli. I am here for you, all of you, but I am not to tell..."

"What is this crazy thing talking about, Aria? You're the First. Don't you know?" Ventus eyed the small figure then Aria.

Aria shook her head, staring at Tuuli. "I... I don't know." After a few moments of silence, Aria asked Tuuli, "Who made you?"

The small figure giggled like a little child, reminding Aria of how playful she used to be herself. "Someone who is seen but not here. Someone who is everywhere yet nowhere."

"Enough with these riddles. What is this place? Who made it? Who made you?" Ventus reached out to grab the little cloud figure but she slipped away from him, making him gasp in anger. "How? I should be able to grab you..."

Tuuli whirled around them, interrupting him. "No, no. You have no power here. No... power..." She whispered the last words in his ear. He turned toward her, but she disappeared and then reappeared in front of them all, still giggling.

Ilex stepped forward before Ventus could respond. "Tuuli, what is this place?"

The tiny figure spun around them, making the air buzz with her words. "This place is Tuuli. I am Tuuli. We are separate yet one. I am the keeper yet this place is all of me."

Tuuli's answers only made Aria's head spin. Nothing was a direct response to any of their questions.

"Come, come! Let's have a tour!"

Everyone looked at each other and then to Aria, who nodded in acceptance.

Tuuli floated in front of the others. As they followed, Aria took in the sight around them. Each cloud was sculpted to look like stone. These "stones" formed castles, peaks, and roofs of houses.

Just as the group relaxed somewhat, Tuuli turned around smiling. "Take your pick." Giggling, she spun around, waving to each high peak of clouds.

Ventus blurted out, "The first thing you say that isn't a riddle makes me even more confused."

Tuuli merely smiled. "Now you pick. You pick a place and stay."

"Stay?" Vindby asked.

"You all stay and never leave," Tuuli replied, her tone light and airy.

"Wait, never leave?" This had to be another puzzle.

Ilex stepped forward. "We might make this our home, but we must get back to the mainland. To help."

"You no longer may leave," Tuuli told him, her voice going from a soft girly tone to a dark, deep one.

"But this is not our home," Ilex said, eyeing her warily.

"This is now home. Mainland is not for you, not for us."

"Who are you to tell us where is home?" Ventus grumbled.

The tiny figure's body started to grow larger, her voice deepening. "This home. No leaving for me, for you. Stay... Rule. One rule. I keep safe, I take care."

"What don't you understand? We are not staying." Ventus also made himself grow, towering over Tuuli.

She only grew larger. "I take care. You all stay forever..."

Tuuli put out her hand and closed her fist, forcing Ventus back to his original size. She then shrunk down her normal size. And in the light giggling voice, she reminded them, "No power here."

19

Omnia and Spero headed back to Solaris—the capital of Spero's homeland, Litore—to see if the shadows had arrived. They were instructed not to take on the shadows or Vako alone and to contact Zelkova if they came across anything unusual.

As the two of them left the group, Spero sensed Omnia was still wary of Zelkova because of what Vako told her. He walked beside the quiet Omnia, who seemed to be deep in thought. He grabbed her hand, shaking her back to reality. Spero smiled down at her. She tried to smile back at him, but her smile didn't reach her eyes.

"You're thinking of what you saw in Zelkova's mind, aren't you? And what Vako told you isn't helping."

She nodded gravely. "I know I shouldn't judge based on what Vako said and what little glimpse I saw of Zelkova in a weak moment, especially compared to the things I've seen her do. What Vako said shouldn't even sway me, but for some reason…"

"Most people judge on the negative even though they have been shown a more positive side to a person," Spero told her softly "I like to think of people like books. You may have been introduced to a few chapters of their past and been with them for a few chapters of their present. But no one truly knows someone's full story. Assuming someone's entire life story from the few pages you've seen, when it could be hundreds of pages long, isn't logical or fair. No one should be defined by their moments of weakness or vulnerability because everyone has them."

She slowly nodded. "So, don't judge someone's life story based on the few chapters you've been introduced to. There's always more to someone than meets the eye."

He smiled and turned from her to the path in front of them. "There is always more to a person than what they show and what others see. Always."

After walking a few more moments in silence, Spero broke it. "We should be there in about a day and a half. I can always move us a little faster when we're in the woods with the leaves under our feet." He hadn't used his powers for half of the day since they were using the trees for cover, but now that the hottest point of the day was over, he helped quicken their pace.

When the sun had set and became too dark for them to see, they settled down for the night. Spero started a fire for them, and Inane laid out their mats and divided food for them. They both sat down near the fire and ate bread. Neither of them spoke, quite the opposite of how he and Omnia usually reacted to one another.

After they had eaten, Inane turned to Spero, her gloomy expression illuminated by the light of the fire. "I overheard you and Omnia talking about Zelkova and Vako. I don't trust either of them. If I had to choose, I trust Vako far less. I understand Zelkova is your hero and is a legend of sorts, but we only know what we've heard from you and stories."

He stared into the flames. "You have seen her in action yet you still doubt those stories?"

He awaited her answer, pondering the differences between Omnia and Inane. Inane was upfront and blunt where Omnia usually spoke her mind more subtly and tactfully. He tried to think of them as different people, but it was hard when they shared a mind and body.

Omnia's voice disturbed his thoughts. It was still Omnia's voice despite Inane's presence, or so he thought. "I see what you are saying. It's just hard for me to trust someone who is so powerful. How do we know she won't turn around and use those powers for evil or selfishness?"

Spero sighed. "You know she didn't choose to have the gifts. They were practically forced on her. To save the kingdoms from all-out war, she did what she had to do, which meant giving up her human life. Everything she knew and loved changed or was lost to her. Have you ever thought of how hard it was on her? She was a human, you know."

"Was," she whispered, barely audible but he had no trouble hearing the single word.

Spero tried to contain his anger, but he could no longer take it. He abruptly stood, walked a few paces away, and leaned his arm against a nearby tree. Upon hearing Inane approach, he sighed and turned around. Without warning, Inane swiftly closed the distance between them. Standing on tiptoes, she gently kissed his lips.

He stepped back, touching his lips in shock. He stared at her wide-eyed. She backed away, the realization of what she had just done evident on her face. "I'm sorry. I... I was reacting to Omnia's feelings. Not my own..."

Inane turned and sat in front of the fire, her face in her hands. Spero paced back and forth, uncertain of how to react to what had happened. It was Omnia's body, but it wasn't Omnia. It didn't even feel like a kiss from her. It was like a kiss from a stranger.

After thinking things over, he went and sat down on his mat, which was laid out beside Inane's. As they both stared into the fire, Spero cleared his throat. "Can you tell Omnia that... that I didn't want the kiss? Even though it may be her body, it wasn't her kissing me." He sighed, uncertain if that was even the right thing to say.

Inane solemnly nodded. "I told her it was all my fault and that I was reacting to the feelings she was giving out. She hasn't responded. I think she might be giving me the silent treatment. I would never get in between you and Omnia. I see what you both have, and it's rare. To be so comfortable with each other so quickly. I don't want to damage that."

They both fell quiet. Night deepened, and the flames dwindled. Without speaking, they both fell asleep. Spero hoped the new dawn would bring about better feelings.

But a new day broke with the ray of sunshine beaming through the trees, and the strained feelings lingered. They ate in silence and packed up the same. As they walked through the forest, Spero finally broke the long silence.

"Omnia, please listen. The kiss, Inane didn't mean... I didn't want..." He fumbled with his words, not really knowing what to say. Omnia continued walking, not saying a word. Spero looked down, walking a few feet behind Omnia. Her long hair flowed behind her, half black, half white. His heart skipped a beat at how beautiful she was. He quickened his pace to come up to her side. "I'm sorry, Omnia."

She nodded and looked up at him but shyly looked away a second later, which made him smile even more. He reached out his hand and took hold of hers. She didn't pull away. They walked like this until midmorning when they reached the end of the woods.

They looked out at the green meadow in front of them and walked out onto it holding hands. Reaching the bottom of a steep hill, Spero turned to see a dark fog following them. They froze at the sight of it. A sense of dread filled his very being.

"Spero," Omnia said anxiously, clutching his hand tighter.

"I see it," he said lowly, not taking his eyes off the darkness.

Both of them instinctively backed up. The dark fog followed, swiftly closing in on them.

"Zelkova, we found some shadows..." Spero whispered on the wind, hoping she heard.

Zelkova and Carya moved toward Silva to put a light barrier around the city as the others went their own way. Zelkova remained on guard. She kept an eye and ear out for the others, not wanting the shadows to overtake any of them or for Vako to hurt someone.

Carya noticed and squeezed her hand. "Everything is going to be all right."

Zelkova sighed. "Will it? I'm not certain."

"It will. You were able to face Tempus."

She nodded at Carya's words but looked down. "It took me over a year to recover, and in that time, Vatten tried to kill you. Others suffered, and all the while, Vako was in the shadows already planning all of this. I didn't see it until it was too late, and now, I'm struggling to stop it all. If Vako is who we think they are, how am I going to deal with that?" Zelkova stopped and smiled wearily at Carya. "I've missed you."

Zelkova wrapped her arms around her, bringing Carya in for a long and much-needed hug. Seconds later, she felt wetness on her shoulder. The tears touched something deep inside Zelkova. Neither of them wanted the hug to end but both knew they needed to keep moving toward Silva.

Zelkova would help move them a little faster than walking but still didn't want to overuse her gifts. Just like when she was human, she knew her powers could have a ripple effect, and she didn't want to take any chances unless there was no other choice.

Zelkova's thoughts were still in a dark place. Even after coming back from the shadows, some of her still seemed to linger there. Her mind felt as heavy as her body. She tried to smile and seem normal for Carya. Zelkova was so happy to have her back, but a lot still weighed on her.

Her mind wandered to how she would confront Vako and, if need be, defeat them. Her brain was so filled with worry she didn't notice when Carya grabbed at her arm, trying to get her attention.

"Zelkova... Zelkova." She shook her head and looked down at Carya, her eyes focusing on the confused expression on her face. "We're here."

Taking in her surroundings, she saw they were at the edge of the city lined with large trees rather than a wall like the other capitals. She smiled at the thought of the people in the city and castle still being close to nature, just like her father had wanted despite Malus and his offspring taking the capital after her father passed. The borders of protection she had once placed were lowered. She had lowered them herself after Malus's death, hoping the nobles would be able to have Councils and come to agreements without war, which they had done for the most part.

Zelkova decided to put up a shield of light then go into the city to see if a stone lay under the castle just as it had in Opima. Carya instinctively stepped back as she knelt and raised her arms. A faint light exuded from her hands and grew outward, expanding the length of the city and wrapping around the castle.

People came out of their homes and stared at the light dome forming over them. Some gasped, others whispered, some pointed, others shook in fear.

Zelkova sighed and lowered her arms, still kneeling. People came to the edge of the light wall to get a better look.

As the people of the city came closer, Zelkova slowly stood, not wanting to scare them. Soon, even the nobles tentatively approached. Zelkova assumed the guards must have told them of the sudden gathering. The queen arrived and people moved to make way as she walked toward the line of light. Once Queen Malin saw the stone figure standing on the other side of the barrier, her eyes grew wide and her mouth gaped open.

After a few moments in silence, the queen dutifully knelt and bowed to Zelkova. People followed the queen's lead, surprising Zelkova. Soon, all were bowing. She looked to her left and saw that even Carya was bowing. She didn't want people to kneel to her. There was no reason to. When Queen Malin lifted her head, Zelkova nodded and smiled.

"I was going to come see Your Majesty once the light shield was up," Zelkova told her, dipping her head in respect. "You may have heard rumors of the shadows, but they are not just rumors. Some others and I are tracking down the source. The source is not from any other country and everyone should keep the peace during this hard time. The light now surrounding the city should keep the dark shadows at bay, but if you step outside the light, you will no longer be protected. If anyone sees shadows, do not approach them. If someone sees a large stone with symbols anywhere, do not touch the stone for your own safety as well as that of others. We are trying our best to find the one behind all of this, and I'm certain everything will go back to normal soon. So, please go about your everyday lives and just be aware of your surroundings."

People began to whisper, and one person yelled out above all the rest, "Where have you been the last two hundred years? Everyone said you had died."

Zelkova nodded. "That is true. My human body did pass away."

People gasped and started talking louder.

Queen Malin cleared her throat loudly, making everyone hush. "Thank you, Zelkova. We appreciate you helping us, and we wish you luck and safety in finding the person behind the shadows. When you have a free moment, I wish you to tell me more of this threat." The queen then turned to everyone. "Let us all wish Zelkova and the others a safe journey with a cheer."

She raised her arms, and the crowd cheered loudly.

The queen turned back to Zelkova once more and bowed slightly, whispering, "I know you can hear me. I don't want to make the same mistakes of my forefathers. I will put my trust in you, but I hope it will not be in vain. Don't prove Malus right, prove him wrong."

Malin turned and made her way back to the palace. The people around her tried to ask Zelkova more questions. It seemed as if the whole of the city stood in front of her. Lines of people stood in the streets, trying to catch a glimpse of her. Even more voices arose from the crowd, trying to ask questions. But Zelkova only nodded and smiled, then turned along with Carya and walked back into the woods out of sight.

Returning to where it all began, where she had once been human made her think of what could have been if things had played out differently. Trusting others had led to her death and Carya's imprisonment. But she needed to trust once again, to not hold others' wrongdoings against the rest. Trying to push the feelings of regret away, Zelkova turned to Carya once the two of them were far enough away from the town. "We'll head into the castle after nightfall to make it easier to hide. Want to sit and rest?"

"Yes. That would be nice."

The two of them sat against a nearby tree. Zelkova reached out her stone hand and touched Carya's water one. Carya smiled at the gesture.

Carya turned to Zelkova with sadness in her eyes, but before Zelkova could ask why, Carya said softly, "I want to tell you about how I tried to reach out for help while you were on the island."

"Please. I want to hear what you have gone through." It had been a long two hundred years, and she wanted to know everything. Zelkova felt a weight of guilt at not finding Carya sooner, at not seeing what Vatten had done.

Carya's expression turned sorrowful. "I tried to reach out to Cedrus a few times when he was in the camp near the border. One day, a girl who looked very similar to me tried to stab him. Thankfully, I was able to stop her without detection from Vatten." Sighing, she avoided locking eyes with Zelkova. "I wanted nothing more than to reach out to you. I saw everything Vatten saw. And when you locked him away..."

"You were locked away as well." She wanted to make it up to Carya. She, too, had been alone and suffered, just as Zelkova had. She hugged her tight, thankful Carya kept her solid form. "I'm so sorry. If I had known, I would have..." The words fell short. There was no fixing what had been done, and she wouldn't turn back time to try.

"Zelkova, you know I have never blamed you, nor will I ever blame you. You were pulled into all of this. Just as I was. And I wasn't going to let you do it alone. We are together now. Let us enjoy the time we have."

There were so many questions Zelkova wanted to ask about Vako, but she was scared of the answers. And she wasn't even certain she was ready to hear them.

Carya continued, describing how she stayed hidden but was able to reach out a few times to others.

Day gradually turned into night. Before dawn, the two of them made their way out of the woods and into the kitchen garden. It had changed from what she remembered. The castle had extended past it. They moved past it, toward where the dungeons should be located. Zelkova was thankful to find them empty. She lit their way with a small orb of light that floated in front of them. As they made their way from cell to cell, nothing seemed out of the ordinary.

When they entered the darkest part of the dungeon, Zelkova saw a small dark figure in the corner of a cell. "Stay a few paces back, just for safety."

"All right," Carya murmured, watching her intently.

Zelkova entered the cell and moved closer to the figure huddled in the corner. Once she got close enough to make out features, she knelt, moving the light orb to hover over it.

The light hit the dark figure, and Zelkova almost fell backward at the sight. It was her as a child. Her long brown hair was tangled, and she had a dirt-streaked face. A dark shadow covered the outline of her.

Zelkova reached out her hand to the child, who shrank back. "It's all right. I'm here to help you. Why are you here?"

The girl lifted her head. Their eyes met. "I'm hiding from Vako," she whispered.

"Vako? Why and for how long?"

"For a long time... I made them mad and they used their power on me."

Zelkova frowned. "Power?"

The girl shook her head. "Ssshhh. No one is supposed to know."

"Who is Vako to you?"

The girl leaned forward and, trying to whisper, said, "My sibling..."

She reached out her hand toward her younger self. "Give me your hand. Let me take you home."

The child smiled for the first time and put her hand in Zelkova's. The second their hands touched, the light from the orb overhead looked as if it were raining sparks of light down on the child. The sparkling lights chased away the shadows.

And after a few moments, the child also faded away as if she had never been there. Zelkova stood up and took Carya's hand. "We must hurry."

"But, wait. Was that true? That Vako is your sibling? I thought..."

Before she could finish her sentence, Zelkova looked sternly at her, shaking her head. "In time, we will discuss Vako, but now we must hurry."

"Hurry for wh—"

Again, Zelkova interrupted her, but this time it wasn't with words. Their surroundings changed as they went from the cell to the outside wall of the castle and then into the woods. In a matter of moments, they were standing near a large stone in the middle of the forest.

Carya blinked. "That was fast."

Zelkova turned to her, about to speak, but her eyes widened. In one swift movement, she grabbed Carya and stepped in front of her, protecting her from the unseen force.

In seconds, a figure stood directly in front of them. Vako looked from Carya then to Zelkova—or so she thought. It was hard to tell with the cloak over their face.

"So, I see you've freed Carya. I didn't even know where she was. You two look so sweet together, I almost hate to split you two apart again."

Zelkova pushed Carya further behind her. Carya's slender form was nearly invisible behind her. She wouldn't let Vako take Carya or her family from her again, not when she just got them back. But fear crept into the back of her mind like a virus that would infect every good thought it touched if she let it.

No, she had to keep her anger and doubt in check. They could be her downfall, and she refused to let that happen.

Vako laughed at Zelkova's move. "Oh, dear sister."

"Don't call me that. You know I'm not your sister. My little brother died when I was four and I know you're not Pyrus." The two of them glared at each other. Then Vako laughed again, and in the next instant, shadows overtook Pyrus and Sten, then Omnia and Spero. "Don't you dare!"

Vako laughed at her again. "Dare? Dare to do what? Now that you know our connection, I think it may be easier to turn you."

"You are not my brother. We are not siblings."

"That may be so. Either way, it changes nothing."

Zelkova tried to figure out how to save everyone and keep Carya safe from Vako. *How can I stay here and fight Vako while saving the others? Can I be at more than one place? I can't do that, can I?*

Vako scoffed, interrupting her thoughts. "It's your move." Vako tilted their head to the side in an animal-like motion. "I really don't see a way out of this for you."

"What is it that you want?"

"Oh, dear. You still haven't figured out that part? Come, come now. I thought we were connected on a deep level."

Zelkova's mind frantically looked for a solution. How could she be at three places at once?

"All right, I've given you enough time." Without any warning, Carya moved toward Vako, not walking but floating.

Zelkova looked from Carya to Vako, panic on the verge of being her sole emotion.

"Oh, dear, I thought you knew I had the power of water." Vako laughed.

Carya hovered ever closer to them. "I can't move," Carya said, fear lacing her voice. "This is worse than Vatten."

Zelkova stared. Panic had frozen her body. She blinked and reached out her hand, trying to pull at Carya, but no matter how much strength she put into it, Carya would not stop moving toward Vako.

"This is quite fun. You had me scared the other day, but it seems I might have found your weakness."

Zelkova glared at Vako. "Which is what?"

"Your kindness is your weakness."

This time it was Zelkova who laughed. Vako tilted their head in confusion, halting Carya's movement forward. "You underestimate the value of kindness. I think that's your weakness."

Zelkova decided to do something she had only tried a few times in the depths of her cave. Hopefully, she would be able to save all the ones she held dear — or die trying.

20

Facing off with Vako, Zelkova knew she had to save the love of her life standing only a few feet away and the others who were countries apart. So, she concentrated on three spots. Zelkova saw where Sten and Pyrus stood near the edge of the ocean, on the beach where they rested as stones. Then to Omnia and Spero in a field near the capital of Solaris. Then back to where Carya was, in the woods of Lignum. Something in the back of her mind made her think of a fourth place. The thought only lasted for a second, but it was long enough to interfere with her concentration.

When she opened her eyes, she looked down at her hands, which had transformed into intertwining roots outlined with fire. Taking in her surroundings, she saw she was in the capital of Solaris standing next to the tree she had planted with an Elemental many years ago. When she had faced off with her uncle, before the fight with Malus had ended her human body, this nature Elemental worked with her uncle and forgot the good in humanity. Zelkova had sentenced it to life as a tree, for it to watch its surroundings and to learn as an observer, much like she had done with Vatten. That had not worked out well. Would this have a better outcome? And why had she thought to come here?

Had she succeeded in what she was planning to do? Was she at the other locations she had sent herself to?

Closing her eyes again, she sensed she was in the other locations, and when she opened her eyes, she could see through her other selves' eyes. Not wanting to impede them, she decided to stay where she was and watch for the time being.

Just before she was about to sit down under the tree, it shook violently. Her eyes widened. Nodding her head in understanding, she lifted her arms, then lowered them down and away from each other.

When her motion stopped, pieces of the tree fell away, as if it was shedding skin, revealing a large figure standing in its place. It stood almost two heads taller than her and much broader, with thick intertwining roots. The roots were intertwined so closely they almost looked like bark. The figure stepped forward and looked Zelkova up and down.

He wore a slight smirk. "Well, isn't that an odd combination? You don't look at all like expected." He spoke with a strange accent, nothing like she had heard before. She didn't remember him sounding like that the last time they met.

She didn't give it much thought, still keeping eyes on her other selves. "So, I didn't catch your name before. I'm fairly certain you know mine."

"My name is Jardin. I would say it's a pleasure to meet you, but I still haven't forgotten what happened last time we met. It was unpleasant sitting here, watching humans running around. Do you know how many vile things I've seen? You wouldn't believe the rubbish humans are capable of. I don't know if I'll ever get some of it out of my head..." Zelkova smiled slightly at Jardin, which made him scowl. "What are you so cheerful about?"

"I've never been called cheerful. I'm far from it. I've just never heard an accent like yours, and some of the words you use..."

"Yes, yes. I can be quite odd," he answered. "But that's beside the point. You might say I'm not from this area."

Zelkova tilted her head, wondering if she heard him correctly. Maybe watching her other selves made her misunderstand.

Jardin chuckled at her confused expression. "No, you heard me correctly. I'm not from the continent, time. Oh, now I'm getting confused..."

"Wait, what?"

"I... am... not..." he said slowly, as if talking to someone who couldn't comprehend his words. She waved her hand, forcing his lips to close shut. His eyes widened in surprise.

It was now her turn to smirk up at him. "What do you mean? Are you saying you come from a different land and time?" Zelkova waved her hand again, making his lips part. "Please explain thoroughly."

"Look, I am from a land separate than this one. Now you're asking yourself, why hasn't anyone ever found it or even heard of it? Someone would have seen a whole other continent. There is an explanation for that. It is hidden with a shield around it. I don't think it's ever been lowered for anyone."

"How did you get here, then?"

"You really want to know everything, don't you?"

"How do you know these things? Are you with Vako?"

"I am forbidden to say. For the fun of it, I'll tell you what little I can. And what little I can remember. I was dying of boredom, so much so that someone brought me here to keep me alive. I've been here for thousands of years. I'm not with this Vako, nor do I know of this Vako. Also, no, your mother doesn't know me."

Zelkova sensed there was more to the story but couldn't tell if he was deliberately hiding it or really couldn't remember. She started to ask more, but Jardin stopped her. "No, no more. I told you. I am sworn to secrecy. No... Now, do what you will with me."

Reaching out, she lightly touched his shoulder. Flashes of other lands came to her mind. A castle made of clouds, so vast it blocked out the blue sky. Then an image of an underwater paradise with walls of seaweed and furniture made of bubbles. Then a large island full of sand, dirt and rocks.

Just as quickly as it appeared, the visions faded, pushing her out of his mind.

Confused by the images and his actions, she stepped back from him. "You have changed. It's like you're a completely different person."

He started at her words and stood. As he walked closer to her, she had to tilt her head up to see his face. He stopped inches from her and whispered, "You..." He backed away with a bright smile and said, "I think you might be onto something there." Jardin turned and walked to where he once stood as a tree. After pacing for a while, he turned to her once more. "I might like you." He saw her shocked reaction and laughed. "No, not in that way. As a friend of sorts. Now that you released me from my prison, which I still haven't forgiven, what's on our agenda?"

"Our agenda? I have a long list, but I don't know what you want to do. You are free to do as you choose, as long as you don't hurt a living being or fight in another war. But I have more questions for you. I just don't have the time to figure you out at the moment."

"You have bigger fish to fry? Then, my plan is to follow you."

"Me? Why me? Don't you have other things you've been wanting to do for the last two hundred years? And bigger fish to fry? I don't understand that wording."

Jardin eyed her up and down again with a sly smile. "There are things I would like to do, but I have a feeling whatever you are going to do is far more interesting."

Zelkova couldn't help but smile. "You're right. You are odd." She was glad he was coming. There was something unusual about him, and she needed to find out just what. But now was not the time.

Looking at his aura, his life force, Zelkova saw no darkness. Only a light green hue that faded into bright white. It was risky bringing someone else into Vako's game because they could be used as a pawn, but there was something about Jardin that made her feel at ease.

"We should head back to the woods of Lignum, below Silva. Come, let's move fast."

Moving through the trees, Zelkova felt Jardin staring at her, but he broke the awkwardness, asking, "Why are we headed to Silva?"

Without looking at him, she continued forward. "To help my other self… Hurry, it's getting worse."

"What's getting worse?"

Zelkova didn't answer, just moved faster through the trees.

Splitting had been risky. She could have pulled herself into nothingness. The other risk was not having enough strength to combat Vako and their shadows. This plan had to work or her reunion with her family would be short-lived.

Zelkova opened her eyes and looked down at her hands to see clouds forming her body. Mixed in with the clouds were light and darkness, giving her a swirl of color. She could see what was happening to her other selves but knew she needed to deal with the situation in front of her. From her vantage point on top of a hill, she had a good viewpoint. Down below, shadows circled something at the bottom. Someone. Two someones.

Relieved the darkness hadn't overtaken them, Zelkova moved swiftly. When she neared the shadows, she noticed they weren't as thick as usual. It was easy to push them aside and walk to the center to reach Omnia and Spero.

The two of them were on their knees, obviously in pain. She knelt and waved her hand in front of their faces. They both glanced up. Their eyes were pure black, iris and all. She stood and stared at the two vacant faces in front of her. The darkness seemed to realize she was there and moved toward the three of them again.

She clapped her hands and then moved them apart, forming a dome of light that covered them. Seconds later, the shadows engulfed the area once again.

When she was about to sit down in front of them, Zelkova remembered she was made of air and could use that to her advantage. Faint clouds moved around Omnia and Spero. Zelkova reached into both their minds to find them in the dark place they had been taken to, just like they had done for her in the past. To make things easier, she would bridge the gap between their minds to reach them both at the same time. She hoped that, connected, Spero and Omnia would be able to help each other through the darkness.

As her consciousness reached theirs, Zelkova was surrounded by pitch blackness. Snapping her fingers, a small orb of light appeared in front of her.

"Omnia, Spero, Inane." With each name, a wave of light extended from her into the darkness. After a while, the light hit something, like a wave of water hitting a rock.

Calling out again, she followed the ripples to find what looked like Spero. It was his body, but it was as vacant as the one she had just seen. She reached out her index finger and touched his forehead. Immediately, her surroundings swirled and changed, taking her deeper into his mind, back to Brandton. A few feet away from her was Spero holding a sword. An older man was screaming at him.

Stepping closer, she could make out the words the man was yelling. "Kill me! Do it!"

Spero trembled, and in a blink of an eye, the man impaled himself onto Spero's sword. The force of it caused him to release the weapon as the man fell to his knees. Spero stared in disbelief at the lifeless body in front of him, the horror of what happened overtaking him.

Zelkova rushed over to his side. She motioned her hands around his head and whispered reassuring words. "He did that to himself. It was not your doing. You killed no one. You have saved and helped so many people. You wouldn't hurt anyone needlessly. You know that is true. Your heart is pure and kind."

His tear-filled eyes turned to Zelkova. Anguish poured from every part of him. Without a second thought, she grabbed ahold of Spero and pulled him in for a hug. He buried his head in her shoulder, releasing his sadness.

After several moments, he lifted his head, and the scenery around them went back to darkness. The orb still hovered beside Zelkova and now Spero as well.

Releasing him, she looked him up and down. He seemed to be almost back to normal, but Zelkova knew he wouldn't fully be himself again until he saw Omnia. With the silent Spero by her side, she called out, "Omnia, Inane!"

With those words, ripples of light spread out. Once again, she waited to see if the light would return to her from a certain place, but this time it didn't. Zelkova was about to call out again when she turned to Spero. "Why don't you try calling out for her? Think of light flowing from you to her while you call her name." He solemnly nodded and closed his eyes. "Remember to imagine light reaching out to Omnia."

"Omnia! Inane!" Pausing to open his eyes, he seemed surprised at the five rays of light extending from his body like ripples in a pond. Focusing, he tried again. "Omnia. I'm here, Omnia."

The two of them waited and watched the waves of light search the darkness around them. Right after the last ray disappeared, a faint ripple came back to them. Zelkova caught a glimpse of Omnia.

"Keep calling to her. Hopefully, the light will get brighter as we near." But after a while, Zelkova stopped Spero from calling out anymore. They waited for a ripple back. Nothing came this time, not even a faint wave. That worried Zelkova. She hoped her next move would work.

Looking to Spero, she smiled slightly, trying not only to ease his fear but hers as well. "What I need you to do is to think of Omnia and only Omnia. Think of how she makes you feel, how you feel about her, how she looks. Anything and everything."

He closed his eyes. As Spero thought of Omnia, Zelkova made a stance a few feet away from him. Her left leg was in front of her body, bent at the knee. Her right leg was behind her, straight. She stretched out her arms wide on both sides.

With one swift motion, she rapidly closed her arms, making a loud clap. The shadows around them followed her movement and quickly dissipated, leaving a bright sunny day in their place. They were standing in a field, much like the one Zelkova had found the two of them in. Spero gasped at the sight of Omnia, who was huddled on the ground near the edge of some nearby trees.

He rushed over to her, with Zelkova following behind. Kneeling, he lifted her onto his lap and hugged her. "Omnia, I'm here. Please hear me."

She made no move to indicate she had heard. Zelkova motioned her hands over her head. Inane appeared next to the three of them, standing apart from Omnia. Zelkova stood in surprise.

Looking at the three of them, Inane slowly backed away. Zelkova gently grabbed her by the arm to stop her from running. "Inane, we are here to help you and Omnia. Please..."

Inane pulled hard against Zelkova's hold, making Zelkova grip her more firmly. Spero looked up at Inane. "Please help Omnia," he begged, gazing down at the woman in his arms.

Inane and Omnia's outlines both blurred with darkness. Spero instinctively surrounded himself with light. He hovered his hand above Omnia, putting rays of light into her. "Please, wake up. I need you..."

Zelkova shook her a little so Inane would look at her. When their eyes met, a wall of shadows hit Zelkova, knocking her several feet away.

Before Zelkova knew it, Inane had reached out for Omnia and Spero. Dark shadows secreted from her outstretched hand. Zelkova lifted her palm toward the three of them, creating white light around them that absorbed the shadows. Inane turned her head to look at her as Zelkova moved toward them.

"You think you're so clever, don't you?" Inane said in a voice that was not her own. "But by splitting up like that, you've left yourself weak. I can easily overtake you now. Don't look so surprised, dear sister. If you can do something, so can I. Well, for the most part. I wouldn't split up my body as you have, but I can control those who have the darkness in them. You should try controlling someone sometimes. You might enjoy it." Inane winked, making Zelkova shudder.

Just as Zelkova was about to reach out her other hand to shine more light onto the three of them, Inane turned with both palms open to Zelkova, hitting her with the strength of a tidal wave. The force knocked her back, but her light still surrounded Omnia and Spero. Inane concentrated all her power on Zelkova, hitting her again and again with shadows.

Vako was right. Splitting into so many places at once was taxing, and it did make her weaker. This wasn't going as planned, and her head was spinning. She managed to catch herself and push against the onslaught, trying to mimic Inane's motions. The darkness from Inane and the light from Zelkova met in the space between their two bodies.

She felt Vako's strength coming through Inane. They were trying to control the darkness in her own body. She looked past Inane to Spero hugging Omnia, whispering to her, trying to bring her back.

Maybe this was the end. Maybe darkness was really going to engulf the world. Maybe everything she worked to prevent would happen and the world she tried so hard to save would disappear.

Despair consumed her, making her weaker, but something pricked the back of her mind, a small voice that could hardly be heard. "You can't give up now. You've only just begun. You know how things will end if you just give in. Now, stop having your pity party, stand up and move forward. Be your own hero."

Zelkova realized she had closed her eyes to concentrate on the voice. Opening them, she saw Inane had moved closer to her. She tried to stand up but fell back down to her knees under the intensity of Inane's attack. Her eyes searched for Spero and Omnia, but they had disappeared.

Panic set in. Had they been killed by Vako using Inane's body? Zelkova found the strength to push forward, to get closer to Inane.

When Inane spoke, it was truly the shadow one speaking. "Come now. You really are trying too hard, all sides of you. Give in. I might even let you live and visit Carya from time to time. That is being overly nice. I've given you several chances to side with me and live. But if you keep going on like this, you are going to die, along with your friends. I care nothing for them but you—you are the one I want by my side. I want you to understand, though, I will kill you if I have to. So, what is your answer? Will you give in now and live with me and Carya, or keep trying to fight and die?"

Zelkova smiled deviously at Vako's words. "What you're offering me is a life of slavery where I must obey you and do your bidding, while everyone who lives in these lands is turned into shadows to endure an endless life of suffering. You really think I would let that happen? I don't care about being enslaved. That's not what bothers me. What really nags at me is that you want everyone to suffer just like you are suffering." Her words seemed to take Vako by surprise, momentarily weakening Inane, letting Zelkova take a few steps forward. All the while, they still pushed against each other with light and dark.

She went on, letting the thought of what Vako had planned for the world and all its inhabitants help her move forward. "If you really are my so-called brother, you should know I would never, ever let you kill innocent people. No, it's even worse than killing them, to let them suffer an eternal nightmare they will never wake up from." She paused, moving forward again, gaining ground toward Inane.

Zelkova's voice got louder as she used the air around her to amplify the sound of her words. "The only reason you are doing all of this is because you're not satisfied with your own world suffering with you. You want everyone here to agonize alongside you as well. Instead of looking inward for your own peace, your depraved mind decided the only way to end your pain is to take everyone else down with you."

She was just a few feet from Inane now. In a rush of movement, Zelkova took Inane's hit full force, but she was able to move close enough to distract her. During their battle, Zelkova had blocked the connection between Vako and Inane. All the while, Spero had been able to wake Omnia. The two of them moved behind Inane and grabbed her arms, stopping the barrage of darkness.

"Now, Zelkova!" Spero yelled.

She rushed forward and placed her hands on Inane's head, immersing Inane in bright light. After a few moments, Zelkova backed away, along with Omnia and Spero. The light dissipated, and Inane's image vanished along with it. Zelkova fell to her knees, and Spero and Omnia rushed to her side. Without a word, she grabbed both their hands, causing the world around them to shift.

Zelkova breathed in deep, trying to regain what little strength she had left in this form.

"We didn't move," Spero said. They were back in the field where Zelkova had found them. "We're in the same place we just were."

Zelkova let out a laugh and a groan. "The place we just left was in our minds."

"Wait, what? All that? It felt so real. You were being beaten pretty badly, and you're saying none of that was real?"

Zelkova laughed again. "I never said that it wasn't real. It was very real. Just because it took place in our minds doesn't make it less so. It actually makes things a lot more dangerous and dying a lot easier."

Spero wore a shocked look on his face. Omnia cleared her throat. "Why are you made of clouds? What happened? And Inane apologizes."

Before Omnia could say more on behalf of Inane, Zelkova motioned for her to stop. "I know none of that was you or Inane. It was all Vako. I am in cloud form because right now, I am fighting not just one battle but three. We should really move on. I need to go help myself." She smiled at the last part. It sounded a little strange to say that.

Before they could move, Spero asked, "Wait, why and how are you fighting three battles?"

Zelkova held up a hand for Spero to stop before he could ask any more questions. "I'm certain you do have a lot of questions and I will answer them, but now is not that time. We must move before…" Zelkova didn't want to voice her fears, so she left it at that.

She lifted the three of them up and moved fast toward her other selves. She tried not to show how weak and tired she felt.

Or how scared.

Her plan was taking a toll, and Zelkova feared what the ultimate price might be.

Zelkova looked down at the shore then at her stone body. Dark and light ran through her first layer of rock like veins beneath skin. Toward the ocean, a black dome sat atop the sandy beach. She stepped forward and the darkness reached out for her, like dark ribbons on a windy day. But the light she shielded herself with drove it away, back toward the dome.

Pyrus and Sten must be trapped in the shadows. The thought of them freed from one prison to just be put back into another one made her heart ache. Closer to the dome, heat radiated from within. Stretching out her hand, she pushed through the shadows. These shadows felt different from the ones before.

Instead of feeling like clouds or mist, they felt like hot tar against her stone body. Zelkova tried to push the tar-like shadows away with the motion of her arms, but her arms stuck to it like flies to honey. Soon she couldn't move at all and could see only a few inches in front of her face. She worried about what was happening to her brother and Sten all the more and pushed at the goo even harder.

"Sten, Pyrus! Can you hear me? I'm here!" Zelkova heard nothing in return as she desperately tried to break free. Anxiety grew as the realization of the situation sank in. She was sinking into a pit from which she could not escape. The light she had put around herself faded, leaving her in darkness.

"Pyrus, Sten! I'm here!" she yelled.

Zelkova wanted to yell out more, but it felt as if her body was being crushed by thousands of pounds of pressure. She didn't realize how weak she would become when she split herself between several bodies. Looking at her other selves, Zelkova saw some of them were struggling as well.

"Pyrus, Sten..." she whispered once more.

Closing her eyes, Zelkova thought of the two of them, trying to reach them through the light. "It can't end like this..."

With more determination, she made another light barrier around herself, illuminating the area. Beyond it, there was nothing but the darkness that tried to envelop her.

Feeling through the elements, there came a sense of warmth from the center of the shadowy slime. Pushing toward it, the area became warmer. Soon, a faint light pierced the darkness. Reaching out her hand was difficult because of the thickness of the shadows, but she was able to push through them.

When Zelkova did, she was surprised to feel someone grasp her hand, pulling. With a strong tug, Pyrus and Sten yanked her into a light bubble. Falling to her knees, she sighed in relief at the sight of them. Examining them, Zelkova could tell they were growing weak and the barrier that held the darkness at bay would not hold much longer.

She stood and was about to speak when Pyrus said, "You seem different..."

"Yes, I had to split into several bodies. Vako attacked you two and Omnia and Spero at the same time. And he is also trying to take Carya..."

The thought of Vako and Carya made pain and guilt sear through her. How could she leave Carya again? And in the hands of the shadowed one. At the want of saving them all, would she lose the love of her life again? All of it was becoming too much for her heart to handle. And that scared her all the more.

Sten crossed his arms. "And this was the best idea you could come up with?"

Zelkova nodded. "Yes. If I hadn't, you two would soon be crushed."

"Us? We're the one who rescued you." Sten laughed at her accusation of weakness.

"You both are strong for having just a little light. But I gather you are both reaching the end of your strength. In a few more minutes, this barrier would break, and the shadows would overtake both of you."

Neither of them responded.

Not wanting to waste any more time, Zelkova stood in between them, lifting her hands above her head. She flattened out her palms and closed her eyes. Rays of lights sprayed out from her body, expanding the barrier Pyrus and Sten had made. As the light barrier grew, Pyrus and Sten mimicked her movement, and the shadows slowly dissipated.

After a while, the shadows were banished, leaving the three standing on the sandy beach. Zelkova's knees gave out, but before she hit the ground, Pyrus caught her. He lifted her up, hugging her under her arms. "If you had flesh, I would say you were looking a bit pasty," he said, looking down at her. They smiled at each other, trying to lighten the situation.

Sten turned to the two of them, trying to grin but his expression turned grim. "I'm sorry to bring down the mood, but it seems we might have more trouble on our hands."

They followed his gaze and saw several dozen Elementals on top of the hill overlooking the beach. Pyrus sighed. "You've got to be kidding me..."

Zelkova stood, grinning. "I'm guessing he wants you dead this time."

Pyrus laughed. "I guess you're right. What are your other selves doing? Could they come help?"

"One seems to be on its way to assist the self who is fighting Vako, the other is still trying to rescue Omnia and Spero. The self facing down Vako is near our hometown and is having a hard time..." She wanted to say more but knew they didn't have time. "I think it's best we take out the weaker ones first."

Sten turned to them. "I agree, but where did all of these Elementals come from and why would they fight us?"

Zelkova turned to face the hoard of Elementals beyond Sten. "It seems Vako recruited Tempus' minions." The Elementals ranged from a few Seconds to Fourths — of fire, water, air, rock and nature. They stood, waiting to see who would make the first move.

Pyrus, Sten and Zelkova spread out, so as not to accidentally strike one another. Zelkova looked at Pyrus. "Do you even know how to fight with your gift?" she asked almost teasingly.

He laughed at her. "It will come to me." With a wink, he raised his arms high. When he lowered them, a wave of dirt shot up toward the Elemental army.

"Well, that's one way of starting things." Sten smiled at Zelkova and then at Pyrus.

The army moved down the hill toward them, hurling balls of flame, rock, and water. Sten stomped his foot, creating a wall of sand to stop the first attack. Things progressed rapidly from there. In a matter of moments, they were each separated from one other and surrounded by a few dozen Elementals each.

Zelkova faced off with two Second water Elementals, several Thirds and Fourths of fire, and one air Elemental.

The bulk of them seemed to be working together, infusing their powers to make them stronger. This was something she hadn't seen any Elemental do before. Most would rather work alone. She tilted her head as she analyzed all their movements.

How the air fueled the fire was mesmerizing to her. With a flick of her wrist, she pulled up and around the Elementals surrounding her, putting out the fire and choking the air. Just as she was about to make another move, her vision blurred.

Zelkova fell to her knees and noticed her other bodies were feeling the same effects. It all seemed to stem from the body with Vako. She tried to see what was happening, but her senses were blurred. Lifting her head, she let out a blood-curdling scream that sent shockwaves from her body, shooting out in all different directions.

21

The shockwave sent Elementals flying. As it neared Sten and Pyrus, Sten disappeared from Pyrus's view. While Pyrus frantically looked for him, he felt someone pulling him by the ankle.

"Hurry, before it hits," he heard. Pyrus realized what Sten was doing and let himself be pulled into the ground to avoid the shockwave.

Pyrus heard screams, and then the wave of sound passed above them. But was it just sound? This Zelkova didn't have air, so it was unclear how she made the wave. He pondered this while they lifted themselves up from underground. Their surroundings had completely changed within those few seconds. The water of the ocean was pushed further from the shore. The nearby grass and trees were gone. Elementals were strewn all over. Some moved while others showed no sign of life.

Pyrus grabbed Sten by the arm. "What happened? Do you see Zelkova? Do you feel her?"

Without looking at Pyrus, he surveyed the aftermath. "I don't see her, and because she is a First, I can't sense her even if I wanted to." He sighed and continued scanning for Zelkova. The two of them started walking, having to step past or over lifeless Elementals. The only ones who kept their form were the stone and nature Elementals. There was scorched or wet sand where the fire and water Elementals had been.

"Zelkova! Show us where you are!" Pyrus called. They waited for some kind of answer, but none came. This worried him. "We should head to where Vako has Zelkova and Carya. We must go back to where it all started."

"Yes, I agree," Sten replied. "I've never seen any Elemental be able to take others out with such ease…"

"She is a First now."

"It's more than that. It has to be. Zelkova is growing stronger than any of us realizes."

"More than she even knows." Pyrus sighed, trying to focus on his movements, wanting to reach Zelkova before it was too late.

But too late for what? The thought made a pit in his stomach.

Staring at Vako, Zelkova couldn't control which element went where when she split herself, and she was far from pleased about being stuck in her watery form. Now that she knew Vako could control water, this was going to be a battle of wills. She hoped they couldn't control water as well as they controlled the shadows.

Vako had been watching and when they saw her in her new form, they let out a delighted laugh, which didn't sit well with Zelkova. "How inconvenient, surprising and amusing all at the same time. I expected a lot from you. This only shows me how strong you really are and how much stronger you can become. If you are to join with me, that is."

They moved Carya toward them again. When Zelkova reached out her watery hand, she saw dark and light running through her arm like veins under flesh. But despite her efforts, Carya was soon by Vako's side, who stretched out their other hand toward Zelkova.

Her body froze in place. "What? What are you...?" She tried not to let the panic she was feeling show, but no matter how much she tried to move, her body would not respond. The shadowed one was controlling her just like they controlled Carya.

Vako pushed Carya to the side, closing the distance between them and Zelkova. Soon Vako was almost face to face with her. The two of them stood around the same height, but Zelkova still could not see their face. Darkness cloaked it, even with how close they were.

"This could be interesting. I've always wanted to test my powers, and I think you will be the best subject to try them on. Every person I tried before was far too weak and died before I could complete the trial. Now. Which should we start with?"

Zelkova looked past Vako to see Carya staring at the two of them. She was trying to will herself free from Vako's grip, but neither of them could move. Zelkova sent a message to her other selves to hurry back to her position as fast as they could. The closest one was her nature/fire self who traveled with Jardin. The other two were still trying to fight the shadows.

All she could do was watch Vako, who started to pace in front of her. They seemed all too happy trying to decide what to do to her. "Ah, I think I know what I shall try."

With a sudden jerk, Vako turned to Zelkova again. The sudden movement would have made her jump if she had been able to move her body. The last time Zelkova was in a situation like this was with Tempus. That was when Carya's human body died, she was imprisoned by Vatten, and then Zelkova was tortured with the element of time. Yes, she gained the gift of time in the end but at great cost. What suffering would this bring to her and those she loved?

Zelkova hated this, hated feeling weak, helpless, and hopeless.

Vako lifted their hand and twisted it. Zelkova fell to her knees, her face turned upward to look at Vako. They leaned over Zelkova, and she could *almost* make out their features. "I think you'll feel more pain in a different form," they whispered.

Vako brushed the back of their hand against Zelkova's cheek, making her think of the time she killed Aoman, her uncle.

After Vako lifted their hand, Zelkova's watery form changed into a flesh one. Zelkova's eyes widened in surprise. Vako took a few steps back to watch the transformation. Their tone took on a hint of excitement. "I like what I see." Zelkova tried to speak but wasn't able to move her lips. "Oh, yes, that's no fun." Vako moved their fingers over her now-flesh lips. "Now try again, what is it that you wanted to say?"

Zelkova glared up at Vako. "You're sick. You know that?"

Vako stepped back and laughed but continued to stare at her. Anger grew inside her as she stared back at them. But fear was there along with the anger. Fear of Vako's power. How could they turn an Elemental into their human form?

"Why don't you show me what you really look like?"

They leaned toward Zelkova. "In due time, I will. But right now, it's all about you."

They lifted their index finger. With their other hand, they reached out toward Zelkova, as if to grab something. Zelkova felt a pull from within. Soon, a small stream of water formed from her body, drawn to Vako's finger. They made a circular motion, pulling more at Zelkova. She screamed in pain.

As they continued to pull the water from her, Vako chuckled. "You see, I can do a lot more to you now that I made you have a flesh body. No need to thank me, really. It was my pleasure."

Zelkova screamed, the pain becoming more intense. It felt as if her life force was being pulled out of her. This pain came from deep inside, so agonizing there were no words to describe the feeling.

In between screams, Zelkova could hear Vako speaking. "Once the water is gone from you, I will take your light, leaving you with darkness. Once your flesh body dies once more, you will be mine to control." With a yanking motion, Vako pulled the rest of the water element out of her. Water in the shape of her heart rested in Vako's hand.

Vako studied the watery heart in their hand. "Oh, this is interesting. I was not expecting the core of your water element to be your heart. Only fitting though, since that is Carya's element." Vako turned to Carya then back to Zelkova.

In the next breath, they crushed the heart in their fist.

"No!" Zelkova screamed, gasping in pain. She glanced at Carya, who seemed to harbor the same feelings.

"Come, come now. The fun part has yet to begin." Vako knelt and hugged Zelkova's naked body against theirs, putting one hand on the small of her back, the other hand on the back of her head.

Still reeling from the pain, Zelkova was shocked by Vako's next move. They leaned close and touched their lips to Zelkova's flesh ones. Zelkova was unable to move away from them while Vako pressed against her. Vako made Zelkova's mouth move for her as if to kiss them back.

"Stop! Please stop!" Carya cried, but Zelkova had no control. Carya had been unable to speak until then. Vako had let her speak to hurt her more. Even though they were face to face, she still couldn't see their features. All Zelkova could see was darkness, despite feeling their lips.

Tears rolled down Zelkova's cheek. Vako pulled away. "I wasn't expecting this kind of reaction from you." Vako leaned in and licked the tears from her cheeks. If Zelkova could, she would have shuddered in disgust. Vako brushed the back of their hand against her arm, looking at Zelkova to see her reaction.

"Now, what do you think Vatten would say seeing you now, or even better, before when you were in water form? I bet he would have fallen in love with you all over again. Oh, come now, don't be surprised. I knew he loved you. It was obvious from my viewpoint." Vako stood up in excitement. "Even better, what would our brother and Sten do if they saw what I'm about to do to you? Too bad they'll be dead before you are."

Zelkova tried to see her other selves but had no connection with them at all anymore. How could that have happened?

"Don't look so worried, my dear sister. It will all be over soon. It won't feel that way, though."

Zelkova glared up at them. Rage and fear fought for precedence inside her. "What did I do to you?"

Vako had been moving toward Carya but turned toward Zelkova again. "You lived..." Their voice was dark and menacing, but as they walked toward her again, their voice changed into more a cheerful tone. "Don't you see, above everyone else, I want you by my side. How can you not see that? Sadly, I have to break you for you to see things my way. I don't mind hurting you if I get what I want in the end."

She tried to think of a way out of the situation, but panic threatened to overtake her.

"What about me?" Carya asked, stopping Vako in their tracks.

Laughing, they turned back to Carya. "You will stay with me and Zelkova, of course. After I turn her, we'll all be one happy family."

Carya interrupted them, "I thought you told me you were—"

Vako waved their hand, shutting Carya's lips. "That was the past, and I said what I had to, to gain your trust. Don't worry, you will know all once you join me."

They turned their attention back to Zelkova and motioned with their finger like before, pulling a small thin line of light from her body. Her body grew weaker, and dark thoughts flooded her mind. She slumped over as Vako released their hold slightly to continue to pull out the light.

She closed her eyes and saw only darkness. Her mind battered her with thoughts of self-doubt and self-hatred. But in the back of her mind, a small light seemed to shine. It was faint, but it was there. Zelkova tried her best to focus on the light through all the darkness.

"Listen... Listen..." Zelkova strained to hear the weak voice call out to her.

Again, she heard, "Listen... Listen... The elements are all around you. In you, never leaving... Take hold... Take back..." The words *take back* echoed in her mind and the realization of what it meant dawned on her. She thought of her other selves and focused on them coming back to her, back into her body. She thought of this over and over again. The pull from Vako seemed to ease, letting her open her eyes.

She screamed, not just from pain but from all the pressure that built inside her. The call to her other selves was released, and it came roaring from her body like a shockwave.

The shockwave knocked Vako off their feet, releasing Carya, who quickly dodged the wave; it knocked down trees and even the stone that took her to different times.

Each one of her elements came rushing back to her — one from a nearby tree, another by the nearby stone. Air came from the air around them, and fire came down in a ball of flame. It hit her, setting the surrounding leaves on fire. But one was missing that she could not get back: water.

She opened her eyes and saw the aftermath of the shockwave. Turning her head from side to side, she saw uprooted trees and the broken stone that Vako placed long ago. Standing, she looked down at her hand to see stone in the place of flesh.

Her head swam, and moments later, darkness swallowed her once more.

Carya scanned for Zelkova among the debris once the shockwave had cleared. Looking around, she saw no sign of Vako, nor did she feel them nearby. In the distance, Zelkova was getting to her feet but fell back to her knees. Rushing to her, she hugged Zelkova, holding her in her arms. She was unresponsive.

"Zelkova. Zelkova, can you hear me? Please. Please wake up."

Carya's tears fell on Zelkova's face, her stone body absorbing the water. Carya watched Zelkova for movements, hoping to see any sign of life. "Zelkova, please, hear me."

She lay her down and kept watch over her throughout the day. The others made their way to where Carya and Zelkova were just as day broke. The light shined through the remaining trees that stood nearby. The trees within a close radius of Zelkova were gone, and the stone had crumbled.

"What in all creation happened here?" Jardin asked, stopping near Carya and Zelkova. "Wait, don't answer. I'm guessing it's like what happened to the Zelkova I was with."

Carya eyed Jardin. "And who are you?"

Jardin bowed then sat down near Carya, who watched over the motionless Zelkova. "I am Jardin. I encountered Zelkova over two hundred years ago. Because of my part in the war, I was turned into a tree to watch my surroundings and learn from what I saw. Somehow, she came to me — her body made of tree and fire — and set me free. Seeing those two elements together was quite a sight to see. I came to help as much as I can, but it doesn't look like there is much that can be done." He watched the two of them with a familiar expression. One Carya could not place.

Jardin fell silent as Sten and Pyrus came into view. Pyrus rushed over to Zelkova and Carya. Kneeling, he touched Zelkova's cheek. The two stone Elementals took a seat beside Carya, and Jardin followed.

Pyrus sighed at the sight of his sister. "I'm guessing all her forms had the same effect the one with us did." Jardin and Carya nodded. "What happened to Zelkova to make her split up? She said that Vako was attacking several of us at a time. What else occurred?"

Carya grimaced at the memory of Vako kissing Zelkova. She shuddered and shook her head, trying to escape the thought. Before she could respond, leaves rustled near them. Moments later, Spero and Omnia entered the clearing. The two of them sat near Carya with somber looks about them.

Jardin stared at the two newcomers. "Have a hard time at it, have we?" He winked then turned back to Carya. "Please, go on."

Carya breathed in deeply, trying to hold back the emotions on the verge of breaking through her exterior.

"Zelkova and I came from Silva after setting up the barrier there and looking for a stone she thought may be under the castle. What we found was a shadow of her younger self who seemed to be hiding from Vako. The shadow called Vako her brother, which doesn't make sense to me. Then we came to the stone here to try and destroy it. That's when we encountered Vako. Zelkova split herself up to help all of you. In return, she was left in her water form, which Vako could control."

Reaching out to touch Zelkova's hand, Carya went on. "Vako was able to control me and Zelkova but somehow was able to take water from her and made her body flesh once more." Carya thought it best to leave out certain details. Like the fact that they had kissed her, along with the confusion about who the shadowed one really was. She hoped to figure that out herself before confronting anyone with her speculation. "Vako started taking what little light she had in that form, and that's when all of this happened. She has yet to wake up."

Sten, who seemed to have had been deep in thought, cleared his throat and looked at Zelkova then Carya. "So, Vako took Zelkova's water element?"

Carya nodded. "Yes, it was in the shape of her heart."

"Should Omnia and I go into her mind like we did before?" Spero asked in concern.

"No, I don't think it has to do with shadows this time but the lack of one of her elements that might be causing her condition. Because Vatten is gone and Zelkova no longer has water, that makes you the First of water, Carya." Sten paused, watching her. "That means you can give her your gift."

Taking in what Sten said, she thought of how Zelkova had first given her water as children. Mimicking what she had seen Zelkova do, Carya placed one hand over Zelkova's head and the other over her chest. Closing her eyes, she imagined water going into Zelkova. A gentle stream of water poured from Carya's hands onto Zelkova's body. The water hit Zelkova, and her body absorbed it. After a few moments, Carya opened her eyes and lifted her hands away to watch for any sign of movement.

Minute after minute went by with no sign. The waiting made her heart ache. She had watched Zelkova for so long. Seeing it all through Vatten's eyes was more painful than Carya had realized it would be. Before their relationship could really begin, they were taken from each other. Was this how things were meant to be for them? Would she lose Zelkova this time? Would she not even be able to watch her live?

She shuddered at the thought, trying hard not to let fear take over. *Zelkova is strong, she will come back to me. She has to,* Carya thought as she held her beloved's hand, hoping for a miracle.

Darkness filled Zelkova's mind.

"Come..." a voice whispered. "Let me show you what you have been asking for."

Zelkova wanted to ask what exactly it was she had asked to see, but her surroundings changed before she could. She saw herself in a royal guard uniform. It was silver in color with gold intertwining, as if roots from a tree. This armor was reserved for only special occasions. In the throne room, her father sat atop his throne at the end of the long room.

She knelt then looked up to him. "Father, you called for me." Her armor glistened in the afternoon sun that streamed in from the windows outlining the throne room.

He looked down from his throne at the top of the stairs and, with a slight smile, said, "My daughter, lovely as ever." She returned his smile. "I have called you here because I have some grave news. There has been an outbreak of what is called Elementals, creatures who can control different elements. They have joined forces with humans to take over each country."

Zelkova gasped.

"I am afraid this has happened before, but this time there is no one to stand against them, and the Elemental leading it all is not going to back down like they did in the past."

She stepped forward with a worried look. "Tell me, Father, what is it that I can do?"

He sighed. "I wish there was something someone could do. But I fear there is no hope. I called you in here to also tell you your brother..." He paused and looked down before speaking again. "He is dead, killed by Ruri and Elementals forces." He breathed in sharply at the sight of tears falling down her cheeks.

This... This couldn't have happened. No, this didn't happen. I am certain of it. This is not real.

"Their army is moving toward the capital as we speak. I'll have the horses readied to take us to the mountains of Montis. Our only hope is that they won't make it that far."

The scene blurred into another vision. This time, it was like she was flying, looking down on the world below. Zelkova surveyed the land and saw no sign of life. Trees that were once lush were now just sticks protruding from the ground, which was cracked due to lack of rain. It seemed Elementals and humans alike no longer inhabited the land she saw.

Once again, the images shifted but this time they shifted to darkness. "Without someone to confront Tempus, he took over the lands and killed the Elementals," the voice from before said from the nothingness around her. "It is true that he had tried to kill them before and was stopped. But this time, things were different. If you were not granted your gifts and hadn't done what you had, that would have been the outcome. Death. Death to all but Tempus. You have been wanting to see what would have happened if you had not been involved. Now you know."

Zelkova was trying to find her voice when a cool rush filled her body and mind. It felt like the slow current of a river, gently carrying her away from the darkness and the voice. As the water rushed around her, she felt peaceful and at ease.

Her mind drifted like she was on the verge of falling asleep, but she opened her eyes to see Carya looking down at her and heard sighs of relief come from all around her. Sitting up, she saw her brother, Sten, Omnia, Spero and Jardin staring at her. She looked down at her hands to see that they were once again stone and felt all the elements within her. Then her eyes met Carya's, who sat up a bit straighter at the notice.

Zelkova grabbed Carya, pulling her in for a hug, then whispered in her ear, "I'm so sorry that happened. I promise I won't let you be in danger again."

Carya sighed at her words, then pulled away. Zelkova froze in surprise. Carya looked her up and down and then slapped her across her face. "Don't you ever do that again. You should know by now you can't save everyone. Next time don't risk yourself for any of us."

The words shocked not just Zelkova but the others as well. Omnia was quick to respond. Sitting up on her knees, she glared at Carya. "So, you're saying our lives mean nothing compared to hers?"

The look Carya gave Omnia scared Zelkova. She had never seen Carya angry before and she didn't know how to react to it or what to expect. "She is more important to me and she's the only one that can save this world from Vako." Carya turned her attention to Zelkova. "We were lost from each other before. I won't let that happen again. Next time don't go off to rescue others, save yourself first."

Zelkova sighed at Carya's words and took her hand in her own, the one she had just slapped her with. She held back a smile. Seeing and knowing the reason Carya was angry made her heart flutter. Now she knew she had one, and Carya was the key to it.

"Carya..." Carya tried to pull away, but Zelkova wouldn't let her. Their eyes locked. "No. Listen, please. The only reason I took on these gifts, the only reason I've made all the decisions I have up to this point, is and always will be to save others." She sighed, knowing the next words would hurt her to admit.

"Don't you think I've wanted to give up? To let humans and Elementals just fade away into the shadows? There have been so many times I've wanted to let go, to stop fighting and let death take me. Two hundred years ago and this time as well. But every time I thought of death, I was brought back by a soft voice telling me to keep going, telling me people needed my help. That is the only thing that got me through. Helping others is what drives me. I cannot let that go, Carya, and you shouldn't ask me to change who I am."

There came a pause where Zelkova could feel all eyes on her, so she went on. "Yes, Vako is gone for the moment. But they will be back, and I will have to face them again. If they repeat the separate attacks like they did today, I will make the same decision to split myself into pieces to help others. I want to have a life with you, Carya but I can't, not until Vako and the shadows are gone. This is my purpose."

The silence around her continued. Not wanting to face the looks of her companions, Zelkova kept her eyes lowered, waiting for someone, anyone, to say something. After several moments of silence, she finally lifted her eyes to see everyone looking down. Their expressions were somber. Omnia had tears in her eyes. Pyrus and Carya looked grief-stricken. Sten and Spero comforted them, looking gloomy themselves. She wanted to comfort them all, but she had no words left to do so.

She was about to turn away when Carya gripped her hands harder. "I'm sorry, Zelkova. I was wrong, and I was being selfish. I never want you to change. I want you to always remain true to yourself."

Omnia sniffed. "I am sorry as well. I have had my doubts about your motivations, but it is clear no one would choose the life that has chosen you."

"If I had known any of this would have occurred, I would have never left Silva. I would have stayed. Maybe that would have changed things for you." Pyrus was about to say more when Zelkova stood up and knelt beside him.

She smiled at him as he turned his gaze toward her. "It's not your fault. Even if you had stayed, they would have found me. It does us no good to think of the past or how things could be different. What we need to do is look forward and make decisions to create the future we want." She winked at Pyrus, making him grin.

"I think we all wish there was another way. A way for lives to go back to simpler times. But I know more than most, once things are set in motion, there is no stopping it. You have made great sacrifices for this world, Zelkova, and I am forever grateful." Sten stared at her, pride written upon his face.

Zelkova stood and smiled at Sten, then turned to all of them. "Things might not be the way we want them, but we have to work with what we have. Don't let the past drag you down or the thoughts of the future carry you away. Let your feet be steady on the ground and learn from the past so you can hope for the future."

She went over to Carya and sat back down. "Now, let us put it to a vote. Shall we go our separate ways as we were or travel together?"

As they all made their choices, their voices filled the cool morning air, but Zelkova only half-heard. Something was amiss... She jumped to her feet. Her heart exploded in her chest, and her body tensed. She felt a change in one element that should be dormant.

Zelkova's eyes grew wide. She saw something the others didn't. At the other end of the clearing stood a form she had thought long gone. Even Vako said they were dead. She mouthed the word, "Tempus," to which the figure nodded.

Zelkova moved quickly, motioning to the people and Elementals around her. First was Carya. She thought of a safe place for her, a place where no one would reach her. She repeated her goal while moving her arms toward her. Her arms went wide and then came together. In an instant, Carya was gone from sight. Then Pyrus and Sten. Again, she thought of a safe place and motioned just as she did with Carya. In a blink of an eye, Sten and Pyrus were no longer there.

Omnia and Spero had confused looks on their faces. Spero asked a question, but she had no time to explain. It was something she had never tried. All she could do was hope what she had just done had worked, and just then, hope was all she had.

Everything seemed to be moving in slow motion. Tempus started to manipulate time around them, meaning she had to hurry. Again, she thought of a safe place for Omnia and Spero. She motioned her arms, and they were soon gone. She turned to Jardin, the last one, but before she could send him to safety, the wave of the time manipulation hit her like a rock wall, throwing her and Jardin against the nearby trees.

As the rush of time spun past them, everything around them changed, but she couldn't let that happen. Gathering all her strength, she pushed herself off the tree and took a wide stance. She spread her arms out wide and closed them together, which slowed the time change. Tempus's power surprised Zelkova. She wondered how he survived and what was making him do this. Revenge?

She was being pushed back when she felt something push against her from behind, stabilizing her. Looking back, she saw Jardin with a determined look on his face. He smiled and winked. "Don't be looking at my pretty face, love. Concentrate on that jerk." He nodded toward Tempus.

Zelkova focused on Tempus. He looked as he had when they first met, but he seemed more weathered and… Zelkova couldn't place what it was…. and then it hit her. His eyes were completely black. He was being controlled.

With the help of Jardin, she slowed time and was reversing Tempus's effect when he hit them with another wall. Even though they were pushed back, they stood strong. Zelkova fought to close the large time rift Tempus was making. She kept closing her arms, but the smaller the rift got, the harder it became.

"All right, I'm going to let go and restart," she whispered to Jardin. "Push against me to hold us up."

Zelkova saw him nod from the corner of her eye. She released her arms and lowered them for only a second before lifting them back up wide on each side. Zelkova dug her feet into the dirt, and Jardin followed her motion. Rock formed around their feet and ankles, reinforcing their stance.

Then in one swift movement, she rapidly closed her arms together, yelling out. Time stopped around them. Zelkova searched to see if Tempus still stood where he appeared, but he was nowhere to be seen. The stone around her and Jardin's feet crumbled back into the earth.

The crumbled stone was nowhere in sight. The trees around them were not the same, familiar trees. Closing her eyes, she focused her senses to see where and what time they were in. They had gone back in time by one or two centuries. Pinpointing the exact time was proving difficult, however.

Jardin touched her shoulder, and when he did, flashes of his past entered her mind. She saw him as a young child — not an Elemental but a human child. The person holding his hand looked familiar, but Zelkova couldn't place them. Fragments of his life came into view of her mind's eye, like that of a muddy stream. Impossible to make out all the stones, despite knowing they were there.

She saw him being taken at a young age, but from where was not shown. Zelkova waited to see who was taking him. As the imaged cleared, she saw an Elemental, Tempus... Following the visions, she saw Tempus had placed him on an island and only visited once after. Jardin was left to fend for himself, which made him become an Elemental at a young age. But she could not see how he received the gift of nature. That was blocked. In fact, several things about him were blocked.

The vision of Jardin faded when he took his hand away. "Zelkova, are you all right?"

She turned and stared up at him. "Yes, I'm fine. I was trying to see what time we're in. Are you all right?" Her eyes searched him up and down for damage.

"Getting an eyeful, aren't you?" Jardin laughed. "I'm fine. It will take a lot more than that to take me down. So, where are we? Or should I say when?"

Zelkova looked around, not just with her eyes but also with the elements. "It seems we've gone back in time, but there's another thing... How do you know we've gone through time?"

"Look, I can't get into all that at the moment. Shouldn't we figure out where we are and how to get back?"

Zelkova eyed him. "Who are you really?"

"Try and read my mind. See what you can get. You'll probably be as confused as I am. Things only come to me in bits and pieces. What memories I do get come in fragments. None of them fully makes sense. It's more like a feeling, a knowing more than anything. That's all I can give you."

"How do you know..."

"Just do it..." Jardin took her hand and placed it on his head. Seconds later, Zelkova saw intertwining visions. One was of him with her uncle, stern and uncaring. Then he would be laughing and acting up with guards, acting completely different. Then an image of him with Sten and

Vatten came next. Zelkova tried to pull away, but something pulled her further in.

There are times when things can't always be explained, a soft voice told her, just like the one she had heard so many times before. *One day all will become clear. But today is not that day. You must focus on taking down Vako. Trust Jardin. He is loyal and will not falter.* This voice had somehow pulled her through dark times.

All Zelkova could do now was trust, something that had been her downfall several times already.

The voice and images faded, and she took her hand from Jardin. His eyes searched her, waiting for a response. "I think we may be in an alternate reality," she said finally.

Zelkova didn't want to ask how he knew Sten or Vatten, not yet, not until they found a way out of this place.

Jardin busted out laughing, so much so he backed away from Zelkova to hold his side. She eyed him with confusion until he looked back at her. "Wait, you're serious? I thought you were jesting."

Shaking her head, Zelkova said solemnly, "We were talking of being in a different time just a few moments ago. Yet you're shocked at this? We seem to be a little more than two hundred years in the past, and what this alternate plane has in store, I know not."

He stared at her in disbelief. "Please tell me you're talking out your arse right now. I've read theories of different universes existing side by side, but to be in one..." He surveyed the area, confused. "Yes, I can wrap my head around being in different times because I've lived in the past. So, I guess that doesn't scare me to revisit it. But this is a whole different level."

"This seems to be Vako and Tempus' doing. I didn't even feel Tempus. I thought he was long dead."

Jardin shrugged his shoulders. "It was bad enough dealing with one, now both. Life just doesn't seem fair."

Zelkova was a little confused by his wording but pushed it aside to focus. "I hope everyone else is all right. I'm not even certain how to get us back to our own plane."

She started to pace with agitation. Jardin put his hand on her shoulder to cease her movement. "You're strong, Zelkova. If anyone can undo what has been done, it's you."

"Thank you, Jardin. Tell me, do you remember anything before the island? When you were a child."

"I hardly remember when I was younger. How did you? Oh, yeah, reading my mind..." He turned away from her.

"Listen, I have an idea, but I'm going to need to know about your past. I know it doesn't make sense right now, but in time, it will. Please." She reached out her hand for him to take.

Jardin gazed down at her hand skeptically. After a few moments of hesitation, he reached out his hand and clasped hers.

"I might be bringing up memories you may not remember," she said softly, smiling encouragingly. "But please don't pull away."

She closed her eyes and focused on Jardin, on his past, his first memories. Her mind's eye moved through space and time. The only thing that came to her were short snippets of memory, not enough to piece anything together. No matter how much she pushed to see the time before Jardin was taken by Tempus, her vision remained foggy. She sighed and let go of Jardin.

"Are you done already?" Jardin asked, frowning. "I didn't feel anything. Did you find anything naughty while searching the depths of my mind?" He laughed.

She smiled at his humor. "Come, we should see if the capital is the same here. I will try and keep us from others' views, so don't make any sudden movements or needless noise."

With an expression of mock shock and hurt, he stepped back, putting his hand over where his heart would be if he were human. "You wound me. I have never been one to step out of line or make any kind of noise above the sound of a hummingbird."

Zelkova laughed again. "Have you ever heard a hummingbird? They may be tiny, but they have a high-pitch chirp."

Jardin crossed his arms. "See, I rest my case."

They both laughed. Despite the situation, Jardin managed to lighten both their moods, easing her tension and heartache a bit. "So, tell me of the others. I hardly met them."

"Well, Sten is strong and sure. Hardly shows his emotions, but that doesn't mean he feels."

"I'm assuming he probably feels more because of that. And the other stone guy is his lover boy?" Jardin smirked.

Again, his words confused her, but his smile was contagious. "Yes, they are a couple. The other stone

Elemental is my brother, Pyrus. He is strong and fair. Has a strong sense of justice. Which means he sees the cruelness of our world more than others."

"The two humans? The girl is like a little mouse."

"I think she's taking it all in. The Elemental world is new to her. This doesn't mean she doesn't care, or see..."

Jardin chimed in, "It means she's very observant and tries to see all sides. But still a tad overwhelmed at times, it seems. I can't blame her. I'm still reeling from being a tree for so long. My roots are still sore." He stretched his back, making groaning noises, smiling all the while.

"Then there's Carya. Strong. And if it wasn't for my elements, she would know more than me. I think she always has known and yet kept it hidden so as not to hurt me or herself. She's deeper than any ocean and is secure in herself. I wish I were more like her."

"You two do make the cutest of couples." He almost giggled.

"Cuties?"

"No, cutest. Like adorable or darling."

His worlds once again left her confused. He kept trying to explain what he meant as they moved on.

They moved swiftly toward where the capital of Lignum existed in their own universe, staying in the cover of trees as they passed small villages. Soon, the city of Silva came into view. It was a lot larger than the Silva Zelkova once called home. The city had twice as many houses and the castle was a lot higher, with tall walls blocking out the town. In the Silva she knew, the castle was open to the woods around it, which divided the town from the castle.

But here they sat right beside each other, divided by the stone wall. This castle had a barrier all around it.

They didn't enter the city but kept to the woods on the far side of the castle. There, a small wooden door opened at the base of the wall. Zelkova pushed Jardin behind her into the cover of the shadows. A small figure emerged from the door and struggled to close it behind him.

Jardin smiled and leaned near Zelkova to whisper, "Isn't that a cute little chap?"

Zelkova nodded and watched the boy, who looked oddly familiar to her. As the boy walked past them to go deeper into the woods, Zelkova's eyes followed him. Before he was out of sight, she turned to follow.

Jardin grabbed her by the arm. "Where are you going? Aren't we going into the castle? The door is ajar. Now is the time."

She shook her head. "No, getting into the castle is easy for me. But there's something about that boy. We should follow him. Come, stay close so I can shield you from view."

With a shrug, he followed a few feet behind her, careful not to make any noise. The boy seemed to be in high spirits as he jumped over logs and ran around trees. The two of them followed close enough to keep him in view but far enough to keep hidden.

Zelkova and Jardin stalked him for several miles until the boy reached a large creek. There, he played in the water and threw rocks. They stood there for a long time watching. Then a loud boom in the distance broke the quietness. Zelkova turned her eyes upstream from the boy and saw a black hole hovering above the ground. The cloaked one stepped through.

Vako looked around and seemed to curse, then with a wave of their hands, a large stone formed over the black hole. Vako touched the stone and vanished on the spot. Zelkova and Jardin weren't the only ones to see what had happened. The young boy had seen it, too.

He started toward the stone, wading through the creek. Right when Zelkova was about to reveal herself to stop the boy, Jardin grabbed her by the shoulder and pointed. "Look."

She followed his gaze to see Pyrus running toward the boy. Pyrus was only a teenager. "Rhus!" he yelled, his voice cracking. "I've been looking everywhere for you. Lunch is ready, come now." He grabbed the boy's hand and dragged him away.

The name shook not only Zelkova but Jardin as well. But everything took a turn for the worst when the boy pulled away from Pyrus' grip and went running toward the rock. He leaped into the creek before anyone, even Zelkova, could stop him, touched the stone and disappeared.

Pyrus fell to his knees, screaming. Zelkova was about to go after the boy, but Jardin put both hands on Zelkova's shoulders, stopping her. She glared up to see his expression had changed. It was dark yet deep, as if everything made sense to him now, but he was still in turmoil with it.

Just when she was about to ask why, he leaned in and whispered, "It's too late. What done is done. There is no turning back. Even if you saved him, who is to say his life would have been any better?"

Zelkova stared up at Jardin, studying his face, his words. "That name..." Before Jardin could answer Zelkova, Pyrus raised his hands in anger. Tree roots burst from the ground near the stone and creek. With a swift motion of his arms, the roots went barreling toward the rock, slamming into it at a high speed and shattering it.

Zelkova's eyes grew wide. How was he able to destroy the stone when she wasn't? This Pyrus had the gift of nature, which her brother never had. "How does he have nature?" Zelkova whispered aloud, staring at Pyrus, who slowly walked back toward the castle.

Jardin had let go of Zelkova and leaned against a tree. He grumbled and answered her question. "It seems all of them had the gift of nature given to them by their mother. I'm also assuming because Pyrus is from this universe and he is related to Vako or is Vako. That is the reason he was able to destroy the stone."

Zelkova turned to him, still dazed. Everything was starting to connect, but there was still one question. "How do you know this?" She stared at him in confusion.

He stared back at her unblinkingly. "Because the name Rhus stirred up some very old memories." Zelkova was about to speak when he held up his hand for her to stop. "You see, it's all clear to me now. I was put on that island as a small boy by Tempus. He found me roaming the woods after I touched that stone. He was trying to keep the balance of things. I didn't belong in your world, and he knew it. I tried to touch the stone I came from in your universe, but it wouldn't work. Seems it was a one-way trip. I hadn't thought about any of that in quite some time. Not until I heard that name, did I recall any of it."

Jardin sighed. She stood frozen, unable to form a response. "You see, Zelkova, I am from this universe. I came to yours and turned into what I am today. I guess that makes me your brother in a way." He huffed out a laugh that filled the air around them, giving Zelkova chills for the first time in ages.

Pyrus was disoriented and almost scared when he disappeared. Knowing Zelkova was responsible made him worry that she might have been taken over by Vako.

In an instant, both Pyrus and Sten were teleported to an unknown land. Looking around, all they saw was dirt and rocks. No trees, no water. Pyrus turned to Sten in bewilderment. "Where are we?"

Sten shook his head, then closed his eyes and focused on the ground around them. "It seems we are on that island we were going to search for."

Pyrus stumbled around in confusion. "So, you're telling me we are no longer on the continent where I was born? We are on an island out in the ocean?"

"It appears so." Sten stood, stopping Pyrus's frantic movement. "Calm yourself. I am here with you."

But Pyrus's mind was reeling. "How big is this place?" He had never heard of an island mass other than his home. How far were they from the ones they loved, and could they even get back? He had to get back to help Zelkova. Pyrus couldn't lose his sister again.

Sten looked around then down at Pyrus. "Not as large as Elementum. About half that size."

Pyrus tilted his head in question. "I've never heard our continent called that before."

"It's what all the Elementals call the lands instead of the country names. We call all of it Elementum. Come, let's go to the edge and see if there's anything in the distance."

"What's the word mean? Elementum?" Pyrus asked as they walked toward the nearest coast.

"It means element in the old language. The language no one speaks anymore."

"No one speaks? Who used to speak it?" He reached out, touching Sten's arm. Sten turned to him. The gaze Sten gave him was something Pyrus had never seen before. It was almost dark.

"I... I don't remember..." In an instant, it was gone, and his expression was back to normal. "Come, before daylight fades."

Before long, they reached the north-west side of the island where the beach had black sand mixed with gold flakes. The water was an aqua color, leaning more toward a blue hue. Pyrus sat down on the shore while Sten scanned the horizon. "See anything?"

Sten shook his head and sat down next to Pyrus. They both sat in silence until Sten spoke. "What do you remember about your little brother? Do you think Vako could really be him?"

"If he is, he can't be from our universe or time. Rhus died right before my mother changed back into an Elemental. He caught a bad cold that turned into pneumonia and passed away at the age of three. We buried him. He had no Elemental gift. So, I'm certain Vako is not him."

"Could he be you from a different universe?" Sten asked instead.

Pyrus nodded, picking up sand in his stone hand. "I guess that's possible. But what I want to know right now is why we're here, how we got here, what is here, and what happened to Zelkova and the others."

Sten stood and walked toward the water's edge. When he dipped his foot into the ocean, a shimmering barrier knocked him back to where Pyrus stood. Pyrus rushed to Sten and helped him up. They both gaped at the edge of the beach and the water beyond.

Sten chuckled. "I guess that means we're not leaving this island anytime soon."

He sat back down and Pyrus followed suit. They looked to one another in concern. "Sten. Why did you and Vatten stop being close? When I was younger, you two were like brothers."

Sten sighed heavily. "I saw him changing, and every time Tempus came back, he tried so hard to find someone to defeat him. But this last time, he was starting to take things too far and became obsessed with Zelkova. I saw that and confronted him many times, but he wouldn't listen. That's when I backed away."

"Do you think this was Zelkova's doing? Making this island?"

Sten considered that for a moment. "I think she put us here to protect us. It's probably hard to worry about Vako turning us into shadows while also fighting him. We don't want her to fight alone, but from her point of view, she feels putting us all someplace where Vako can't reach us is the only way to protect us. We need to support her decision, and if that means staying here, then I'll do that. I'm uncertain who made this land. But I can feel it's safe. We're safe."

Pyrus smiled at Sten and then leaned over and hugged him. "Every day you make me fall in love with you all over again."

Sten laughed and embraced Pyrus but then flipped him over so Pyrus was lying on his back in the sand. Sten lay next to him, propping himself up on his elbow. He cupped Pyrus's cheek, pulling him in for a long, passionate kiss.

23

Zelkova walked toward Jardin, who was still leaning against a tree. As she neared him, she extended her arms and hugged him. Zelkova had never thought she would be reunited with her younger brother. The only thing she knew was that they had to get back to her universe, to find and stop Vako. When she pulled away from him, Jardin was smiling down at her.

"So, now what do we do, sis?" he asked.

She released him and stepped back. "We find a way back to my universe; we have to stop Vako and, now, Tempus."

He made a sound of agreement. "Who do you think Vako is? They are not me or Rhus from your time. Nor are they you or Pyrus?"

Zelkova shook her head. "Just because Vako was here doesn't mean they're from this universe or this timeline. If it is Pyrus from this timeline, he might not have turned into Vako yet..." She didn't want to go into detail of who she thought Vako really was; not yet, not without more information to go on. If it was who she suspected, things were only going to get worse.

Zelkova and Jardin started back to the castle in the hopes of finding something there. On the way, Zelkova asked, "Should I call you Rhus or Jardin?" She averted her eyes, not wanting to meet her brother's gaze.

"Just keep calling me Jardin. I'm no longer Rhus and haven't been in a very long time."

They continued walking, but Zelkova soon stopped in her tracks, grabbing Jardin's forearm to halt him as well. They both stood motionless as Zelkova surveyed their surroundings.

"Someone has found us," she whispered.

Before she could say more, that someone came up behind them. As they turned, Zelkova's eyes focused on Tempus. He looked like a teenager and was not the same Tempus in Zelkova's universe.

"Neither of you belongs," the young man whispered, leaning in. "I felt the ripple in space and came searching. Come with me. It's not safe for either of you out here. Come." He motioned for them to follow.

Zelkova nodded for Jardin to follow as well. After a moment, he wearily trudged behind them. They walked slowly behind Tempus, who seemed to be moving them through time like she had in the past with Spero and Ilex. Soon, they were at a cave entrance at the bottom of a mountain.

Jardin looked at Zelkova, whose eyes followed Tempus as he stepped into the cave. The surface rippled as if he were stepping into a puddle. Jardin pouted, his posture slumping, so she grabbed his arm and dragged him behind her like the child he was imitating. Very brother-sister-like. She smiled through her annoyance and worry.

They stepped into the ripple. Immediately, Zelkova felt the shift in time, which meant they were in a time bubble just like the one she made on top of the mountain. This trick helped keep them hidden. To an outsider's eye, this was nothing but an empty cave.

The young Tempus motioned for them to sit down on the ground beside a burning fire. Zelkova looked around the cave, seeing tables lined up against the stone walls. Piles of books on one, writing quills and paper scattered over another, and a large map lay across a third. A fire burned in a pit in the center of the cave, casting shadows all around. Vako would probably not be looking for them because they got what they wanted: Zelkova out of the way.

Tempus had been rifling through papers, but he turned and sat down in between Zelkova and Jardin, who sat on opposite sides of the fire. Jardin kept a watchful eye on both Tempus and Zelkova.

After Tempus had warmed his hands by the fire for several moments, he turned to Zelkova, wearing a hint of a smile. "So, from what I've gathered, one of you is from an alternate universe. One is from here but isn't at the same time. Quite odd, but I'm confused about how you got here. I felt a portal open, but when I got there, I saw nothing. Then there was another opening that seemed to last a little longer, but once again, I saw nothing when I reached the area."

"I see, what else do you know? Or think you know." Jardin smirked.

He eyed Jardin then Zelkova. "I sense a connection between you two but can't place it. So, I have a question, and

I hope you answer truthfully. How did you get here?" He pointed at Zelkova, tilting his head in question.

Zelkova smiled slightly at the question. "You are much different than the Tempus in my universe." She paused, sighing thoughtfully. "Long story short is that someone from this universe, but in the future, has made their way to mine and is now trying to destroy it. To get me out of their way, they somehow sent me here. Now, I need to find a way back home so I can stop them from killing everyone and everything."

Tempus leaned toward her with childlike curiosity. "Tell me, why would they destroy your world? And who would have such power? Elementals are not ones to start wars." He thought better of his words and said, "Well, at least most aren't. But who would be able to rip through time as you say and kill everyone?"

"I wish I could tell you more, but I can't alter anything here. Therefore, I cannot share details, least of all with you." She sighed and gazed at the fire, which was burning wood, something she hadn't seen in a long time.

Tempus glanced at Jardin. "So, you are from here, yet aren't. Can you explain?"

Jardin nodded. "Yes, but first, how do you know all of this?"

Tempus frowned. "Wait, you said I'm the one you want to tell the least to. Why is that?"

Before she could answer, Jardin spoke up. "Because you are time, are you not? Oh, don't look so surprised. I may be a nature Elemental, but it doesn't take a genius to figure out who you are. You look human, but you are much more than that."

Tempus' eyes widened in surprise but then his facial expression changed completely when he chuckled. He even slapped his hand on his knee in a fit of laughter. "You got me. So, that's the reason then. I guess I'll answer your question on how I know. The reason I can tell is because I see everything here, all the Elementals and humans alike. There's nothing happening or going to happen without my knowledge. But when I saw you two, I could only see you as a child. As for her, I could find nothing in the past or future." Tempus thoughtfully put his hand to his chin.

Jardin mouthed, "What are we doing? We should leave," to Zelkova.

Zelkova nodded to Jardin and then turned to Tempus. "So, what my friend and I need to do is find a way back. Maybe see if there is another portal somewhere nearby or..."

Tempus sat up straight. "Make one," he said with a sparkle in his eye. "Oh, what a lovely idea. I have been quite bored as of late."

Tempus jumped up and ran over to the map to study it, and it was only then that she realized he had the same hint of an accent as Jardin.

"Tell me, Tempus —"

Tempus froze. "How... How do you know my name? I never gave you my name."

Zelkova shrugged. "The Elemental of time from my universe is called Tempus. I only assumed it would be the same here."

He laughed nervously. "You had a question then?" He turned back to the map, but he wasn't looking at the papers, just rummaging through them. His hand shook slightly. From excitement or nerves?

"Are the Elementals here friendly? So much as to give gifts to a human?" Zelkova was uncertain how this question would affect things, but she was hoping to find out who Vako was. She stood and neared him. Looking down at the map he had laid out, she saw small islands off the coast, one on each side. Pointing, she asked, "Who inhabits these?"

Tempus sighed. "I guess telling you this won't affect you. I'm certain you have the islands, maybe you use them in a different way. An Elemental and their kind each have an island, while the humans stay here. Well, that is for all but me and two other Elementals. We live with the humans. I can blend in, and they can go unseen. The Firsts keep the elements in balance by rejuvenating this island of Elementum once a year. To your other question, some Elementals are friendly to humans, others not so much. That's why we all try to stay in our own areas."

Tempus continued to study the map. He was deep in thought when Jardin pulled Zelkova to the side. "Are we sure about this barmy?" He pointed his thumb to Tempus and whispered in a softer voice, "I know I'm new to this helping people thing, but shouldn't we limit our time and be selective in who we interact with?"

"I thought you would want to change things, to save your home," she whispered back.

"I know if you foresaw a way to save this place, you would try." He paused, studying her face. "So, am I correct?

You have looked into the future here and saw that even if you saved it, there would be another way it all ended?"

Zelkova stared at him in surprise. "How?" She paused to look at Tempus, who was still studying the map. "How did you know that?"

"You told me to watch and learn. So, I did. I watched you and others. Even though I found no fun in it. The trees I sat with were more entertaining." He laughed, scratching the back of his head. That motion made her think of Cedrus.

Zelkova had to remember. Jardin knew more than he was telling and remembered. "Find anything?" She went over to Tempus and looked over his shoulder again, surveying the map along with him. "We need to find a place that doesn't have humans or Elementals. A place where there is no danger to the surroundings."

"What about," Jardin motioned the area around him, "here?"

"Yes, we could do that," Tempus said after a moment, "but there is a chance the mountain will crumble or be taken into the portal as well."

Jardin huffed. "Then why not just make another island and do it from there?" He crossed his arms in agitation.

Zelkova stepped forward, putting her hand on his shoulder. "That might just be the answer we are looking for. I should be able to make an island where no humans or Elementals are. Good thinking." She smiled at him, and he returned it.

Tempus frowned, confusion written on his features. "Wait, only Firsts can make something like that. How could you have so many elements?"

Jardin nudged Zelkova. "This guy is more dimwitted than I thought."

Tempus and Zelkova both stared at Jardin in question, asking in unison, "What?"

"Clueless?" They shook their heads. "Loused up? Discombobulated?" Once again, they shook their heads. Jardin sighed heavily. "Doesn't understand quickly?"

"Why didn't you just say that? And I am not what you called me. I just have a lot on my mind, is all. But again, how can you have so many elements?"

Zelkova interrupted Tempus. "I do have more than one element, and I am strong enough to make an island, even though I've never made one. I don't want anyone here getting any ideas."

"Right," Tempus said.

"Doesn't understand dimwitted," Jardin muttered in annoyance.

"Now that that is settled," Zelkova said, "we should move fast. The longer we're here, the more things will change."

Carya's watery heart raced when her surroundings changed. The determined yet frightened look on Zelkova's face made her worry even more.

Once her vision cleared, she found herself underwater in a large bubble, bigger than the pond she was in with Vatten. There were a lot of smaller bubbles connected, streaming out in different directions. The bubble let her walk around on the ocean floor. Within it, she saw what looked like walls made of water with seaweed for privacy.

She roamed around, looking for any sign of Zelkova or anyone else who might be there. After a while, she sat down on a stone in the center of the largest bubble. Carya's anxiety increased at the thought of being alone again. Had she lost her love after finally finding her again? Could this be how their story ended? Being separated once more.

Amid the silence that enveloped her, there came a faint noise. It almost sounded like singing. She stood and went toward the noise, which seemed to be coming from the other side of the dome she was in. She drew closer and saw something like a well shaped out of stones. Carya warily looked down into it, but there was only darkness.

"Hello?" she whispered.

The noise stopped in response. Carya stepped back right before a geyser burst up from the well. After the tower of water flowed back down, a small amount remained, floating above the well, forming a figure.

A small sprout of water neared Carya. "You are here, I see," it whispered in almost a hiss, sounding a lot different from the singing a few moments ago. "Have you come to play with me?" The voice was almost childlike, but the hiss made her wary. When she didn't answer immediately, it demanded, "Have you, have you?"

But Carya interrupted it with a wave of her hand. "Where am I, please?"

Its facial expression turned sour. "Rude. Rude indeed. Very." It floated back and forth as if pacing. "You are here, here you are. There you were, are no more. Here now, here forever."

Carya grew worried. "Can you please tell me the name of this place? Who made it?"

The watery figure laughed, sending chills into Carya. "This place, Unda. I, Unda. All, Unda." Its voice became deeper, darker. "Someone seen but not here. Someone everywhere yet nowhere." Its voice returned to its normal hiss. "Come, Unda show. Let's play."

It ran away without a reply from Carya, who had no choice but to follow. She trailed behind the tiny figure that floated in front of her, all the while wondering where Zelkova was and who had made this place. After walking a while, looking at the different bubble domes, the figure stopped in a smaller one. Water oozed in from the ocean, which then turned and went back into it, making a circular waterfall.

Unda turned toward her, hissing, "You pick. You stay, now home."

Her mind whirled in every direction, trying to find answers to the situation she was in. "Home? No, I need to get back to — "

It started speaking loudly, shocking Carya. "No. Home, here. Live. Live forever. No leave. Never."

Carya was taken aback by its words. So many questions ran through her head. Where was Zelkova? How did she get here? How would she get back to the mainland?

She moved to the water wall and reached her hand into it. A jet of water sprayed her back.

The watery nymph floated overhead, circling her. "No leave. Stay, home. Play with Unda. Never leaving."

Spero and Omnia were back at the border of Solaris, in the garden of the castle. Omnia hugged Spero's arm. "How did we get here?" she asked. "And where is here, exactly?"

Spero sighed in disbelief. "This is my hometown of Solaris. I don't know how we got here. If I had to guess, Zelkova saw a threat and moved us here because of it."

Omnia's tension eased. "I see. I thought she was trying to kill us, that Vako was controlling her."

He laughed. "No. I think she's too strong for that."

"Can you contact her? Or Nati? Whatever happened to Arbor?"

He looked away from her. "Arbor has been missing for a while now. Zelkova doesn't know what happened. The only thing we could think of was that the shadows took him. I can contact Nati, but neither she nor the others know where Zelkova or the others are. Can you sense Zelkova?"

Omnia shook her head. "I can't sense her at all." Everything that had happened made her worry. All of this was almost too much.

Spero took her hand. "Since we're here, we should go speak to the king and queen, then I can give you a tour before the sun sets." He smiled warmly at her. She smiled in return but faintly, thinking of everything that could go wrong and had already gone wrong.

The two of them headed into the castle. People waved at Spero, even coming up for a handshake or a pat on the shoulder. Omnia was in awe of how everyone seemed to know him and he them.

At the end of a large hall, two guards stood on each side of the wooden doors. When they saw Spero, one grabbed him by the shoulders and gave him a light shake that Spero returned. "Where have you been? You were supposed to be here days ago. Come, I'll tell the king and queen you are here." Everyone was so much nicer and more relaxed than in Silva.

The guard opened the wooden door then closed it behind him. Omnia noticed the intricate carvings in the wood. It was so fine and detailed, she doubted it was done by a human hand. The level of skill seemed otherworldly.

They were ushered into the large throne room, which was bright from the midday sun streaming in through the tall windows that almost reached from floor to ceiling. Omnia shielded her eyes with her hand for a few moments while they adjusted to the light.

Spero bowed, which brought Omnia back into the moment. She curtsied and bowed her head respectfully. Spero came up from his bow with a smile, and King Abram stood to greet them.

"Spero, it is nice to see your smiling face again! It has been a while, and this castle is less melancholy when you are here." The king grabbed Spero, bringing him in for a hug, which surprised Omnia. In Silva, none of the royals showed emotions to each other, much less to those beneath them in station.

Omnia cast her eyes down, uncertain of how to handle the position she was now in. Queen Selah approached Omnia, and she went into a deep curtsy, not knowing how else to respond.

A slight smile played on the queen's face. "My dear, you already bowed. No need to keep repeating yourself."

Omnia tried to return the smile. "Yes, Your Majesty."

Queen Selah had a similar hair color to Spero. Her complexion was fair with a few freckles scattered about her face, making her lovely in Omnia's eyes.

Selah smiled as Omnia stared. "My, my. Aren't you a beauty?" She turned to Spero. "I can see why you are fond of her."

"So, tell us what has occurred," Abram requested. His hair was brown and chopped short. His complexion was a darker tone but just as youthful as Selah's. "We have heard much through stories of people who have traveled."

King Abram showed them to four cushy chairs near the farthest window to the right. They all sat, and Spero told them all of what had transpired since he had left. As he spoke, Omnia admired the room around them. On the far end, there were the two throne chairs on a platform a foot higher than the floor and flanked by windows on either side. Each throne was carved out of what looked like one piece of wood. At the top was a design of a sun, as if to show that the sun was shining on them both.

Quite pretty, isn't it? Inane voiced inside Omnia's mind.

Yes. I've never seen a room so ornate.

It just shows another way an Elemental can use their gifts. Omnia could feel Inane smile.

That's what makes me nervous.

The power of an Elemental?

No one really knows.

Just like that of humans, Omnia. No one truly knows another person's minds.

Omnia went back to admiring the room.

The floor was made of red wooden tiles that glistened from the light streaming in. The ceiling and walls were very similar to the floor but had more of a green tone. The walls were just as intricately carved as the door. Within the designs were more suns and all kinds of different flowers. From the ceiling hung wooden orbs with ornate carvings of flowers. There were six orbs throughout the large room, and each one had different flowers carved into its surface. The orbs looked like they were upside down bouquets.

Omnia was brought back to the conversation when all three of them stood and walked over to the far-right window. Not knowing what was going on, she followed and looked out to where they pointed.

"See that large hole in the ground?" King Abram asked.

"Yes."

"There used to be a large tree there. It had been there at least two hundred years and it was looking healthy." He paused to gather his words. "Well, it was there one day and gone the next. No one chopped it down. There would have been evidence of that. The whole tree, even the roots, were gone."

Spero appeared to think it over. "That was probably the Elemental I was telling you about. Zelkova—she came upon another tree Elemental we met briefly."

The two royals stared at Spero in bewilderment. The king blinked. "Are you telling me that the tree was turned into an Elemental by Zelkova? It just uprooted and walked off?"

Spero smiled brightly. Then Queen Selah moved a little closer to the two men. "Where is Zelkova? Is she going to put light around our city as well? Like you said she did to Ruri and Silva?"

"Yes, she is held up at the moment, but once she is free, I'm certain this will be her first stop. Omnia and I can try to put light around one building, maybe this castle. But it won't be as strong as Zelkova's. We don't have the power to cover the whole city as she does."

We don't have the power rang through Omnia's mind.

Is that jealousy I'm feeling from you? Inane asked her.

No. I just wish I could help more.

Yes, Omnia. But I feel like there's more to it than that.

Before they could speak more, Spero turned to Omnia. "I said I would show you around the town. Come." He extended his hand for her to take. They bowed before leaving Abram and Selah in the throne room.

The halls were a mix of stone and carved wood, showing how the stone and nature element can come together. As they walked down the ornate hallways, Spero told her, "After we walk around a while, we'll try and put light around the castle. Then we'll eat dinner with Their Majesties."

Omnia turned to Spero in alarm. "Dinner? But I'm hardly…"

He smiled down at her. "Not to worry. Before we go to dinner, you will have a chance to bathe and change clothes. You might be Inane by that time, though."

"That's fine."

I'm excited, Inane voiced in her mind. Omnia almost scoffed. Inane disliked putting on airs more than her.

They went through the castle and out the doors into the streets. The houses were either made of wood or brick, and sometimes a mix of both. The wide streets were either dirt or cobblestones. The atmosphere seemed more cheerful than Silva.

Spero spoke happily about his city. The townspeople continued to greet him and he would take a moment for each one as they went on.

"The people love you. It's as if you're the king," Omnia voiced softly.

"My family has played a big part in this city. We've been here as long as the royals. We also own a lot of land that feeds the majority of the city."

"I hardly see any poor people."

This place is quite different than what we're used to. It's refreshing. Omnia could feel Inane smile.

"We provide homes and jobs in our fields, letting them have food for their families until they're set up."

"That's amazing. Do the people treat your whole family as they do you?"

"Some. It depends on each person. Like with anyone." Omnia's heart warmed at how kind Spero and his family were.

It was nearing dark when they returned to the castle. He stopped at a door and turned to her. "This is your room for the night. They should have the bath ready for you and clothes laid out. Take your time. I will come and knock on your door when we are to go to dinner." He took her hand and kissed the back of it. "Till then, my lady." He lifted out of his bow and winked at her. Her heart raced at how charming he could be. He smiled at her expression and then turned to go down the hall to his room.

Once he left, she put her hands to her cheeks, feeling the warmth. She shook her head and opened the door and then locked it behind her. As Spero had said, there was a bath near the fire in the hearth awaiting her. She was thankful for it. It had been a while since she had had one, and she needed it badly.

After undressing, Omnia sank down into the warm, refreshing water. She thought back on the day. On how Spero showed her the city. His warm smile as bright as the sun.

He is handsome, isn't he? You're heart flutters so much when he's around.

Oh, stop it.

Someone is in love.

You've known that. This is all too much, isn't it? Vako, Zelkova, all of it.

It is. But we don't have a choice. It's either help or become shadows. I'd rather help.

*But are we really helping? I feel out of place. Don't you?
You only come out at night. Like a bat.*

I like bats. They're great hunters. And can be rather cute.

Omnia laughed. *I only have a few moments in the bath.
Now, hush.*

You started it.

No, you did. Now hush.

They both laughed. Omnia enjoyed the few moments
before Inane traded places.

After the bath, Inane combed her hair and pinned it
up in a braided bun. Once she was fully dressed and ready,
she moved to the full-length mirror and looked at herself.

Inane almost stepped back at the sight. She hardly
recognized herself. The fancy cream-colored dress made her
skin tone look darker. The dress was finely made with
intricate beads and needlework. She sighed at the beauty of
it all, not just her dress but the castle and city. Everything
seemed to ooze beauty and thoughtfulness. Something
neither her nor Omnia was used to. Omnia had gotten used
to the servants' area.

After sitting for a while, waiting in silence, she heard
a knock at the door. Inane stood and unbolted the door then
reached for the handle but did not turn it. She was frozen by
the thought of who or what stood on the other side. Omnia
assured her it was Spero, but Inane had a bad feeling that
still made her hesitate. Inane didn't know where this feeling
came from. It was as if something was loaming in the
distance, unseen, waiting to pounce, and not knowing
where Zelkova was made the feeling worse.

She sucked in her breath and opened the door to see Spero smiling. His eyes brightened at the sight of her. Inane eyed him up and down. He looked as he had on the day they first met, very regal, with royal clothing that almost shined with its gold leaf. He extended his hand, and she took it.

The two of them started down the hall. He took her arm, interlacing them. She smiled slightly at the ease with which he always did things. He never had a second thought of hesitation, always so sure of himself. Omnia's feelings flowed through her as they reached a door in the middle of a large hallway. When they entered, Inane was taken aback by the sight.

The room was lit by what seemed like hundreds of candles, glistening off the crystal chandeliers, sconces and candelabra. Above the painted tile fireplace sat a mirror that illuminated the room even more. Inane didn't think the night could be so bright.

Spero bowed and she curtsied to the king and queen who stood next to a lavish table full of food. The table was almost as long as the hall and full of all different kinds of items, most she didn't even recognize.

As the four of them were served, they chatted happily, trying not to bring up the topic of the shadows or Vako. Queen Selah turned to Spero, asking, "Have you paid a visit to your mother yet?"

He solemnly shook his head. "I haven't yet."

"Oh, dear boy. I will never hear the end of it from her if you don't. My lovely sister will take it all out on me. So, tomorrow before you set the barrier, go see her."

Inane looked from Spero to the queen, just realizing they were related. The affection between them made sense now.

Abram laughed. "I'm certain he will, all in good time. They didn't even have time to make the barrier today because Spero has to stop and talk to every person he sees." They all laughed, knowing it was true. He couldn't walk past someone he knew without stopping and speaking a few words of greeting.

I'm nervous to meet his family, Omnia commented.

I am as well. And I'll only be in your head.

Want to trade places?

I don't think so. He's your lover boy. It's all on you. Now it's your turn to hush. I'm busy eating all this lovely food. The food ranged from sweet roasted meats and stewed vegetables. Meat pies, and all kinds of baked goods.

After Inane and Spero left the king and queen, Inane glanced at Spero out of the corner of her eye. "Omnia wants to know about your mother."

He looked down. "I thought I told her, did I not?" She shook her head, and he smiled. "Well, you can meet her tomorrow, then. Come, let's get some rest." He saw her to her door, bid her goodnight and went to his room.

When Omnia woke in the morning, she dressed in a dark blue dress and shoes that would be more suitable for outside, just in case they needed to run. She hoped they wouldn't. After a while, she heard a soft knock on the door. She opened it to see a smiling Spero dressed in his regular attire. Brown pants and a green shirt with a matching jacket inlaid with gold leaves.

"Are you ready, my lady?"

Smiling, she took his hand. "I am."

He wrapped her arm around his as they walked toward the breakfast room. "We will have a small meal. No one is joining us, so we will be able to talk freely."

"Sounds lovely."

When he opened the door for her, her eyes welcomed the view. The walls were covered in embroidered flowers on the upper half, with gold leaf patterns on the lower half.

The fireplace was similar to the one in the dining hall, with its tile and mirror on top as well. Spero pulled out a chair for Omnia and she took the seat. The food spread out in front of her was just as lavish as the night before, making her mouth water since she hadn't been the one who had tasted it all last night.

She filled her plate with all kinds of goodies, making it almost overflow. Spero laughed at the sight of her plate. "I'm glad you have an appetite about you."

She grinned. "Well, yes. We have done quite a bit of walking. And who knows when we'll get meals like this again." She sighed, thinking of the uncertain future that loomed overhead.

"Come now," he said lightly, "let's think of only this moment while we are in it. Not the past, nor the future." He reached for her hand. "Shall we do that?"

She nodded in reply as a smile came across her face.

They ate cheerfully, living in the moment. Spero made her laugh and told her stories of the city. After they were done with breakfast and tea, he guided her to a nearby chair. She took a seat, tilting her head in confusion as he stood before her. Despite his speech about living in the moment, he grew tenser by the second.

"Spero, what's going on?"

He interrupted her by kneeling. When he took her hands in his, she felt a slight tremor flow through him. She grinned at the thought that he wasn't always as composed as he seemed to be.

His eyes were bright when they met hers, brighter than she had ever seen. "Omnia. I know we have only known each other for a short time, but every moment I'm with you, all I long for is to remain by your side, always. You are brave, sweet and strong. I could wander all five countries and not come across someone who makes me feel as you do. I can't imagine life without you, nor do I want to. Please do me the honor of becoming my wife, so that we may spend the rest of our lives together."

Before she could answer, he pulled a ring from his pocket. It was a round black stone circled with smaller white stones, set in gold. Words would not come, but tears flowed freely down her cheeks. She smiled at him and nodded. Grinning, he slid the ring on her finger.

He embraced her. "I hope those are happy tears." They broke their embrace to look at each other. Tears were still falling down Omnia's cheeks, but they had slowed to a trickle. He wiped them away with his fingers, grinning wide. "Can I hear your answer?"

She smiled and nodded. "Yes, I would love to spend my life by your side." But it wasn't that simple. "But I'm a maid. You are a lord…"

He shook his head vigorously. "No, no. Don't insult me so. I don't care about titles or what others may think. I want *you*. I want to be with you."

Omnia smiled, knowing he wouldn't give up.

He helped her to her feet, saying, "Now, let's try and go make a barrier." Spero took her hand and led her to the door.

She stopped. "Wait, aren't we going to meet your mother first?"

Spero shook his head. "No, I think it's best we do this first. We can see her afterward."

"Do you want me to meet her?" Omnia cast her eyes down.

"Of course, I want you to. I want the two most important people in my life to meet. But the barrier must come first."

They walked outside and made their way to a low wall with no windows. Omnia turned to Spero, taking his left hand in her right. "I think we will be stronger this way."

He beamed. "Good thinking."

Together, they knelt and lifted their heads and hands in unison. Omnia closed her eyes and thought of light surrounding the castle. Light poured from their hands and extended outward. It was fainter than Zelkova's and a lot slower. What took her a few minutes took them over an hour to just cover the castle.

When they were finally done, Omnia tried to stand but shakily fell back to her knees. Spero rushed to catch her. "Omnia, are you...?"

Before he could say more, a wave of lethargy washed over her, filling her limbs with lead. Suddenly, keeping her eyes open was impossible, all her energy leaving in a rush that left her dizzy.

The darkness is coming… Brace yourself. Warn others, an unfamiliar voice whispered before everything went black.

Zelkova, Jardin, and Tempus headed north-west toward the border of Montis and Ager. Zelkova was somewhat surprised the borders here were similar to her world. With help from Tempus, they moved fast through the lands as he manipulated time around them. She didn't want to show him all her powers, not yet, so she kept her abilities to herself.

Jardin tried to lighten the mood. "So… What do you all do for fun here?" Tempus didn't answer so Jardin went on. "Come on now, I'm trying to be chums here."

Before Jardin could go on or Tempus could respond, Zelkova looked at Jardin. "I know where your accent came from, but some of the words you use aren't from here or my world. Where…?"

Jardin held up his hand. "Now, now. Don't try to spoil the surprise. You can't know everything. Where's the fun in that?" He winked at her and laughed. Zelkova didn't like being kept in the dark. It made her worry.

They went on in silence, the quiet sometimes disturbed by Jardin sighing, clearly bored. "Come on, can't we at least talk some?"

Tempus and Zelkova both said, "No," simultaneously. Jardin rolled his eyes but laughed. Amid his laughter, Zelkova and Tempus had stopped, as if searching the area for a sign of something. Jardin opened his mouth to speak again when a fire figure moved into view.

Zelkova's eyes widened at the sight of it. This fiery figure had a womanly shape that made her think of Kasai — an Elemental she hadn't spoken to in a while. But this definitely wasn't Kasai.

The figure neared Tempus, floating above the ground. "Tempus, what is going on? What are these things?" The newcomer looked past Tempus to Jardin and Zelkova.

"My dear, Ember, do not worry your pretty head about this—"

"Don't dear me," Ember rudely interrupted him. "I want to know what is going on, and you *will* tell me." Ember's eyes grew wide, freezing Tempus in place.

Zelkova tilted her head and stared at Ember, trying to figure out if she was able to control humans' bodies or if Tempus was that scared.

"Ember... Please," Tempus gasped.

She was about to move when Jardin grabbed her arm. She looked back to see him shaking his head. She then looked at Ember, who stared back at Zelkova. Ember seemed to be trying to freeze her as well. Zelkova pretended to freeze in place, not wanting to let Ember know it wasn't working.

"Tell me," Ember said softly. "Who are you? I felt you, but you are not from here."

Zelkova didn't say anything, just stared back. Ember neared Zelkova, the look in her eyes almost evil. Ember

brushed her hand against Zelkova's cheek. "You are quite...
unique." A devious smile came across her face as she leaned
into Zelkova. "Now tell me. Who are you, and where are you
from? If you make me ask one more time, it will be the death
of you."

Zelkova was about to answer when Jardin blurted
out, "You're a charmer, aren't you? I kinda fancy that."

Ember's smile widened, and she moved toward
Jardin, who stood a few feet behind Zelkova. Jardin grinned
as she brushed the top of his shoulder, gliding her hand
across to the other shoulder, walking behind him. Ember
then turned and stood next to him. She looked up at him
with a smile, and he returned it.

How could she freeze Tempus and come into his time
bubble? Who was this Ember person?

Ember turned again to Zelkova, standing in front of
her. "Now, what is your answer?"

Things could turn out badly if she knew of her origin,
so she decided to keep everyone's knowledge of her to the
bare minimum. Zelkova did the only thing she could think
of. With a wave of her hand, Ember froze.

Zelkova couldn't help but smile seeing Ember's
expression frozen in a look of shock. "I am sorry. I can't let
my existence change things here." She sighed at the thought
of doing what she was about to do. But before that, she
turned to Tempus and closed his eyes. He was still frozen,
but not by Ember.

She motioned to Jardin to stay quiet. He nodded in
understanding, and Zelkova moved her hand next to
Ember's head and closed her eyes.

It looked as if she was sewing in mid-air, but she was searching. Once she found the right memories, she made a pulling motion with her hand, removing her and Jardin from Ember's mind. Making it as if they were never there and she never saw them. After a few moments, Zelkova finished and waved for Jardin to approach her. He wordlessly linked her left arm with his, then she linked her right arm with Tempus, who was still frozen.

With each step Zelkova took, they moved several yards at a time. It was different than what Tempus did. He seemed to be manipulating them through time, whereas Zelkova was manipulating more than just time. The whole world bent to her will in that moment. Jardin stared in open awe.

Soon, they were at the mountains that stood between them and the shore. These mountains were not there in her dimension. Their mountains were more east. She stopped the three of them at the foot of the mountain and looked up, gauging the height and width. Tempus was still frozen. Zelkova didn't want him to see her moving the way she was.

And now she was about to do something she hadn't done in two hundred years, let alone with two people in tow.

"Hang on tight and do not move," she whispered in Jardin's ear, "or you might get stuck."

He looked at her in confusion. Then a wide smile crossed his face. When she stepped into the mountain, everything went dark. He gripped her arm harder.

"You've got to be bloody kidding me," he gasped as they moved through the darkness. "I feel like we've been in here for hours."

"It's only been a few minutes."

In the blink of an eye, they came out into a field. It was a splendid view with lush green grass all around. The sun was setting, turning the sky a pink-purple color. Zelkova waved her hand in front of Tempus, unfreezing him.

Tempus turned to Zelkova with a look of confusion mixed with anger. "What happened? How are we here? What did you do? What happened to Ember?"

Jardin jumped in with, "You're a cheeky one, aren't you? I would advise you to stop asking questions you know you shouldn't know the answers to. Now, we have little light left, and I say we get a move on."

Zelkova and Tempus just stared at Jardin, not quite understanding "cheeky." Then she cracked a smile and linked arms with him. "Good idea, let's go."

She waved for Tempus to follow. He did, obviously still confused about what had happened. Tempus moved them along in a time bubble toward the shore. They soon reached a high cliff overlooking the ocean.

"This is perfect, but once I start making the island, we must hurry. Tempus, once Jardin and I are on the island, help me open a rift in space from here. It will be safer for you."

He nodded. "All right."

Zelkova went to the edge of the cliff and looked out into the ocean. She took a wide stance and slowly raised her hands. Out in the sea, the surface bubbled in reaction to her.

Jardin and Tempus watched the gradual process. The sun was just about to set, and they would be left with only a few minutes of light. She raised her arms higher and within moments, a rough patch of ground emerged from the watery depths of the ocean.

Zelkova turned to Tempus. "Remember, we need to move fast. Thank you so much for your help."

Tempus smiled and bowed his head in response. "Be safe on your journey. I hope you reach your home dimension."

"Thank you." She grabbed Jardin's hands then moved them through the air toward a small patch of earth just past the incoming waves. Tempus's mouth dropped open, finally realizing she had more than one gift. Zelkova was glad this Tempus wasn't as bright as the one in her timeline.

He shook his head in disbelief as they landed and moved his hands away from each other, forming a black line. They both motioned as if pulling something apart, opening the slit into a circle.

Zelkova sighed and nodded to Tempus in thanks once again then turned to Jardin and grabbed him by the waist. "Hang on tight." He grabbed her arms as best as he could but was too tall to wrap his arm around her. They both stepped into the darkness that wrapped around them. "Think of our land. Nothing but our land."

Moments later, Jardin said, "Uh-oh."

Zelkova looked up at him, and he smiled sheepishly.

Their atmosphere cleared to reveal a desert wasteland. The sun had long set, and it was hard to see their surroundings. Zelkova knelt and placed her hand on the earth, which shook greatly in reply.

Jardin widened his stance so he wouldn't fall from the tremors. "What did you do?"

She glared up at him. "What did I do? What did *you* do? Darn it, I said our land. When I said our land, I meant our time as well. I didn't know I had to be so specific." She took her hand away from the ground, and the trembling stopped.

He laughed. "I'm sorry. I tried my best. Where and when are we?"

Zelkova crossed her arms, still glaring up at him. "We are in the future, thankfully in our dimension. But what made you think of this time?"

Jardin awkwardly looked down. "Well, in all honesty, I was trying, but it was like someone placed a thought into my head. Like someone whispered, *future.*"

She sighed and kicked at the dirt in frustration. "Odd." She tried to think of what and who Jardin was. He was truly an oddity. "But we shouldn't stay long." Right after the words left her mouth, she fell to her knees, holding her side in pain, wheezing.

Going over to her, Jardin knelt and wrapped his arm around her shoulders. "What's going on? You should never kick the dirt like that. Is it getting back at you for your outburst?"

Zelkova laughed, which made her cough. "No... Something's wrong here..." She tried to stand but fell back down. "Something's lost... Someone's hurting so much..." Everything inch of her hurt. Her mind became heavy. It was like every element was calling out to her, seeking her help.

Zelkova fell into black nothingness as pain ran through her whole being. It was almost like she was back on the island with Tempus riddling her body with the pressure of time itself. She couldn't move or speak, and everything was off. This wasn't a dream, nor was it reality. The darkness around her shifted and changed.

When her vision cleared, she found herself in an unfamiliar place. It seemed to be underwater. She saw what looked like bubble domes in the distance spreading out in all directions. Some domes stood higher than she could see. She almost laughed at the sight of them and then remembered the vision from Jardin's memory. Zelkova started moving toward the domes but not by her admission. No matter how much she tried to stop her body, it kept moving.

She thought maybe she was dreaming, but if it was a dream, it was a very vivid one. It felt so real. Zelkova was soon pushing through the bubble, which sealed back behind her. She immediately looked around for any sign of life. After walking around several domes, Zelkova sat down near a well, then yelled, "Carya!"

Zelkova was surprised at her outburst. She had no control over her voice. It was like her body and mind were two different people. Surely, this was a dream. It had to be.

Her voice cried out again, "Carya! Please. I'm sorry."

She was just watching through the eyes of this person. There was nothing she could do to stop what was happening, just watch it play out and hopefully wake up soon. After sitting there for a while, a small figure floated toward her. The figure didn't have much shape to it, but it almost looked like a very small child.

"Unda here," it hissed. "Carya come. Questions, questions, she will ask."

Zelkova felt herself nod her head in response. They waited and soon saw Carya in the distance. She stood and rushed toward Carya, grabbing her and embracing her. But in a split second, Carya shoved her back and slapped her across the face. Zelkova wanted to cradle her cheek in shock, but her body only looked down as if she were a child being scolded.

"Do you know how long I've been here?" Carya demanded. "How long I've waited?" Zelkova shook her head, but it seemed like Carya didn't want a response. She continued without much of a pause. "I've been wait—"

Zelkova rushed to her and whispered something in her ear. She could not hear what she was telling Carya; only that her facial expression drastically changed from anger to sadness and confusion.

Pulling away, she said, "Carya, I will answer all this soon. I promise. Please let me take you to her."

Carya hesitated only briefly. "Please do.."

Zelkova took her hands, and in an instant, Carya was gone, leaving Zelkova and the small watery creature who floated away. Zelkova went back into the watery depths, and darkness soon swallowed her mind.

Jardin found shelter in the only place he could: the only trees left in this wasteland. They had long been dead, but it was the best he could find. Leaning against a tree, he held Zelkova in his arms, hoping if a human came by, they would look like a rock and a tree. But her other elements didn't help with this effect.

He sat with Zelkova all night and half of the next day. The sun was high in the sky when she finally moved. He sat up straight. "Zelkova, are you with me?"

She groaned. "I think... I hope... So strange..." Zelkova groggily sat up and put her face in her hands. "What I saw felt so real... Was I here with you the whole time?"

Jardin put his arm around her shoulders. "Yes. You collapsed in the middle of nowhere. I brought you here so we could have cover."

She nodded, keeping her face in her hands. "Thank you. I just had the oddest dream. Everything felt so real."

He scooted closer to her. "Do you want to tell me about this dream of yours?"

Zelkova looked at him, and the look on her face made Jardin stare. To see the grief and confusion made his heart wrench for her. It made him want to help her all the more. He hardly remembered his sister. That part of his life was still fuzzy. But having her in his life again warmed his rooted heart. He hadn't had a person he could truly count on in ages. It was a nice change. And Jardin knew he would do anything to protect her.

"I was in the ocean, I think, or maybe a lake. I saw bubble domes under the water where Carya was. I wasn't the one moving my body and I had no control over what I said. Everything felt so real. But my body was here the whole time, right?"

"The whole time. That is quite a pickle you're in. But shouldn't we be getting out of here?"

She shook her head. "I feel movement. We should stay here until dark. Just to be safe. We don't need anyone finding us in this time."

Something rustled a few feet away from them. Jardin looked to his left and saw a man with black hair emerge from somewhere unseen. He went past them out toward the wasteland. Jardin sighed in relief when he disappeared from view, but Zelkova put her finger to his lips and whispered, "There seems to be a lot of movement under us. You picked a nice spot. We really can't move until they settle down."

Jardin sighed, sat back against the dead tree, and moved more brush around them to cover them from sight. There was an imbalance in the air, making him feel uneasy. It was as if the elements were seeking to be rejuvenated from their decimated state, wanting to wake but unable to do so. If this was their future, what would become of them? The thought almost scared him.

Zelkova whispered, "I feel something amiss in this time, but my gifts are not responding as they used to. Something is wrong here, but this is not my time and the longer we stay, the more things will change."

"But would it be for the worse?"

"That is always unknown. One small decision by anyone could have a mass effect on the world, and no one would be the wiser. I can't even tell what makes this happen.

What choices lead to all of this. My gifts aren't seeming to work. And if they do..."

"Would you wish to know?"

Knowing wasn't always better. In trying to make things better, sometimes it made things worse. Jardin had found this out the hard way. One day, he would tell his sister of his past and future.

Ilex and Aria, Ventus and Vindby stopped following Tuuli and instead went to the border of the cloud city to see if they could leave. If Tuuli was right, they were no longer able to. They reached the edge of the clouds, and when they came to a certain point, a strong gust of wind knocked all of them back.

"What is going on?" Ventus grumbled.

"Let us connect our power and try pushing through," Ilex suggested.

"If we have to." Ventus groaned.

They all agreed and started to unite. As each of them put more energy into moving out of the city, a stronger force pushed right back. No matter how much effort they put into getting around the force, they didn't move an inch.

"How is this happening? Why aren't we able to leave? We're trapped. This was all a trap. This must be Vako or Zelkova." Ventus floated back and forth.

Before anyone could answer, Tuuli appeared out of thin air. "No one leaves. Not safe. Must stay. Stay till safer. No one leaves. Ever."

"I wish I knew what was going on. I'm worried about Zelkova." Ilex hadn't been able to contact her since they arrived.

"You're worried about her? You should be worrying about us. We're the ones stuck here. Like prisoners. This has to be a trap," Ventus voiced in anger.

"If it were a trap, we wouldn't be kept safe. I think that's what all of this is. To keep us safe from something we can't see." At least that's what Ilex hoped.

"I agree. If it were Vako, we would be dead. This has to be Zelkova or something that had been placed here long before any of us. I am surprised I never knew of this place," Aria said.

"I concur. We would have long been dead by now. Brother, you are over worrying. We are all in this together. Stop thinking of only yourself," Vindby added.

"You act like I'm in the wrong. This situation is insane. We have no idea where we are or who made this place and put us here."

Tuuli once again floated around. "Come, pick rooms. Pick homes. You all stay. This home. Home forever." The word forever was elongated with a musing tone, making Ilex feel like Tuuli's words rang true. His heart sank at the thought.

He started to feel the loss of his friends who he had known for over two centuries. And the thought of Zelkova fighting Vako alone made him worried. Dark storm clouds from a looming storm seemed to hang over all of them.

"Omnia!" a hushed, sweet voice said. Who was the voice? "Omnia, Omnia."

She opened her eyes to see Spero's smiling face staring down at her. She instantly returned the smile. "Hi."

"My fiancée awakens. How do you feel? It seems you used too much energy when making the light shield."

Omnia sat up. "What time is it?"

"Not quite lunchtime. Slow down, you need to rest."

"We're going to be late to meet with your mother. I feel fine now. Please." She looked up at him, pouting.

You act like you're not nervous. I'm proud, Inane told her.

Now is not the time.

Inane laughed. *Aww, acting so grown up. So proud!*

"All right, if you're certain you feel better." He extended his hand, and she took it.

The two of them walked the streets of Spero's hometown, and the smile and warmth coming from him made the feelings within her grow.

You do love him, don't you? You don't even have to respond to that question. I feel what you do, and I know the answer. How genuine he is, how he puts others before himself. The way he treats people and stands up for what's right. And don't get me started on how he looks at you. I can feel your heart racing at the mention of it.

Omnia flushed. *You are making it hard to concentrate and making my heart race even more than it should.*

Oh, dearest. You know I like to tease you. And besides, who else can you tell your deepest thoughts to? Like how you think of him at night when I'm trying to sleep.

Inane. You're making me as red as a tomato.

Inane only laughed.

"Are you feeling all right? Should we turn back?"

"No, I feel fine. We're close, aren't we?"

"We have arrived."

Raising her gaze, Omnia saw a lovely home made of ornate wood. The wood paneling was similar to what was in the castle, but this was more intricate. She wanted to look further. It seemed like the wood was trying to tell her a story. There were figures carved out that looked like different Elementals encircling a human. How ornate it all was made it almost lifelike.

But the door opened, and her attention was drawn elsewhere. Standing in the doorway was a woman with hair the same color as Spero. Her smile was just as bright. And before Omnia knew it, the woman embraced her in a hug. This woman was much taller than Omnia. Gazing up, she saw a lovely freckled face.

The lady pulled away, saying, "I've heard quite a bit about you. It's so nice to put a face to the name. Please come in!"

As Omnia was ushered in, she saw a family crest above the door. It was of a large tree with stones on either side, and a bright sun in the background. The tree leaves were green and the stones were a dark tan, making the crest standout among the brown wood. She followed them into a lovely indoor garden where lush trees and flowers awaited them, along with an array of food, some of which she had never seen before.

"Mrs. Aurum, this is all so lovely." She still couldn't help but stare at all the different kinds of food, one in particular. The bright pink fruit in the middle was cut into star shapes.

I'm jealous you get to eat all this lovely food. My — I mean, our stomach is growling at the sight of it. You have to try it all for me. Please, Inane begged.

I will do no such thing. Being a pig when I first meet his mother will not stand well. You will get your turn to try the food. Maybe tonight.

If you say so, Inane said softly.

Now, please, hush. I need to concentrate. I want to make a good impression.

"Oh, my dear. No need for formality. And it wouldn't be missus. My husband took my name when we married. I was more well-known than him. Anyway, call me Aleece."

Omnia remembered Spero telling her he had several siblings and that his father had passed. But today, it would be just him, Omnia and his mother.

"Mother, this is a lavished setting you have set out for us today." Spero smiled at her as the three of them took their seats around the table.

"I have been doing a lot of gardening lately."

"Mother has a large vegetable garden, which is where all these came from." Omnia watched as Spero looked over the array. But then he stopped, spotting something. Her eyes followed his gaze, which seemed to land on the pink fruit. "Mother... are those?"

"Now, now, dear. Aren't you hungry?"

"No, Mother. Where did you get those?" Spero asked, suddenly stern, which was rare. "You know you're not supposed..."

"Spero, now is not the time to speak of such things." Aleece cut her son a severe look that sent chills down Omnia. She froze, not certain how to alleviate the tension rising between mother and son.

Omnia, I don't think there is anything you can do. All you can do is watch. They are mother and son, after all...

Inane was right. She was still an outsider to this family. Yes, she was to marry Spero, but that could change if she said the wrong thing, which scared her.

You're not going to lose him, Omnia. I was just suggesting you stay out of this one until you know them better. Wait... Isn't that fruit from the story? The one Zelkova made the seed for, where it tastes different to each person but no one had seen it in two hundred years? Where? How?

Omnia remembered that story. It did seem to be similar.

While Spero and his mother went back and forth, Omnia reached out for the pinkish fruit. The taste from the juices was salty and sweet at the same time, something different than anything she had ever tasted. *Omnia. Omnia... Spero and Aleece are staring at you.*

Coming out of her daze, she noticed they were staring. "Are these — are these from your story, Spero?"

"Yes... Yes, they are. That is what my mother and I were speaking about."

"How did...?" She put another piece in her mouth, giving Spero's mother time to answer.

"Great-grandfather was able to find the seeds. He's kept them in the family this whole time."

"And we were not supposed to plant them, Mother," Spero said, his tone still harsh.

"I have one plant, and that is it. I will show you by giving you your wedding gift early." Aleece reached to the seat next to her and placed an intricate box on the table. The box held the same emblem as the one Omnia saw above the door. Spero's mom opened it to reveal seeds cased in gold. "You two now have the seeds. These have been passed down generation after generation."

A look of surprise flittered across Spero's face. "Out of all your children…"

"You are the one I choose to give these to. You and Omnia. And then you will pass it down to your children."

You're blushing, Omnia.

Hush, she told Inane.

"These are lovely and it's an honor."

"Now, let's eat and get to know each other more," Aleece said, smiling sweetly at them.

After they ate, they went into the indoor garden for tea. A table was set in the center of a garden that was shaped like a circle. The ceiling was made of clear glass, something Omnia had never seen. On the outer circle were trees that reached for the glass. In the middle was rose and other flower bushes. In the center near the table were more flowers, large blooms giving the whole area color.

This is amazing. I want to know the names of all these flowers. Look at that one, it's multicolor.

Omnia was just as much in awe as Inane.

Once seated, Aleece turned to Omnia. "It's lovely to meet you. Spero has told me so much about you. I am sorry you are having to go through all of this with the shadows and light. I can't imagine how hard that must be. I am glad you have Spero with you to help during this time so you are not alone."

Aleece's words shocked her. No one had ever said what she just did. It warmed her heart. "Thank you. I am glad to meet you. Spero has been so kind. I never knew such compassion before I met him."

"That means I've done my job." Aleece smiled brightly. "Out of the eight of my children, he does have great compassion, which can cause jealousy among his siblings. Being the middle child also doesn't help with that. Do you have siblings?"

"I do not..." Omnia wanted to tell her she was only a maid, but surely, she knew.

Don't sell yourself short, Omnia.

Thank you, Inane. You are like a sister to me.

"You will have many brothers- and sisters-in-law. When you meet them, let me know if they treat you in any way short of kindness. Now, let's talk about the wedding."

Once the sun had set, Jardin moved the brush away from them so they could survey the area. Zelkova stood and looked around. Near where they had been sitting was a hill. It looked as if something had been buried under the dirt, but now was not the time to see what it was. They had to find a place to open a crack in time without anyone near.

She turned to Jardin. "Come, let us go east."

Because her gifts were not responding as they should, they moved slower, not like before in the other world.

"Are you feeling all right?" Jardin asked after a while. "You seem a little logy."

Zelkova laughed at the strange word he used. "Sometimes, I don't understand what you are saying. It's as if you're from a different world entirely and not just the one we came from." She sighed. "Something is off; I can't quite figure out what it is either. It's something with this time."

They walked until morning when they saw a large city looming up ahead. Tall buildings reached toward the sky, similar to the ones she had seen over two hundred years ago when she first touched the stones. The city had a similar pattern. After a few moments, it dawned on her. The large city was none other than Opima.

"What is it?" Jardin asked. "It's as if you saw a ghost. The city does look quite odd, I'll give you that. The buildings are so tall. And what is it that they're made out of, metal-like swords? This place doesn't feel right."

Zelkova nodded, not taking her eyes off the city. "Come, we need to move away from here. We should be near the coast by nightfall."

As they walked, she hoped he wouldn't push his question further. And he didn't. There had to be a way to prevent this future. Mentally, Zelkova tried to reach out to the nature around them, but what she felt disturbed her. It was as if something dead was reaching out, hoping to be resurrected. It sent a chill through her. She realized she must be feeling through all the elements.

"What on earth could have made this happen?" Jardin asked.

She kept walking, not answering his question. Zelkova knew the answer but was searching her mind to see if there would be a way to avoid this outcome. Everything she saw was limited, and what it showed was not a favorable outcome. Her heart kept seeking out the elements, hoping they would respond. Then she felt a small life force within a forest near the center of the country.

Jardin touched her on the shoulder, and in the next instant, Zelkova saw visions.

Her mind filled with images of an unknown world. It was like nothing she'd ever seen. Even in the few times she had seen the future, it was nothing like this. The grass at her feet had a pink hue. Past the field, huge buildings loomed, larger than what she had just seen. And in the bright blue sky flew enormous birds. She shook her head. No, not birds. She couldn't figure out what was flying through the sky, but it wasn't natural. It seemed manmade.

When Jardin took his hand away, it left Zelkova in a daze. "Are you all right? Did you see something?"

Her eyes refocused. She tried to find the right words, but nothing came out of her mouth.

She reached out and hugged him, seemingly surprising him. "I'm sorry," she whispered. "Thank you for this time." She pulled away and started walking again.

Taking a few large steps to catch up with her, he said, "Wait, you can't leave it like that. What did you see?"

She shook her head. "I can't tell you that much. I saw your future. It seemed bright and exciting." Her heart felt like it was being pulled out of her chest again. She hated herself, hated that she couldn't change his fate, couldn't change this world or the others. Zelkova would save everyone in every timeline if she could.

"There's more to it than that. I know you don't want to change the outcome of things, but I am here for you if you want to talk about all that is bothering you." He smiled at her.

She nodded and smiled faintly back. "Thank you. I am glad you are here and we have this time together."

Right before the sun was to set, they made it to the beach. No birds were in the sky, and no breeze to bring in the freshness of the salty air.

"So, what are we doing here?" Jardin asked, peering around, confused on why this location

She glanced at him then to the ocean once more. "I'm going to make a small island like before."

When Zelkova raised her hands, she screamed in pain and collapsed to the ground. Jardin went to her and shook her, trying to wake her. He reached into the ocean for water, but it was dark muck. Jardin threw it back, disgusted.

"Come on, now is not the time. If you think you can leave me here all alone, you're daft." He shook her once more.

To his surprise, she floated out of his arms and into the air. He stood and watched as each element circled her. A cloaked figure came near and he froze. It looked like Vako, but something was off. Jardin couldn't quite put his finger on the difference, but it didn't seem like Vako, despite the cloak.

The figure's voice was distorted, almost like they were speaking underwater. As it came closer to the floating Zelkova, it said, "I am sorry to do this. I need some of her strength. I am not completely whole."

Jardin moved in between Zelkova and the cloaked one when he froze. The person reached out their hand, which was made of water, not black matter like Vako. "Sorry. I had to freeze you. I just need help."

In just a few moments, the person was standing under Zelkova. She floated down into the cloaked one's arms. Zelkova opened her eyes, and a gasp escaped her lips when the person sat her down on her feet. It seemed as if they were speaking without words. Maybe through their minds? He couldn't tell, just that they were staring at one another.

After a few moments, Zelkova nodded and knelt, holding her hands out. The cloaked one mimicked her and knelt as well. As they connected hands, all the elements floated around them.

Soon, the elements enveloped the pair, and Jardin could no longer see either of them. While he stood there, he could feel great power coming from the orb that swirled around the two. It was like earth, nature, fire, water, air— everything's cries ceased, and the sense of death no longer loomed.

The elements slowly parted to reveal Zelkova and the cloaked one. They both still knelt but soon stood and held each other's hand while they outstretched the other. When they moved their hands in a circular motion, a rip in time opened in front of them. Zelkova turned to the cloaked one and nodded as the other one bowed in thanks.

Zelkova motioned for Jardin to come near, and he discovered he could move at last. "What's going on?" he asked walking near them.

She smiled at him and reached out her hand for his. "I will explain it all when we get to the correct time. We must hurry while we can."

Jardin nodded and took her hand. He stared at the cloaked one who stood watching them go into the rift.

This time, Zelkova did not warn Jardin of his thoughts as they stepped from the future to the past. Their surroundings changed to a lush green forest. Jardin smiled at the sight as it eased his heart. He sighed in relief and saw Zelkova was also smiling.

"So, what happened back there? Who was that? Was it Vako?" Jardin breathed.

She stared back at him. "That wasn't Vako. It was someone else who needed help. I did not ask their name. I was helping them regain their energy as they, in turn, helped us get back here."

"How do you know it wasn't someone like Vako going to destroy the world?" Jardin asked, frowning.

Zelkova looked down, smiling. "That world was already destroyed. They showed me their goals and all I could do was trust them. I know it probably wasn't a sound decision, but at the time, I did what I thought was right. I hope I won't be let down by my actions. I guess only time will tell." She looked up at him again and winked.

He laughed, scratching the back of his head in confusion.

"Come, we need to move. I need to go put barriers up and find more of those stones."

Jardin nodded and fell into step beside her. "So, sis."

She looked up at him in surprise. "Yes?"

"When will I meet this world's Pyrus? Officially, that is. I barely saw him before we all parted again."

Zelkova was moving slower than before. "I hope soon. I'm glad I'm able to have this time with you, though." She smiled, and he returned it.

Concern for her filled him. What they had just been through clearly took a toll, making her weak and slower. Then he worried about that other cloaked one and Vako. Jardin wished there was a way he could help her more but knew, right now, the best he could do was be there.

They traveled a while until they reached Solaris. When they entered the city, they saw a small orb of light surrounding the large castle. Zelkova had made herself and Jardin undetectable to the human eye. The people would see a blur, then rub or blink their eyes and they would be gone. That's how they entered the castle.

They searched for Omnia and Spero in the large rooms. The atmosphere of the castle was invigoratingly full of life. Flowers were rushed from one room to another. Servants were busy gathering plates, silverware, and drapes. A feast was to be held, it seemed. Not wanting to startle anyone, Zelkova guided them to where she felt Spero. Thankfully, he was alone in a drawing room, reading a book.

The two of them entered, and Zelkova lifted their haze. When Zelkova cleared her throat, Spero's head shot up. He grinned brightly and stood. He gave both a warm hug and then stepped back, eyeing each of them in turn. "Where have both of you been? We couldn't find any of you anywhere. And you never really introduced us."

Jardin laughed as he thought of where they had been. He also liked this redhaired fellow. Not everyone had such a cheery disposition about them. "How long were we gone? Oh, yes. I am Jardin. Nice to meet you." He vigorously shook Spero's hand.

Spero's smile widened. "Nice to meet you as well." He paused and then answered, "About a week or so, I think."

Zelkova shrugged when Jardin eyed her in confusion. She then looked at Spero. "So what is the occasion for the feast?"

Spero brightened, so much so Jardin blinked at the brightness he was radiating. Jardin giggled at the sight of it. Zelkova nudged him to act serious.

"Omnia and I are to be married in two days." He beamed with excitement. "I asked her to marry me right after we arrived here. By your doing, I assume. I know it may seem like a short courtship, but I can't think of life without her. And with Vako still out there..." He shook his head. "Right now, she's getting fitted for her dress. Oh, you haven't met my mother! She'll be at the wedding, and you can..."

Zelkova held up her hand in protest. "I think it's best I keep out of sight, don't you? I don't want people getting worried, thinking my presence might bring Vako. I will put a light dome around the rest of the city and the nearby fields. Then on your wedding day, I will meet you before the ceremony to bestow you both with gifts." Before Spero could say more, Zelkova smiled at him. "I would like to speak to Omnia beforehand, though. There is something I need to speak to her about."

Grinning, he nodded. "She will be back in here once her fitting is over. We are going to have tea. Would you both like to join?"

Jardin jumped in with, "Of course! I haven't had tea in ages! Love the stuff. It's like sweet water."

The three of them sat and chatted while waiting for Omnia. For the most part, Spero spoke of the wedding and plans for the future, beaming brighter than the sun.

Jardin yawned, sprawled out on the long sofa. Even though it could seat three people, its size still looked and felt tiny compared to his long-limbed body. Zelkova rolled her eyes, to which he only winked.

The door opening brought Jardin out of his lull. He jumped to his feet, startling Zelkova and Spero. Jardin rushed over to Omnia and swung her in the air. "Congrats! Now," he sat her down with a smile, "where's the tea?"

Omnia was taken aback. "Nice to see you, too."

Spero went over and kissed Omnia sweetly on the cheek and then led her to a table near the open window. They all sat down and waited for the tea to be served, some more impatiently than others.

Zelkova laid her hand on Jardin's leg, stopping its bouncing. "You do like tea, don't you?"

He nodded. "Yes, quite. I do get easily excited, I know. But also, when the tide turns serious, so do I." He winked at her but then turned as the door opened. He jumped at the sight of the tea tray and was held back from knocking the poor women off her feet by Zelkova, who laughed at the sight.

Once the tray was set down, Spero served everyone. Zelkova turned to Omnia with a smile. "I see congratulation are in order for both of you. Would you allow me to make you both wedding bands?"

Omnia beamed. "That would be lovely!"

After speaking on that for a while, Zelkova turned serious. She sighed. "Omnia, I wanted to speak to you about Inane. Now you are getting married and I can search for Vako without having to put you in harm's way. Even though I am grateful for all of your help, I would not be here without you two and Spero. It's time to relieve you of the gift of dark and light. Same with you, Spero. It's a burden I don't wish on anyone, and when you two have children..." Omnia blushed, but Zelkova went on despite it. "I don't want future generations having the gift from Yin and Yang. That is something they would have been against. It's up to you when you want to be rid of it. I would suggest before the wedding."

Omnia looked down at her hands, probably talking to Inane. Jardin had drunk several teapots worth of tea, which made him almost giddy. The tea had the same effect on him as mead would on humans, it seemed. Zelkova shook her head at the sight of him.

Zelkova turned to Omnia. "I will give you a day to think about it. I will come again in the morning to receive your answer." Omnia solemnly nodded. "Now, do you have a place I can hide this big fellow?" She pointed to Jardin, who sat there grinning.

Spero showed Zelkova and Jardin to a large room full of rugs. Zelkova led Jardin in with the temptation of treats, but once inside, Zelkova pulled two little twig dolls from behind her back and handed them to him. He greedily took them, smiling. Jardin loved tea and would soon remember why he stopped drinking the stuff.

26

Zelkova and Spero left the room. "He should be all right in there for a while. He missed his childhood, and I think that's why he reverts back to it sometimes. I'll come back for him once I put the barriers up. Thank you so much for your help. I do mean that." She reached out and hugged him. "Now, I have a request of you."

"Anything," he said immediately.

She laughed. "You haven't even heard my wish."

Spero smiled. "Stories of you and my great-great-grandfather have been passed down since he was around. How can I pass up a request from you? It would be an honor."

Zelkova smirked, thinking future generations might not think the same way. "I was hoping to give you more of the gift of nature. That way, it will stay strong throughout your bloodline."

He beamed. "Thank you. That is most gracious of you."

Again, she thought of future generations. "I will put a cap on it. If someone is of ill mind or severe temper, it will not bloom within them."

"You always think of everything."

"Thanks again, Spero." She placed her hand on his head and closed her eyes. And with that, the light and dark left his body by the top of his head and went into Zelkova. A green hue formed an outline around Spero, but in an instant, it was gone.

When they both opened their eyes, they smiled at each other. Zelkova took him by the shoulders, saying, "Your kindness will guide nations."

"Zelkova, what is your plan for Vako and the shadows?"

She sighed at the thought and the dread it brought. "I'm not quite certain, but stay inside the light barrier. Once I do face off with them, I don't know what might happen. I will try my best to control the outcome, but even with what I can see, there is always a consequence of fighting Vako. Vako won't go without a fight, and to let them have their way would mean the end of the world."

Spero put one hand on Zelkova's shoulder. "Whatever occurs, we will all know you did your best and that you saved us all. Without you being here, Vako would have already taken over the land with the shadows and we would not be talking right now. Believe in yourself. I know you will do your best. And you always think of everyone who lives on these lands, not just Elementals or just humans but the greater good for all."

Zelkova nodded at his words, tears falling down her cheeks. The knowledge of how much he believed in her touched her heart. She just hoped she was able to live up to it. "Thank you for your encouragement." Giving him her brightest smile, she bowed and backed away. "I should go put up a light barrier."

As they parted ways, Zelkova longed for her past life. Her life as a knight of her father's guard, going out on adventures with Carya, not having this weight on her shoulders. She walked outside the castle and out of town. Keeping the view of her from others' eyes, she knelt several yards from town, wanting to take in some of the farmlands with the town.

Once she was kneeling, she extended her arms and focused on the light coming from her and surrounding the lands and town. She tried to push away the doubt eagerly trying to seep into her mind and concentrate only on good thoughts, on the happiness of the people in the village, of the upcoming wedding.

The image of flowers filled her mind, petals floating through the wind on a warm spring day, filling the air with the scent of life. As the light flowed from her hands and made a dome of light over the land and town, people came out to watch.

Afterward, Zelkova moved to a remote spot at the edge of the woods. While she rested from the drain of light, she formed gifts for Spero and Omnia. She laid her hands on top of her knees, palms up. Closing her eyes, she focused on what she wanted the rings to look like.

She imagined the circular ring, black and white metal intertwining, together yet apart. When she opened her eyes, a shiny ring glittered in each hand. Satisfied, Zelkova moved onto working on a surprise for Omnia. This would be her first and last gift of this kind, and she hoped it wouldn't cause an effect that would hurt the world.

Jardin came out of his daze in a room full of rugs. In his hands, he held two dolls. He laughed at the sight of them and stood from the floor. Exiting the room, he had to duck his head to avoid hitting the doorframe. He saw no one about and immediately went in search of Zelkova or Spero, all the while trying to not scare anyone who might come upon him.

When a group of people carrying flowers neared him, he backed against a wall and shaped himself like a tree. Once they passed, he looked again. He could find no sign of anyone he knew.

Something or someone felt like they were calling out to him, but he couldn't figure out what or who. He left town, thankfully only having to hide a handful of times. He went toward a thicket of woods near town.

As he entered the small forest, a dark fog neared him. He froze at the sight of it. It came closer and closer, and soon, the shadowed one stood in front of him. "You heard me call. Good."

"What do you want?" he snarled at Vako.

"I heard you are my brother. Oh, how I've missed you. I never knew where you had gone, and to see you here, and as an Elemental at that, well, I am quite surprised."

Jardin glared at Vako. "You are the one who put me here. I touched a stone you made. I found happiness here, but that happiness has nothing to do with you. What do you want?"

Vako made a noise that sounded suspiciously like a giggle. "Oh, but isn't it? Isn't all of this my doing?"

Jardin refused to be played and asked again, "What is it that you want?"

"You know who I am, don't you?" Vako asked, eyeing him closely.

"Yes."

"Yet you haven't told Zelkova. Interesting, why not?"

"Answer my question first, and then I might talk." His anger was growing at a rapid pace.

"Calm down, all in good time. What I want at this moment in time is for you to join me, dear brother. I want us to be family again. I've missed you."

Jardin busted out laughing. "Us? Family? Join you? Surely, you're joking. I don't want to become a shadow or a slave to your will."

Vako's low laughter interrupted him. "We are family whether you like it or not. If you join me now, I promise I won't hurt you or Zelkova."

"Your promises mean nothing to me." Vako tried to speak, but Jardin spoke louder. "I won't play by your rules. I am removing myself as a game piece in your twisted game. I will not let you use me as one of your pawns. If you want to kill me, do it now. Because I will never join you."

Vako laughed again. "You are already a pawn in my game. You always have been and always will be. And that is why I won't kill you yet."

And with that, Vako and the shadows vanished out of sight. Jardin heard rustling leaves behind him and turned to see Zelkova leaning against a tree. Jardin stepped back in surprise. Zelkova pushed away from the tree and walked toward him.

She smiled slightly. "So, you know who Vako is?"

Jardin's mouth dropped, but no words came out.

"I've had an inkling for a while. I understand why you didn't tell me. You hadn't even met Vako yet, but now that you saw them..." She paused and then went on. "I hope everything works out all right. I am nervous about all of this. It's far worse than Tempus, and now that Tempus is somehow alive and with Vako, it only makes matters worse. I think you should go be with Father and Mother in the forest. They are already protected there."

Jardin grinned. "Already protected?"

Zelkova nodded. "Yes, I put up several kinds of barriers around the forest two hundred years ago. Our parents would be happy to see you."

He shook his head. "No, my place is by your side, at least for the time being."

They walked back in silence. Jardin was glad Zelkova didn't push the topic of Vako's identity. She must know he wouldn't and couldn't tell her. Just like many things about his past.

Jardin's cheeriness had all but faded after the encounter with Vako. He was in deep thought over the future and what tomorrow might bring with the rising sun. What he had seen in the future concerned him. Was there anything he could do to change that outcome, to help Zelkova?

Right before they were to enter the drawing room to see Omnia and Spero, Zelkova put her hand on Jardin's shoulder. "Let us not allow the thoughts of tomorrow distract us from today."

He nodded and tried to smile at her words, but his thoughts were still elsewhere.

They opened the door, and Spero's smiling face greeted them. "Come! We have dinner laid out. We hoped we could have dinner with us four."

They all sat around a table and ate very little. No one spoke much until Spero asked, "Where are the others? Will they be coming to the wedding?"

Zelkova shook her head. "I'm afraid not. They are in safe places, away from Vako. So, where is the wedding to be held?"

"Out in the gardens. Zelkova..." Omnia paused and looked down, then stared straight at Zelkova with great determination. "I don't care what Inane is about to say. I don't want her to leave me."

In the next heartbeat, the sun shift, and day became night. Omnia became Inane. They could all tell by the expression of her face that the two of them shifted and switched places.

"As for what Omnia said, I understand her reason behind it," Inane said, her tone deeper and more serious than Omnia. "But I am her and she is me. No matter if she has light and dark, I will always be with her. This is her life to live. Not mine. It never has been."

Zelkova nodded. "I understand both sides, but I hope both of you come to a decision together. I will come to Omnia again in the morning. I am sorry for this, but it's safer for you and Spero not to have these gifts. Vako will be less likely to come after you."

"We will be ready," Inane said seriously.

After dinner, Spero and Jardin sat and played cards near the fire while Inane and Zelkova talked. They walked through the moonlit garden that was to hold the wedding.

Inane and Zelkova walked in silence until Inane finally broke it. "I understand why you gave Omnia light and, in turn, made me. I wanted to talk to you about Vako. He told Omnia about her family, and I feel she is too shy to ask. So, I'm doing it for her as a wedding gift."

Inane smiled. It was one of the few times she had seen her smile, and it was lovely. Zelkova couldn't help but smile back. "I did know her family, but her family's past doesn't make her future. All she needs to know is that her parents loved her and wanted the best for her. By all rights, she is a princess, and don't listen to anyone who says otherwise. Omnia and Spero should look toward the future with great expectation and joy."

"Omnia knows, but she doesn't want to lose me. I've tried to explain it to her."

"Understandable. But she won't be losing you."

"Yes, I'm a part of her."

Zelkova took Inane's hand. "And forever will be."

They talked further into the night until Inane retired to her bedroom. There, Omnia and Inane had a long conversation on what their choice would be.

Inane was adamant about her stance.

Omnia, I am you and you are me. No matter if you have the gift of light or dark, I am and will always be with you. I'll be that voice in the back of your mind, telling you to do daring things you won't take the chance to do. This is your life to live with Spero. You will need both your nights and days to be together. You have to think of him now as well. You are soon-to-be husband and wife. You were yourself before me and you will be after as well. Please think logically, Omnia.

Inane could feel Omnia wanting to scream.

I don't want to think logically. Without you, what is the point of it all?

The point is to live the life you are meant to live. You can't let this stop you from having a happy life. Be reasonable. Inane sighed, not wanting to fight.

The night went on like this, going back and forth with little sleep.

27

In the morning, Zelkova made her way to meet Omnia, but as she walked down the corridor, Omnia was standing in the middle of the hall, a dark outline about her. Zelkova froze. Would losing Inane make Omnia so sad and angry she had now only one thought, to kill the one who was going to take her away?

Zelkova had to think fast. With a motion of her hands, all the doors were sealed, leaving them alone in the hallway. She didn't want any bystanders to get hurt. Then she made an air and light bubble around them.

"You..." Omnia said, dark fog seeping from her to curl around both of them. "All of this is your fault. You want to take my sister."

Zelkova sighed, knowing the reason for all of this, but then she felt something coming from Omnia, something she had never felt before. A stronger, darker presence. Omnia's darkness had gotten stronger, but how?

"Omnia, please, listen. I'm trying to do what is best." Zelkova tried to approach Omnia, but she wasn't having it.

She extended her hands toward Zelkova, and black fly-like flakes flew toward her. Zelkova quickly covered herself in light, but the darkness forced its way through. That's when she knew—Omnia was letting Vako use her body and act through her. Zelkova fell to her knees as Omnia walked closer.

"You thought you had everything worked out, didn't you? But you didn't realize how Omnia had come to depend on Inane. Now they are with me." It wasn't Omnia's voice that was coming through but Vako's. "They'll be together forever."

Zelkova tried to stand but only got to one knee. "I won't let you take them... Omnia. Inane..." She struggled against the darkness Vako was feeding through Omnia's hands. "Listen. I won't let you two be apart. I know I want to take light and dark from you, but I'll try my best to let you be together like sisters."

"Lies!" The darkness only grew thicker. Her pain only fueled the shadows. So much suffering, so much sadness seethed in the darkness.

Zelkova looked up at Omnia's form. "Please, listen. You two won't be together like this. You will only suffer, and what about Spero? Will you make him suffer as well?"

"Enough!" Vako's voice came through, while at the same time, Omnia shouted, "No!" and Inane yelled, "Must stop!"

Zelkova found the will to push herself to her feet. "Inane, Omnia, fight him. You are both strong, but together, you are stronger. Fight Vako, reclaim your body!" She inched forward until she reached Omnia. Every inch of Zelkova's body screamed, feeling like she was being pressed into a vice. But she reached Omnia and wrapped her arms around her.

Zelkova noticed she had closed her eyes, but she opened them to see her and Omnia bathed in bright light.

Vako was gone, but so was Inane.

After the fight with Vako, Zelkova found herself in a dark place without knowing how she got there. Voices came from all different directions, screaming in pain, screaming for help. *Where am I? Who is there?*

Zelkova tried to fill the area with light, but nothing would appear. Was she in her mind or somewhere of Vako's making? She couldn't tell. "Is anyone here? Where am I?"

She waited for an answer and heard a faint voice. "I'm here. It's me."

"Who? Who is here? Where are we?"

"Inane… I'm here. I think we're in your mind," the voice said a little more clearly. "I think you might have had too much darkness. You must push through this."

"I'll try again." Zelkova concentrated on the light.

Light flowed through her mind, bringing with it a wave that washed over every inch of her surroundings. Zelkova blinked at the brightness and saw a figure standing nearby. Walking closer, she saw Inane.

"So, you're are now in my mind."

"It seems so."

"Good, now I have something to show you. Shall we go?"

She stared at Zelkova in confusion but took her hand anyway. As their hands touched, their scenery changed.

Jardin heard voices out in the hall and decided to see who it was. When he got to the door, it wouldn't open, not even an inch. He kept trying to push the door open but again, it would not budge. Putting his ear to the door, he could hear the conversation on the other side.

"What? What is it?" Spero asked anxiously.

Jardin shook his head. "Not good. It seems Omnia was so upset about losing Inane, she let Vako take control of her body. Vako is now fighting Zelkova through Omnia."

Spero stepped back in horror. "No, please, no." He went to the door and desperately tried to get it open.

Jardin put a hand on Spero's shoulder. "It won't help. Zelkova put a seal on everything to protect everyone. It won't lift until she lets it, or..." he trailed off, not wanting to say the words.

Spero turned to Jardin, anger in his eyes. "Or what?"

He sighed. "Or she dies. Which I'm certain won't happen. It's Zelkova. She'll save Omnia. Don't worry." Jardin tried to smile, but he knew Spero was too worried to find peace of mind at the moment.

They both waited at the door, Jardin conveying what was going on while Spero stood nervously beside him. It seemed like hours had gone by, but it had only been a few minutes when the barrier lifted, and the door cracked open.

The two of them rushed into the hall to find Omnia lying on the floor and a figure covered in shadows a few feet away. Spero rushed to Omnia and picked her up. She was out cold and laid unresponsive in his arms.

"Omnia, are you all right? Speak to me."

Jardin stepped toward the dark figure on the floor. He knew it must be Zelkova but also knew he couldn't help. He didn't have the gift of light. He watched Spero take Omnia into the drawing room and lay her on the sofa.

Spero joined Jardin as he continued to stare at the figure. "What are we going to do?"

"Wait, just like before."

"What do you mean, before?" Spero asked, frowning. "You were waiting for Zelkova before?"

He shook his head. "Yes and no. Long story."

"What if the darkness spreads?"

"Let's cross that bridge when we come to it, aye?" He patted Spero on the head like someone would a pet.

The figure grew smaller and smaller, and within a few moments, the darkness was gone, along with the figure it enwrapped. The two of them stood in shock, not knowing what just happened, or where the body went. Jardin started to get worried and began pacing the floor. Spero didn't want servants to see, so he dragged him into the drawing room where he began to pace again.

"Where could she have gone? Has she ever disappeared like that before? From all the stories you've heard, has she done that?" Jardin stopped and stared at Spero, almost begging for an answer.

He shook his head. "The only time I know of is when her body was split, and she called herself back together. In all the stories I've been told, that's all I remember."

Jardin mumbled, "Yes, I remember that as well. So, could Vako have taken her? Should we make a search party?"

Spero sighed. "Think, it's Zelkova. What would she want? Would she want humans to leave the safety of the light barrier to find her? Don't worry. She will come back, I am certain."

Jardin resumed his pacing, watching as Spero went over to check on Omnia, who was starting to open her eyes. Her hair had turned fully white. He fell to his knees and hugged her while she cried.

"Oh, Spero. I'm so sorry. I wasn't thinking. I'm so sorry. I could have hurt someone." She sat up straight, almost pushing Spero away. "Wait, where is Inane? I can't feel her. No..."

Spero hugged her again. "I don't know what happened. We don't know where Zelkova is. We saw a dark figure lying on the ground, but it faded away. I'm sorry."

She tried to smile, but it didn't quite reach her eyes. "Don't be sorry, it's all my fault. There is no reason for you to be sorry."

He shook his head. "I'm sorry you are hurting."

Omnia hugged him back tightly. "Thank you. I am so grateful you are here with me. Thank you for being by my side."

Spero smiled and lightly kissed her on the lips. "Always."

"All right," Jardin said, ruining the moment. "Enough. Save it for your wedding night, will you? We have something more pressing at hand. I know you both want alone time, but we need to find Zelkova. You are the only two I know who can help me. I have no bloody idea where the others are. So, it's up to the three of us to figure out where she went." Jardin crossed his arms.

"We will help look for her, but we *are* getting married tomorrow," Spero said firmly. "Again, Zelkova wouldn't want us to risk going out and being taken by Vako. Then she would have to come to rescue us even though we were trying to find her."

Jardin sighed in defeat and sat near the window and stared out. He jumped up in an instant and looked at Spero as he thought of a way to look for Zelkova. "Show me the highest point of this castle." He didn't wait for Spero to responded. He just grabbed his hand and dragged him out the door.

Spero laughed and then led the way with Omnia following behind them. He showed Jardin the highest tower and climbed a shaky ladder to the roof. Up top, Spero hugged Omnia to him while Jardin looked out for any sign of Zelkova or anything out of the ordinary.

After a half hour, Spero told him, "We're going back downstairs. We have some last-minute details to take care of for the wedding."

Jardin didn't respond, so focused on searching through the nature element. Spero patted him on the shoulder on the way down, and together, he and Omnia left.

Jardin remained on top of the tower until nightfall, hoping to find a sign of Zelkova. Right when he was about to turn and climb down the ladder, a light gleamed at the edge of the forest past the fields. He smiled, knowing it must be Zelkova and she would show herself soon. He was sad at how the humans were so easy to give up on their search for Zelkova, but they trusted in her power as well. Even though he had been human once a long time ago, he never fully understood them.

With this in mind, he made his way to the drawing room, picked a random book off the shelf, sat down near the fire, and opened it. Instantly, the pages turned on their own. He dropped the book into his lap as the pages continued to whirl.

It finally stopped, and he stared at the blank page it landed on. As he slowly picked up the book again, a vision came into his mind's eyes. It was him but in flesh form. He was standing in a field, and weird objects floated around in the sky. Almost like birds, but not… There were large towers in the distance that made him think of giant wide square trees. He stepped forward, and the vision faded.

When he looked down to see the book, it was no longer there. Where did it go? Surely, it hadn't just vanished.

"Are you all right? You've been sitting there all night," Spero asked, somehow beside him without Jardin even realizing it, hand on his shoulder.

Startled, Jardin looked up and saw that it was morning. "Yes, I'm fine. Big day, right? Getting married and all that." He stood and wrapped his arm around Spero's shoulders. "I didn't mean to zone out all night. I was hoping to give you a bachelor party."

Spero stared at Jardin with a dumbfounded look on his face. "Zone what? Bachelor party?"

Jardin laughed. "Never mind that. Let's get you ready to walk down that aisle."

Omnia was sitting in her room, eating a light breakfast, thinking of the day before. She still wasn't certain why she did what she did or what had happened. The only family she knew was Inane, and she was gone. She didn't know how to move forward. It was as if half of her was gone. Like there was a hole in her heart. As she sat deep in her thoughts, someone came into the room.

Turning in her chair, she stared at the young woman who seemed to be around her age. She had long black hair and a pale complexation, opposite of her dark tone skin and light-colored hair. Heart beating faster, Omnia stood and moved closer to the young lady. The woman stood a few inches taller than Omnia and had more of a serious yet elegant look about her.

"Are you just going to stand there all day or are we going to get you ready to be married?" she asked.

Immediately, tears poured down Omnia's face, and she was in Inane's arms in seconds.

Omnia half laughed and cried as the two of them hugged. "You're here."

"Don't cry. I'm with you. I told you I would never leave you. That we would always be together."

Omnia buried her face in her shoulder and in between sobs said, "But how? Zelkova took you."

"Come now. It's Zelkova. I am her wedding gift to you." She held out two beautiful rings. "Along with these."

Omnia stepped back and studied her and then the rings. "How long are you here for?"

Inane laughed. "How long is anyone here for? No one knows their year of death. I'm here as long as I'm alive."

Omnia smiled. "Wait, so you're not just a vision, right?"

She shook her head. "No. I am real. I'm not certain how she did it, but she did. We are sisters. Always will be."

Jardin stood by while Spero dressed. The door opened, and as if second nature, he turned himself into a tree-like figure to blend in and hide from human eyes.

A woman laughed. "Jardin? You couldn't be more obvious if you tried."

Jardin turned to see Zelkova in the doorway smiling at him. She looked different somehow. He went closer to her, staring.

"You're making me feel very self-conscious," she said, her smile turning into a frown.

He lightly touched her shoulder. "Your skin..." He looked closer, narrowing his eyes. "Your stone almost looks like skin."

She laughed and brushed his arm away. "Come on, you know that can't be." She went over to the closest mirror to see. After a second, she turned back to him. "See. Nothing to be scared of. So, where is Spero?"

Eyes still narrowed, he said, "He's behind the doors there." Pointing to the closed doors, he sat down on the large sofa. "He'll be out once he's dressed. Glad you're back. You had me worried." He thought back to Zelkova's skin. Were his eyes playing tricks, or did she find a way to turn from human to Elemental? Zelkova sat on a chair adjacent to the sofa. "I'm sorry to have worried you. I should have sent you a message."

Jardin crossed his arms, almost pouting. "That would have been nice."

He was about to say more when Spero opened the doors. He was dressed in his royal attire. His pants and jacket were white with a red shirt and green vest. The form of his family crest was seen throughout his outfit. A mix of forest green and a tan color like that of dry dirt were woven in leaf patterns throughout, along with highlights of red on the sash that draped across him. A large tree crest was the centerpiece. A shiny medal hung down from his neck, the meaning of it unknown to Jardin.

"Where's the medal from?" Jardin asked, eyeing it.

"It was given to me by the last king of this kingdom for saving a family's life from a fire that overtook their home."

Jardin watched the exchange between Zelkova and Spero. She lightly hugged him. "Spero, you look handsome. I am glad I am here to see this day with my own eyes. Thank you for letting me be a part of it."

"I'm glad you were able to return in time. What happened? The doors were locked and there was the shadow. Then you were gone, along with Inane."

"In Omnia's grief, Vako was able to break through and control her. When I connected with Omnia, I took the gift of light and dark from her, which also meant taking Inane as well. But we can talk more about that later. There's a wedding we need to get you to at the moment."

They left the room and headed to the garden where Spero would stand, awaiting his bride. Zelkova and Jardin stood in the shadows where she hid them from view. Behind Spero was a water fountain. On either side of the guests were lovely flowers of all different colors.

"Aren't those tulips? But it's not the season for them." Jardin pointed out.

"I'm assuming it's his family's doing."

"They have the gift of nature as well?"

"Seems so." Zelkova watched the crowd.

Jardin eyed the garden. Where Spero stood waiting was a lovely arch that had blooming wisteria. As they waited for Omnia, something shifted in the air. If it was Vako, Jardin hoped they would hold off until after the wedding. He couldn't place where this feeling came from and looked at Zelkova to see if she felt it, too, but nothing indicated that she did. Music started, and every eye turned to the back of the garden where it connected to the castle.

Omnia emerged from the cover of the walkway. Her long straight white hair gleamed in the afternoon sunlight. Omnia's champagne-colored silk and lace dress showed off her figure, the train flowing behind her. The long flower-embroidered lace veil hung loosely around her, held on by a silver tiara. Inane walked behind her, her black hair a stark contrast against her light purple dress.

Spero's face brightened at the sight of her. He straightened to his full height and smiled. Every eye was upon her as she flowed down the aisle. Once Omnia reached Spero, he took her hands, and they turned to the man dressed in white who was to oversee their vows. Inane stood a few feet away holding Omnia's bouquet of purple tulips.

As they stood facing each other, holding hands, the man turned to each one, asking them to repeat after him. They would pronounce their name and say, "I, Spero, take you, Omnia, as my partner in life. With all the breath within me, I will live for you. Our souls will forever be intertwined in this land and the next."

Omnia repeated what he had said, tears flowing down her cheeks. "As we live our lives, we will live for each other, never wavering in our hearts or minds. Our hearts are now connected, and our love is now a never-ending circle. Let no man break us apart."

Each one repeated the other. "As a flower grows from the ground, and the wind blows through the trees, our love will live on through the ages. Forever yours, forever mine, forever thine."

They put the rings Zelkova made on each other's ring fingers and smiled as each ring formed to the perfect size.

Spero lifted her veil and kissed Omnia's lips, leaving her flushed. After they parted, everyone cheered. Right before they walked up the aisle as husband and wife, the sky shone bright, and light mixed with white rose petals rained down on them. Everything looked as if it were bathed in gold. Omnia and Spero laughed and smiled.

Jardin leaned into Zelkova and whispered, "Was that you?"

She nodded, their eyes following the wedding party into the castle. She sighed and looked up at Jardin. "Are you certain you won't stay here? This was your home for so long. I don't know what will happen if I have to face Tempus and Vako at the same time. I might not be able to protect you."

He put his hand on her shoulder. "I have lived a long life, and I met my sister and learned many things. What more could I ask for? My choice is to help you in any way I can. No matter the outcome."

"As you wish." Instead of following the procession into the castle, she turned to town.

"Wait, aren't you going to say goodbye to them?"

Zelkova shook her head. "In my own way, I already did. They have their own life to live. Now, let's go before Vako decides to crash their wedding because I'm here."

Jardin could tell she wanted to stay, but as always, she put others before her wants and needs.

Jardin solemnly followed Zelkova out of town and the light dome. Zelkova walked toward the eerie feeling that seemed to loom around them. It seemed to be centered in the fields where people and Elementals were enslaved over two hundred years ago.

Dark fog filled the area as they drew closer to the fields. "Is there no way I can talk you out of following me? I don't want to lose you, not now when I just found you."

"If something is lost, is it to never be found again? Just because something may be lost doesn't mean it's lost forever." Jardin winked at her and walked past her.

She smiled and followed him into the dense fog that was taking over the land. As they moved forward, the fog darkened, and the air became thicker. This time, she might not be able to save the ones she loved. Was she strong enough to face them both? She tried not to let doubt creep in, but there was no stopping it. Doubt crept in every corner of her mind, filling her with fear of the unknown.

Jardin placed both hands on each of her shoulders. "No matter the outcome, you have always done your best, and in the end, you will save us all. Just think what would happen if you didn't take a stand, if you didn't fight back against the ones who want to plunge this world into darkness. No one would be alive right now. I wouldn't be standing before you. Think of all the good you've done and will do."

Zelkova stared up at him, knowing he had seen more than he had been letting on. How did he know what she was thinking?

When they could no longer see anything around them, no grass, no trees, they stopped walking.

"Jardin, thank you..." Before Zelkova could go on, they heard laughter coming from the midst of the darkness.

"Such a cute sight to behold. Too bad it mustn't last. I was enjoying it." Clapping, the shadowed one emerged with Tempus at their side.

Tempus looked like death in human form. His eyes were sunken, and he had pale skin with a gray hue. Was he even alive?

"Come, come now. Don't look so surprised at seeing Tempus. Yes, I did imply he was dead. And for the most part, he is." Vako turned to Tempus, who was slumped over, not focused on their conversation. Vako snapped their fingers in front of the frail figure who jumped and fixed their eyes on Zelkova. He moved his arms to open a time vortex, but Vako put his hands on top of Tempus's. "Down, boy, we have to discuss a few things before you do that. Why don't you tell Zelkova what happened to you after she so sweetly let you live?"

When he opened his mouth, dark matter seeped out, like he was breathing out the shadows. "After I was transported back to the island, Vako turned back time on my body, making me a baby once again. As I aged, Vako gained control over the body you see before you. Now I do their bidding. I am not alive, nor am I dead." Tempus coughed, making darkness ooze out of him even more.

Vako laughed at the sight of Tempus twitching and groaning. "Don't worry about him, that's just his way of trying to fight my control. He should know after all this time that it does no good." They leaned in and whispered a few unheard words to Tempus and then laughed again as they wrapped their arm around his shoulders. "You really should have killed him, would have helped you out a lot. Because now, not only will you face off with me but Tempus as well. I wish you would have joined me back when I asked. It would have been so simple if you had. Why do you always have to make things so difficult? Not only for yourself, but for others around you. Do you ever think of them?"

"How dare you!" Jardin stepped forward angrily. "Who are you to say such things? Zelkova always thinks of others. She could have disappeared and left this world to its fate, but she stayed to fight you."

Zelkova reached out to stop Jardin from moving forward, glaring at Vako. "Tell me, since I am to die at your hand, why do all this? Why use Carya and Vatten against me?"

Vako giggled as they raised their hands to their hood. "I used them against you because I loved one, and the other used me and you. And for Carya, I still hope there will be a happy ending for the two of us. I also wanted to play with both of them. Not just for your sake, but mine as well. For you see, I do all these things not just for my benefit, but for yours as well." Vako was about the lower their hood but slowly lowered their arms to their side. "You know, you aren't the only one the Elementals manipulated for their pleasure. Have you thought of your other dear brother? The one who seems to have weathered the best here, but maybe not so much back in my world?"

Zelkova sighed impatiently. "What are you talking about?"

"I know you don't know what happened. Not completely. You've only seen fragments. Can you be certain what you saw was even from my world? You do know there are several worlds besides ours? I've seen them. Don't worry, this world I chose to have fun with first. Mostly because it had you. You see, not every world had you in it, so very boring if you ask me."

Tempus coughed again.

"You see, Zelkova, all of this, two hundred years ago and now, is all happening because you exist. Everyone who lives here would all go on living normal lives if you weren't here. Tempus wouldn't have gone to such great length if you hadn't been there."

Zelkova looked up from the ground where she had been staring for some time, thinking, searching. She laughed at Vako and Tempus, clapping condescendingly. "I commend you on your effort, but nothing you say matters. So, what I would suggest to you is to go back to your world and take your negativity with you because it's not welcome in mine."

There were two things they didn't know. One, their world held no power over her. Two, they had only been in her life for a few pages, versus the thousands upon thousands of pages in the book of her life. Zelkova was stronger than any mental tricks he could throw at her, so she silently dared them to try their best.

In a split second, Zelkova had vanished and then reappeared in front of Vako, her hand against their chest. Light poured from her palm into them. At the same time, Zelkova tried to shield Jardin with light and shadow his image from Vako and Tempus.

Vako hissed and moved back. "Tempus, do it now!"

Tempus stretched out his arms and put his palms together, then rotated his hands outward, making a wide rip in time. It sucked things from the surroundings. First leaves and twigs, then rocks and large limbs.

Zelkova mimicked Tempus's movement but backward, trying to close the time rift. "Don't do this!" she screamed, still trying to close the rift as Vako helped Tempus open it wider. Jardin stood behind Zelkova, letting her use him as an anchor. Jardin put his arms out toward Zelkova's and wrapped his limbs around her.

"Start moving and I will help you have more force," he whispered in her ear.

She nodded and moved her arms out wide. She put her right leg back, and Jardin mimicked the movement. She breathed in deep, and as she exhaled, she moved her arms rapidly closed. Once they clapped together, Zelkova and Jardin were pushed backward, and Vako and Tempus were blown out of sight.

But the wind from the backlash of the tear closing pushed Zelkova and Jardin further away and further apart. Zelkova's vision blurred. She could no longer see where she was or how far had she been pushed back. What was happening to her and Jardin? Would she defeat Vako? Or would all this end with the world sinking into darkness?

28

When the dust cleared, Zelkova could see the world around her had changed. It was a bright day, and people were happily tending the nearby fields. Before she could hide from human eyes, she heard a voice behind her. "Is that....?"

Turning, she saw flame-like hair atop a smiling man's head. Before she could say a word, he grabbed her and hugged her tightly, as if she would disappear if he didn't grip her tight enough. Tears formed in Zelkova's eyes as he pulled away and looked her up and down. "I knew you were not dead! This time and place is quite unexpected, though." He hugged her again. "I'm so happy to see you! You have no idea how we've missed you. Is Carya with you?"

Zelkova shook her head. "She isn't here with me at the moment." She looked around to see what time she was in. It seemed to be almost ten years from when her flesh body had died. That meant the man in front of her would now be around thirty-two. "Is this the first time you've seen me since then?"

He smiled his signature bright smile. Staring at her, he spoke softly. "Yes, you look very different. I'm so glad to see you! What have you been doing these last ten years?"

She tried to smile back at him, but the thought of what she was doing, and what she had gone through then, made her want to scream. She had not been the only one hurting, and that only made it worse. "It's good to see you as well, Cedrus, but where I've been and what has happened is a longer story than either of us has time for."

Cedrus laughed. "You're back now. We have all the time in the world."

She stared down at her feet, not quite certain how to go about it. She wanted to tell him everything, but that could change things. Even if it might be for the better, was it the right thing to do? Zelkova wanted to talk with him, to spend time with him, but she knew that path was not hers to take. "Cedrus, you of all people know that sometimes I can't say what I've done or what I've seen."

With a questioning gaze, he asked, "You can't even tell me the smallest of things?" Tilting his head, his grin grew. As a laugh escaped his lips, he said, "As long as you're back, that's all that matters."

She shook her head, almost in defeat, wishing she could spend days with him, even hours. But she couldn't be selfish, no matter how much she wanted it.

His expression changed completely. "Something's happened, hasn't it? You're not really back, are you?"

Zelkova shook her head again sadly, taking in the image of him. His defeated expression changed to worry. Cedrus was always so caring.

"There has always been something I've wanted to tell you." He sighed and hugged her, whispering, "Thank you. Thank you for not running away. For protecting this land

and all of its inhabitants. You didn't have to fight for us, you could have turned and walked away and lived your own life. But you didn't do that. You stood and fought for what you thought was right, despite what it cost you."

His words wrapped around her water heart like warm sunlight. Cedrus always knew what to say. His heart was bigger than anyone she had ever met. If she lived to be a thousand, she doubted anyone would shine as brightly as he did.

Cedrus released her then looked her straight in the eye. His well-known smile returning, he said, "Whatever you faced or are facing and whatever lies ahead, you will always do the right thing for everyone. You are not doing all this for glory. To you, there is none. I believe in you. I trust you and the decisions you make." He paused and brushed a stray tear that ran down her cheek and went on. "Now, go beat the crap out of this person who has brought such a sad look to your face. You should always smile." He winked at her and embraced her once more.

Zelkova would always hold him in her heart. Just like all those who she had lost but hoped to find once more.

"Thank you, Cedrus. You always know what to say. We will see each other again. Never let that smile fade." She hugged him tightly and reluctantly parted ways. He walked toward the fields, waving at the people he neared. And she walked toward the cover of the nearby trees.

Right before she entered the woods, she saw a large stone that matched the ones she'd seen before. Did she hit that rock in the future and that was what brought her here? She reached out her stone hand and touched the surface.

In seconds, her surroundings rapidly changed. When her vision cleared, she just wasn't in a different moment in time but also a different area of the continent near the entrance of the capital of Ingens.

There was always a reason for the place she found herself. What was the reason for being here?

Spotting horses heading her way, she ducked under a tree for cover. On the other side of the road, a dark figure appeared out of nowhere and stepped out in front of the riders. As the horses reared up, the men flew off but hardly hit the ground. It was as if something had cushioned their fall. As the three of them stood up and brushed themselves off, the figure approached them.

"What were you thinking, jumping out in front of the horses like that? We could have gotten hurt. What is wrong with you?" Malus angrily stepped toward the figure.

"We don't have time for this..." another man started, but before he could finish his sentence, the cloaked one reached out their hands, palms open. When they closed them into fists, two other forms appeared on the ground in front of Malus and his men. Then in an instant, the cloaked one was gone, leaving behind Malus and his men with Ilex and Cedrus lying unconscious at their feet.

That was when everything started to blur and change without her touching a stone, just like it had before. Now that she thought about it, it felt as if someone was moving her through time to see certain things. But who? It didn't feel like Vako or Tempus' doing. Who else would have the gift of time? A third person she would have to face?

When Zelkova's surroundings cleared, she was on top of the floating island. Zelkova could tell it was moving, but she didn't feel any Elementals on it, and no sign of Vako or Tempus. But how did she get there? Had someone moved her there?

She walked to the side and looked over to see a thick black fog covering the land. Small orbs of light stuck out of the fog.

The realization stung. Backing up from the edge, she searched for Vako, for Jardin, but felt nothing. Zelkova had closed her eyes to get a better sense of things, and when she opened them, a figure stood in front of her. The sight made a shudder run through her.

"How?" was all she could manage to say. What stood in front of her didn't make sense, but then again, didn't it make perfect sense?

The figure approached Zelkova while the island continued to move above the dark fog-swathed lands. "I understand what you are thinking. I've thought it myself."

"I bet you have." Zelkova's voice shook despite her best efforts. Trying to hide her feelings would do no good. This person knew her feelings better than anyone.

"I'm not Vako, but you know that, don't you?" The figure smiled and stepped a few feet closer to Zelkova. "Now. I should explain why I'm here, or maybe how I can be here. It is confusing. Even now, I still get confused. I guess I'll tell you my name, even though you know it. But I still try to have manners, even after so long."

Zelkova eyed the figure in front of her. They were mostly made of light but had other elements flowing through them. The sight of them still surprised her. She hoped this meeting would help change the tide.

They dipped into a low bow. "You may call me Zel," they said, straightening. "Short for Zelkova. It also takes on another meaning, but that's for another story." They paused, watching Zelkova's reaction. "You had hints of this in your subconscious, yet you act surprised." Zel laughed and went on. "I would do the same thing. And given time, I would tell you how all of this happened and how I came to be here, but in time, you will know the answers to questions you never knew to ask. So, right now, I'm going to tell you why I brought you to this place and time. In the near future, you will feel like you are defeated, but I want you to know it will all work out. Don't lose hope, even when things seem hopeless. Keep fighting, and never give up. Things will become clear. I brought you here to show you a glimpse of what is to come."

"And what if I don't want to see what you have to show me?" Zelkova continued to stare at them.

They stopped and looked down, gathering her thoughts. Then with a grim expression, Zel went on. "I will show you anyway. You will face something you never would expect. You were will be hurt beyond imagining."

Hurt beyond what she had already felt? The thought of it made her heart ache. "Why come and tell me all this then? I have looked into some of the future; it is blocked from me. And seeing what may lie ahead might not change the outcome."

Zel shook her head. "You know as well as I do that we don't do things to change what might or will happen. We fight through whatever the universe hands out."

"Yes, I understand that, but why tell me?"

Grinning, Zel went on. "Because I helped you in the past. Remember those voices, telling you that you could handle what Tempus threw at you and that giving in would not bring about what he thought?"

"And in the cave..." All those times she had heard a kind voice speaking to her was this figure in front of her.

Knowingly, she smiled. "Yes. You were the one leading yourself out of those dark situations, and in the future, you will do much more of it. Remember, others' actions are always out of your control. No matter how strong we are, some things are out of our reach, and we must accept that. That is what I came to really say." Zel motioned with her hands. Seconds later, the ground beneath them became translucent, showing the fog-filled land below and the island they stood on.

"Yes, there is a lot out of reach." Zelkova had been telling herself this for decades. Zel should know this.

"Some things are out of your control, and if you go to change things, the world will pay the price for it. Do you understand what I am saying?"

Zelkova nodded. "Yes, I must face all these sorrows and not go back to try and change things, or everything will turn out for the worse. I've known this for quite some time." Maybe Zel wasn't who she said she was. Yet she still trusted her.

"Be brave, no matter what you face. Not just for you, but for everyone who lives in this world." Zel paused in thought. "I've already said too much. Now, you must get back to your own time."

"To face what is to come..."

The two Zelkovas stared at each other, and before she could ask what she was thinking, Zel answered it. "I can be here at the same time as you because we are both time."

With those last words, everything started to blur, and she knew she was being sent back to her time, to face the future, no matter what sorrows it might bring.

Vision clearing, Zelkova saw she was near the castle of Ingens, where she hadn't been in over two hundred years. Last time she had gone to each capital, she had bypassed Ingen in the hopes of avoiding Malus. She knew what she had to do and had very little time to accomplish it. Only two more cities to put a light barrier around. Only two…

But a lot could happen between now and then. She just hoped she had enough time.

Time was a tricky thing and a lot could happen in a matter of moments that could change the whole world and everyone in it. Zelkova hated to admit it, but she was scared. She never let herself feel this emotion—fear. It was such a strong feeling. Much like anger, it consumed all other emotions and left someone unable to control their actions. Fear and anger were not something she wanted to get used to feeling or using. It would lead to an ending she could not recover from, and Zelkova had others to think about. She wasn't the only one living in this world. How would they cope if she lost? She knew the answer to that question and even if she were to win, the people would still end up suffering.

Guilt crept into her mind along with self-doubt. All these feelings she had been keeping at bay hit her like a stone wall, and she fell to her knees, holding her head in pain as tears fell down her stone cheeks. She might not win, and even if she did, she might leave this world in such a state that no one would be able to live. Everything, this time and last time, was her fault.

She should have never lived…

Among the negative feelings wrapping around her, she felt a warm sensation on her shoulder and heard a soft voice say, "Now, this is not a sight I ever thought to see. It hurts my heart to see you in such a way. Whatever has put you in this state, don't let it overtake you. No matter what thoughts fill your mind, don't listen. You are stronger than they are. You know better than anyone that without you, we're all dead."

Zelkova looked up to see Jardin's large figure leaning over her like a shade tree on a hot summer day. The sight of him brought a smile to her face and ease to her heart. "Thank you, Jardin. How did you find me? Where did you end up?"

The doubt and feelings still weighed on her, but she was not one to show her emotions to anyone. Zelkova had gotten used to hiding and fighting her emotions alone, and right now, she had to focus on the shadowed one.

"After facing Vako and Tempus? The fog cleared and you were gone, along with the two of them. I searched the area but found nothing. So, I walked toward the nearest city you needed to cover in light."

"So, here you are?" She looked up into his eyes. "I feel you know more than you are saying." She tilted her head in question, waiting for his answer.

He just laughed, scratching his head, a very human movement. "We should head to the city. It will be night soon and seeing the dome cover them when it's dark might freak people out more."

The word *freak* confused her, but she didn't comment on it. She stood, and they both headed toward their next stop. They were on the outer edge of the city where farmlands encircled Ingens.

Once at the edge of the fields, Zelkova knelt and spread out her arms, palms facing the city. Jardin stood behind her and watched. He had never seen her put the light barrier around the cities. As light shot from her hand and spread out around the city, she lifted her head and opened her mouth. And on an exhale, a small orb of light floated out of her mouth toward the center of Ingens. Once the orb was centered, it spread out to meet the light extending from her hands.

Jardin watched in apparent awe. She closed her eyes and concentrated on the dome connecting. Once finished, Zelkova tried to stand but fell back to her knees. Immediately, Jardin put his arm under hers, helping her to her feet.

"We should move on, shouldn't we?" he asked.

"Yes."

He helped her around the light dome and toward Montis and then to Petra.

It took a few hours for Zelkova to recover from making the barrier. Even though she was helping herself and Jardin move faster through the lands of Ager toward

Montis, they still moved slower than before. Using her gifts so often and with such intensity was starting to take its toll.

Throughout the day, pieces came together in her mind on how all this was going to end, making the doubt and fear within her grow. Zelkova dreaded what she and the ones she cared for might soon face.

Jardin finally disturbed the silence that filled the night. "I have a question." He didn't look down as they kept moving. It was as if he was asking the question to the air around them rather than her.

"What is your question?" Zelkova looked up at him, but he kept his gaze forward as if he didn't want to see her face when he asked his question.

"If you could stop all of this, if you could go back in time and end all of it before it started, would you?" Still not looking at her, he stared out into the dark forest.

She cleared her throat and then, after a pause, said, "Would I go back and stop Tempus before he started? Or even Vako? To maybe even save the other world? That is a hard question to answer. If I could do so without any repercussions, yes. But who's to say something worse wouldn't have taken their place? Or that the outcome would have been better for everyone. In the end, no one really knows."

"But you do know…"

The truth was painful. Even though she knew he wasn't looking at her, it felt like all eyes were on her. Zelkova knew the outcome, knew what would happen. But she couldn't focus on what she couldn't or wouldn't change.

"That is true, but changing history doesn't mean it's for the better. All we can do is learn from past mistakes and not repeat them." Zelkova knew Jardin was looking for more, so she went on. "Let's say I went back and stopped Tempus from starting the war. Then Vatten wouldn't have wanted to give me the gifts, and I would have stayed normal. Two hundred years later, I would be dead and Vako would have still come. Just at a different time."

"And without you here to put up light domes and to stop Vako," Jardin continued to interrupt her, "every living thing would be dead, including yours truly."

Silence filled the air around them as the heaviness of the reality settled on both their shoulders. "Since I answered your question, I now have one for you. I felt it the first time we met before I turned you into a tree. You've seen things beyond these two worlds. I know you can tell me very little, but do you have the gift of time? Is that why I get this feeling from you?"

Jardin laughed at her question. "Me, have the gift of time? Thankfully, no. I'm not certain I would handle it as well as you. But to give you more of a detailed answer." He paused, either gathering his thoughts or searching for the right words. "As you've said, there is always cause and effect. Consequences of others' actions and decisions affect the world around them."

Zelkova frowned. "I don't think I've ever said that."

"Maybe not yet." He winked.

"So, you're telling me you are an effect of someone's actions? My actions?"

Smiling, he almost laughed. "I can't say more than that." His expression and voice softened. "No matter what happens, I want you to always know that I am thankful for this time. Getting to know my big sister means more to me than anything, no matter what I face in the past, present or future. I will keep the memories close to my heart."

Zelkova stared up at him, not certain how to respond, wanting to ask for more. Instead, she took his hand in hers, returning his grin. "I will always cherish this time as well. Spending time with you brings light into my dark world."

They smiled at each other and moved forward toward the border. So many thoughts ran through her mind, and her heart ached at the thought of Carya, Sten, Pyrus, and Ilex. She knew where they were and was thankful they were all safe from Vako and the shadows.

All she could do was hope they would forgive her for pushing them away. Even though it was for their own safety, that didn't mean they wouldn't be upset with her decision, especially since she hadn't given them a choice in the matter or even told them why. Zelkova considered doing the same with Jardin, but for some reason, she decided not to and that scared her.

They traveled for serval days until they reached Petra; neither of them wanted the journey to end. The sight of the big city saddened her. She had not kept up with humans and their affairs for some time, and this city was proof of that. It was now a ghost town. It lay in ruins, so much different from the mountain city she used to know. Zelkova had loved how they took the stones around them to build Petra, making this city close to the element. The two of them entered through the main gate that hung on its hinges.

The villagers had returned with Crag, but after his death, his people must have left. She was so curious she almost looked into the past but knew that would change nothing. What happened was already done.

Jardin looked back at her since she had slowed and was now trailing behind. He opened his mouth to say something, but a sound from a small nearby shack stopped him from speaking

An old lady came out from the cover of the barely standing shack and neared the two of them. She must have had bad sight because the look of the two of them didn't scare her.

"I was told you would come," the lady said in a gruff voice weathered by the years.

"Is that so? Who told you this?" Zelkova eyed the lady. She had an uneasy feeling.

"I was to tell you what had happened to all of the people who lived here. Yes, once the king passed so long ago, most left, but some stayed." She coughed and then went on, nearing Zelkova. "For the ones who stayed, they were all taken over by this black fog."

The old woman coughed again, but this time, dark mist poured from her mouth. It reminded Zelkova of Tempus. This woman was being controlled. Zelkova immediately stepped away, gesturing for Jardin to do the same.

"I was told once you came, I would be freed from this pain." The woman hacked ever few words now, filling the area with a thin layer of the dark fog. "That was over a hundred years ago…I have been waiting."

Zelkova formed a light bubble around Jardin as the two of them moved further away from the women. "I can help you…" Again, Zelkova felt guilt creeping in.

"No, no one can help. But now… Now… I can be at peace."

Jardin looked from the lady to Zelkova. "That old bat thinks where she's going is peaceful! From what I've seen, what Vako has planned is far from peaceful!"

She nodded at Jardin's words, knowing the dark shadows only brought more fear and hate. This made her realize the thoughts that had been filling her mind recently had been what too much darkness had brought out. Zelkova had let the dark overcome the light within her. She had not been keeping them in check like Yin and Yang had told her. Surveying her surroundings, Zelkova saw the fields below had been covered in shadows and were rapidly moving toward them.

Turning to the lady, she circled her hands, as if making an orb. Then she shot her arms forward, shooting a beam of light from her hands at the woman. The light surrounded the old lady, casting out the shadows surrounding her. "Now, now you can be at peace. You have waited a long time to be free."

The lady's body gradually faded away, granting her peace at last.

The uneasiness Zelkova had been feeling grew. She was scared she wouldn't be able to keep Jardin safe. She had lost so many people she cared about. This time, Zelkova would say how she felt. Immediately, she turned to Jardin and was right in front of him in a few steps. Looking up, she smiled and then hugged him "No matter what, we'll always be connected."

He hugged her back. "A brother and sister bond that will never be severed, no matter where we are."

It seemed both knew something was coming and wouldn't speak of it. A question hung in the air like smoke: did they both know the same thing?

Soon, the shadows crested the wall and moved toward them. It stopped near them and out of the fog stepped Vako and Tempus. The sight of them made Zelkova shiver in fear yet shake with anger at the same time. Panic crept its way inside again, making her wonder if she would be able to defeat them. How could she defeat both?

She shook off the fears and focused on what she had to do: protect Jardin and everyone else from Vako. It was as simple and as complicated as that.

"So, you found our guest," Vako said, studying her. "It took you longer than I expected. I was hoping this would be one of the first cities you were to visit, but it seemed to be the last. But it's all right. We can deal with you better now."

"Better how?" Zelkova's nerves were raw. This game of cat and mouse was tiring.

"I wasn't quite certain how to beat you. I was still trying to learn about you and find your weakness, but I think I've found it. I must say, though, I am proud of you, putting up light barriers I can't seem to break through. Kudos to you." Vako clapped their hands mockingly.

Zelkova glared at them. "I'm glad you find them impenetrable."

"Come, come, we can be friends, can't we?" Vako stepped forward, and Zelkova and Jardin automatically took a step back, not wanting Vako to gain any ground.

"Oh, look, Tempus, it seems we have scared her," Vako said.

"If you say so," Tempus whispered.

Vako started to laugh.

Jardin was getting angry at the banter and started moving forward, but Zelkova held him back by squeezing his hand. "So, are you going to end me now? Is that what this show was about?"

Vako's cloak had always hidden their face. Even now, it shadowed their features, though it seemed to have slipped out of place slightly. "I have had fun with this game we've been playing, but I am starting to get tired of the chase. I want to have you as my pet now."

"Your pet?" Jardin yelled, animosity clear in his tone. His voice got progressively louder. "Are you kidding me? Are you bonkers or what? Is that what all this is about? Really?" Jardin made to bridge the distance between himself and Vako, but Zelkova quickly grabbed his arm, firmly holding him back. "I can't believe all of this is because you want Zelkova as a pet, a plaything to bide your time."

"Aren't you a tough guy? Did I hit a sore spot?" Vako wagged their finger at Jardin. "Zelkova knows there's more to it than that. She's like a prize at the end of a race."

Jardin leaned down and whispered in Zelkova's ear, "No matter what, beat their arse." His whole body trembled with the force of his rage.

Zelkova grinned. His words sounded funny to her, but she got the gist of them. Nodding, she breathed in deep, trying to prepare for what was to come. She wouldn't look into her future, not this time. This time, she would be facing not just one person who could control time but two. The thought made her uneasy.

"So, if you win, I will become your so-called pet and shadows will take over the lands?"

"Why, yes. Of course. Sounds like a plan to me." Vako chuckled.

"And what do I get if I win?"

Vako let out a blood-curdling laugh. Chills raced through her body. "I highly doubt you will win, but I guess to make things fair, what is it you want if you do win?"

"When I win, I want you and your shadows to disappear from this world and all those you have touched to be freed. I want there to be no trace of you. I want it to be like you never existed."

"Well, that's far worse than mine. At least I'm going to let you live. All right, enough of this. Playtime is over." Vako raised their hand, and shadows flew toward them.

Zelkova wrapped herself and Jardin in another bubble of light, which diverted the shadows but not the other attacks. A hand reached out from the earth under her feet, grabbed her by the ankle, and yanked, trying to pull her under. She kicked at it, but before she could dislodge its grip, several hands reached up, all trying to grab her.

Roots shot up from the ground next, trying to grab her and Jardin. They both fought against the roots and ground trying to subdue them. Zelkova motioned her hands and set the roots on fire, making certain not to set Jardin ablaze as well. She stomped the roots, making them recede into the ground but not for long. The roots wouldn't stop until the source was taken care of.

She turned her attention to Tempus instead, knowing he was the weaker of the two. She wouldn't be able to let either of them live this time. For the safety of everyone, she would have to end them. Taking someone's life was not something she did lightly, but Zelkova had no choice.

But Vako's strength matched and, in some ways, exceeded her own.

She moved her hands together then apart. Tempus fell to his knees, screaming in pain. Vako looked from him to Zelkova. She wasn't certain if Vako was shocked or angry by their laugh, but she wouldn't give them enough time to find out. Zelkova repeated the motion, trying to pull Vako's shadows off Tempus.

"What are you doing?" Vako snapped. "Trying to kill him?"

She widened her stance and spread her arms out wide and then moved them, making a large circle of light. Vako mimicked her motions, making a dark circle.

"You won't win!" Jardin yelled.

"You, Jardin, really know how to make things awkward, don't you?" Vako snarled.

"It's one of my qualities that I pride myself on! Thanks for noticing!" Jardin yelled over the rush of wind

Zelkova had produced as she tried to knock Vako off their feet.

Tree limbs and roots crawled over the wall behind Vako and Tempus, the one boarding Montis. Vako had the gift of nature, stone, time, water, dark and light. But what they lacked, Zelkova had. Wind and fire.

Now was not the time to play fair. Time to get dirty.

Zelkova called on all the elements for aid. She pulled water from their surroundings, the humidity in the air, and from a nearby well to fight off the hands and roots trying to pull her and Jardin under. Then she moved the air around them, which pushed back the shadows. And with a snap of her fingers, the tree limbs and roots caught fire.

Whatever Zelkova did, Vako counterattacked. After a while of Zelkova trying to free Tempus, Vako fed more darkness into him, pushing back Zelkova's attack.

Then, Tempus entered the fight.

Tempus opened a rift nearby, but each time, Zelkova was able to close it. It was hard keeping control of all the elements. Her body felt weak, and it was becoming harder and harder to manage. Trying not to show her shaking hand, she reached out and touched Jardin, giving him the gift of rock to be able to push back against the sinking sand threatening to entrap them. He had been fighting off the roots the best he could, but he, too, was growing weak.

So much was coming at her at once, and it was becoming taxing. Vako was throwing all they had at them. Roots and tree limbs tried to entrap them. The dark shadows encircled them and the ground underneath them sank. On top of that, Tempus kept opening time rifts.

Even though Zelkova had more gifts, there was only one of her and two of them. There was strength in numbers, but would that help her stop them from destroying the world? She was also worried about Jardin getting hurt in all the chaos.

Without warning, the ground around them shook, nearly knocking her off her feet.

She looked to her right and saw that Jardin had placed his hand on the ground, which was the source of the shaking. As the ground shook, the dirt under them became solid. Zelkova quickly mimicked him, but so did Vako. The ground cracked in between the two groups as the shockwaves became more intense.

The few buildings that still stood crumbled and collapsed as the ground continued to shake and split apart. The crack in between them widened and gradually broke apart. Renewed by their efforts, Zelkova put more force into moving the ground where Vako and Tempus stood, further away from them.

It wasn't long before the ground underneath Vako and Tempus started to give way, along with the stone wall behind them. Within moments, the wall and the ground fell to the fields below.

Dust and shadows filled the air in a cloying thickness. Zelkova stared into the night air, hoping beyond hope to see only fields lying beyond. As everything cleared, she sighed at the sight of the barren fields and nothing else.

Her body tensed in dread. Deep down, she knew it wasn't over yet, no matter how much Zelkova wished it were so.

"It's not over yet, is it?" Jardin asked in a hushed tone.

"I'm afraid not."

As the words left her lips, dark fog filled the air, right before Vako lifted themselves up, with Tempus in tow. Zelkova moved herself and Jardin further back into the town with a swift movement of her fingers. The hope she held for a matter of seconds was now gone.

She readied herself for an onslaught. The situation they were in made her curse herself. Wishing she had been stronger, that Jardin wasn't here with her in danger. The lingering thought of her existence had made all of this occur.

Zelkova shook her head, dispersing the thoughts that would consume her if she let them. Movements swift, she called on the different elements all at once. Answering her call, the wind blew in a strong gust, the trees uprooted nearby, and fire sprouted up in a bright blaze along with a water geyser.

As Vako and Tempus neared, something shifted around them. Her eyes widened in surprise at what was about to happen. Time and space near them were starting to fracture. Turning, Zelkova saw a small rip in time opening next to Jardin. Her heart sank in fear.

Taking action, she hurried to close it, but both Tempus and Vako were opening it, their combined force greater than hers. This couldn't be happening. Zelkova couldn't let this happen. To lose someone else because of Tempus, because of Vako, might break her.

She knew not to let fear overtake her, to cloud her judgment, but the emotion grew stronger by the moment.

"Hold on!" she yelled to Jardin. "Root yourself!"

Without asking any questions, he immediately dug his roots in deep, bracing himself. Zelkova grabbed Jardin's hand just as the vortex started to pull him closer.

To her left, Vako was using multiple elements at once. Now it was a battle of tug of war, and Jardin was the rope.

This can't be happening. Fear was the frontmost emotion, pushing out reason, making her second-guess her actions. She couldn't lose Jardin. They had just become close.

As she pulled with the gift of nature, stone, and air, Vako, in turn, pulled with nature, stone and then wrapped Jardin in shadows. Zelkova lost her grip on Jardin.

Thankfully, Zelkova had already put a layer of light around Jardin moments before, but the shadows would soon penetrate that barrier. And in an instant, it did, and Zelkova could no longer see Jardin but could hear his screams clearly.

Before she knew it, Jardin was being pulled into the time rift. Zelkova pulled him back, but inch by inch, he went closer to the vortex that awaited him. She couldn't lose another brother, not again. Her heart ached. If he did get sucked in, he would be covered in shadows, bringing the darkness to whatever time and place he landed. Jardin would become a shadow creature, only feeling hate and fear. She couldn't let that happen.

"We both know how this will end," Jardin whispered. She couldn't see him, but she could hear him with the gift of air. "I am not afraid." There was a slight pause until he continued in a soft voice. "I will always remember our happy times. You have to stay and fight. You have something Vako doesn't. You care for others, for this world.

And that is how you overtook him. I will leave it to you, my sister. To end this."

Zelkova couldn't lose him, not now. This couldn't be happening; how could she stop it? Her mind raced with possibilities and far-flung hopes, her watery heart pounding against her stone body.

"No!" she yelled, all of her frustration seeping into the elongated word. In response to her voice, everything and everyone stopped moving, even the elements and the time rift froze.

But not everyone. It was nearly unnoticeable, but both Vako and Tempus were moving ever so slightly. They weren't completely frozen like everything else. A pressure filled her body as she slowly walked closer to Jardin. She had completely stopped time for the first time, and it was taking its toll on her. Every step felt like she had walked a hundred miles. Motioning, she unfroze her brother.

"Jardin... I..." She was only a few feet away, but her chest felt tight. Even though her body was made of stone, she still felt pain of the flesh, and everything hurt.

"Zelkova, you take too much on yourself," he said faintly through the shadows. "Don't put guilt on yourself when none of this is your fault. You being here didn't bring this about. No matter how much time passes, we will always be family. Remember, when someone lives in your heart, they are never truly gone. I will always be a thought away."

A tear slid down Zelkova's cheek. In the corner of her eye, she saw Tempus and Vako moving more and more. Her strength was fading, and she couldn't hold time still for too much longer.

"I'm sorry," she told Jardin, her voice wavering. "I should be able to do more. I should…"

Jardin laughed through the shadows, a laugh that eased her aching heart. "You should save everyone and everything? It's all right, Zelkova. You are strong, but we all have weaknesses. I don't blame you. I am glad we met, and I am glad you turned me into a tree for two hundred years. I would take none of it back. I cherish every moment. Stop being burdened by what you think you could have done and think of the fond memories that were made, not on what could have or should have happened. Everything will turn out all right. You'll see."

Time resumed its normal pace once more. She stumbled back, lightheaded from the exertion. Exhaustion pulled at her will.

"How could you?" Vako asked her in wonder. "We were trying to start time all the while you had it stopped. How can anyone…" Vako groaned in anger at the situation. They extended their hand, forcing Jardin into the rift.

Zelkova was struggling to close the rift and hold onto Jardin with both Tempus and Vako fighting against her. In a blink of an eye, fire sprouted from the ground toward Vako and Tempus, but right as they stepped back from it, Vako sent Jardin whirling toward the rip in time and covered Zelkova in shadows, roots, and stone.

She couldn't let Jardin take the shadows with him, for his sake and for the world or time he would end up at. With darkness surrounding her, she made a pulling motion, pulling the shadows from Jardin as he entered the rift.

"I'm sorry." She sent the words into Jardin's mind as she pushed against the elements surrounding her. "I will find you."

With great regret, she clapped her palms together, closing the rift. Zelkova wrapped her arms around her middle and forced herself to breathe in and out. The shadows, roots, and stone around her mimicked the motion of her breath, sinking in and then expanding out. Vako took advantage and motioned for the elements around Zelkova to crush her.

For everything Zelkova did, Vako seemed to have a counter. It was as if Vako knew Zelkova's moves before she did herself. As the elements tightened around Zelkova, suffocating her, she closed her eyes, letting herself feel the loss and pain.

But grief soon turned into anger.

She screamed and threw her arms out wide, casting the elements away in a burst of energy that knocked Vako and Tempus off their feet. While they were down, Zelkova walked toward them, intending to finish this once and for all.

Vako quickly pushed to their feet. They swiftly motioned their arms, and roots erupted from the ground to wrap around Zelkova and yank her into the ground up to her waist, immobilizing her.

She struggled to break free as Vako leaned down and whispered, "You should have learned by now. We are equally matched."

As they lifted, Zelkova saw their face for the first time, and the sight chilled her to the core. She had expected someone familiar, but what she had just seen was completely different.

Vako laughed. "Really, don't look so shocked. I thought you already knew we have a lot in common."

Zelkova shook with anger, her emotions making the ground around her tremble. What they had just done to Jardin, to their own brother, made the water within her boil.

Her watery eyes turned completely black, and seconds later, Tempus fell to his knees, crying out in pain.

Vako knelt next to him, then looked at Zelkova. "What are you doing?"

Tempus turned his head toward Vako and smiled. "Do...it...Zelkova...Kill me...Set... me...free..." he said in between gasps.

Zelkova heard him and nodded as she emerged from the ground. Had their control over the stone element weakened, or had her will outshone theirs?

"Be free, Tempus..." She waved her hands, one over the other, and within a matter of moments, Tempus' body turned to ash and floated away on the breeze Zelkova created, setting him free at last.

Vako stood and the air around them thickened, so much so Zelkova could hardly see around them, even with the gift of light and dark.

"How dare you? I wasn't done playing with him!" Vako yelled.

"He suffered enough, Vako! And how do you think I feel? I won't let you continue!" she yelled through the darkness. Vako had locked not only Sten and Pyrus away but now Jardin.

Vako laughed. The shadows looked as if they were rippling in response to the hollow sound. Suddenly, Zelkova fell to her knees, unable to move. Vako slowly walked closer and lifted her chin with their finger.

"When will you realize that I don't care about anyone, just like they didn't care about me!" Vako said in a rough voice. "Everyone is selfish. Why shouldn't I turn my back on them like they've turned their backs to me?"

"But this world isn't the same as yours. These people have done nothing to you…" She was about to say more when Vako interrupted her.

"Oh, but isn't it all the same? People's cruelty is seen everywhere. No matter where you go, it's there. Like your own shadow, it follows you relentlessly."

"And for that reason, you want everyone to live in endless suffering?"

"They would bring suffering on themselves with or without me. We all suffer in life. I'm just making it come to some faster."

"So, you killed your world and everything in it? With your shadows of sadness and rage."

Zelkova's words only seemed to fuel Vako's anger. They raised their hands and pushed them toward Zelkova, enveloping her in thick, dense shadows. She had never felt such strength from Vako before. Had they been holding back this whole time?

She screamed as fear and anger filled her mind. Zelkova had already been feeling these emotions but now they raged through her. It was as if they were a flood and she was the tree limb being swept away by the rushing current.

"Playtime is now over." Vako's voice held a hint of humor. He paused as Zelkova screamed again. "You will end up as shadows just like the rest."

Gasping in pain, unable to form words, she reached out to Vako with her mind. *You will live alone forever. Is that what you want? It's not too late to turn back. To save the ones here and live among them in peace.*

A brutal laugh cut off her words. "Ha! Being alone is better than living with people who will only end up hurting me more than I could hurt myself. I think I'd rather face eternity alone than have more of the judgment and hurtful words humans can lash out. And you! I hoped you were different, but I was proven wrong again. You fooled me!"

Vako pushed more shadows onto Zelkova. The agony she had felt before wasn't even close to the pressure and pain that filled her body. It felt like a mountain lying atop her, and she was a tiny lizard about to be crushed. Vako grabbed onto Zelkova's elements and yanked them from her like before. Sharp stabs filled her body. Even without being able to see, she knew Vako had driven spikes of darkness into her.

A soft voice reached her mind. *Be strong. Think of where you want to be in this whole world and think not of the pain that fills your body or the anger that fills your mind. Let peace and love fill you... Now think....*

Zelkova tried to do as the voice said, to fill her mind with thoughts of where she wanted to be in all the world. She thought of where she had sent Carya, of how she would be with her if she could. Above all else, her smiling face filled her mind.

There came a shift in the air around her and a movement of her body. The pressure lifted. When she opened her eyes, a familiar smiling face greeted her.

It seemed her desire to see Carya had transported her to where she was, just like she had done when she split herself into many forms.

"Are you real? How?" Zelkova tried to reach out to Carya's face but fell to her knees.

Carya ran and grabbed Zelkova before she could hit the ground. Zelkova looked around, her vision blurred. All she could see was deep water surrounding them. She could hear Carya's voice trying to reach her. Zelkova's stone body surged with pain. Her insides felt as if they were burning, her mind full of heaviness. The elements within her were acting against her. *What's happening?*

Then everything went blank, sending her mind into a void.

30

Zelkova opened her eyes to see herself outside her own body. Darkness surrounded her, but a small glimmer of light reached out to her body. Leaves started to float around her, then water and stones...

All the elements circled her. One after the other, each seeped into Zelkova to be absorbed. Even though she was floating above herself, Zelkova could feel the warmth of the different elements restoring her strength.

She heard a voice and saw a faint light in the distance. Leaving her body behind, she floated toward it. As Zelkova got closer to the light, the voice became clearer and louder. "Zelkova! Zelkova!"

Someone was calling her name, but who? She couldn't tell, so Zelkova moved ever forward. Gradually, the light became brighter, so much so she had to squint.

Her surroundings changed. A figure stood in front of her in a large flower field with the sun shining behind him. The flowers were all different kinds and colors, their sweet smell filling the air. She gasped at the sight of the man standing in front of her. Looking down, she gaped at her hands. Zelkova expected them to be stone, not human flesh.

The man smiled, his red hair set aflame by the sun. "You act so surprised. I wasn't expecting to see you this quickly either." His smile warmed her heart and tears ran down her face as she went to embrace him.

"I'm happy to see you as well. But come, we don't have much time."

She stepped away, taking in the sight of him.

"If I didn't know you so well, I would think you've fallen in love with me." He laughed and then went on. "I am here to give you a message."

"Wait, where is here?" Zelkova interrupted him before he could go on. "I don't feel like I have my gifts, and you look so young!" She smiled at Cedrus as he continued to smile at her.

"That's true. At this moment, you don't have your gifts because everything is in harmony here. There is no need for Elementals."

"But where is here? And why am in this body?"

His grin became larger as if he had a secret just waiting to be told. "You aren't really in a body right now. Because you are dead."

Dead? Am I truly dead, after all this time?

"Wait... What?"

"Now, now. We don't have time for all of your questions. This place is called Caelum. It's in between realms. It's what holds everything in place, a divider if you will." She was about to speak, but Cedrus held up his hand. "As I said before, I am here to give you a message. You must go back to your world. Everyone needs you. Without you there, Vako will take over more worlds. They will never fill the void within their heart and because of that, they will always search for new worlds to envelop in shadows. For this reason, you are being sent back to your body. You will have a hard time but remain strong. Time will pass. Pain will ease, but I am sad to say, it will remain your constant companion. You must push through and always remember to be true to yourself. Even though things may seem out of your control, believe that in time, everything will become clear."

"But who is saying all of this?" Zelkova wanted to ask more but refrained and waited for Cedrus' answer.

"In time, all will reveal itself." He stepped forward and hugged Zelkova tightly. "Now, go back and remember, you are never alone. Remain strong and true. Goodbye, Zelkova." He kissed her forehead, and in an instant, she was back hovering over her stone body in the darkness. Zelkova breathed a sigh, and as she exhaled, she floated into her body.

The sight of her old friend made her more nostalgic than she had been. Zelkova had missed him, his humor, his smile, the brightness of him.

Her thoughts were interrupted when a soft yet worried voice hummed in her ear, but her body and eyes felt like they weighed a ton. Couldn't she sleep a while longer? With reluctance, Zelkova's eyes slowly peeled open. When her eyes adjusted, she realized she was in the library of Silva's castle. Two books rested on the table near the window.

Zelkova sat up and pushed to her feet, and as she neared them, she noticed one had a bright outline where the other had a dark outline. Reaching one hand to each, the pages suddenly turned in both books, as if reacting to her.

After the books finally settled on a page, Zelkova leaned over them and was hit with two visions, one filling her left eye with the other filling her right.

One vision showed her kneeling in front of Vako, her head thrown back as Vako once again took elements from her. They were speaking, but Zelkova couldn't hear what they were saying. The vision expanded, showing her they were on the island. Without warning, her body fell limp, and darkness expanded into the world below.

The second vision was similar to the first. She was in the same position in front of Vako. But as Vako started to pull out elements, Zelkova stood and slowly bridged the distance between her and Vako. Even though it was only a few steps, each one seemed like a mile. They still tried to pull out her gifts.

When Zelkova was close enough, she hugged Vako, whispering words to them that the present Zelkova couldn't hear.

The visions faded, but she still stood in the library. Something was off. This place still felt like a dream. This couldn't be reality. Was she dreaming or maybe in a different reality? Her thoughts felt like a poorly built nest, with each thought intertwining but not connecting. It must have been from… Her eyes widened at the thought.

Cedrus had said she had died…

The thought that Vako had killed her made her freeze with fear. Unblinkingly, she looked around the room, as if trying to find an answer to all her questions. Again, Zelkova looked down at the two blank books open before her. She glared at them as if trying to will them to show her something.

She was taken aback as they responded to her by flipping through pages, both at the same time as if a strong wind were blowing them both over. Closing her eyes, Zelkova thought of what she wanted to see. "Show me how to fix this."

When she opened her eyes, the books showed her the same vision again, but her perception was different.

There were two versions of herself. One covered in darkness, the other in light. Anger and hate came from the dark outlined one, but mixed in with the hate was great sorrow, so much so it felt like her heart would break from it. The other had strong feelings of love, hope, and peace, so much so that it healed her broken heart.

The two figures reached out to one another and, in an instant, became one. The bright light that came from them combining made her blink. The vision faded, and she was back in the library, again uncertain on how to leave this place.

Was she even meant to leave the library?

Zelkova went toward the doors that led out to the main hallway. Reaching out her hands, she laid them on the doorknobs, not stone hands but ones of flesh. Stalling for only a moment, Zelkova stared at her hands. After a moment, she turned the knobs and pulled back the doors to find a large forest.

Instantaneously, she was pulled from the library, which then disappeared, leaving her in the thick lush forest. The trees were so tall she couldn't see the tops, their trunks wider than three people standing shoulder to shoulder. The sight warmed her heart.

A figure approached, and as it neared, the outline became clearer until she could see that it was not human. The form was half black, half white.

Zelkova whispered, "Yin, Yang?"

The figure nodded, and when they spoke, it was two voices in one. "We are sorry we were unable to help. Neither of us knew of Vako's strength and it seems you have witnessed it as well. They are a force not to be taken lightly. Even though we are gone from your world, we will always remain in your heart, guiding you. We are greatly saddened by placing this burden on you. To not just face Tempus once again, but now Vako, along with having to keep the balance of dark and light. Only you know the great responsibility you hold, and you mustn't let it overtake you, Zelkova."

"I'm sorry things turned out the way they did. Sorry I wasn't able to save you both."

"We do not blame you. You are not at fault. We are glad we bestowed our gifts to you. No matter what, keep the balance, no more of one than the other. Keep all the elements stable and equal. One day, we will see you again. We'll be waiting for your arrival."

Just like the room before, Yin and Yang disappeared, along with the forest, leaving her in darkness. From within the darkness came images from memories, like moving art displayed in front of her. The first images were of her and Carya as children, their first meeting, her saving Carya from the river, giving her the gift of water. Then them as teenagers playing with their gifts in the same river, one with stones, the other with water. After those came Carya holding Zelkova in her arms.

She didn't remember that last one, though...

Was that present day? Zelkova looked lifeless as Carya rocked her in her arms, her face twisted in sorrow.

Pain pierced her heart at her love looking so distraught. The scene changed, showing her and Carya standing in front of her father, along with Cedrus, Ilex, and Malus. Immediately, tears fell from her eyes, wetting her cheeks. Her life played out in front of her.

A memory came to mind, one Zelkova was not a part of. One of Cedrus and his wife, marrying and forming a family. So many happy faces at Cedrus's table warmed her heart. Their smiles and happiness were contagious, even after the images faded.

Next came Ilex. To know he had turned into an Elemental and that Aria had never left his side made Zelkova's eyes glisten with pride. The two of them had overcome so much in so little time, yet they hadn't let it break their connection. It gave her hope for her and Carya. It then showed Ilex and Aria along with Ventus and Vindby in a large cloud castle. So, they had found what they had been searching for, after all. She hadn't heard anything since they'd left because they were blocked from the elements.

The images flowed, showing the four of them acting like a family, even making Third and Fourth cloud Elementals, forming an ever-bigger family. Something none of them had ever experienced brought joy to each of them and Zelkova's heart ached, knowing she couldn't be with them.

The next one made her freeze. Malus and his family. Some of his children played happily while excluding the one who played longingly in the corner, occasionally looking up to his father and the others, only to shrink back in fear of being caught. His caramel skin and hair reminded her of Carya, along with his warm innocent heart that was strong against the harshness the world threw at him.

Everything stopped and then went black. She waited to see if it would show more or if her scenery would change, but after a while, nothing happened.

She stepped forward, and more images appeared. These came faster, so fast she could hardly make out what they were. It showed everything becoming a wasteland covered in darkness. The next images were of a lush forest with clear flowing rivers. Back and forth it went, from devastation to rejuvenation. The images sped up even more, making her head hurt.

Falling to her knees, she held her head in her hands. Voices invaded her mind, not just one but dozens—no, more than a dozen. Too many to count. They all repeated the same thing.

"Things will fade into darkness, but the light will remain. Everything will change but will continue forward. Look for a tree among the rubble. The rose among the thorns."

An image filled her mind. It was of a lone tree standing among large buildings. She had only seen it once long ago. The sun loomed overhead yet the tree sat in shadows. The wind blew the dried-up dirt around, making the area look as if it were in a dust storm.

Her mind shifted to another tree. It was dead yet leaves still clung to the limbs. Behind it loomed a mountain. From that place, she felt someone or something calling to her, but her attention returned to the tree when a bright light struck it, sending her into bright nothingness.

Carya sat with Zelkova in her arms. No matter how much she tried to rouse her, no sign of life came from her, no movement, no fluttering of the eyes. Her heart sank at the sight of the love of her life lying lifeless in her arms. She trickled water over her, trying to find any injury to see if it could be healed, but she found none.

She sat there with Zelkova, rocking her, hoping the movement would bring out some sign of life. With every moment, her heart became heavier and heavier. Carya thought she had felt sorrow before, but this, seeing Zelkova like this and not being able to help, tore at her.

What had happened? Was it Vako? Tears ran down her watery face onto Zelkova's stone one. The soundlessness around Carya felt earth-shattering, almost breaking her mind like her heart was.

This couldn't be the end, not when they had just found each other again. So many thoughts ran through her mind. So many memories of the past and hopes for the future ran concurrent, fighting for precedence. She wished she had more time, more power to help her love. Carya screamed, hugging Zelkova tighter.

And then something unexpected happened.

Water began to float from the ocean outside toward Zelkova, like a thread through a needle. It encircled them both. Then leaves came from a tree near the well. After that was small pebbles from the ground.

Carya stared in a daze as flames streamed in beside the water. Then, out of nowhere, came light and dark, intertwining to join the other elements surrounding them. She was still holding Zelkova tightly, but the elements gently pulled Zelkova away from her. As Zelkova floated, encircled by the elements, Carya stood watching, hoping the love of her life would be brought back to her.

After what seemed like ages, the elements seeped into Zelkova, one after the other. The last to enter was light, which shone so bright Carya shaded her eyes and whirled around. Blinking, turning back to look, she saw Zelkova standing in front of her, but something was different. Carya's eyes widened at the realization that Zelkova had somehow changed.

The intricately carved armor glowed and underneath lay black inlay with gold flecks, making it even brighter. The dark and light of the armor intertwined, but this was different. Before, her elements seemed almost a mess about her. Now, everything flowed and ebbed in harmony. Her hair was still pointed leaves as before, but it now flowed to her mid-back, where her human hair used to reach. Her eyes were now white with sky blue pupils instead of black. This new version of Zelkova had a different demeanor. More determined and peaceful. But at peace with what?

It was like she had shed her old skin for this new one and came out someone different. Stronger. Wiser.

Carya noticed she had been staring at the beauty of Zelkova and was brought back to the moment, at the sound of a little laugh. Before she could move, Zelkova had stepped forward and wrapped her arms around Carya, pulling her in tight.

She lifted Carya's chin toward her and leaned down, pressing her lips against Carya's. She knew she would never get enough of these kisses. How Zelkova looked at her made her melt inside, always had. Their kiss became more passionate as Carya wrapped her arms around Zelkova's neck, pulling them closer. Carya could tell they both wanted this moment to last. Take things further, to love one another. They'd never really gotten the chance to truly show the other how they felt, and that hurt Carya the most. What she wanted more than anything was to go back and love her more.

Suddenly, Zelkova's body froze, making Carya look up at the emotionless Zelkova. Fear shot through her. Had she had been taken from Carya once more?

"Zelkova, are you all right?" she asked anxiously, shaking her. "What happened? What is happening?"

31

Zelkova couldn't respond to Carya's voice, only focus on the images. Whoever was sending these to her was much stronger than she was. No matter how much she tried to push it away, the images became stronger, repeating faster and faster each time they replayed in her mind.

She almost sunk to her knees at the sight. It was of her family, friends. Carya. Ilex. Each one waiting, stuck, unable to move from their own lands. Their feelings reached her, stabbing at her heart. They all felt sadness and loss, but loss for what or whom?

"Now is the time to say your farewells for only a time," a voice whispered in her mind.

Zelkova tried to cry out at the voice, to ask what it meant, to ask who it was. Was it Vako? Did they do this to her? After the vision repeated several more times, she blinked and recovered her senses. A panic-filled Carya stared at her.

"I'm sorry, Carya."

"What happened? When you first got here, it was like you died and then this. You were frozen. What is going on? No sugarcoating. Tell me everything." Carya crossed her arms, her features switching from panicked to determined.

Zelkova smiled at how she could push away her worry to take on matters at hand. She had always admired how strong Carya was. She kept her eyes on Carya, not wanting to lose sight of her again. And with a sigh, she told her of all that happened since they had last been together. Of how she found out Jardin was her brother, then lost him in a fight with Vako. Of how she released Tempus, who was being controlled by Vako's shadows. A lot had happened, and it stabbed at her heart.

They had sat down on a rock bench Zelkova had formed and when she was about to tell Carya of the vision that had frozen her, Carya grabbed her hands and asked, "Wait… Are you telling me while I held you in my arms, you were actually dead?"

Zelkova nodded, casting her eyes down to her feet, not wanting to look Carya in the eyes, not wanting to see the emotions on her face. Despite her efforts, someone would always suffer.

"Why can't someone else save this world?" Carya asked bluntly, causing Zelkova's head to jerk up in shock. "Can't someone else fight Vako? Why risk your life each time? Can't we just run away together and forget everything else?"

Zelkova smiled sweetly at Carya. "You know there's more to it than that. If someone else could take on Vako, I would gladly let them, but I think this goes much deeper than either of us knows right now. Someone else is trying to push me further and I'm not certain who or why."

Zelkova hated lying to Carya. She knew full well that Zel and other forces were interfering, but she still wasn't certain why. Her future, among other things, had started to become blocked. Their timing came at the worst moment. And why did she not have control of any of it? If they had such power, they should take on Vako.

Carya sighed. "Then at the least let us help you. Me, Sten, Pyrus, Ilex. Let us help you against Vako."

She shook her head. "No..." Pausing, she thoughtfully sighed and then smiled at Carya. "I can't lose any of you. If Vako can do that to me, just think how easily they could kill all of you. It's not that I discount your abilities. You saw how Vako toyed with me. I don't want to imagine what they could or would do to any of you. I'd rather risk my life than risk any of yours." Carya opened her mouth to speak, but Zelkova held up her hand. "I understand, but the world needs as many Firsts as it can get to survive if Vako takes over. Maybe to restart..."

Carya put her watery finger on Zelkova's stone lips. "I'm sorry. I wish we all could have been more help to you. I wish you didn't have to carry this burden alone."

Zelkova shook her head and smiled. "But that's the thing. The one thing I have over Vako. I'm not alone." She winked at Carya. "Even though you all may not be by my side, you are all with me. Through the elements, I can feel you. So, when I face Vako again," she took Carya's hands in hers, "meditate on your element. Focus your strength on reaching out to every living thing. You will know when the time is right."

Carya grabbed ahold of Zelkova's arm, knowing she was about to stand. "Don't go, not yet. When will I see you again? When will we have our chance?" Her emotions showed as she looked at Carya, wishing there was another way. "It's going to be worse than last time, isn't it?" Carya asked.

"Last time, I thought you were dead. For over two hundred years, I searched for you." She knelt in front of Carya, taking her hands in her own. "My heart ached, and I found happiness in nothing. I was a walking shell of myself without you. I... I'd rather not say how things may end..."

Carya's voice shook, her emotions showing through her features. "Please... I want to know."

"But what will knowing do? It will only make your suffering longer." She stood and took Carya's face in her hands. "I don't want to leave you. I want to stay by your side forever, but that's not possible right now. I will return for you. I may be gone from your view, but it doesn't mean I'm gone from this world. I will come back for you... I love you, Carya. No matter how much time passes, my heart will never change." She leaned in and kissed Carya gently on the lips.

Standing, Carya rushed and hugged Zelkova from the back. "I love you, Zelkova. I know you are doing your best. You have a will that burns like the hottest fire. A great heart that flows through everyone you touch like a gentle breeze. Your bravery is like a well-rooted tree, never shaken. Your love is grounded like a stone, never moving, never wavering. Your passion for life is like a strong river current. And the kindness you show shines so brightly that it almost blinds those who come in contact with it. But then you have deep sorrow and guilt that weighs heavy on you, like a dense dark cloak that weighs on your shoulders. But always know I will be here. I will always love you. No matter how much time passes, I will be waiting for your return."

Zelkova knew Carya was trying to bury her emotions, just as she was. Turning, she embraced Carya. This hurt more than any physical pain ever could. This was worse than death itself. Knowing the love of her life would be waiting, no matter what. Would she be better off dead to her?

"Thank you for your strength and understanding. I will come back to you. Some water Elementals may come here. To save who I can, I must do this. Guide them. They will be scared and confused; but remember, you are now the First of water."

Carya gazed at her, everything starting to sink in, and nodded. They kissed once more, neither wanting it to end but also knowing it must.

Zelkova decided to leave the same way she came. She had only tried it a few times and hoped it would not mess with the delicate balance of the elements. She knelt and told Carya to step a few feet away. "I'm going to try and travel to where Sten and Pyrus are through the fabric of time and space. It's harder than it sounds."

I could be split into several pieces, never fully coming back together, she thought to herself, hoping that didn't happen.

Carya's face changed to one of concern, but Zelkova tried to laugh and smile, hoping it would ease her worries. "Don't worry. When have I ever tried something and failed at it?"

Carya smiled. "There was that one time when you first picked up the bow."

Zelkova laughed. "Very true. I'm not the best at archery, but no one's perfect, right?" They both laughed. Seeing Carya smile warmed her heart, and she had to push the thought of not seeing that smile again out of her mind. "I'll see you soon. And Carya…"

"Yes?"

"Remember that you are my heart."

"I love you, Zelkova."

Tears rolled down Carya's watery cheeks. She couldn't leave her like this. It might be her last chance to hold the love of her life in her arms.

Standing, she rushed over to Carya and kissed her once more, needing to feel her. Wrapping her arms around her tightly, Zelkova sent images of how she would spend time with Carya. All the flower fields she would have made for her and the time they would have spent in them. This, this was the hardest thing she had ever done. She hated to leave her.

Leaving these images in Carya's mind, Zelkova whispered, "I love you, too," and wiped away her tears.

Releasing Carya, she turned and closed her eyes, pushing all her worries from her mind to think of where she was and where she wanted to go. She imaged herself in the underwater bubble and then she thought of Sten and Pyrus on an island of stone and dirt.

Repeating the images in her head, she moved her arms in a circular motion then pushed them outward. After completing the movement several times, the air around her shifted.

Opening her eyes, she stood in a vast desert. Dry heat filled the air around her. There, looming in front of her, were large stones. Her surroundings reminded her of when she was in the shadows and thought she had touched a stone. What time was she in? Was this land after for her or before for them? All of this time and different universe weighed heavy on her mind. Zelkova tried to stand but fell back down, images of Carya filling her mind, making tears roll down her stone cheeks. She hated knowing Carya was feeling the same way and could do nothing about it.

Pushing her feelings deep down like she had done time and time again, Zelkova rose to her feet and moved toward the stone domes in the middle of the vast sand lands. A few feet away from her destination, the sand next to her started to shift and change. After a few seconds, Sten was standing tall and broad in front of her.

"Took you long enough," Sten said, glaring down at her. "We were wondering when you would show up." He wrapped his arm around her shoulder and pulled her toward the domes. "We've been waiting, hoping to see you. We still feel something is off. So, I'm guessing Vako is still out there and you have come to ask us to stay here? Am I right?"

She looked up at him and, with a smile, nodded, not wanting to speak the words.

"Ha, I thought so. Come. Pyrus is anxious to see you."

She stepped through the stone dome to find something different inside. The large room was decorated with intricately carved stone furniture. A long table seated for six. The table and chairs had leaf inlaid into the stone surface. Hanging above it was a large chandelier made solely of sand that seemed to shift and change its shape as she moved toward the center of the room.

In the center of the room sat four extravagant stone chairs, every inch of them engraved with figures that seemed to move, as if telling a never-ending story. She stared at them as she heard a voice come from behind the chairs.

"I'm so glad to see you!" Pyrus stood and rushed to her side. "We've been waiting for you to appear."

She was still spellbound by the furniture. "Seems like your taste in the extravagant hasn't changed."

He laughed. "We haven't seen you since you sent us here and that's the first thing you say?"

Zelkova laughed along with him. "I was just stating..."

Sten jumped in. "The obvious. His appearance is the only thing that has changed about him, I assure you."

All three of them laughed, filling the large room with their short-lived moment of happiness. Pyrus turned from Zelkova and whispered, "You've come to tell us that we have to stay here, haven't you?"

Zelkova's moment of surprise was brief as her expression changed to a slight smile. "It seems we'll have to be apart for some time once again. I wish things had turned out different. I wish I were stronger, to be able to take on..."

Pyrus turned on his heels and soon had Zelkova in an embrace. "Don't say it. Never think you haven't done enough. You have given up on your own happiness to make certain others don't suffer as you have. To think of others is the greatest strength to have." He pulled away and placed his hands on top of her shoulders. "You are carrying a great many burdens, none of which you ever complain of having. For that, we are grateful. I just wish we could have helped more. I want to stay by your side more than you know. But for some cruel reason, all of this landed on you." Tears rolled down Pyrus' stone cheeks.

Sten moved in and patted the top of her head. "Even though we will be miles apart, we are all connected through the elements. We will stand beside you always." He paused and smiled down at her. "We believe in you, Zelkova. We will be here awaiting your return."

"I wish we could come and help you. I'm scared for you." Pyrus sighed heavily.

Zelkova nodded. "I know. I am nervous as well." She hated to admit that, but it was true. "When the time comes, you will hear me calling. Focus on your element. Also, prepare for guests. Other stone Elementals will soon be joining you."

"I am not fond of guests," Sten grumbled.

Pyrus and Zelkova laughed, their tension easing. Pyrus moved one hand off Zelkova's shoulder and onto Sten's. "You would say that."

"Don't worry, Sten, none of them are Seconds. You can kick them out when they get to be too much."

"Tell me, Zelkova, what is your plan?" Sten asked as the three of them walked back to where she had entered.

"I'd rather not say. You never know who's listening."

The thought of her plan frightened her. What it meant for her, and what it could mean for the others. She would be taking a chance but hoped beyond hope that it would work.

"True."

The three of them stood, none of them knowing what to say. Farewells had never been a thing between them.

"Zelkova," Pyrus said in a hushed tone. "Remember, we all love you."

"Go finish Vako once and for all." Sten pulled Pyrus to him, who was on the verge of tears.

"We will see each other again. Oh, and Sten."

"Yes?"

"You'll be a First again for a while."

Before he could respond, Zelkova knelt and once again manipulated the time and space around her. This time, she focused on Ilex and Aria. Seconds later, things shifted around her, but this time, it sent her into darkness.

32

Muffled voices could be heard coming from the darkness, but one rang out loud and clear above the rest. "What the hell? How are you not sinking to the sea below? How did you even get here?"

"Ventus, don't be so loud. She isn't fully here yet."

"Vindby, do I look like I give a flying flip? Let my voice mess her up. Who does she think she is, locking us here?"

"We don't even know if it was her. Calm down, would you?"

"Telling Ventus to calm down is like telling the wind not to blow." Zelkova opened her eyes at Ilex's voice. She looked around. Clouds surrounded her, but they looked like huge castle columns, not clouds. She smirked, thinking she must look strange and out of place, like a rock among pillows.

She laughed at the thought, which made the others stare back in confusion. "I agree with Ventus. I probably look ridiculous here. Like a fish out of water, so to speak."

"Tell me, why are we stuck here? Who made this place? I demand answers!" Ventus glared at Zelkova.

"Good to see you again, Ilex. Aria. As well as you, Vindby and Ventus." She bowed her head, knowing this would only annoy Ventus. "All will reveal itself in time."

"That's not an answer!" Ventus burst forward, his dark clouds coming toward Zelkova like a strong gust of wind. But he went by her like a breeze, hardly moving her hair. He turned around, went up in front of her, and glared down at her.

"Come now. We should all be past this by now. I don't want to waste time subduing you." Zelkova stared right back at him, like an owner would their dog, to gain authority, to make them submissive.

He darkened at her words. "I've been in this world far longer than you. You will show me the respect I am due! I am a Second and you... you are..."

"A First..." Aria whispered. "And would wipe you off the face of this world if need be. I would stop while you still have air about you."

He continued to glare at Zelkova but then huffed and backed away, his eyes not leaving her.

She smiled at him and then turned to the other three. "I have come to say my farewells and to tell you more air Elementals will be joining you. At least for a time." She raised her hand to stop the questions. "I don't know for how long. I can't tell you who made this place or why none of you are able to leave. There is a fine balance, and if someone steps out of line, the whole world could come crashing down. Even some things seem to be out of reach of my knowledge. And I'm certain no one wants the world to end, do they?" She winked at Ventus, knowing he grew more annoyed by the second.

Ilex was about to speak, but Zelkova went on. "I'm sorry I have left you all here for so long without answers. Even though I have come, I still don't bring answers. And I am sorry for that." Zelkova bowed her head remorsefully. She wished she had answers, wished she wasn't being blocked.

"So, what is it that you can tell us?" Ilex smiled at her. Just his mere presence eased her heart of some of the stress it held.

She considered what answers she could give him without making a dent in the timelines. Sighing, Zelkova searched the distance. "Things must be kept separate for the time being. It is the way things must be. Yes, it will cause hardship, mostly on the humans. But I am trying my best to ease what suffering I can, though I fear not enough. If things could end a different way, I would give anything to help it along the way. But sad as it is, I see none."

"What about your life? Would that save us all?" Ventus asked. Zelkova didn't look at him, but both Ilex and Aria looked sad at the question.

She shook her head but then nodded. "I already have in a way and I will do it again. I can speak no further about the future. Just know I will do what I can, but Vako is far stronger than I realized. If I am to die again, I doubt I will come back from it this time." She shook her head, knowing she had said too much. "Anyway, I have a request. Listen to your element. You will hear my call. When you do, concentrate on me and your element. I will need your help. Please, no questions. I wish I could say more. Really, I do."

Zelkova sighed again and adjusted her focus on the four cloud figures in front of her. "I wish I could have spent more time with you all."

Vindby smiled at her. "But even good things must come to an end."

Ventus still glared at Zelkova. "I would say more like *good riddance*."

Ilex went up to Zelkova and hugged her. "It seems like all we do is say farewell."

"It just means we get more hellos."

He still wore a concerned expression. "I hope one day to never say goodbye."

Aria went up and hugged both Ilex and Zelkova, whispering, "This is not goodbye or farewell. It is only a short parting, to which we will all be together again soon."

Zelkova smiled. She liked the sound of that. "Please stand back."

Vindby frowned. "Why?"

A small cloud figure formed next to Zelkova, turning to her. "You come I see. I see you come. First time for you."

"Oh, lovely. Now this thing is here. It's been spouting nonsense since we got here," Ventus grumbled.

"And what is your name?" Zelkova asked in a soft voice.

"Tuuli. Tuuli is pleased you here. It begins."

"What begins?"

"The end..." Tuuli almost hissed, then faded away, leaving everyone stunned.

"The end? End of what?" Ventus shouted.

Zelkova couldn't help but think that Tuuli meant the end of her. The figure intrigued her. Where did it come from? It didn't feel like a normal Elemental.

"What does it mean Zelkova?" Ilex asked quietly.

"The end of what we're all used to. Things are going to change, whether we want them to or not."

They all became quiet, which was interrupted by Zelkova speaking softly. "I will miss you all. Please take care, and remember to think on your elements."

"Wait, what are you going to do? How are you going to defeat Vako?"

"You'll know when it happens. That's all I can say. I must go. Time is running out."

Ilex and Aria had a sorrowful look about them. Vindby showed concern and Ventus looked greatly annoyed, making her smile. "I hope to see you all sooner rather than later."

Unlike last time, she didn't kneel but continued to stand. Closing her eyes, she concentrated on her destination. This time, the air around her changed at a more rapid pace.

Opening her eyes, she was on the beach near where Pyrus and Sten had once stood as stones. Now that she knew who was behind the stones, finding each one should be easier. Kneeling, she put both palms on the ground, closed her eyes once more, and thought of the stones.

In her mind's eye, she clearly saw a map of all the lands, and within a few moments, dots appeared on the map, showing where each stone lay. Thankfully, there were only a few left to destroy, but she had to move fast so Vako wouldn't face her at each rock. Thinking of how to reach each one using the least of her gifts, Zelkova decided shifting was too much of a risk. She didn't want to cause a rip in time.

Moving as fast as she could with the air behind her and the ground underneath her, she headed to the nearest stone in Cedrus' hometown. Zelkova didn't use space or time to move faster, knowing that if she were attacked while using it, it could cause a rift.

Something neared her as she passed by Solaris. She came to a full stop in an empty field, and the dirt around her billowed up from the suddenness. Once she had fully stopped, she searched the elements and soon found what searched for her.

Out in the middle of the field stood a large flamed figure nearing her location. They stared at each other as the distance between them decreased. Zelkova hadn't seen Kasai in a very long time. She respected this Elemental just as much as Sten. He didn't dislike humans and didn't think highly of all Elementals. Kasai was blunt and distanced himself from others. He was as reclusive as she was, probably even more so. She bowed when he stood in front of her.

He inclined his head in response. "I've felt a shift for quite a while. What is it you would have me and my kind do? I am here to help in any way I can."

Zelkova smiled at Kasai. His mannerisms had remained unchanged since their first meeting. She admired his quick-to-the-point bluntness. Nodding, she answered, "I need you to gather all fire Elementals and retreat to the deepest caverns that lead to the inner layers of this land. The shadows will not reach you there." She didn't want Vako to know of the place, so she formed a map of the lands and the location of the cave with air and clouds.

Kasai's eyes watched her motion and then nodded that he knew the site. "Is there anything else you need from us, from me?"

"Move fast to that location, and once you are there, you may feel me calling through fire. When I call to you, I need all of you to focus your elements on me."

He shot her a questioning gaze but didn't ask questions, only nodded in acknowledgment. The two of them parted ways, one headed south-west, the other north.

As night fell, Zelkova found herself just above Whaleslength. A small fishing house stood near the road. The outline of the house seemed darker than the landscape that harbored natural shadows from the moon's rising light.

Nearing the house, she saw dark forms off in the distance. The sound of wooden wheels on the road passed the house. Shifting her stance, she looked past to see what seemed to be the fisherman bringing home an empty wagon. Her eyes focused on the two shadows. The family of the man. He must have been at the market selling goods when they found the stone. But where was the stone?

She shook her head. Right now, she had to save the family and make certain the man didn't turn into a shadow himself, then she could find the stone. Moving her arms, she put a light barrier around the farmer and his wagon, just enough to combat the darkness but not enough to startle him into awareness. Then, she put a stronger light around the figures and the fish house.

Zelkova called to them in their minds. *Think of the sun shining. A gentle breeze caressing your cheek. The coldness of water on your lips after a long summer day. The stars that brighten the night's sky. The warmth of a nice fire in the dead of winter. The smell of freshly picked fruit that fills the air in spring. Think of happy times.* She sent images to their minds, clearing the darkness that loomed there.

The shadows dissipated, leaving only the darkness from the night sky. The fisherman reached his house to see his family standing outside, awaiting him. Even though they were stunned and confused, that soon faded with the sight of his return. Zelkova smiled and moved to search for the rock, knowing it must be near but hidden for it not to have been touched until recently. Looking around, she saw a freshly placed fence keeping in some sheep. She was surprised the shadows hadn't overtaken the animals.

Going into the woods next to the fence, she soon came upon a stone that was smaller than the rest, which confused her. All the ones before this were larger. Was this one of the first or one of the last?

This must have been one of the last Vako had opened, meaning they had started to weaken. That might be one of the reasons Vako had wanted Tempus.

Stooping to one knee, she reached out her hand and touched the surface of the rock. This time, she was pulled into a different time with a rush, instead of fading like the other times before. The speed made her head spin as she tried to adjust to her new surrounds. Blinking and shaking her head, she saw she was in a place quite different than the one she had just left.

Everything around her was lush and new. The sun glistened through the tall evergreen trees. The field she had been in was no longer there. In its place stood a large lone tree among much smaller ones. Nati emerged from it, looking somewhat different. She couldn't place her finger on what the difference was, almost like she was new. The expression Nati wore was one of shock and almost anger.

"What are you doing over here? I thought Sten was to keep to his borders. That was the deal we made. Did he not tell his Elementals?"

Zelkova shook her head as she searched for what time she had stumbled into. Before she could find out, Nati gasped, bringing Zelkova back to the present. "Wait, you look different..."

The other elements must have given her away. At first glance, she did look more stone than anything. She had been searching that whole time and now figured out she was close to the new beginning. She smiled in shock but also knew Nati shouldn't know of this encounter.

Waving her hand in front of Nati's face, she changed the image of her in Nati's eyes and memory. She now looked fully stone with flowing dirt for hair.

Nati frowned. "I'm sorry. For a second there, you looked different."

Zelkova smiled. "I get that a lot. I think it's the play of light. Please forgive me for trespassing. I had only recently learned of the rules and found myself here. Many apologies." Zelkova bowed to Nati, who was, by all rights, a First.

The land was so fresh. Things must have been much different. Everything looked bright and vibrant. Zelkova wanted to look further back than this, but this wasn't the time.

"It can take some getting used to. Just don't make the mistake again. Now, move along, will you?" Zelkova bowed once more and backed away, back to the stone. Reaching down, she touched it, and with the same rush, she found herself back to where she had left, near the fishing house. Night air surrounding her.

This time, she didn't release the stone. Concentrating, she sent quick vibrations into the surface. It soon crumbled and fell to the ground. Zelkova motioned her hands above the loose rocks, turning them into fine grains of dust, leaving nothing behind. Sighing, she thought of the three more stones that were left. Only three...

She then moved up toward the northern part of Ruri where she felt another stone waiting. It took her another day to reach where the rock stood seemingly untouched. It stood on top of a stony ridge where only goats were seen. She was thankful for that. Goats probably didn't rub up against it because of its position.

Sighing, she put her hand on the stone, noticing it was larger than the one from the day before. The scenery slightly changed around her. Turning, she looked down the ravine to see armed guards riding below. Strange. She floated down, making certain to blend in with the stones around her.

When she got closer, Zelkova noticed the colors of their gear: red, gold and green. Litore soldiers. Even stranger. She listened on the wind. These stones seemed to send her to a place and time she needed to see.

"Are you certain they said to meet here, sir?" one of the men asked. "This could be a ruse to trap you."

"There is always a chance of someone being untrustworthy, but we mustn't think they are unless they give us a reason. Not everyone is out to trick others." Cedrus' voice reached her like a song sung by the most elegant of birds.

"I understand, sir. Who are we supposed to meet here again? You said you would tell us once we reached this place."

Cedrus laughed. "I understand your duty is to guard me, but trust me, I am in no harm here." The sound of rustling leaves swiftly killed the conversation. The three men palmed the hilt of their swords, ready to draw them at any hint of danger. "Calm down, men. There's no need for your weapons. Trust in me as I trust in all of you."

Cedrus walked a few paces away from the men, telling them not to follow. Zelkova moved a little to see who he was meeting. The sight warmed her heart. Arbor stood hidden in the trees beyond. Cedrus and Arbor spoke in whispers.

Why are some stones leading to when Vako had already found the timeline with me in it? Why did they keep opening time rifts?

The question loomed in her mind as she stared at the two. Zelkova wanted so badly to go down and speak with them but wouldn't chance the impact it could have. She had already made too many ripples. Making more could cause a tidal wave.

She started back toward the stone but right before she reached it, she saw a shadow in the corner of her eye. It was headed straight toward Cedrus. Zelkova reached out and clenched her fist, stopping the shadow in place. Cedrus and Arbor remained unaware of its presence. She pulled her arm to her, forcing the shadow to move closer. It soon stood in front of her. The shadow hung in the air like a cloak hanging next to a fire to dry.

She shook it as if that could shake the answers from it. "Who are you? Why are you after them?"

"I want to go back," it hissed. "To my life before…"

"What life before? I can help you."

It lifted its cloaked arm to point at the two standing on the ground below them. Zelkova moved further up the ridge. Finding a flat area, she moved the shadow next to her, then motioned light around it. With a pulling motion, she removed the darkness from the figure.

After a while, the shadow in front of her took on another shape. She continued the motion, giving light and remove dark. Her eyes widened, tears almost immediately streaming down her cheeks.

"I was so lost…"

Zelkova hugged him tightly, stopping him from saying more. She wiped her tears away and looked at him, taking him by the shoulders. "I'm so sorry, Arbor. If I had known you were wandering around through time, I would have looked for you. I thought you were with Vako and the other shadowed ones."

He shook his head. "I was with Vako for a time, but... I can't remember what happened. How I got here." He looked down at his past self. That Arbor and Cedrus had obviously finished talking and parted ways. "I remember that moment. What we spoke about. I missed those times."

"Maybe your thoughts of the past brought you here somehow."

He shook his head at her words. "I don't know, Zelkova. All I know is that I'm here."

"Come, let us get back to our time. Hold on to me, and don't let go."

He nodded solemnly and held her arm as she moved them to the stone. She touched it, and their surroundings shifted. Once they were back to their time, Zelkova went about destroying the stone. "Stand back."

He did as requested, and like the others, she destroyed the stone into dust. Once finished, Zelkova walked over to Arbor and put her hand on his shoulder once more. "Again, I am so sorry."

The knowledge of Arbor being trapped and knowing she could have helped him sooner had she been aware tugged at her heart.

He shook his head. "No, you didn't know."

"Here, let me at least help you not be haunted by thoughts of the darkness." She placed a hand on each side of his head and let her thoughts enter his mind, casting out the remaining darkness with the light of hope.

Once all traces were gone, she interlaced her arm with his. "We should go see Nati and the others. I will move us fast, so hold onto my arm."

Seeing Arbor again and having him back was a relief. He was safe now, and that was all that mattered. But guilt tried to slip in along with the relief. Guilt always seemed to be her companion.

Despite that, she focused on helping her friend, and in a blink of an eye, they were in the forbidden forest. Instantly, Nati and Fraxinus moved toward them with worried expressions.

"Arbor! We've been so worried!" Nati embraced him as Fraxinus patted his shoulder. "Where did you find him?" she asked Zelkova. "Last I heard from you, he was lost and you feared the shadows took him."

"It seemed I found him by chance, but there might be other forces at work."

"Other than Vako?" Her father turned toward her in question and concern.

She merely nodded, not certain how to explain the events that happened in such a short amount of time. So many thoughts filled Zelkova's mind, and the weight of the world seemed to fall on her shoulders. She had to defeat Vako and help the Elementals and humans.

Zelkova's eyes were downcast as she whispered, "I have long put a barrier around this area. It has kept the shadows out so far, and I hope it will continue to do so. I am not certain how this next battle with Vako will turn out. I fear I will not be able to stop the shadows from consuming the lands. I have long sent word that all should seek refuge in the cities with the light domes. Those who fail to do so might become shadows. This is only a precaution, but I hope things will turn out for the better."

Her father placed his hands on her shoulders. "This must be a heavy burden on you. One that weighs on your heart and mind. I can't imagine how any of that feels. As your father, I feel at fault for this. I am sorry you're going through this."

Zelkova tried to smile back, but her heart only sank more as she thought of the future. Breathing in deep, something that had become more of a habit than a necessity, she tried to ease the tight band around her chest.

Her mother hugged her along with her father. Zelkova sighed as love extended from them and wrapped around her like a soft blanket. Nati whispered in Zelkova's ear, "Thank you."

She looked at her mother in confusion. "For what?"

"For being my daughter," she said softly, caressing Zelkova's cheek. "For being who you are."

For the longest time, Zelkova had tried to bury her emotions. But hearing her parents say those words made them rise to the surface. Again, she pushed them down, trying to focus on what had to be done.

Zelkova smiled at her parents before releasing them. "I want all of you and the other Elementals to think on your element when I call. When the time comes, will you all answer me?"

Arbor and her parents agreed. Her heart ached as she walked away from them.

"Wait!" Arbor rushed to her. "Can't I come with you?"

"Sadly, no. Stay here and help the others. You bring calm to those around you. I will miss that." She sighed.

"I have a feeling this is goodbye, isn't it?" Arbor eyed her.

"Is there such a thing as a goodbye?" She tried to bring a lightheartedness to the air by winking at him. "I will see you all again."

The thought of not seeing her loved ones again haunted her thoughts. But she hoped what she said would come true.

Spero woke to a bright new day. He rolled over and hugged Omnia, whispering sweet nothings into her ear. She laughed, smiling in the way that always took his breath. Before they could truly enjoy the moment, a loud knock on the door ruined it.

He kissed Omnia's forehead and then went to answer it, all the while putting his shirt on. "Coming!"

When he opened the door, he saw a red-faced guard with a stern expression. "Sir." The man slightly bowed. "There are hundreds of people entering the city. The townspeople are gathering at the gate. They want answers about why these people are here. The people coming in from outside are bringing letters from Zelkova. What should we do, my lord?"

Spero nodded. "I see. Give me a moment, and I will meet you at the castle gates."

"Yes, sir." The guard bowed and briskly walked down the hall.

As Spero closed the door, he turned to Omnia, who was already up getting dressed. He smiled and walked over to her. "Let me help you, my lady."

She giggled as his hands found the laces to her dress. "So, what Zelkova warned you about has started? And the king has put you in charge of all things Zelkova and light related?"

Spero knew this was a great responsibility. But it was true he knew more about Zelkova and the elements. There were other things the king had to do for the good of the people. That's what his subjects were for.

He sighed. "It seems so. The people are going to be on edge, but we have to keep them calm. We can't turn others away just because Zelkova was only able to put light around cities. The king knows very little of the light and has never met Zelkova, so he thought it best I be the face of this since I have the most information on the matter." He leaned forward and kissed her cheek. "We will all have to pull together."

She nodded as he pulled away and started putting on his boots. "Spero... Zelkova left without saying much to us. Why do you think that is?"

He stood and adjusted his ornaments in the mirror but was mostly looking at Omnia, who smiled knowingly. "She probably knew I would want to help her and so would the others. But we have to believe in her; she's doing this for all of our safety, trying to limit as many casualties as she can by taking on everything herself."

Omnia wrapped her arms around herself. "Zelkova is facing Vako all by herself... to protect all of us. Why don't we go after her?"

"And do what? She took our light gifts. She could imprison us with barely a thought."

"It must be so lonely for her." Omnia sighed.

Spero hugged her tightly from behind. "Yes, she has a lot on her shoulders and is bearing it all alone. We must do what we can to help here."

Omnia solemnly nodded. After they were fully dressed, the two of them made their way to the main gate of the castle. Shouting came from both sides. Some people were even crying. Omnia looked up at Spero in concern. He shook his head, sadness filling him.

Spero went over, put his hand on one of the guard's shoulders who was visibly shaken by the events that were unfolding. Then he whispered in the man's ear. Nodding at Spero's words, the man went up to a plank atop the gates that divided the castle and town. Once he stood at the highest point, the guard addressed the crowd.

"Citizens of Litore," he said in a loud booming voice that almost shook the ground. "Be you from far and wide or here within the city, I beg your attention. Be still! Lord Aurum will now speak." The man turned and nodded to Spero. Putting away the note the inhabitants had received, he walked up the steps to the plank and stood next to the man with the booming voice.

Spero cleared his throat and surveyed the large crowd in front of him. "Good people of Litore, listen to my words! I have looked over the parchment Zelkova has sent out. As you all know, darkness is spreading across the land. This light barrier around the city is to help protect us all, including those who live outside the city. It's impossible to put a barrier around the whole country, so we must share our food and home with our countrymen."

Spero scanned the crowd, still seeing worried faces among them. He hoped his words were reaching them all.

"Do not close your hearts to those in need. We are all in this together and should help one another. We are all afraid in these dark times. Coming together will make us stronger, not weaker. Most of these people who come in are farmers. They can help us grow the food we will need. We will all get through this together. Please let us open our hearts and homes. I will be opening my home to those who are here seeking shelter. I hope for all of you to do the same!"

Spero slightly bowed to the crowd of people below him and then walked down the stairs to greet people. As he walked through the gates into the crowd of people, he almost had a glow about him. Even though he no longer had the gift of light, he still held the power to brighten the darkest of days with his mere presence.

While Omnia watched Spero, Inane came to Omnia's side. Inane stood a few inches taller than Omnia and had raven black hair and fair skin, opposite of her, yet they shared similar features.

"How's married life?" She smirked and then winked when Omnia blushed. "That good, huh?" Face getting even hotter, she nudged Inane to stop. She only giggled at her prodding.

The crowds were all whispers and laughs. The words Spero spoke seemed to ease some of the building tension.

Omnia only hoped it would stay, that way people's fears would continue to ease and give way to hope.

As if reading her mind, Inane leaned over and whispered, "It won't last."

Omnia looked up at her in surprise. "Why do you say that?"

"Because I am not really of this world. I see things a tad different than you, Omnia. I can still see people's aura. Even though most everyone before us wear smiles, a good amount still has a dark outline around them, which means they are still distrusting and will be quick to become angered or scared. I wish we still had the gifts of light and dark to help ease their minds more."

Omnia stared at Inane, saddened by her words. She had hoped what she saw was true.

Inane gently smiled at Omnia's expression. "Don't tell me you didn't notice?"

Omnia shook her head. "Spero's speech seemed to brighten the people."

"I'm certain you noticed in some way. How Zelkova's soup made you feel at home. How about when she listened to the townspeople and told them stories in turn? The fragrance on the wind?"

"How could you notice all of that and I didn't when you were part of me?" She scanned the area to find Spero further enveloped into the crowd.

Inane put a hand on Omnia's shoulder and gazed out into the sea of people as well. "I think your thoughts were on something else, or should I say someone else?" Inane giggled when Omnia's cheeks flushed once again.

After Spero finished speaking with the group of people, he made his way back to the gates of the castle where Inane and Omnia stood waiting. He took a spot next to his wife and waved at the people as the gates closed. Once the doors were shut, he sighed. "This doesn't look good."

"No, it doesn't," Inane agreed grimly.

"Even though I have eased the people's tension some, they will easily turn back to fear and anger."

Omnia grabbed Spero's arm. "Why would they fear their own people?"

Spero smiled down at her, making her heart leap. "Even though these people are from the same country, they are not known within the city. To them, they are strangers, and what people don't know or understand brings out fear and even hate. It can and will cause chaos. People tend to look out for themselves and their own, not wanting to share or help others during times like these. But I don't think most of the farmers will ask for much. The poorest of us all can be the richest at heart."

"But some will help, won't they?" Omnia asked, concerned.

"Yes, there will be a few willing to share and open their homes. But for the most part, people let irrational fear push out anything logical. Even if they were or are caring individuals. There will be a great number that will be selfish and greedy. I wish it wasn't the case. I wish Zelkova had let us keep the gift of light to combat people's fears."

"Is there anything we can do?" She hated the thought of people at odds with one another. Fear of what could happen started to rise in her.

"I will talk to the king. I already have plans to help crops grow enough to feed everyone, even in winter. That will help combat fear. We also might be able to build smaller homes for those seeking shelter. Even letting the wealthy stay in the castle if they give up their homes to those in need. But that will be unlikely."

Omnia looked down, thinking. Growing up, she had seen firsthand how greedy people could be. But surely, there was some way to prevent it all. "If it's human nature to fear, would light help that much? And even if it did, what would happen to future generations?"

Inane placed her hand on Omnia's shoulder. "You're right. Zelkova can't control everything. We have to do our best and teach who we can."

"And it's not fair to expect that of her as well," Spero chimed in.

They stood there, wondering what lay in store for them and their people.

Zelkova left the forest where her parents stayed and made her way up to the mountain, she had made her home for so long. Once she reached the top and neared the entrance of the cave, she turned and looked out at the vast land below. Opening her mind, she called out to Kasai. *Kasai, are you and your Elemental kin deep in the caves? Headed toward the center?*

She waited for an answer as she looked out at the lush forest below, thinking of all the people and Elementals lives that seemed to lay on the edge of existence. The fact that her actions would soon decide the outcome of all living things weighed heavily on her.

Soon, Kasai answered her. *I think it's quite interesting how you now communicate with us all through our minds. You never cease to amaze me, Zelkova. Yes, we are nearing it.*

Good. Do you think it will be to everyone's liking to live there for a while? Zelkova closed her eyes, viewing what Kasai saw through his own eyes. The fire Elementals were floating down a dark cave lit by their flames, which cast shadows off the walls. Sighing, she released the image and opened her eyes.

Yes, we think we will like it here. Zelkova?

Yes, Kasai, speak freely.

Is there no other way? Must it be like this?

She could feel the tension and worry in his words. *I wish there was another way, but I can see none. This is the way to save the most lives. The worst enemy is yourself, which is very hard to overcome. I will do my best.* Before Kasai could say more, she closed the communication link between them.

Lifting her hands, she put her palms together, then pulled them apart, changing her flat hands into fists. The ground shook slightly in response as the caves closed to the surface above, making certain the darkness would not seep into the core of the world and to the fire Elementals.

Zelkova made different motions. First, she moved her fingers as if playing an instrument. Next, Zelkova started swaying, first with her hands, then her arms, then her whole body as if it were made of water, not stone.

Zelkova repeated the movements for a while. The sun set, and the moon rose to take its place. As her energy started to wane, she stopped and walked to the cave she had called home. She gazed around, taking in the space where she had spent so much time, knowing it might be the last time.

It was quite sparse. Against the back wall were bookshelves carved out of the stone wall. In front of it sat a fire that burned without fuel to feed it. She had kept it simple, quite different than her own mind.

Leaning against the stone wall for support, she made her way to a bookshelf. Sinking to her knees, she removed two books and looked them over. They had been a source of insight and grief over the long years. They had even guided her actions when she was human. Then thinking of the past, Zelkova remembered how much these books played a part in her role in the Elemental war. How Vako used them to trick Vatten, and Vatten had used them to fool her. Despite not knowing who made the books, she now knew how to use them. The thought of it brought tears to her eyes. The past can truly repeat itself. She sighed and was about to stand when she heard movement behind her. Turning on her knees, she saw nothing.

When she was about to stand, a voice called out to her in her mind, filling her body and mind with gut-wrenching pain. Before grabbing her head, she waved her hand over the books, making them disappear.

Words gradually came through the pain. *You opened yourself up. Not the best idea. I've been looking for you. You've been hiding well.*

If you found me, why aren't you here? Zelkova gasped as the pain increased.

You made a strong barrier. I can only reach you this way. When will you come out and play?

Zelkova scoffed at Vako. *Play? Ha. I'm done playing. I am going to end this so-called game of yours!* Zelkova thought of blocking Vako, and within a few moments, the pain and voice were gone. She staggered to her feet, catching herself against the cave wall. It still worried her, how much Vako could control her. Every time they met, they seemed stronger.

The thought of how she asked everyone to think of her when she called crossed her mind, but the moment wasn't right. She could only call on them once, so she had to wait and bide her time. Thinking of what she must now do, Zelkova turned to the center of the cave and raised her arms. As her arms moved higher, a shape formed from the stone, raising as her arms did. It took the shape of a table.

Zelkova stared at the flat-stoned form in front of her, eyeing it with contempt, as if this thing held the blame for all of what had been and what will come to be. Stepping forward, she placed both palms on the table, far apart from one another. Closing her eyes, she summoned her thoughts into action.

One hand glowed with a bright light while deep darkness covered the other. The light and dark then seeped into the stone from her hands, making two separate book-shaped outlines. Sighing with a heaviness that few could fathom, she stepped back and walked to the entrance of the cave.

Turning back, she looked at the table once more. Zelkova stretched out her hands to one side of the wall then the other. Small flames came to light, floating next to the wall, casting shadows. She clenched her fist, extinguishing the fire on the floor near the bookshelf.

She exited the cave, then with a swift movement, she crossed her arms in front of her, closing the entrance behind her. Now to the two remaining stones. Closing her eyes, she sought out the first of the two, which laid at the border of Ager and Lignum.

In a split second, she was gone from the cliff, leaving only moonlight in her wake. Zelkova moved within time and space, trying her best not to leave ripples behind her. Thoughts of the past and future riddled her mind. The past clung to her like a growth on her heart, making every heartbeat feel like her last. But did she even have a heart now? If so, was it made of stone? She shook those thoughts from her mind, but the thoughts of the future came flooding in next, like a great tidal wave, almost drowning her with pain.

Because of the muddled thoughts clouding her mind, she almost ran right into the large stone. She blinked rapidly, raising her chin to try and see the top. It towered above her, the darkness coming from it making her cringe.

The stone in front of her was the largest she had seen from Vako. Why was this one so much larger than the others? The only way to find out was to see where it took her, but the feeling in the pit of her stomach made her reluctant. Something didn't feel right. This one was far more dangerous than the previous ones.

Reaching out her hand, she slowly leaned toward the rock. Closing her eyes, she felt the pull and shift as things changed around her. Sighing, she opened her eyes to something quite unexpected.

A dark void filled the space, but it wasn't like Vako's shadows. Turning in place, she looked at her surroundings. There were dots of light all around, and she felt as if she were floating. When she turned to look behind her, she saw a world covered in darkness. The shadows seemed to be reaching out, trying to expand to other planets.

Gasping, Zelkova realized she was among the stars, in the sky past her world or, in this case, Vako's world. This is what Vako's darkness looked like from the heavens. This is what they had planned for her world and the others. If they were to defeat her, they would move onto other dimensions.

Everything everywhere would be covered in shadows.

If Zelkova were to leave this world as it was, the shadows would make their way to the other worlds. It would take a long time to do so, but it would eventually. The shadows were made to search out any living thing and cover it with darkness.

Looking to her left, she saw the sun in the distance. Moving her arms toward it, she made a swaying motion, moving the sunlight toward the shadowed-covered world. Her left arm repeated the movement while her right arm turned toward the world. Light came out from her, shooting toward the world. The brightness of this light exceeded the sun. The purity of it enveloped the planet.

After Zelkova had placed the warmth and light from the sun, she put a barrier around the darkness of the world, blocking it and the shadows with a strong light shield. Once the beam from her hand had stopped, she started a swaying motion again, which moved the sunlight within the planet's surface layer. She hoped this process would eventually overtake the shadows, leaving the world anew. Hopefully, life could find its place once more.

Looking past this planet, she focused on a world that seemed to be calling her. A familiar voice rang out, so faint only she could hear it. Whoever it was seemed to have known this. Her heart ached. If she were to go, she would be leaving her world behind, leaving it to Vako…

Cupping her hands, she whispered into them, "Soon, I will find you. It may be years, but I will come."

Closing her eyes, Zelkova focused on putting light into the air in her hands. She pushed the light and air orb away from her. It floated toward the far-off world where the voice was calling.

Zelkova then looked at the rock that had sent her to literal outer space. The stone that floated in front of her was small, almost the size of a throwing stone. Because of its size, she almost missed it. It was the smallest of the stones from Vako. Reaching out her hand, she grasped it, and her scenery rapidly changed once more. The pull of the time vortex she fell through was far greater than any before. It felt as if her body was being pulled apart by unseen hands.

Struggling, she concentrated on the time and place she wanted to land at. Her mind started to swirl just like the view around her. It felt as if someone or something was trying to control the depth of time. But would Vako really try such a thing? As her surroundings continued to shift, a voice spoke to her.

Come to me... Focus on me... The voice was soft, yet strong. Calming, reassuring. The scene around her finally stilled and came into focus. As Zelkova blinked, a form came into view. It was like the one she had seen before. Her future self? It felt the same but looked different this time. It had a bright form with a dark outline. Zel had lost the elements they had before.

"It's you..." Zelkova's voice was unsteady, not quite like her. She felt as if someone else was speaking for her.

The figure moved closer to Zelkova. "We must speak quickly. Vako looks for not just me but you as well. They have grown more powerful in recent days and are eager to seek both of us out and destroy us. We two are the only things standing in the way of Vako's plan."

She narrowed her eyes on the figure in front of her. "And how do you propose we stop Vako?"

"You know the answer. You have already started the process." Zelkova waited for the form to speak again, knowing there was more they needed to say. Sighing, the figure spoke again in a weary voice. "I may not have told you all the last time we spoke. I am not you from the future. I am from the same time as Vako."

"The same dimension and timeline as Vako?" Zelkova asked, making certain she heard the form correctly.

Nodding, the figure went on. "Yes, I am Vako's other half. Their lighter half. When they became as dark as they are now, I was cast out, becoming what you see in front of you now. I am your missing piece of the puzzle. I have been watching you and skipping through time to counter Vako's doing, but I have grown weaker as they grow strong. With each person they take with the shadows, Vako takes their strength."

"And why have you waited till now to help me fight Vako?"

"Because neither of us was ready. It can take a while to accept one's death, a second — no, third time, does it not?" The figure tilted its head, waiting for her response.

"So, that's why you lied last time we met, shifted your form and blocked my sight? You were the one that waited so long for fear of dying. I've long accepted my death. This time is no different."

"I waited because I had to help you, so you would not turn into someone like Vako. Think, we have met more than these two times. I may have looked different in those forms since I have weakened."

Zelkova thought of the voice calling to her when Tempus had first tried to kill her with his power. Then when she was giving in to the pain in the cave behind the waterfall. Several more scenes came to her mind's eye as she thought of the past. "You were waiting till I was stronger. But now you are weaker. Why not call on me earlier?"

"Because it's not my strength that matters, but yours. And now that you have found your missing pieces, you can be complete." The light form reached out their hand and bright light flashed in Zelkova's eyes.

The images that filled her mind was of Carya, Pyrus, Jardin, Sten, Arbor, Ilex, and Aria. As the visions of their faces came to her mind, a soft voice said, *Your family is what makes you whole. Without them, you were left empty and bitter. Vako's darkness would have taken this world along with you. Even though you pushed them away for their own safety, it's not just for their wellbeing, but yours as well. They give you strength and without them in your life, you would be more apt to give into the darkness. They can be your weakness as well as your strength. The dread you feel is the fear of failing, but you must believe you are able to face what is in front of you.*

The voice and images faded from Zelkova's mind, leaving Zel standing in front of her. "Are you ready, Zelkova?"

"There is one last stone I need to find."

"It awaits you on the island Vako has made their home…"

Zelkova sighed, thinking of what needed to be done. Was it even feasible? "What's your real name? Now that you say you are part of Vako and not my future self."

The light figure seemed to almost shrug, saying, "My true name is of no importance. Come, we must go to Vako on our terms before they find us." And with that, the form waved its arm and their surroundings swiftly changed.

Zelkova thought of all the people and Elementals who were depending on her success. If she was not able to do what needed to be done, the world as she knew it would be gone. It would turn into the one she had just come back from. Covered in darkness, all life sucked into nothingness.

And the souls that once knew peace would forever live in torment.

Zelkova blinked and the view in front of her changed to one of pine trees. She could feel rock and moss underfoot. They were on the island she had escaped over two hundred years ago. For the most part, it looked the same. All but the ground. It was covered in a dark mist, which made the air around her thick.

"Come, we must find the stone." The light figure, Vako's other half, floated toward a line of trees that stood near the center.

Zelkova followed, making certain all her senses were on guard. Vako could attack at any moment, and she couldn't risk being taken by surprise. As they went through the woods, the mist thickened into a darker fog. The figure was like a beacon lighting her way. As it got progressively darker, they reached a clearing where a large dome-shaped stone stood.

On top of the stone stood Vako. "Welcome to my home. The isle of Umbras as I call it. I've lived here for over two hundred years. Right under your nose, Zelkova. Seeing you both here and now is no surprise. I felt you coming." Vako gazed at the figure in front of Zelkova. "And you, it's not like you're subtle. I could see you coming from a galaxy away." Turning to Zelkova, Vako jumped off the stone.

Their cloak flew back, fully revealing Vako's face for the first time.

Zelkova was taken aback at the sight in front of her. Zel turned and stared at her, along with Vako. "This... You..." Zelkova couldn't believe her eyes.

"Now, now, what is this? You didn't tell her?" Vako looked to their other half.

"No, I thought she had put the pieces together before now."

Zelkova looked back and forth between the two of them, but then fixed her eyes on Vako. Their face was a mix of stone with dark and light running through, different from their hands, which was made of shadows with cracks of light underneath. Most shockingly, their face was split in two. One half was much like her own and the other half resembled Pyrus.

"It is how you see it, Zelkova. You knew we are the same. So, I am thinking you were not aware of our brother?" Vako started to move closer, but their other half stepped in the way. "It was the only way to save him... He lives in the recesses of my mind. I made it comfortable for him there."

"He knows nothing of what you have done? Nothing of the shadows, the world you destroyed, or that you are trying to kill mine?" Zelkova glared at Vako, fists clenched in anger. She couldn't believe what she was seeing. What Vako had done before this was horrible, but this was hard to even fathom. Absorbing their own brother was on another twisted, disgusting level.

"I'm doing this for him, for all of us! Once each world, each dimension is under the cover of my shadows, everyone will be united. No more wars, no more loss. Everyone will feel the same as I do."

"Fear, pain and anger? What kind of life is that? Floating in an abyss of negativity is not a life, nor should anyone live an eternity without freewill, without love!" Zelkova started toward Vako but was held back by Zel standing between them.

"I am uniting all! Everything will become one! To feel as I feel. Don't you see this is how it all has to be!" Vako glared at Zelkova. "How can you want this world to stay like this? Full of war and death?"

"Because there is also peace and love. War and death are a sad part of life, but at least they would be living. Making choices of their own, living a life with free will. Not a slave to hate."

"Enough of this! I will take you both into my fold!" Vako moved the shadows around them, making the fog thicken.

"Zelkova! Go now! I will hold Vako. Hurry to the stone!" Vako's light side screamed to her

Zelkova ran to the large dome-shaped rock. In one blink, she was in front of Vako. The next, she was reaching out her hand, touching the stone.

When her hand reached the smooth surface, Zelkova felt as if she was thrown into a whirlwind with images swirling past her. She tried to grab onto one, to stop the storm around her, but she couldn't control her surroundings.

It was as if she were falling through time and space, but there was nothing for her to grasp to stop her descent.

She tried to grab ahold of something to stabilize herself, but nothing worked. As Zelkova was trying to figure a way out of the whirlwind of time, she felt a push. And in one movement, her body felt as if it had hit a brick wall.

Slamming against something hard, her vision went black for a few moments. Blinking, she noticed her movement had finally stilled. Looking at her surroundings, she saw she was in the middle of a bloody battlefield. Focusing, she saw Vako holding a blood-drenched sword. Dead bodies were strewn around them.

She had seen this scene before, but this time, it was wasn't through Vako's eyes. The knowledge that Zelkova from a different timeline had caused so much pain and destruction weighed on her. It could have easily been her if she had let hate lead her actions. The knowledge shook her to the core.

Trying hard to move toward Vako, she found she couldn't. It was as if a force was keeping her in place. She yelled, but her words found no sound. All she could do was watch her other self become Vako.

As Carya was struck down and darkness enveloped Vako's sword, all Zelkova could do was stand there. She tried all the elements, tried screaming. Nothing worked.

But then a thought flashed into her mind. This wasn't like the other stones. She hadn't been transported to a different time or place. She was in Vako's mind, in their memories.

She tried to figure out if there was a way to control their mind since it was similar to her own. Right when she was about to try different methods, her surroundings changed. Zelkova was thrown into black nothingness and then once again hit another memory like a brick wall.

Groaning, she focused, taking in what was before her. Zelkova was in a bedroom, one that looked familiar, but she couldn't quite place it. Not until she saw a figure enter the room did she remember what room she now stood in. It was Malus who entered. He had aged since she had last seen him face to face. She was relieved he could not see her, but then worry set in. Why he was in Vako's memory?

Zelkova turned and Vako walked right through her, as if she were a ghost. Turning again, she saw the two of them talking. Malus' voice filled her with a pang of loss, even if he did turn on them. After all these years, Zelkova felt that maybe she could have done something different. Maybe her actions led him down his path...

"Who are you? How did you get in here?" Malus unsheathed his sword and pointed it at the cloaked figure in front of him.

"Calm yourself. I am here to ensure something we both want." Vako lifted their hand and moved two fingers, bending Malus' sword. Malus dropped it and glared at the cloaked one. "I want to help you, much like Tempus once did, but you will reap more of a reward this time."

"And what reward would that be?"

"The world." Before Malus could respond, Vako moved forward and placed a finger on Malus' temple.

Zelkova could not see what Vako was showing Malus, but his expression changed. A scowl turned into a devious grin. "And what do you want in return for this great gift?"

Vako laughed. "The death of our mutual enemy."

Before Zelkova could hear any more, her view shifted, and she was again thrown into a whirlwind of memories. Plummeting through the images, one caught her eye and she somehow grasped it with all her might.

Zelkova felt like she was going to be split in two, but she wouldn't let go. This was her way out. Breathing deeply, she pulled herself toward it with everything she had. With one more tug, she was thrown into the image she had been holding onto.

Tumbling, she gained her footing. She now stood in a dark forest. Overgrown brush made it hard to push forward. As she made her way slowly through the thick forest, a soft voice reached her. "Hurry, Zelkova. Come back."

It was Zel. They must be having a hard time with Vako. Pushing through the brush faster, she saw a small rock extending from a small pond. Ivy crept up from the water's edge, rapidly moving toward her.

Zelkova knew she didn't have time to fight, so with all her strength, she jumped from where she was, several yards from the water's edge, into the pond, barely touching the stone.

Blinking, she was back on the island of Umbras. Looking around, she saw thick darkness and a small light in the fog. Stretching her hand toward the stone, Zelkova focused. Soon, warm light gathered on her open palm and shot toward the rock, but it was blocked by shadows. Before Zelkova could even take a breath, she was pulled back into the deep fog.

"You think you can defeat me! I've given you so many chances to come with me, to be by my side. And this is how you thank me?" Vako's voice filled the air.

She looked around, trying to see Zel, but only a faint light could be seen in the distance. "Vako, you don't have to do this to make your pain end. You don't have to be alone anymore. Let light back in and we can be true siblings, living with both Pyruses. You don't have to bring darkness to the world to feel whole."

All she could hear was deep, dark laughter that echoed around her. "I know you feel like you are alone, that the world was against you and the only way you could fix it was to make everyone and everything feel the pain you were feeling, but that's not the answer."

Zelkova was interrupted by a harsh voice close to her ear. "Don't act like you know my feelings. You have not lived the life I had. You are me, but we are not the same." There was a long pause, and the darkness around her became even darker. Like a black hole, sucking in all the light. "How can you love these people? The Elementals? Can't you see that no matter how many chances you give them, they will still turn to their fear and hate in the end? I'm just speeding up the process. They will end up destroying themselves and each other in time. Why not just go ahead and bring the destruction now rather than await their long progression of darkness that will happen either way? You see as I do. You know what is going to occur, but the difference is that you hope they will prove the visions wrong, where I know they will prove what I am saying. Give in to the knowledge of the future we have seen. I am right. I am just bringing everyone into the fold before they bring it upon themselves."

Zelkova's vision was taken over by images of the past, where she had fought in a needless war. Most wars could have been stopped by both sides coming to a compromise. She hadn't seen that then. She had only known she had to fight and defend her king and homeland. But when she had received more gifts, she saw there was more to life and that war was a waste of it.

As those thoughts and images ran through her mind, she blinked, and in an instant, Vako stood in front of her. Zelkova cringed at the sight of their face, a mix of her and Pyrus, which brought a sense of dread along with it.

"You've got all of this wrong, Zelkova." Vako came closer, putting their hand on her cheek. The coldness of it made her freeze. How strong they were compared to her. Vako continued. "I am saving these people from long suffering. With me, they will all be together, feeling the same as everyone around them, together in their pain. Oh, and that thought you just had." Zelkova stared at Vako as they went on. "As you have become weaker, I have become stronger. Your feelings for others will always be your weakness. I only care for myself. I learned long ago that caring about others will always turn out badly."

This time, it was Zelkova's turn to interrupt them. "No... You are the one in the wrong. The ones I care about are my strength, not my weakness."

Their eyes locked. Vako came inches from her face. "Let me show you how weak you really are," they whispered, dark matter oozing from their mouth.

She tried to move back, but Vako moved their hand closer, placing their palm on her chest. Darkness started overtaking her body and mind. Thoughts of anger and hate swarmed her mind; the images that overtook her were not her own but Vako's.

She found herself standing near a crying child. As she tried to get closer, dark fog enveloped the child. A voice came from the darkness. "Come, come now. It won't be that easy."

Zelkova started to wake back to reality. She had been so close to finding the small innocence still within Vako, but her mind hit a rock wall.

Coming back to wakefulness, she felt herself move but not by her own admission. Vako was controlling her body once more. She frantically looked for the light side of Vako. Zel. But there was no light in the darkness around her, only the outline of deeper darkness.

Her eyes turned toward Vako. Vako had taken off the cloak they had adorned for so long. "Let me show you how my world turned against me."

Zelkova was unable to move her body as an even darker fog enveloped her. As the darkness covered her body once more, images came into view. She saw herself, no, Vako as a child, being dragged out into the hall of the castle by her father.

"I've told you time and time again, dresses only!" he yelled. "You are not to wear pants. Girls only wear dresses and boys only wear pants."

The younger version of yelled, with tears of anger running down their face.

The vision abruptly faded to yet another where a young Vako stood in a field with a fire blazing near her. In the middle of the fire stood a long pole and tied to the pole was a nature Elemental.

Their mother.

She screamed in agony. To her right, her father, along with several other men, stood watching. But they didn't look on with horror like she did. They were engrossed in a cheery conversation, smiling and laughing; the screams of their mother did not seem to reach their ears.

Tears filled her eyes as she looked at Vako's younger self who was sobbing, not just in sadness but in anger. People really are a product of their own circumstances. All the events in their life, the ones she had seen before and now, led them to what they were now. Knowing only darkness, all the light taken from their life, made them into Vako. No one was there to pull them out of the darkness of despair, and they were not able to help themselves.

Her thoughts were cut off as her scenery changed once more into another field. The sound of swords clashing rang out. Twigs, fireballs, and rocks flew through the air, making everything a blur. As she looked around, she recognized this vision from before. Again, she saw Vako with a bloody sword in hand.

Across the yard was Carya being cut down, which made everything around her go dark. An idea crossed Zelkova's mind. Did Carya not have an element? Did Vako not know they could have saved her? Would they go back and try and save Carya and themselves?

"Vako. Vako... Please listen. There might be a way." Her words were cut off again as the shadows around her faded, showing an even darker figure emerge from the fog. The elements around her spiked in response to Vako, sending a warning through her body.

"What is it that you want to say?"

Zelkova was surprised they were letting her speak. "Did you know you could have given Carya one of your gifts and she would have turned into an Elemental when she died?" She awaited Vako's response, uncertain of how they would react.

"I can only give *gifts* if I were given them in the first place."

Silence fell, neither of them speaking, both of them staring at each other, daring the other one to say something. *They took the elements, how could Vako do that?* This thought tugged at the back of her mind.

The quietness was finally broken by Vako's unusual voice, the voice Zelkova now realized as two, not one. "I take that back. I was given dark and light, but the others were not given to me willingly." A smirk came across their face, and her stomach churned.

All Zelkova could do was whisper, "How?"

"How did I take the other elements?" Vako laughed. "I took over their minds. Showing them that if they didn't give me their gifts, they would die. Of course, that was a lie. They died either way." Vako almost giggled as they recalled their actions. "Let me show you how."

Zelkova was still unable to move but was still able to call nature. Immediately, roots shot toward Vako. They quickly put up a rock wall, stopping the roots' progression. "You really think you can hurt me now? Yes, you may look different, but I have grown stronger, where you have grown weak. Have you not realized that yet? Come, let me show you."

The dark fog once again overtook her, filling her mind and body. Images came out of the blackness that surrounded her. First, she saw her mother. It was her in her flesh form, but the flesh seemed to be rotting off her. Next, her father came up to her, then both of her brothers, all in human form but decaying. Flesh, hanging limply on their muscles, fell to the ground. Clumps of hair soon followed as they walked toward her. The four of them reached out to touch her, grabbing at her stone body, trying to pull her into the depths of the fog.

She tried not to focus on what she knew was not real, even though it felt very tangible. Zelkova tried to focus on the question that kept coming to her mind. *Why*? Why was Vako playing with her? Prolonging the end? What were they getting at?

Maybe Vako was lonely, and this was their way of stalling. Because if Zelkova was gone, who would they confront? Everyone else would give in to the darkness.

"Vako... You don't have to be alone!" Zelkova cried out as the shadows grew thicker. Thoughts ran through her head, trying to destroy the light she held within her. Hope, love, peace. "Vako! Listen. You don't have to be alone. You can go back to your world, cast light back into the darkness. Remake, create." Zelkova was screaming over the buzzing in her ears. It felt as if every inch of her was covered in bugs, even in her ears. All she could hear was the bugs as they tried to devourer her stone form.

"Vako, listen. We can fix this. It's not too late." Zelkova heard a deep laugh in response, casting out the sound of the buzzing. "Please, listen to me. You are not alone."

The fog, bugs and decaying people vanished and, in its place, stood Vako. Zelkova's stone body hovered in front of them. Anger contorted their face. "You think you can help my loneliness? That all of this is fixable? Like I'm a cut that needs to heal? Do you hear yourself? What I don't understand is why you want to save all this. Saving things that will only end up hurting and hating you. These people, Elementals who turn on their own kin, why risk your own life for theirs?"

"Because everyone has a choice, a choice to do better, to make the right decision, to change their path. There is good in the world. There was good in your world." A large rock smashed into Zelkova's chest, pushing her back into some trees, knocking the breath from her. Vako still had ahold of her, and she was unable to move. They were right. Their strength had grown. They must have absorbed Zel to make themselves stronger.

Zelkova lay among the trees, watching Vako's form come closer. "This has to stop, Vako. I won't be your plaything forever. I can help you if you let me."

"Just as you are helping yourself now? Or how you helped Carya who was imprisoned for two hundred years, or your bother who waited for an eclipse you could have made? What about Jardin? It's your fault he is where he is now. Is that what you call *help*?" Zelkova let out a small laugh. "Why do you laugh?" Vako snapped.

"Because you are still trying to make me hate myself by pushing all of this onto me. But deep down, you know this is all on you. I have faults just like anyone, but I did not make the shadows, nor did I lock my brother in stone."

Vako stopped in front of her, and with a swift movement, Zelkova was standing inches from them. "You still don't understand, do you? I am you and you are me. Everything I've done, you would have also done if you were in my position. We are the same, me and you."

Zelkova was tired of letting Vako push her around. She had tried to get through to them, and it wasn't working. Now was the time to try another way.

"Vako, there are other ways. You made the choice to do all of this, not me. We are completely different." She fought against Vako's control more vehemently.

Vako's eyes widened in surprise then a smirk came across their face. "So, you haven't really been trying this whole time? You've been letting me think I had control? Now, this is going to be fun." Their smile widened even as their eyes narrowed. She cringed at the sight of their distorted face.

She stared at them, moving her fingers and then her hands. The air around them thickened as their intensity started to grow. After a few moments of their staring contest, Zelkova won her freedom, despite how hard Vako tried to control her.

"Is that all you have, sister?" Vako laughed.

"You still call me sister after everything?" Smiling, Zelkova lifted herself up off the ground.

Vako reflexively moved back, and Zelkova moved toward them. Their eyes locked on each other, watching the other's every movement. They moved in a circle. Zelkova floated above the ground with the help of air, where Vako used their shadows.

Zelkova was getting tired of playing this game Vako so eagerly wanted to continue but wasn't keen to make the first move. "Vako, you don't have to do this. We can still go back and save your world. But I can't do it alone. Maybe we can find your Carya." A burst of rocks came jetting toward her. She threw up her arm, blocking the spray. "Listen! It's not too late. Don't you want to go back to your happy days?"

Water and stones shot from the ground around her, hitting her in all directions. She made an air shield around her, trying to think of how she could get through to Vako. They were almost equal, but she had her family and friends to help her.

To draw on them would mean the end. Not just the end of her but the end of everything.

The image of the future she had been to floated in her mind, along with Vako's world covered in shadows.

Zelkova knew she must try harder to get through to Vako. No matter how Zelkova thought about it, there seemed to be no other way. And this time, she would not look into the future to see her own death, not again. With a push of air, she sent the rocks and water bombarding her back to the ground. And with a swift motion, she was in front of Vako.

The shadowed one was taken aback, but before they could move, Zelkova had her arms around them, holding them tight with not just her embrace but with the elements Vako held in them. Closing her eyes, she rested her forehead against Vako's. They fought to pull away, using every element they had, but Zelkova would not relent. She had to push through their guard to break it. She had to force her mind through the deep anger and sadness that filled them and find their core. To find the light inside them, to bring balance to their thoughts.

Light and dark must coexist. Or her plan would unravel.

Zelkova touched her forehead to Vako's and dove deep into their mind, quickly passing through their memories, fears and thoughts. She had to search fast before Vako pushed her out. *Faster*, she thought. She had to move faster. She had to find what she was looking for.

Shadows were trying to overtake her mind, trying to push her out and drive her insane in the process. Zelkova surrounded her mind with light and dove into the deepest parts of Vako's mind she could.

Immediately, she saw darkness like she had never seen, moving forward in the fog surrounding her. This had to be the right place. It's what Vako said themselves. They had locked Pyrus in the back of their mind, saying it was pleasant for them there. This was anything but pleasant. This was hell. The darkness seethed with anger but mostly fear. Fear of being alone, fear of failing.

Zelkova continued forward, moving fast, not wanting to be pushed out before she found him. She searched the darkness for what seemed like hours. As she moved through the fog, she could feel Vako's claws in the back of her mind, trying to pull her out, but she had to keep going.

Finally, she spotted something in the distance, but she couldn't make out what it was. It was almost shapeless, like a blob of something just sitting there. As she approached it, it became clear that it wasn't shapeless but was many shapes circling each other. If she still had her human form, the image in front of her would have made her throw up.

It was Pyrus' dismembered body, each limb floating around the other. Zelkova looked away, not wanting to see anymore, the sight of it too much for her to take. Vako was truly cruel and selfish, but she knew the reasons for their madness and hatred. Waving her hand, the limbs knitted back together, creating a form. When she looked up, she saw her brother with half of his face missing.

Zelkova slowly moved toward him. He stood motionless. Reaching him, she wrapped her arms around Pyrus. His body was long gone. This was just his mind and very little of it was left. He was hanging on by a thread, and what was left was in so much pain, so much sadness.

"It's all right, Pyrus. Be at peace, my brother." Zelkova kissed what remained of his forehead, and a white light enveloped him. She released Pyrus, letting his body slowly fade away. Seconds later, a bloodcurdling scream nearly deafened her and the mind she was in sent her flying out.

Zelkova hit her body hard and fell back to the ground, her mind whirling. But before she could gather her thoughts and stabilize herself, Vako lifted her up, their dark shadowed hand wrapped around her throat. She put her hands on their wrist. Glaring at her was Vako's now half-missing face.

"How could you? You killed our bother!" Vako yelled, their voice harsh and no longer two. The whole island shook in response. "He was all I had left! And you took him from me! Why? Why would you do such a thing!" Vako's pain radiated off them like turbulent waves in a storm.

"Vako, listen." Her voice came out as a gasp as their grip tightened. "You are not alone."

"Ha! You know full well I have nothing left but my goal. Come to think of it, I've added something to my long list of things to do. Before I kill you, I will kill those you love, so you know how much pain you've caused me." Vako started to back away but kept a thick dark fog around her throat.

They were about to fade away when a faint light emerged from the darkness and slowly made its way over to Zelkova. In an instant, Zel pushed herself into Zelkova's body. She hadn't been taken by Vako?

Zelkova gasped as Zel became one with her. *I have fought and avoided Vako for over two hundred years,* Zel told her faintly. *I am tired. I give my last light of life to you. Become stronger, Zelkova. Become what Vako is not, and by doing so, you will save us all. Even though it may not seem like it, you will have done the right thing. What lies ahead is what is brought about by those left behind. There will come a time when you question everything, and when that time comes, dear Zelkova, remember my words. All that has come and will come to pass was not all your doing. There were other forces in play that you do not yet know. Remember me in the future, and do not look at your past in despair, always hope for the future, dear one. Now, go and take back your world from the hands of darkness.*

Zelkova breathed in deep. Light streamed into the dark fog around her and Vako, coming from all living sources — the trees, grass, stones, ground, water, air, animals, people, Elementals. She took a little bit of light from every living thing. When she opened her eyes, Vako was staring at her. To combat the light, they started pulling darkness from everything around them.

Bright light surrounded her as deep darkness surrounded Vako. Zelkova tried to reach out to Vako again, one last time. "Please, Vako, you are not alone. We can fix all of this! Together!"

"Ha! There is no together! You have ruined every chance. I've given you so many opportunities to join me. You've brought this on yourself and your world." Vako raised their arms, and the ground started to shake once more, loose pebbles, dirt and tree limbs flying through the air.

Zelkova looked through the elements to see if the world below was also being affected. She only got a glance before another attack of dark fog mixed with loose rock, trees, and water hit her. She sunk to her knees, trying to push the elements back, but Vako's anger was fueling them, giving strength to their power.

The world below was being torn apart. The elements were in chaos, about to rip the world apart. If she were going to stop Vako, it was now or never. Going to one knee, she looked up at Vako, who was concentrating all their energy into forcing the elements to destroy the world.

She had to finish this, but deep down, she knew she was dragging the process out. Not just in the hopes of helping Vako but also saving herself as well. In that moment, Zelkova knew she was being selfish. Who was she to put her life before others, to say her life meant more than all the humans and Elementals combined? Shaking her head, she stood up, forcing the elements back.

Slowly, Zelkova put one foot in front of the other. She had no right to put herself above all the others. Everyone had their place in the world, and no one had the right to live more than another.

Vako was so absorbed in destroying the world below, they did not see her slowly creeping toward them. Right when Zelkova was about to reach Vako, they turned and pushed her back with dark fog.

Zelkova groaned as she hit the ground several feet away from Vako. Lifting up to her elbows, Zelkova stared at Vako, who was no longer looking at her. The pressure on her body felt like ten-ton rocks sitting on her chest.

Determined to end Vako now before the world below was completely destroyed, she called through her mind and the elements to reach out to her family Elementals. Fire, Kasai; Nature, Nati, Fraxinus and Arbor. Then air, Aria and Ilex along with Ventus and Vindby. Then to rock, Pyrus and Sten. Zelkova took a deep breath and focused on water. Carya...

Her eyes teared up at the thought of Carya. How could she ever forgive Zelkova? How could Zelkova ever forgive herself? Was there really no other way? She couldn't think of one, besides the plan that had already been set in place. Zelkova wasn't ready to say goodbye, not again. She had just gotten her loved ones back, and now she had to leave them again.

Sighing, she opened her mind to the others, and within moments, the Elementals sent her their energy. Closing her eyes, Zelkova let the tears fall down her cheeks. This could be the last time she would ever feel their souls. The ache of loss ran through her. After gathering the others' strength, she stood and moved toward Vako again, reaching out for Pyrus and Sten in her mind.

Zelkova could feel overwhelming love through their connection. Wordlessly, she pushed cherished memories into their minds. Memories that had been forgotten as she got older, but once she connected with the elements again, they had come flooding back. Like when they were younger playing by the river. How the four of them, Sten, Pyrus, Carya and Zelkova would roam the forest. Sten teaching them how to use their gifts as Pyrus watched and fell in love with Sten, who was oblivious for a long time.

The last memory she sent to Pyrus and Sten was all of them together, laughing, happy. She then switched to her father and mother, sending out images of happy times. When their family was whole long ago, before her mother turned back into an Elemental.

Then to Carya. She had only just found Carya and to part ways with her again tore at her heart almost as much as when she thought Carya had been taken from her the first time. This time, Zelkova would be the one leaving. There was no way around this, not if she wanted to save everyone. Zelkova had very little time to say her goodbyes. Her strength was already waning, and she had to take out Vako or this world would end up like the other one.

Carya? she whispered in her mind. Once connected to her, she sent images to her. Each image was of times they had shared together as humans. Their first kiss, and their first words of affection. Then she made it where they saw each other in one another's minds. Zelkova took Carya in her arms, hugging her tightly. "No matter what the future holds, no matter how long or how far apart we are," she whispered in her ear, "we will always be connected. I will always be with you. Please remember that, Carya. And know that I love you."

Before Carya could respond, Vako lifted up her body, momentarily distracting her.

Focus on your element. Focus on spreading it throughout the land, Zelkova whispered to every Elemental.

Zelkova opened her eyes. Bright light illuminated them in the surrounding area. Vako took an involuntary step back. She had broken their hold and had started moving toward them. The elements responded to her beckoning, and their vibrations could be felt all around.

Vako looked at Zelkova in confusion. The elements now surrounded her. She moved closer and closer. Vako kept trying to move back but a force held them in place.

Zelkova's gifts were heightened, and she could hear everyone's thoughts, including Vako. *How did Zelkova go from being weak, almost beaten, to this? So strong and certain?*

"Because I am not alone," Zelkova answered easily. "I have others on my side who love this world just as much as I do. And together, we will save it from the hate and sadness you wish to spread."

Vako was about to speak again but was unable to move their mouth. Their eyes widened in surprise and perhaps a touch of fear.

"You have long spoken your piece. I will hear no more." Zelkova stopped in front of them. Stepping forward, Zelkova started to merge with Vako. The feeling scared Zelkova. This would be the end for her. She may never see the people she loved again. But there was no turning back now. The light and dark merged into one. Zelkova could feel Vako's body disappear. She then felt them in her subconscious. Just like where Vako had placed their Pyrus...

Zelkova merged with Vako, taking in their hate, fear and sadness; as she placed Vako in the recesses of her mind, Zelkova knew Vako would try everything to escape. She shifted through time and space, bringing herself to the mountain where she had formed the table, where the two books lay.

She stood in front of the table, one palm on each outline of the books. Zelkova knew what she was about to do would change their world greatly. Even though it wouldn't be like Vako's world, the people who lived through it all would suffer in the end. Zelkova hoped she was making the right decision. Suffering for a time was better than death or never being at all.

Doubt filled her mind. What right did she have to make this choice for everyone? They might want to die rather than suffer. Zelkova shook her head, knowing those thoughts came from Vako, who was going to fight her all the way.

Sighing, she called out to all the Elementals once more. From the Firsts to the Fourths, she called to them. "Thank you all. We will wake to a new world."

She knew what she was doing would put all Elementals into a deep sleep, but for the world to go on, for humans to live on, she had to do it.

Zelkova focused on the books under her hands. She could feel Vako trying to emerge. Her body shifted between her own and theirs. She groaned as she battled for control, all the while trying to focus on the books. If she could do this right, everyone would be safe.

The world would be safe, wouldn't it?

She fell to her knees, still fighting for control. Struggling against Vako's inner attack, she concentrated on the two books again.

Focusing, a bright light engulfed her right side, and deep darkness engulfed the left. A strong gust of wind pushed the remaining elements away. She could feel it working, her body fading while the Elementals fell into a deep sleep. Tears rolled down her cheek as she thought of it all. The past, present and future. As each element whirled in the enclosed cave, the form of Zelkova and Vako vanished, leaving nothing but the stone table and the two glowing outlines of the books.

It was another summer morning; everything started out normal. He, Omnia, and Inane were taking breakfast on the terrace, something they did when the weather permitted it. Everything had been relatively calm since their wedding. It was as if the last few months had not occurred, and it was all a bad dream. But if that were the case, he would have never met Omnia.

The people in the city were still getting used to the farmers and rural citizens of Litore. But everyone was still on edge at the thought of the shadows attacking at any moment, not to mention the unknown of what would happen afterward.

Omnia took his hand. Looking up at her, he smiled, and she returned it. "Spero, you seem deep in thought. Would you like to share, or was it just a passing fancy?"

Spero laughed at her words and then sighed, deep in thought again. After a few seconds, he looked back at Omnia and Inane. "I was just thinking of all that had happened in the last few months. Our whole world has changed. We've gained so much, but will we lose it all in the end?"

Omnia looked shocked at his words. "Everything that comes to pass is what will come. We've done our best and will continue to do so. Even if the moon is shut out by darkness, we will go on. And you of all people know having the right attitude can make all the difference."

He nodded and tried to smile at her, but worries still floated in his mind of what all could happen.

"No matter what occurs, we have each other now," Inane said.

And as if on cue, the earth shook slightly.

Immediately, the three of them stood and walked to the edge of the light dome. Outside the border, everything was pure chaos. Loose dirt and rocks ranging from pebbles to large boulders flew through the air. Water sprouted from the ground in thick, powerful streams. Trees were being ripped from the ground. Spouts of fire shot from the earth. And strong gusts of wind blew it all around.

As he studied the chaos, Spero saw something he hadn't noticed before. "Come!" he yelled, heading to the highest tower, the one Jardin had used to look for Zelkova.

At the top, he saw another light dome past the thicket of trees. It was more pronounced now because of the dark fog rolling in. He pointed, showing Omnia and Inane. "Zelkova put light protection over the fields. I wonder if she connected us to it someway."

His eyes widened when he realized something. Turning to Omnia, he took her by the shoulders, hugging her tight.

"What is it, Spero?" Inane whispered.

"This darkness, I fear despite Zelkova locking away Vako, the shadows may stay for quite some time..."

"How do you know she sealed them away?" Omnia stared at him, fear coating her features.

"I can feel it somehow. I feel a shift in everything deep within me. The war still rages on for Zelkova and Vako."

"Not in this world..." Inane voiced, her tone hushed.

Omnia turned and stared in question. "What do you mean?"

"When Zelkova was making me, I got a rare chance to see inside her mind," Inane told her. "It was a split second, what I saw. I think she wanted to share it with someone, with us." She paused and forced a smiled for them both. "If what I saw was what she had planned, Zelkova made a plane of existence solely for her and Vako and, as you said, Spero, sealed not just the shadowed one away but herself as well."

The three of them stood there in silence, wishing she had asked more of them, all the while hoping for a better, brighter future. Spero understood why Zelkova had never fully told anyone of her plans. Vako could have gotten wind of it by several means. He tried to understand her stance on the situation, but looking out into the field of shadows with one dome of light in the distance made him worry for Elementum and its inhabitants.

When all was finally still and calm, the world changed before them. After the great dark fog had receded, the other elements seemed to shift and vibrate, as if in response to something. After the darkness was gone, a strong gust of wind pulsated through all the lands.

The vibrations from the ripples of the wind almost knocked them to the ground. Staggering, he looked around at the land outside the protective shield. Darkness mixed with faint light seemed to be at war, swirling around one another.

"What's happened?" Omnia asked anxiously.

"I think it's over..."

"The real battle now begins," Inane said softly.

Standing, he tried to make out this new world before them, but images hit him, throwing him into a land of visions. The surrounding area was bright, just like they had been when Vako took them, but there was no darkness to be found, only the three of them.

"Live life well," a voice said through the whiteout in front of them. "Do not take more from the elements than what is needed. Live in peace, and look to one another in kindness. The dark and light will fade from your world, but before that happens, many will be overcome with fear. Do not let it spread, or it will ignite like wildfire, leaving nothing in its wake. Future generations will look to you three. You must be strong and understanding. Times will be tough but lean on one another and your people."

Despite her words, his heart ached, knowing this was the end deep down. He would not see or hear from her again. And for her, she may never see her loved ones again. He hated that thought but knew there was nothing he could do.

"Spero, be an example for others to follow. Show kindness and strength in hard times. Give people hope because without it, what is left?" There was a moment of silence. "Take care, you three. I look forward to watching you all from afar. I will be gone from this world, yet always present. Omnia, from you, future generations will grow.

Take pride in who you are. Don't look to the past for answers. There is nothing there for you. Look toward the future, which will be filled with the love you lost at a young age.

"Inane. You, too, will find what you seek in this world… You will grow into a much-needed guide to those around you. And never discount love. You never know where it might come from. Believe in yourself and know that you have a purpose. Never doubt that."

Spero sighed as he felt a hand on each shoulder. "You carry a heavy burden, but you are strong, and because of this, I know you will lean on those around you when you need to. Never let your hope wane because it will shine brightly for your future children to follow. Thank you, Spero, for being a guiding light."

"No, Zelkova. Thank you. Thank you for everything," he whispered back, hoping his words reached her.

With those words, a light breeze brushed his cheeks, and in the next moment, they were back in the present, standing on a tower, overlooking an ever-changing world they now had to lead out from the shadows...

Vako fought her all the way, still seething with anger, loss, and fear. Her own feelings were what kept them in check. To combat Vako, her emotions had to be the polar opposite to balance the small plane of existence they were now in. Forever balanced. She pushed away the feelings she wanted to focus on, such as the loss of Carya and her other family and friends. Zelkova needed to concentrate on her love for them and the peace the elements gave her.

Despite what she had seen of the future, there had to be a way to change it. She hoped she was not the cause. Hoped the humans would live in peace with the Elementals once they awakened. The things she put in motion should restore and keep balance.

If she did it right.

Again, the feeling of despair threatened her mind. Zelkova needed to sink into a meditational state. To think of peace and love. To remember those she had lost, but never think of that. Not the loss but of the happy times. Not the kisses she never gave Carya or the words she never spoke to Pyrus. But of the ones she did have with her love and her beloved brother. To think of the times she shared with them, replaying them in her mind. Keeping them and the emotions they brought out alive in her mind and heart.

The love and happiness would fill her very being, from now until the end of time as she floated with Vako in the abyss.

The ones Zelkova left behind, the lives she had touched, kept her story alive.

Omnia and Spero had a long, happy life together with laughter-filled halls. Their several children played among them. Each told their children and grandchildren the stories of Zelkova and the Elementals. Of how the darkness came, and how it would one day go just as quickly.

The Aurum family continued to be a shining beacon of hope through the ages. Until the world changed.

Darkness came and went, along with the boundaries of light. Even though Spero, Omnia and Inane were not able to see the darkness fully fade, their grandchildren were there in their place. The tales of Zelkova and Elementals also faded into legend. The stories passed down changed from truth to folklore and fairytales, that were told to children who could not sleep. But those too faded into myth.

After the darkness left and the barriers lifted, people from the cities roamed the countryside once more. One border remained in Lignum, which no one was able to pass. Hundreds of people tried different ways to break through the light wall, but nothing worked.

Despite the stories and warnings not to take more from the land than needed, to use it as a source of life. To respect the elements as living beings, they did the opposite. Future generations used and abused the elements that gave them life. The air they breathed. The water they drank. The earth that nourished them.

After centuries of taking advantage of what the lands gave, the elements revolted. Storms raged, earthquakes, floods, tornados, furious fires and the widespread death of crops and trees devastated the land. None of which had ever been an occurrence before when Elementals were around. They had maintained the balance, but when the elements were used up, the equilibrium of it all set off a chain of events no one could have foreseen.

Zelkova had reset the elements in their purest forms for humans to live off of, for a thousand years or more. But the greed of one cut that time in less than half. Despite everything, the world continued and people went on, changing their habits to work around the extreme elements.

But there are consequences to every action. And some actions, little and big, can be world changing.

www.ingramcontent.com/pod-product-compliance
Lightning Source LLC
Chambersburg PA
CBHW051508250626
47156CB00001B/15